SAVING
YOU

Saving You

Hidden in Plain Sight

A Novel

Val Guildthorne

For those who dare to dream,
And for those who dare to wake up.

Prologue

The rain was soaking them to the bone, almost punishing in its intensity. The brief respite they had that morning was clearly over. She had always hated the heat of summer, but she would have preferred the sun shining mercilessly above their heads to the deluge that was making it difficult to see a few feet ahead. From that moment on, she would always associate the sound of thunder with the bloodshed taking place before her eyes. Screams were coming from every direction. Lives were brutally taken away by a war that seemed to mock romanticised poems of heroism. The tattoo playing in her ears had nothing to do with a military drum and everything with her frantically beating heart. If only it were loud enough to swallow the noise of the battle raging around her.

"I have to find you shelter. Anything. God, I have to find a way to take you away..." His voice, full of panic, sounded almost foreign to her ears, so different from the controlled aristocrat she was used to.

"It's only a few yards away, on the hill," he continued without turning, his voice carrying above the rain. "There, you'll be safe. Once I know you are away from danger, I'll come back and fight."

"You'll do no such thing. I came here to save you from committing the greatest mistake of your life. And you are not coming back out here!" she panted, out of breath, trying to keep up with his long, hurried strides.

"You shouldn't have come here, for me..."

"You can't be serious! You couldn't have expected me to do nothing, knowing that you..."

BOOM!

A deafening noise drowned her words. The deflagration hit them, propelling them from behind and throwing their bodies a good distance from where they were a few seconds before. He tried to protect her from the worst of the fall, but it was too late. They fell to the ground with a bone-rattling thud.

The last thing she thought before darkness swallowed her was that *that* was how it should have ended.

Chapter One

Eight months earlier
London,
November 1814

"Unbelievable." Lady Victoria Gallard regarded Baron Whintrope's retreating back with a mixture of incredulity, astonishment, and righteous indignation. "You were right. Was that the third time Baron Whintrope asked me to introduce you?"

"Fourth," replied Lady Ivy Kington, Countess of Everleigh. "I told you he wouldn't remember me. You owe me another shilling."

Lady Victoria sighed. "I just don't understand how it's possible that you have to be introduced time and again to some people of the *ton*. It must be something in the air we breathe. We are all so self-absorbed. You are a Countess, for goodness's sake!"

"Let's not talk about this tonight, shall we? Take a walk around the room with me. I'll even forgive your debt." Ivy smiled at her friend, grateful when she nodded and dropped the delicate subject. It was a recurrent joke between them to bet on whether Victoria had to repeat Ivy's introduction to the person who approached them or not. The outcome was often disheartening for Ivy and, since the bets started, Victoria's pockets have been considerably lighter.

The fact was, people knew *of* Ivy. She was a peeress in her own right, a rarity among the ranks of the British *ton*. Ivy was the Countess of Everleigh, a title bestowed on her at birth. Her father, Rafael Kington, was the Duke of Rutherford *and* the Duke of Blythe, the Marquess of Wiley, and a list of other —for him— minor titles so long that back in the days, with a special dispensation dated 1720, King George I had allowed some of them to be passed directly to all her great-great-grandfather's children, daughters included, prior to the death of the Duke holding them, lest most of them would have been lost among the various Earldoms and Viscountcies.

Her lineage traced back to the Conquest, after which her ancestor was given his first estate. After him, a sequence of notable men and women, with cleverness and a considerable dose of luck, always found themselves on the winning side of history, adding titles and lands to the family collection. All that explained why Ivy, at two-and-twenty and unwed, carried the title of Countess of Everleigh. Her brother Gregory, at seven-and-twenty, was the Marquess of Burnam.

Such an illustrious family was bound to attract the *ton's* attention, always looking for mishaps and scandals and secretly hoping for the fall of the mighty. And few were mightier than the Kingtons. Obligingly, they didn't disappoint. Both still regal and beautiful in their fourth decade, Ivy's parents were an unfashionable, and sometimes scandalous, love match. They were utterly devoted to each other and not afraid of showing it to the world. After all, who would dare ostracise a double Duke?

Her brother Gregory, on the other hand, was devoted to women, plural, and halfway down the path of becoming a rake. A couple of inches over six feet, with his dark hair and a wicked smile that lit up his equally dark eyes, he didn't have to try very hard. He carried around an air of carefree exuberance that made him instantly likeable to everyone. It was rare to find him not surrounded by friends. He had a good heart, with a soft spot for his little sister, Ivy.

Ivy shared his brother's dark hair and eyes they had both inherited from their mother's side and was on the tallish side, but the resemblance ended there. There was nothing wrong with Ivy's appearance per se. It only seemed she didn't draw the same attention as the rest of her family. Looking at herself in a mirror, Ivy saw a pretty young woman with a nice figure, slightly slanted dark brown eyes, a straight nose, and a mouth with a lower lip fuller than the upper one. Her brown hair wasn't curly but wasn't straight either. In short, she didn't see anything out of the ordinary. And maybe therein lay the problem. They lived in a world where the standards of beauty were either fragile-looking blondes men married or extremely exotic women they admired from afar. Her looks, combined with a shy attitude towards strangers, didn't seem to leave a lasting impression.

"Fine," Victoria agreed begrudgingly. "I will drop the matter for now, but, before I do, let me tell you this one more time. You are sweet, intelligent, and caring. Don't ever let anyone make you feel you're lacking. *They* are. Good sense!"

Victoria gave Ivy's arm a gentle squeeze, and Ivy acknowledged her friend with a smile, uncomfortably accepting her praise. The situation wasn't so dire as Ivy depicted in moments of discouragement. In fact, promenading slowly around the room, Ivy nodded and politely waved to different acquaintances and friends. It was only the more distracted members of the *ton*, and often gentlemen, who seemed in constant need to be reminded. Hardly flattering, though. She didn't walk around waiting to be ogled by lascivious lechers like some sort of succulent roasted meat but feeling invisible wasn't pleasant.

Halfway across the room, Ivy and Victoria came up to two of their best friends, Misses Elizabeth and Grace Winter, who greeted them with welcoming smiles.

"Hello, Ladies," Ivy said. "Lovely evening, isn't it?"

"Lady Quindsley will be elated. It's a crush tonight." Miss Grace Winter fanned herself with her dance card, having misplaced her fan somewhere, as usual. "Personally, I can't fathom why the *ton* thinks a ball is a success only if the guests have to spend the evening apologising for bumping into each other, pretending not to sweat for the heat."

"Now, now, Miss Winter," Ivy reprimanded in her best impression of a governess's voice. "You know young ladies aren't supposed to talk about body fluids. How gauche!" She disapprovingly wagged her index finger, eliciting pearls of laughter from her friends. Grace made an exaggerated chastised expression.

The four of them then fell into an easy conversation, smoothed by years of friendship. Victoria had been part of Ivy's life for as long as she remembered. They had grown up together, spending summers roaming their adjoining estates. They had made their debut the same year. That very night, they had met Grace Winter. Her sister Elizabeth was two years younger, but she had effortlessly become part of their little group later, her personality too vibrant and cheerful to be ignored. The three older girls had bonded over similar circumstances that had become apparent after that first season. They found themselves in a curious position. They couldn't be labelled 'wallflowers' because their rank and wealth didn't allow it. Victoria's father was an Earl, and Grace and Elizabeth's sire was so flush in the pocket that the Prince Regent couldn't do anything else other than bestowing a Baronetcy on him to keep him on his good side.

Nonetheless, they weren't considered diamonds of first water either. Which was absurd when one looked at how beautiful Victoria was, with her blonde hair and blue eyes. Ivy suspected she could have been crowned *la belle* of the Season if she didn't stubbornly spend most of the time by Ivy's side.

No, they weren't wallflowers. They weren't *Incomparable*. They were somewhere in between. Not the worst place to be, just…not very exciting. And the *ton's* marriage hourglass was inexorably draining.

Ivy and her friends were in the middle of planning an outing for the following day, prompted by Ivy's pressing need to visit a bookstore when Lady Quindsley's butler announced the arrival of a tardy guest. Ivy could hear the man's booming voice over the chattering rising from the crowd only because they were standing near the staircase leading to the ballroom.

"His Grace, the Duke of Blakeburne."

All eyes of those within hearing distance turned towards the man standing at the top of the staircase, Ivy's included. Gasps of surprise travelled across the room. It was easy to discern the reason why. Next to Rutherford-Blythe, few were the titles as powerful and revered as the one of the Duke of Blakeburne. And the current Duke wasn't merely an aristocrat. He was also a decorated Army officer, with various medals to show for his valour in fighting against Napoleon. Ivy had been almost convinced he was a myth, having never seen him in the flesh. Apparently, he had spent the last few years —when on English soil— in the country, managing his numerous estates. Ivy knew all that thanks to her brother Gregory's impressed ramblings and various ladies' whispers. Seeing him now right before her, she couldn't blame them for being fascinated by him.

Even unaware of his military career, it would be impossible not to notice the air of command exuding from him. Shoulders held impossibly straight, he perused the room like a divinity observing mere mortals. Ivy would have archived him as one of the many arrogant Lords, but no, he was handsome too. Extremely handsome. Ridiculously so. He was young, younger than his reputation had led her to believe. A little over thirty, or near five-and-thirty, if she had to make a guess. His dark hair was kept short, but not overly so, hinting at curls that, being allowed, would surely be unruly. It contrasted dramatically with his eyes, of the purest green Ivy had ever seen. It was not the colour, as remarkable as it was, to make her pause. It was something behind those eyes, difficult to grasp. In those emerald orbs resided a general aloofness and a cold glint that made him seem unapproachable. Ivy immediately scolded herself for her fancy thoughts. How was she to know what was behind his eyes? All the books she read were starting to muddle up her brain, to borrow her brother's favourite insult for her.

His bored gaze swept over the ballroom, predictably passing over her, not deeming her worthy of a second glance. He was immediately approached by the delighted host and hostess, with whom he exchanged a few words, after politely bowing over Lady Quindsley's hand. Captivated eyes —Ivy's included, she was forced to admit— followed his every movement across the room, where he stopped to greet another Lord, one who was his polar opposite in every way. Sebastian Sinclair, Viscount Bellmore, was a well-known and even better-liked figure in the *ton*. He was admittedly a very handsome man with ash-blond hair and blue eyes, constantly alight with mischief. Ivy had been acquainted with him for years since he was one of her brother's best friends. Their interactions had never gone beyond polite greetings and dinner conversations, so the Viscount didn't fall in the category of 'those-who-didn't-remember-her', but he couldn't be considered a friend either. The same couldn't be said for Blakeburne. Bellmore was currently smiling at the Duke and, even with his back turned to her, Blakeburne's posture seemed to relax slightly by being in the Viscount's presence.

"Dear me, where was he hiding?" asked Elizabeth. "Never mind that. Is he married?" she added, voicing what all unmarried, and more than a few married, ladies were wondering. Ivy wasn't one of them. *Really, she wasn't.*

"Ah, I see Lady Quindsley's guest of honour has arrived. To answer your question, Miss Winter, Lord Blakeburne isn't currently married or affianced. Good evening, Ladies. Sister." Her brother Gregory stepped in front of Ivy and her friends and bowed gracefully in their general direction, eliciting curtsies from the women in return.

"Good evening, brother. How nice of you to join us. I gather you were aware of our mysterious Duke's plans of being here tonight." Ivy greeted her brother with a light kiss on his freshly shaven cheek. "You must be excited to see your hero," she added with a cheeky grin.

"He is not my hero, Ivy. I am not a child. I simply admire his military career, that's all. Everyone does. And yes, Bellmore told me he was planning on being here tonight. Apparently, his mother cajoled him into making an appearance."

"Even Dukes aren't immune to a mother's request," Ivy replied, still watching the Duke from the periphery of her eyes. He was conversing with Viscount Bellmore, now holding a glass of champagne in his strong hand. *Stop staring at him, Ivy!* she reprimanded herself. *Don't be like all the other marriage-minded women, salivating over a handsome man!* Admittedly a very handsome man, but still...

Regaining her wits, she turned to Gregory, blocking the unsettling view of the Duke of Blakeburne. "I reckon you are here to pay your due for losing the bet." She smiled broadly at her brother's resigned sigh.

"I didn't actually lose that bet, and you know it. Technically, in the English version of the *Divina Commedia*, Ulysses says—"

"I don't care what the translation says. You insisted on quoting the original version, so you must follow what Dante wrote. Now it's time for me to collect. Dance the supper dance with your sister," she finished with her best version of an evil laugh. Her friends reinforced the point by nodding eagerly. While her brother didn't share her deep love for books, he had always been very curious, even as a boy. Despite their age difference, more often than not, he and Ivy were found arguing over something. From the constant bickering as children, they had now moved to mature discussions.

"Fine. Let's get this over with. Next time, however, be prepared for retaliation, sister dearest," Gregory grumbled while leading her on the dance floor and taking the first steps of the waltz. Maybe they were not so mature after all. Her smile broadened even more. She loved this time spent with her brother, even if he didn't share the sentiment.

The waltz was a fairly new —and sometimes frowned upon— addition to the dancing repertoire. Lady Quindsley would rather eat her feathered headpiece than being found not at the height of fashion. If stodgy matrons found it scandalous, even better. For her part, Ivy loved the new dance. Not having to repeatedly change partners during a set allowed a connection with the other person, pleasing her shy nature. And if it annoyed Gregory to dance in such closed proximity to his sister, that made it even more pleasurable.

❊ ❊ ❊

Gabriel Sherborne Eastham, the fourteenth Duke of Blakeburne, was absent-mindedly perusing the room, already devising a way to leave without being intercepted by any acquaintance or, God forbid, his mother. Her constant nagging about him always being out of town and not in London searching for a wife was starting to irritate him. He had spent the months after his return from the Continent administering his estates scattered all over Britain, managing the vast Blakeburne fortune, as he had been doing since his father's ultimate passing, six years before. Parliamentary issues had finally brought him to London, where his mother and younger brother were enjoying the Season. Without hundreds of miles between them, there was no avoiding Her Grace's insistence that he attended *ton* events. And Blakeburne, a great military man according to his soldiers and superior officers alike, knew when to choose his battles. Ergo, there he was, at the great crush that was Lady Quindsley's ball, saved from boredom only by his friend Bellmore. He and the Viscount went way back, having met their first year at Eton and having been friends ever since. It had been Bellmore, already a Viscount at the time, to singlehandedly decide, upon first meeting him, that they were going to be like brothers. Why? Because he had liked the globe he had brought with him from Blakeburne. Gabriel, then Marquess of Addington, had always been a quiet and reflective boy and concluded that it was as good a reason as any other to befriend somebody. From that moment on —and despite their obvious differences— they spent years being inseparable. They even bought their commissions together, joining the Army at the same time, much to the disgruntlement of the old Duke.

"It's good to see you finally in Town, Blakeburne. This year's Season promises to be even duller than the last one if that's possible. Glad to have a fellow man to share this tediousness with." Bellmore sipped his whisky slowly, savouring the taste. Lord knew where he got it. Lord Quindsley was renowned for locking his spirit cabinet and serving only champagne and lemonade at his balls. Then again, the young Viscount's reputation of effortlessly charming everyone he set his eyes on was almost legendary. The cabinet didn't stand a chance of remaining locked.

"Just what I wanted to hear," Gabriel replied, suppressing a sigh. Looking at the couples twirling around the dance floor, he recognised various acquaintances, even after his years away. Nothing ever changed among the upper class. He had never cared much about Society. His time was too valuable to be wasted in idle chatter and inferior spirit.

His eyes paused on a young couple following the steps of the waltz the orchestra was playing. He knew the man from a time, years ago, when he had stopped by his table at White's to chat with Bellmore. The Marquess of Burnam, heir to the great Rutherford-Blythe title and a surprisingly pleasant fellow, was now dancing with a brunette, laughing at something she was saying.

"Who is Burnam dancing with? He seems to be having a good time. From what you told me of him, I didn't get the impression he was looking to get leg-shackled."

Bellmore laughed. "Far from it. If he's going to be ready for the parson's mousetrap in ten years' time, I'll be surprised. No, the Lady is his sister, the Countess of Everleigh. A nice enough lady, even if I haven't had many interactions with her so far. A bit shy, she is. Unmarried, in case you are wondering," he finished with a wink.

"I'm not." He wasn't interested. He only noticed her because, amid a sea of affectedly disinterested faces, her smile was genuine, lighting up her whole face.

Gabriel knew of that family's peculiar title-spreading succession rules, but he had never given it a second thought before. Now, looking at Lady Everleigh, he wondered about the life of an unmarried Countess. She didn't seem different from any other miss attending the ball. She didn't even stand up in appearance. She was pretty, with dark hair like her brother and a pleasant, curved figure, her bearing one of a lady of good breeding. Nothing, however, indicated a sense of entitlement or snobbery towards others, at least from where he stood. Not that a dance with her brother was any real indication.

The gong announcing dinner interrupted his thoughts. Gabriel, reluctantly, started seeking Lady Quindsley or Lord Rutherford-Blythe. Lady Quindsley insisted on that overly formal practice, 'mostly for smugly cataloguing her guests', according to his mother. As the highest-ranking peer, it was his duty to escort their hostess to dinner, but a double duke outranked even him. Spotting Rutherford-Blythe approaching Lady Quindsley and his Duchess wife on Lord Quindsley's arm, Gabriel was now left to escort the Dowager Marchioness of Whiteridge, a surly, if somewhat amusing, old lady.

"Here you are, young man. Chop chop. I'm not getting any younger here." Lady Whiteridge was one of the few people who could get away with reprimanding him and calling him a 'young man'. He, a thirty-year-old decorated Army Major and a Duke. "My deepest apologies, my Lady. In my eagerness to reach you, I kept on stumbling on my own feet." Gabriel replied with a serious face.

"Don't be cheeky with me, Blakeburne. I know your mother well. I could make you regret it," she replied threateningly, even if amusement shone in her light blue eyes.

"I am duly chastened. Now, please honour me by letting me be your escort. Shall we?" Gabriel offered his arm and started leading Lady Whiteridge to her place at the big dining room table. He was pulling the chair out for the old Lady when the commotion started.

"A rat!" someone shouted.

"There's another one!" a lady shrieked with an impressive piercing cry, falling into the nearest man's arms, who was barely able to catch her before she hit the ground in a dead faint.

Other, more sensible, guests moved out of the way and let footmen run around trying to catch the three —yes, there were three— rodents that were merrily scurrying under the dinner table and chairs. Gabriel found himself behind a group of people, all watching the unfolding of what could potentially represent Lady Quindsley's fall from the pedestal as one of the best hostesses in London.

Two burly liveried young men were trying to corner the rats, mindful not to overturn anything in their hunt. When, finally, one of them emerged victorious. He turned to his employer, proudly displaying the three wriggling creatures dangling from his hands by their tails, which revealed themselves to be small house mice. From above the shrieks and cries of some shocked ladies, poor Lord Quindsley swiftly dismissed the footmen from the room, ordering to get rid of the disturbance.

Gabriel was patiently waiting for the admittedly entertaining racket to end, when he heard the woman in front of him, of whom he could see only the back of the head, say, so low that she could only have been talking to herself, "I know Lady Quindsley calls her three children 'little animals', but I thought she meant it affectionately, not literally." And that was it. Gabriel couldn't help it. He started to laugh.

Chapter Two

*B*other. She had said it aloud. Ivy prayed for a hole to open under her feet and swallow her whole. Not only she had said that horrible thing, but someone had overheard her. She didn't dare turn her head around to see to whom the deep, throaty laugh belonged, hoping for once that the man was one of those who usually dismissed her. That luck wasn't on her side became apparent when she felt warm breath near her ear, followed by a deep voice whispering, "Oh, I don't know. I've seen the portrait gallery once. I admit finding some resemblance with great-aunt Gertrude."

Ivy put a hand over her mouth to stifle the laugh threatening to burst free but couldn't avoid looking over her shoulder, to put a face to that marvellous voice.

She froze. Green eyes, the greenest eyes she had ever seen, met hers. Darker than the colour of a grass field, it was a shade she had never believed existed in human irises before. They were currently bright with laughter. There was a guarded quality in that amusement that made Ivy's curious gaze reluctantly move to catalogue the rest of the man's face. His green eyes were surrounded by thick dark lashes, set under straight dark brows, the same colour as his hair. Of all people who could be standing next to her, it had to be the Duke of Blakeburne. She should have turned around and pretended the exchange didn't happen, but something made her say instead, "Portrait sittings must be interesting."

The Duke smiled. It was a thing of beauty, that smile. Like the rest of him, his mouth was beautiful, with straight white teeth. But what made Ivy stare was the feeling that the Duke didn't let the world see it very often. No laugh lines marred the sides of his eyes and mouth, marking it as a rare occurrence. Blakeburne opened his mouth to reply, but he then caught himself. He straightened to his full height, and his whole countenance sobered. She particularly felt the loss of the laughter in his eyes. He shook his head slightly and turned away from her. Ivy shouldn't have felt hurt by his rude dismissal —they haven't even been introduced to one another— but deep down, she had to admit she inexplicably was. It was a good thing, however, that the Duke had put an end to their peculiar conversation because, a moment later, her father joined her.

"Ah, there you are, Ivy. Crisis averted, it seems. Your mother was wondering where you were. She couldn't see you from the other side of the room."

"I've been standing here, looking at the scene." Ivy dared to send a look over her shoulder, but the Duke had disappeared. She spotted him leading Lady Whiteridge to her seat. Fortunately, no one else seemed to have witnessed her talking to the Duke. Innocent as it all had been, the *ton* was unforgiving of unmarried ladies talking to bachelors without proper introductions. Ivy wasn't keen on the idea of tarnishing her reputation because of a few unwise remarks, especially for a man who had turned away from her without a second glance.

15

Their host's voice rose above the guests' conversations. "My Ladies, my Lords, apologies for this unpleasant ahem...accident. I assure you, it has been someone's..." He sent a dark look at the door leading to the kitchen. "Bad idea of a joke. Please rest assured that this household adheres to the highest standards in all things. Now, let's all take our seats and enjoy the meal."

Ivy was led by her father to her place before joining his wife and sat on Lady Quindsley's left. The Duke of Blakeburne was with them, with her mother placed on his right and Lady Whiteridge on his left.

After that unorthodox beginning, the meal proceeded uneventfully. Ivy was distracted by the lively banter between her brother, the Earl of Covington, and Viscount Bellmore. They were discussing some talented young portraitist the Earl had met the week before.

From time to time, while enjoying the various courses prepared by Lady Quindsley's indisputably gifted Cook, Ivy felt someone staring at her. A particular green-eyed someone. Surely, she was imagining things. There was no way that the Duke of Blakeburne's interest was fixed on her. More likely, he was trying to understand what his friends were talking about so animatedly. After all, history taught her that she didn't exactly leave a lasting impression. She had no reason to think that time would be different. She could always wager with Victoria later.

※ ※ ※

After dinner and after having left the men to their cigars and port, the ladies were chatting in groups around the ballroom, waiting for the dance to restart. The main topic of discussion was the 'mice tragedy', obviously. Nobody was ready to leave on that account, claiming that "even if it was unpleasant, they couldn't leave dear Lady Quindsley alone in this time of need!" Ivy barely suppressed a snort. What they wanted was not to miss anything else that could occur at that ball, to discuss it in greater detail the next day.

"Time of need, my a—"

"Ivy Emmaline! Watch your language! I've raised you better than that!" the Duchess of Rutherford-Blythe reprimanded her daughter sharply under her breath.

"I'm sorry, Mother, it was a slip of the tongue. I must be more tired than I thought." Ivy was standing with her mother, Victoria, and the Winter sisters. She silently chastised herself for the umpteenth time that evening for voicing her thoughts without restraint. It was true that she had been raised with a lot more freedom than any other lady of her status, mainly because of her parents' belief that women were as capable and crafty as men. Nevertheless, Ivy had always tried to uphold her best ladylike behaviour, mostly out of respect for her parents and for her own title. It had never been a challenge. Until that night. Something must have destabilised her.

What that something —or rather someone— was, became evident when the men joined them. One particular group was stealing the scene. Ivy had to admit she could understand why the ladies were staring. *La crème de la crème* of British aristocracy was crossing the ballroom with confident strides. Confidence given by wealth, prestige, and the power to influence decisions of Prime Ministers, Kings and Queens.

First was Ivy's father, the Duke of Rutherford-Blythe, also known as the 'Double Duke'. A handsome man at eight-and-forty, he exuded that kind of self-assuredness that came from more than having worn the coronet for almost three decades. It came from experience, from the way he wielded that immense power. Underneath all that, there was the deep satisfaction of being unconditionally loved by his wife and children.

In stark contrast to that stood the flamboyance of youth. Viscount Bellmore and Ivy's brother Gregory attracted the hopeful interest of every matchmaking mama, debutant, and more than a few married ladies, who were drawn to good looks, charisma, and connections.

Ivy, however, was drawn to the fourth man approaching. The Duke of Blakeburne. His face was as beautiful as it was emotionless. If Gregory and Bellmore attracted stares, you could actually feel women's thoughts, plotting how to gain an introduction to the elusive Duke.

As the group approached, Blakeburne's eyes took in the ladies before him, his expression not betraying any sign of recognition. He was the incarnation of the perfect gentleman, a Duke to the bone, mighty and unapproachable. Despite all that, a frisson of awareness travelled down Ivy's spine, together with the inexplicable desire of seeing what lay beneath all that ducal splendour. Ivy wanted to believe, however fanciful that sounded, that she had had a glimpse of it earlier, in the dining room.

Her father kissed her mother's cheek as if they hadn't just dined together. Ivy and her brother were used to that kind of behaviour and, after many years together, the entire *ton* had come to accept that the Duke and Duchess of Rutherford-Blythe were not going to conform and hide their love behind closed doors. That didn't make it less scandalous for the stodgier members of society.

After releasing his wife, the Duke turned to his younger counterpart. "Your Grace, let me introduce you to Misses Grace and Elizabeth Winter, daughters of Sir Winter and good friends of my family's; Lady Victoria Gallard, daughter of the Earl of Gallard. And this is my daughter Ivy, Countess of Everleigh. My lovely wife, you've already met at dinner." The ladies dropped in formal curtsies, to which Blakeburne replied with a polite bow.

"Enchanted. His Grace is fortunate indeed to have all these beautiful ladies among his family and friends."

Ivy knew better than to be charmed by his rehearsed words. It was to be expected from a man like him. To prove her point, what followed was a string of trivial remarks on the weather and upcoming social events, to which Blakeburne responded with unwavering, if detached, politeness.

When the orchestra started to play, making various people around the room form couples and take their positions, Ivy's father took his wife's hand and put it in the crook of his arm, leading her for a dance. Baron Whintrope appeared at Elizabeth's side to claim the dance he had previously written down in her card. Bellmore grinned and addressed Grace, who blushed. "Would you do me the honour of this dance, Miss Winter?" At her whispered assent, they too were off.

The ever-suffering Gregory sighed and turned to Victoria. "It seemed they are all paired up. We might as well take their example and dance."

"Always the charmer, Lord Burnam. How could I refuse such a heartfelt request?" Victoria's reply was so frosty, Ivy's eyes snapped to them with curiosity. Just like Victoria and Ivy, she and Gregory had known each other since childhood, their relationship one of close acquaintances, if not friends. She would later puzzle over the strange development in Gregory and Victoria's interactions she had been observing lately. At the moment, she was facing another, more immediate problem. Intentionally or not, she had been left standing alone with His Grace. Her family probably thought they would follow directly behind them, but the Duke didn't seem so inclined. Frustrated and a bit angry at the fact that he stood stoically silent beside her, not even wasting breath in conversation, she opened her mouth to take matters in her own hand. At the last moment, the insecurities and shyness that had been plaguing her for as long as she could remember took root, replacing her indignation. Why would he want to dance with her? He surely had relegated what happened before dinner as meaningless chatter. She should do the same.

Looking around, Ivy spotted her Aunt Evelyn and Cousin Eleanor making their way to her. Given that she had never been that close to her cousin, there was only one reason that explained the eagerness in her steps. And that reason was the over-six-foot tall, dark-haired, breathing statue beside her.

Eleanor was beautiful and aware of it. Since she was a child, she had always been praised for her dark blond hair and unblemished skin. The only thing she and Ivy had in common was their brown eyes, about which Eleanor constantly bemoaned, wishing she had inherited the light blue ones from her maternal grandmother. Being only two years younger than Ivy, Eleanor seemed to feel the constant need to point out the differences between them. The comparison was, obviously, rarely flattering for Ivy. She didn't think of her cousin as a bad person. She was simply a little vain and self-centred. Hardly surprisingly, if one looked at her upbringing. As the only child of the Duke of Rutherford-Blythe's younger brother, she had always been spoiled by her good-natured father. Uncle George, the Earl of Northcott, thanks to the over-abundance of titles in the family, never resented being a second son. On the contrary, he seemed pleased with his lot in life. He had married a beautiful heiress and had been blessed with an even more beautiful daughter, prosper lands and holdings, without the burden of ducal duties. *"There are not enough riches in the world to tempt me to trade my life with my brother,"* he always said. His wife did not share his placid view of things. Ivy had always had the impression that the Countess of Northcott covertly resented that Ivy carried the same title as hers since birth and that the same privilege did not extend to her daughter Eleanor. Therefore, in her mind, a match with a Duke — or a Marquess in case of ducal penury— was crucial to outrank Ivy. That made their current purposeful march across the ballroom rather self-explanatory.

Before her relatives could reach her, Ivy felt a hand lightly touch her forearm. She turned questioningly towards the Duke of Blakeburne. "I beg your pardon, my Lady, but I have to bid you farewell. Enjoy the rest of your evening." And, without waiting for her response, he turned on his heels and walked away.

Well, then.

"What did you say to him to make him leave?" asked Eleanor, narrowing her eyes accusingly.

"Now, now, Eleanor, don't berate your cousin like that. His Grace has been standing beside her for a while. Surely, he has given Ivy enough of his time. He has to renew his acquaintances," Aunt Evelyn said, coming to Ivy's 'rescue'.

"He could surely have spared a few minutes more to be introduced to *me*," replied Eleanor, as if it were inconceivable that the Duke had something better to do than wait for her. Ivy sighed. That evening couldn't end soon enough.

Chapter Three

The following morning, Gabriel was in his study. Correspondence from his various estates across the country was already pouring in. At least the people in his employ were efficient. He was opening the ledgers to plan the renovations for the next quarter when his mother breezed in without knocking.

"Good morning, Mother. What can I do for you? I will be down shortly to break my fast. I only wanted to have a look at these first." He didn't even raise his eyes from the letter he was reading.

"Good morning, Gabriel. Is there a particular reason why you left the ball early yesterday? You didn't even come to find me, and your brother has barely seen you the whole evening."

"I did what you asked me to. I made an appearance at the ball and conversed with guests worthy of being conversed with. I never agreed to stay for the entire evening."

"You spent the time talking to Bellmore! One could hardly call it mingling."

"As I said, people worthy of being conversed with. Not that I owe you a list, but I also talked to Lady Whiteridge and Lord and Lady Quindsley."

"The hosts and a Dowager Marchioness who is seventy if she's a day! Seeing that you are being deliberately obtuse, let me rephrase that. Have you been introduced to any eligible lady? Or men of noble families with a daughter of age?" At his disinterested shrug, her mother let her irritation show. Always the picture of elegance, she would have never let anyone outside her closest family see her losing her composure like that. The Duchess of Blakeburne more and more resembled an indignant hen, her feathers ruffled by her unruly offspring. Not that Gabriel would ever tell her that. He wasn't that brave.

His mother levelled him with that look mothers all over the world must have perfected since the beginning of time. The one that mixed disappointment with long-suffering patience of having been burdened with such a progeny. He wasn't even the 'unruly child'. That honour had always belonged to his brother Edward. Until their mother had deemed it was time for the Blakeburne line to be secured by an heir. Then her perfect, dutiful firstborn had transformed into a slippery eel.

Truth be told, he had been introduced to some eligible ladies the previous night. One, in particular, came to his mind. A smile tugged at his lips, remembering Lady Everleigh's embarrassment in realising that Gabriel had overheard her comment about Lady Quindsley's children. It had been an entertaining diversion from an otherwise tedious evening. Not her embarrassment, but her wit in joking about what for other ladies would have meant a run for the smelling salts, as the dining room floor demonstrated. Nothing worth putting his mother on alert for, though. But he should have known better than to think something could escape her notice.

23

"I hoped to hear it from you, but I don't have all day to talk in circles. I have an appointment with my modiste. Really, Gabriel, try to spare my nerves." Her nerves had never had a problem in her life, but that was another thing Gabriel had no intention of pointing out. It would only prolong the conversation. "Lady Quindsley told me you were seen talking to Kingtons. A bit of an eccentric lot, but one is hard-pressed to find a more titled family in the whole Kingdom. The daughter is a Countess even if, at two-and-twenty, I believe, she is still unmarried. One wonders why." He had been wrong. His mother wasn't a ruffled hen. She was a bloodhound, scenting even the faintest marriage trail.

"She's a very proper lady. Not a hint of the slightest *on dit* about her. Not feeding gossips is a good thing, mind you, especially for a respectable lady seeking a husband. It isn't desirable to have to constantly quash rumours about one's wife…." Gabriel soon realised his contributions to his mother's analysis could consist mostly in murmurs of assent. He tried surreptitiously to resume reading his correspondence, keeping a distracted ear to what she was saying. He had learned the hard way what a total lack of attention to the Duchess's machinations could mean. He had found himself agreeing to attend two dinner parties and a ball before he even realised what he was nodding about.

"What I find strange is that, more often than not, when I talk to gentlemen, they insist they've never met Lady Everleigh, which is impossible. She has been out for years! And with her family exploits and notoriety —not to mention her surely enormous dowry— she should be one of the most sought-after ladies in the *ton*." That made Gabriel focus his attention back on his mother, whose brow was now furrowed. Gabriel himself found it difficult to reconcile the image his mother's words were portraying with what little he had seen of the Lady. Sure, she appeared reserved, shy even, but he *had* taken notice. He mentally shrugged. He certainly would not give his mother strange ideas by showing that his curiosity was piqued.

Suddenly, the Duchess sprung from the chair and rang to summon the butler. "Oh dear, look at the time! If I don't leave now, I will be late for my appointment. Remember that tonight is the Winters' musicale."

"Musicale?" Gabriel's eyes widened in horror.

"Yes, Gabriel. I told you about it days ago. Do try to keep up. You agreed to accompany me, remember?" She rose with her customary elegance. "Have a good day, dear."

Gabriel watched his mother's exit, aware that any objection would be futile. He sat back with a thud when the door closed behind her. *Hell and damnation.* That made it two dinner parties, a ball, and a bloody *musicale* he had agreed to attend. He frowned at the papers laying on his desk as if they carried the blame for it. For a military man, he really ought to pay more attention to what happened around him.

❀ ❀ ❀

Later that night, Ivy was looking for Grace. And she wasn't the only one. That evening's musicale was held by Elizabeth and Grace's parents to show the *beau monde* how accomplished their daughters were. But while young Elizabeth basked in the attention and looked forward to the nights when she could impress the *ton* with her talent, Grace was another matter entirely. The older sister had to be systematically cajoled by her mother to perform in front of their guests. Sometimes her nerves got so bad, she failed to appear at all. Once, she was even found hiding in a linen closet, close to hyperventilation. Other parents would have taken pity on her and spared her the dreadful moments. Not so the Winters. Lady Imogen Winter couldn't be persuaded that her daughter's chances of a good match would not be jeopardised by sitting among the audience and not singing in front of it. That, *despite* her efforts, Grace was still unmarried at two-and-twenty was really baffling for her.

As it happened, that night Lady Winter was once again in search of her daughter. Coming up unsuccessful, she tried to hide her exasperation behind a polite mask, stopping to converse here and there. Ivy, hoping to save her friend from another of Lady Winter's rants, decided to search for Grace herself.

She felt her friend's pain. She counted herself lucky that her family couldn't stand that kind of musicale, let alone be the hosts of one. Otherwise, she couldn't promise she would not be found in search of the nearest linen closet as well. Stepping outside the room, Ivy was relieved to see Grace standing in the hall, drawing deep breaths, trying to gather enough courage to cross the doors that led to what Ivy had heard Grace often describe as 'the dentist of all *ton* events'. It was really a shame that she had to suffer thus before every performance. While Elisabeth could pleasantly carry a tune, Grace had been gifted with a sweet melodious voice, which unfailingly left those who listened to it completely enraptured.

Inspecting her friend, Ivy assessed the situation to be dire. She hadn't even noticed her approach.

Gently touching Grace's arm, Ivy searched her mind for something to say.

"Grace, dear…"

"Are they all waiting for me? I can't do it, Ivy. I'm sorry, I simply can't." The misery in Grace's voice was heart-breaking. Ivy knew everything about being shy in front of judging strangers, but that was something else. That was paralysing fear. Grace was staring at the people conversing inside the room, wide-eyed and unblinking.

"You've done it numerous times already. You know everything will be all right. You have nothing to fear." Grace was shaking her head, fear overriding logic.

"They'll all be watching, waiting for me to make a cake of myself and laugh behind my back. Or worse, in my face. No, I won't sing, I can't!" Grace turned on her heel, 'linen closet' written all over her face. If Ivy thought she could get away with it, she would have let her go. Hell, she would have helped her find a hiding place. But, over the years, she had come to know Lady Winter. It would be better, for all concerned, if Grace went ahead with the performance willingly and not kicking and screaming. Metaphorically speaking. Mostly.

"What if…" Ivy took a resigned breath, "I accompany you with the pianoforte? Will it help?" Grace's face cleared, and she clapped her hands, hope shining in her eyes. "Oh Ivy, would you do it? Really? It would help me immensely if you were there diverting some of the attention on yourself! Oh, thank you!" Ivy watched her friend scurry away, almost in fear that Ivy would retract her offer. She won't. She won't let her friend down. That didn't mean she was looking forward to it. At all.

"I would rather sprint down Hyde Park naked at dawn than play in front of those snobby people…" she said to herself, groaning. Now it was too late to have a change of heart, not after seeing the relieved look in Grace's eyes.

"What a fetching image." Ivy jumped at the sound of a male voice. "I'm sure many people in there would prefer it to any performance, no matter how masterfully executed." *Oh no, not again*, thought Ivy, closing her eyes and silently willing him to disappear. *Can a footman please find me a shovel? I'll dig a hole myself. Thank you very much.* Ivy recognised the voice. Even after only having heard it the night before, the timbre of the Duke of Blakeburne's voice was very distinctive. Did this man emerge from the country with the sole purpose of witnessing her most embarrassing moments?

Unfortunately, shovel or not, she couldn't ignore the looming presence behind her. She turned and faced him directly. *In for a penny…*

"Do you make a habit of eavesdropping on private conversations, Your Grace?" The Duke was watching her with a serious expression. In contrast, his emerald eyes were sparkling. Ivy could not determine the meaning behind that glint. Amusement? Judgment? Superiority towards her half-witted behaviour?

"If by 'private conversations' you mean stumbling across people talking to themselves, then it seems it's becoming a pastime of mine. A rather entertaining one at that. One seems to discover secret wishes and surprising animal ancestry." Ivy felt her cheeks redden at the reminder. How ungentlemanly of him to point it out. The current conversation was rapidly taking a downturn. Better hide behind politeness. Ivy dropped into a curtsy.

"Good evening, Your Grace." His smile gave away that she had not been as subtle as she had hoped. *Drat*. He inclined his head in response to her belated greetings.

"Have you just arrived?" Ivy asked haughtily. Anything to regain her footing. If he could be hoity-toity, so could she. He may have been a Duke, but she was a Countess. A Countess who had to admit he was an extremely handsome specimen of a Duke. He was dressed in a dark blue superfine coat that enhanced his powerful shoulders and slim waist. He was impossible to overlook. Hence her question about his possible tardiness. That the performance had yet to begin was inconsequential.

"No, my Lady. I just stepped outside with a cigar. Now, if you don't mind heeding my advice, it would be better for you to go back inside the room before our absence is noticed. You have a pianoforte to play, I believe."

Ivy gave an elegant nod, begrudgingly admitting he was right. She was turning towards her fate when his deep voice stopped her on her track.

"Why did you do it?"

Ivy turned to face Blakeburne again. He was watching her as if trying to solve an enigma. Or maybe as if he were dissecting an interesting bug. With this Duke, one never knew.

"I beg your pardon?"

"If you hate it so much, why did you offer to play?"

She furrowed her brows. Wasn't it obvious?

"Well, obviously, Grace needed someone to help her overcome her fears. Right now, I'm what she needs. What kind of friend would I be if I didn't come to her rescue?"

With those final words, she left an oddly puzzled Duke of Blakeburne. Seeing Grace frantically searching for her, she went to take her place behind the pianoforte, suppressing yet another sigh.

❧ ❧ ❧

After the first notes out Grace's mouth, all guests were entranced. There was a reason why these events gathered so many members of the *ton*, and it wasn't for Lady Winter's refreshments. Even some renowned rakes were spotted in attendance, men who usually wouldn't be caught dead at this kind of events but who —despite their mastered ennui for life— enjoyed good music. The music room was filled to capacity, all eyes trained on Ivy and Grace. Elizabeth had already received her round of applause, and now Lady Winter was looking rather pleased while her elder daughter's sweet voice filled the room. Ivy hid a smile. Her nervous friend was gone. In her place, a self-assured, talented young woman stood in her stead. It really was a crime that such paralysing shyness overcame her before every performance. Listening to her—and seeing those enraptured faces— made Ivy's 'sacrifice' worth its while.

While she was playing, Ivy's eyes were repeatedly drawn to the back of the room, where the gentlemen who couldn't find a seat stood. There, tall and more imposing than any other men in attendance —or so it seemed to Ivy— was the Duke of Blakeburne, whose gaze was unnervingly fixed on Ivy, the same intense expression on his face she had noticed in the hall. Their eyes met and held. A strong current travelled between them, reaching all across the room, and Ivy wondered if other people could feel it as well, so powerful it seemed to be. She was lucky her skills in playing the pianoforte were adequate enough to allow her to play well-known pieces without really paying attention.

It was Blakeburne who finally looked away when the person beside him said something to him, allowing her to be freed from the shackles of their battle of wills. Only then Ivy did notice Viscount Bellmore standing near the Duke. The blond-haired aristocrat, she noticed, was staring slack-jawed at Grace. *"My God, she is magnificent,"* she saw him mouthing, awe washing over his face. Her smile broke free, seeing one of the reputedly most refined men in the *ton* made almost speechless by her friend.

When the set ended, the room filled with resounding clapping. From behind her, Ivy saw Grace give a start as if waking from a dream. Unfortunately, with a splash into reality, fearless Grace vanished. She quickly disappeared among the guests rising on their feet to partake of the rich buffet, her time as the centre of attention clearly over. Ivy stood from the stool and slowly made her way to join her mother, who was waiting for her.

"Well done, darling. I know how you dislike these public displays. It was sweet of you to come to Grace's aid."

Ivy shrugged. "I didn't do anything special. She loves to sing, and she deserves to have her voice heard."

"I beg to differ, Ivy. It's time you realise your kindness is a very precious gift that few can honestly say to share with you. Stop selling yourself short."

"Mother, this isn't the place to have this discussion. Again."

"I'll repeat it as many times as it will take for you never to forget it, daughter." Ivy knew it was pointless to argue with the Double Duchess. Her Mother was her children' fiercest and staunchest supporter. It was wonderful to be loved so much, and Ivy would never take it for granted, but sometimes it made it difficult to make her understand.

Since childhood, her lack of self-esteem had been a puzzle for most. A Countess by birth, growing up in a loving, exceptional family, she shouldn't question herself constantly.

Besides being very harsh on herself, she always felt particularly lonely when those thoughts took root in her mind. Ivy was aware that most of it was of her own making, that she couldn't see herself clearly and only through a veil of constant doubt. That, combined with the unpleasant feeling she got every time she felt invisible and overlooked among her peers, made her doubt her mother's objectivity.

Her parents and brother's attempts to make her see past all that was infused with a touch of bewilderment. If she had to be honest, a big reason for it was that their personalities were so big, those insecurities were completely out of their sphere. Then, she felt immediately guilty for not appreciating how lucky she was, and she hated herself for it. And the circle began anew. When those jumbled thoughts hit, her mind wasn't a peaceful place.

Ivy was spared from continuing that uncomfortable conversation by someone walking right past them. Her embarrassment was complete when she realised that the person —who most likely had overheard her mother's well-meant tirade— was none other than the Duke of Blakeburne. *Again.* The man was quickly becoming the bane of her existence. Their eyes met behind the Duchess's back, as they did during the performance, while shivers ran through her. His expression was as unreadable as ever. Why wasn't that man ever where he was supposed to be? Or rather, why was he always underfoot at the worst possible moments?

Ivy braced herself, but he simply looked away and continued walking. Small mercies. What she was feeling was relief. She couldn't possibly be disappointed that the Duke hadn't once again remarked on something embarrassing about her. She scoffed at the thought, winning a puzzled look from her mother, who turned towards the source of Ivy's distraction. She felt her knowing eyes burning into her, but Ivy refused to acknowledge her. In desperate need of a diversion,

Ivy took her mother's arm and steered her towards the tables on the opposite side of the room.

"I am positively starving. Look at those pastries! Don't they look delicious?"

❧ ❧ ❧

With a glass of unexpectedly strong punch in one hand, Gabriel observed Lady Ivy Kington. The Lady was a constant surprise. It seemed his fate —where the Countess was concerned— was to stumble upon her in the most peculiar situations. He had pushed their first encounter at Lady Quindsley's ball to the back of his mind, catalogued as a pleasant, but not memorable, episode. Then, that night, while returning inside after a fortifying cigar to face the evening to come, Gabriel had heard Lady Everleigh trying to coax a very recalcitrant Miss Winter into taking her place for the night's entrainment. If the lady who had to sing was so reluctant, the evening didn't sound auspicious for them all. He was in for a surprise, however. And it wasn't that Miss Winter could actually sing. No, it had been Lady Everleigh. From his experience with the ladies of the *ton*, it was rare to find someone ready to be put on the spot if they weren't sure to look their best. Not for someone else, and certainly not if there was the possibility of being outshined. A possibility the Countess was undoubtedly well aware of, being friends with the other woman.

Once Miss Winter had left, Gabriel had found himself approaching her. He knew it was most improper and very dangerous for them both. A woman could be compromised by far less than being alone in the company of a man. And a man could find himself in front of a priest before knowing what was happening. And the loftier the titles, the bigger the scandal. He couldn't help himself, however, and certainly not after overhearing something he was sure he wouldn't soon forget.

I would rather sprint down Hyde Park naked... Even now, his body was reacting to the image that had conjured. He couldn't put it out of his mind. Gabriel was able to picture it perfectly. The morning mist rising from the green grass caressing her ankles… The light of the rising sun just enough to illuminate the white of a flimsy camisole and that of her skin, revealed by the obliging fabric, blowing behind her in her run... He could have been a gentleman and found another way to the room without alerting her of his presence, sparing her any embarrassment. Instead, reminiscent of the last time they had such an unexpected conversation, he had come upon her from behind. He had been barely able to keep the lust out of his voice while teasing her. It was worth it to see the light blush colour her cheeks. It was a pity seeing it gone so soon, hidden behind her unfailing aristocratic upbringing. Seeing her so composed helped him clear his mind of lustful thoughts as well, leaving it open to another interesting aspect of the conversation he had heard. It seemed the Duchess of Rutherford-Blythe agreed with him on the uncommon kindness of her actions if what he had heard from *another* overheard conversation was anything to go by. How sad was it that the only conversations that didn't bore him these days were the ones in which he wasn't directly involved?

"Blakeburne? Are you even listening to me?" Gabriel was forced away from his scrutiny by a mildly irritated Bellmore trying to talk to him. And not for the first time either, apparently.

"Sorry, Bellmore, you were saying?"

"Let me say that the sight of the Duke of Blakeburne distracted and woolgathering is so out of character it cannot be a good sign. Is Britain in danger? Is Boney just outside those doors, waiting to be announced?"

Gabriel glared at him. "I don't *woolgather* like an insipid poet."

"Ah, now *that* scowl I am familiar with. You had me worried there for a moment, old chap. I'd really like to know whom you were staring at so intently." When Gabriel didn't answer, Bellmore, who was used to his less than chatty friend, searched for the answer on his own.

"Don't tell me you are giving in to the Duchess's pressure to find yourself a bride?" Bellmore made a disapproving sound. "I would have thought a man like yourself, nerves of steel and unparalleled courage, would resist a bit longer. Now, let's see if I can find the woman who put that look on your face, my friend."

"What look? And you'll be looking all night, for there's no woman." Just because he was even now thinking of a way to talk to the Countess again, it didn't mean he was interested in her. At least not so much as to tempt him into thinking about marriage.

Bellmore ran a hand over his chin, pensive, his mannerism overdone, as usual. Suddenly he brightened as if he had found the solution to all of Britain's problems. "Now I see. I can't say I blame you, old chap. Lady Ingram is rumoured to be delightful company, but you know that better than most, don't you?"

Taken aback by the unexpected conclusion, Gabriel's eyes searched for the Lady in question. Sure enough, a little to the Countess's right stood Lady Ingram. A few years older than Gabriel, the Baroness had been widowed for almost a decade after his much older husband had died from a fever, leaving his young and beautiful bride free to enjoy the perks of widowhood. And enjoyed them she did. After shedding the black mourning garbs and society's strict conventions, Arabelle Ingram had been collecting young and virile lovers. Gabriel had been one of them, many years before. They had met shortly after her year of mourning and had entered a mutually beneficial arrangement. For Gabriel, it had been doubly satisfying. Their sexual encounters had not only allowed him to accommodate the needs of a young Marquess, but they had also annoyed his Father, the Duke, who had valued spotless behaviour above all else.

Gabriel had, however, voluntarily put an end to their liaison when Lady Ingram had started to fancy herself in love with him, picturing a future as the next Duchess of Blakeburne. That, together with an exacerbation of the war between Britain and France that meant he was likely to be called away at any moment, had pushed Gabriel to sever all ties with the young widow. He still remembered the exasperation he had felt the night he had broken the news to her. It had come after a week of her trying to convince him to sell his commission, something he absolutely had refused to do. The shouting matches —or shouting monologues, because future Dukes didn't yell— that had followed could be heard from the outskirts of London. Gabriel still thanked his military training that had sharpened his reflexes. Otherwise, he couldn't be sure the pointy cane of a porcelain shepherdess wouldn't now be permanently embedded in his forehead. That kind of behaviour really was intolerable, and it only served to reinforce Gabriel's decision. No amount of physical pleasure made up for those shenanigans. Gabriel didn't suffer hysterics well.

From what he had heard a few months afterwards, Lady Ingram's disappointment had been short-lived, and Gabriel had been replaced with a young, if not dull, Viscount's son. He was glad no hard feelings lingered, for he hadn't spared much thought for the Lady after they had parted. He had seen her in passing over the years but, having spent much of his time either on the Peninsula or at one of his estates, that night was the first time they found themselves in the same room since their liaison ended.

As if she could feel someone watching her, Arabelle lifted his face and met Gabriel's eyes, the look of surprise swiftly replaced by pleasure. Silently cursing the rules of society, he was forced to acknowledge her with a slight nod. Otherwise, others around them would wonder what had brought the Duke of Blakeburne to give the cut to the Baroness. If there is something he abided even less than hysterics, it was gossip.

Dukes don't make people talk about them, if not in admiration for said Duke's actions or in fear of repercussions of their own. Even now, years after his death, his father's voice still had the power to echo in his ears.

Gabriel quickly looked away from Lady Ingram's hopeful gaze. He didn't need the headache that would accompany rekindling their affair.

"It was a long time ago. And despite her undeniable charms, I don't have the time nor the inclination to get reacquainted."

"With whom you won't get reacquainted, Blakeburne?" Gabriel turned at the sound of his mother's voice. She wore a richly adorned burgundy gown, which complemented her pale skin and light blond hair. She didn't seem old enough to have raised two adult children, the only concession to time a slightly round figure. That said, she still attracted gentlemen's eyes wherever she went. His brother Edward had written to him more than once how he was repeatedly accosted by men who hoped to become their new stepfather, trying to gain the Duchess's favour through her son. Said son was even now standing at her side, a male mirror image of their mother, with light blond hair and hazel eyes.

"Good evening, Mother. Edward. How are you two enjoying the evening?" Gabriel placed a perfunctory kiss on his mother's cheek and nodded at his brother.

After greeting Bellmore, the Duchess answered him, "The Winters' is one of the few musicales one attends with real hope of going home with the hearing intact." Gabriel found himself nodding, pleased that, for once, the conversation didn't immediately start with an account of the night's eligible women. "One can always count on Dorothea Winter for a guest list filled with the best of what London has to offer. I have already counted at least ten young ladies who would make a splendid Duchess of Blakeburne." Or maybe not. Gabriel could see the merriment dancing in Edward's eyes. He knew how much it annoyed Gabriel to be subjected to an endless parade of potential brides. But Edward also knew Gabriel would never disrespect their mother. But did the young pup ever come to his rescue? Of course not. To make matters worse, he was saddled with friends like Sebastian Sinclair, Viscount Bellmore.

"I think, Your Grace, that something, or rather someone, has already caught your son's eye. Maybe you will have more luck than me in prying this information from the Duke." If looks could incinerate, the one Gabriel shot his so-called friend would make his ashes easy to sweep under a rug. Unrepentant, Bellmore launched himself in a passionate discussion with his mother on who would be the most likely candidates. Wanting to curb that tiresome topic, he addressed his brother. "How is the design for Blakeburne Manor coming along?" Despite giving out the air of idle second son, Edward was a talented architect, and Gabriel was more than happy to let him oversee the renovations of the ducal seat. It was something to keep his brother's overactive mind busy and far from that slippery slope he had seen many young aristocrats fall into. And if it was one less item on the seemingly never-ending list of things Gabriel had to manage, all the better.

"Good. If Mother doesn't have any other spur-of-the-moment requests, I think I'll start hiring hands from the village so that they can begin next week."

"My requests are perfectly understandable, if not necessary!" interjected the Duchess.

"Four more cherubs at the corners of the ceiling in the great hall is not what I'd call *necessary*, Mother."

She regarded his son like she couldn't believe she had bothered to raise such an offspring. "Nonsense, of course they are." *Cherubs*? And more than one? Gabriel mentally shuddered. Draining his glass of punch, he decided he had earned another moment of solitude.

"If you'd excuse me, I'm stepping outside for some fresh air. I'll be on the balcony when you're ready to leave." Without waiting for acknowledgement, Gabriel walked to the nearest doors leading to a balcony. There, the only sources of light were the one filtering from the room and the full moon shining above his head. He already felt his muscles relax. He would never let it transpire, but he really loathed having to attend *ton* events. It was a waste of good time he could spend

37

replying to letters or making decisions on the multitude of issues that required his attention daily. Hell, he could even go to his club or read a book. He would prefer it ten times more than making vapid conversations with vapid people. If he weren't reluctant to disappoint his mother, those people in there wouldn't be able to link his title to a face. He didn't even like cigars all that much, either. He didn't enjoy the cloud of smoke clouding his eyes and his mind. It was something he had always seen his sire doing, another trait he had associated with being a Duke. He couldn't stomach more the one once in a while — much to what he was sure would be his father's disgust—, but Gabriel had to admit it did have its perks. He wasn't unwilling to exploit it as an excuse to leave everyone behind and spent a few minutes by himself.

He was so lost in his thoughts that he didn't hear the steps approaching until a voice tentatively whispered his name.

"Blakeburne? Blakeburne, are you there?" He instinctively turned towards the feminine voice. Before he could spot its owner, a hand tugged sharply at his arm. Taken by surprise, he stumbled to his right, only to be unceremoniously pulled in a dark alcove he hadn't noticed until that moment. He and his assailant found themselves in complete darkness. Two slender hands covered his mouth before he could speak.

"Shh. Please, Your Grace, don't make a noise." Gabriel stood still, not trying to free himself anymore. He could step away if he so wished, his strength no match for the woman. If not for the unexpectedness of the action, he wouldn't have bulged from his previous position. He was almost certain he recognised the voice whispering in his ear. More intrigued by the moment, he wondered what the Countess of Everleigh was up to. His breath was warming the cold palms still pressed against his mouth, his lips grazing them. He could feel the shivers running down her arms at the contact. She moved slightly, and a ray of moonlight confirmed her identity. He looked into her eyes. He couldn't see much, but he noticed they were beautiful, dark, and surrounded by thick lashes.

They were pressed indecently close, almost touching, and Gabriel felt his body react. He didn't peg her as a woman in search of an assignation, but appearances could be deceiving. After all, what did he know about her? Was it a plot to trap him, compromising her reputation by being found alone with him? He stiffened at the thought, his lust momentary forgotten. He won't stand idle, waiting to be discovered and forced to marry a chit who would come up with that kind of ploys. He tried to take a step back. "I don't know what you think you're doing, my Lady, but—"

"Shhh! Will you be quiet, you big oaf!" She interrupted his righteous indignation with an angry whisper. He was taken aback by her vehemence. Certainly, a woman trying to be compromised wouldn't throw insults at him?

"Who's there? Blakeburne, darling, is that you? Come on, don't make me chase you," said the voice in a seductive tone. The small, voluptuous figure of Lady Ingram appeared, illuminated by the candlelight from the music room.

"You like to play, don't you? All right, I hope my prize will be satisfactory." Lady Ingram's words were clearly meant to seduce but didn't stir anything in Gabriel, if not anger. His mind was too occupied, searching for a way out of that predicament. The situation didn't look good from where he was standing. It was either being found in the company of the Countess or meeting the Baroness halfway. Hiding didn't sit well with him, but the Baroness was a complication he didn't want in his life at that moment. And while he was evaluating the lesser of two evils, Lady Ingram was getting nearer. His mind was still working furiously when Lady Everleigh huffed in exasperation.

"Oh, for God's sake. Lord save me from fools." She stepped around him and into the light.

❀ ❀ ❀

"Lady Ingram! I didn't see you there! Are you outside admiring these beautiful stars as well? It's so rare to be able to enjoy such a clear night. It's almost a pity to be forced indoors, don't you agree?" Ivy stepped in front of Lady Ingram, effectively blocking her path. A flash of irritation passed over the older Lady's face, but it was quickly hidden behind a mask of politeness and, if Ivy wasn't mistaken, a touch of contempt.

"You are absolutely right. Lady Everleigh, isn't it? Why would one go outside on a balcony at night if not for stargazing?" The cheek of the woman! Ivy knew why Lady Ingram was there, and it wasn't for the constellations. From the conversation she had fortuitously overheard, it was something else she was looking for.

Having felt the beginning of a headache but unwilling to leave her friends' musicale too soon, she had been making her way to the French doors leading outside, hoping that fresh air would alleviate her discomfort when a name had captured her attention. Behind a large potted plant, Lady Arabelle Ingram had been confabulating with Mrs Lavinia Higgins, a notorious gossip and, from what Ivy assumed, one of the lady's closest friends.

"Of course, it's going to work, Lavinia. You only have to wait for me to give you the signal with my fan, like this." Lady Ingram had opened her fan behind her back. "You'll come out on the balcony, looking all shocked, and it's done. You'll be looking at the future Duchess of Blakeburne."

"How do you know he will be on the balcony? You haven't even talked to him directly tonight. And even if it all went according to your plan, how can you be so sure he would agree to marry you and not try to wriggle his way out of it?" Ivy had thought Mrs Higgins was making an excellent point. At least one of them had been showing some sense. She had borrowed deeper on the other side of the plant, waiting for Lady Ingram's answer.

"Don't you worry, my dear. He will come. I saw how he looked at me from the other side of the room when he was talking to the

Viscount. Positively scorching! I sent him a look that said I was amenable and if I know him, and I do..." Her voice had been full of innuendo. "He won't be able to stay away. Believe me, I'm never wrong about these things."

"That I don't doubt. But marriage?" Mrs Higgins still hadn't sounded wholly convinced. Wise Mrs Higgins.

"He will propose." Lady Ingram's voice had instead oozed confidence. "Blakeburne values honour above all else. He won't allow it to be besmirched by anything in the world." Ivy had heard enough. Lady Ingram had never figured much in Ivy's thoughts, being a staunch supporter that people could do whatever they wanted, as long as it didn't hurt others. But her little speech didn't sit well with her. Obviously, she knew stories of women —or men— who were forced to wed to avoid scandal. Hell, it was the main reason gossipmongers existed. But trapping someone, banking on their sense of honour, was not only distasteful but simply wrong.

Ivy had left her place behind the plant and resumed her way to the balcony. Should she warn the Duke? Maybe she could find an excuse to approach him? Then again, if Blakeburne and Lady Ingram had really wordlessly planned an assignation, perhaps she should let nature take its course. While weighing her options, she had finally reached what she had come to consider her alcove. That secluded spot had so far remained virtually undetected by other guests. Ivy had spent many an hour sitting on the marble bench when balls or musicales became too much.

The familiar dark surroundings had been having their usual calming effect on her when a large shadow had appeared. Its owner had followed, leaning on the balustrade. Ivy had stiffened, recognising those powerful shoulders. She had embarrassingly ogled them all evening. Of course, of all the corners of Winter House, the Duke of Blakeburne had to choose the same balcony to meet with his lover. Ivy should have expected it.

She had to give it to Lady Ingram: her signals had worked like a charm. There had stood Blakeburne as she had predicted. Only, he hadn't looked like a man on a secret rendezvous. Not that she was familiar with how men should look on such occasions, having never had one, but she would have expected for him to look a bit more...enthusiastic? Expectant maybe. Blakeburne had been resting his forearms on the balustrade, his gaze on the dark gardens before him, an unlit cigar playing between his fingers.

Right that moment, Ivy had felt a sort of kinship with the mighty Duke. He, too, had seemed in need of a reprieve from the constant chatter, like it didn't come completely natural to him to stand among those people inside. Just like her.

Kinship or not, she had been sure he wouldn't have appreciated her witnessing his private moment, even though most of their interactions had begun with him manifesting behind her. She had been stepping into the light to make herself known, to excuse herself and hastily retreat inside, when Lady Ingram's voice had stopped her on her track. *Bollocks!* So much for staying out of other people's affairs. She had looked back and forth between the Duke's back and the open doors, trying to judge his reaction. When he had made to turn towards the newcomer, Ivy had been able to see his face clearly. The look of surprise on it had made her act on instinct. Moving quickly, she had grabbed his arm and pulled him into the darkness with her, covering his mouth to stifle any protest.

The alcove was spacious enough when alone, but the Duke's strong body had taken up all the room available. She had found herself almost pressed to his front, the tingling that she always felt in his presence stronger than ever. His warm breath on her hands and his presence alone had been enough to make her feel engulfed by him. That close, she could have slid a hand in his dark hair to find out if it felt as silky as it looked. Or, even more boldly, she could have stood on tiptoe and pressed her lips to his. By then, it had been undeniable. She was deeply attracted to this serious, uptight Duke.

She had felt the moment he had recognised her. Obviously, the tingling had been one-sided because she had felt him stiffen and try to put some distance between them. That had made the attraction turn into anger. Couldn't he see what she had been trying to do?

"I don't know what you think you're doing, my Lady, but—" At least he had had the decency to keep his voice to a whisper. She had taken a huge risk. If someone had found out they were hiding together, hell would break loose. She should have shoved him back directly into Arabelle Ingram's welcoming arms without involving herself in scandals that hadn't concerned her. That taught her for making rash decisions.

"Shhh! Will you be quiet, you big oaf!" she had said urgently.

Meanwhile, behind them, Lady Ingram's voice had been coming nearer and nearer. Finally, Blakeburne had seemed to realise the predicament they were both in. Ivy had been able to see his mind working. The way he struggled to come up with a solution had made her realise she had been right all along. There had been no assignation. When she saw the other woman open her fan behind her back, she had known that, in no time, the balcony would become more crowded than a market square. With that, she had come to another realisation. She was the only one who could do something to stop that absurdity.

"Oh, for God's sake. Lord save me from fools," she had murmured under her breath.

That was how she now found herself talking about stars and constellations with the unpleasant Lady Ingram, who had the nerve to look at her with condescension. As if she were a naïve little girl, clueless to what went on in the adult world. She was a maiden, but she wasn't that sheltered. She was a Kington, after all. Her family believed a person was truly free to choose only if they really knew what that choice was about. Thanks to her parents and brother, she had had an unconventional education. Nonetheless, Ivy hated confrontations of any kind. The Baroness's —and yes, even, the Duke's— behaviour was getting to her nerves, making her act very uncharacteristically.

"We once had the honour to have the famous astronomer, Sir Horatius Wilde, at Wildrose Manor." Ivy continued her ravings. "Apparently, it's the perfect spot to observe an unencumbered night sky. He and my father forged a deep friendship and still exchange letters to this day…." Heart pounding, she was still rambling about the sky, hoping to keep Lady Ingram occupied. Or bore her enough to make her leave. She prayed the Duke had the sense to stay put and not make a sudden apparition, like a poor excuse of a stage actor. More so when, following Lady Ingram's flawless plan, Mrs Higgins made her dramatic entrance in what was quickly becoming the farce of Ivy's evening.

"Oh, dear heaven! I have no words for what I'm seeing! Lady Ingram and the Duk— Lady Everleigh?" Ivy cringed at Lavinia Higgins's high-pitched, piercing voice. If that evening was a farce, it really needed better actors. Her feigned exaggerated shock transformed into real surprise upon seeing Ivy instead of the handsome Duke.

Her loud exclamation succeeded in drawing the attention of those within hearing distance. Which was almost everyone in attendance that night. Ivy once again became the centre of attention, with the guests wondering why all that fuss for two ladies conversing.

"It really must be a beautiful evening outside if it distracted from the feast Lady Winter had spread out for us," Ivy's mother said, emerging with Imogen Winter herself from behind the small cluster of people gathered at the balcony doors. She regarded Ivy quizzically, but years among polite society had taught her to wait to be in private before enquiring.

"Lady Ingram and I were just returning inside," Ivy replied, using it as an excuse to steer the other woman towards the doors. "I was just telling her of Father's friendship with Sir Wilde and the summer the scholar spent with us at Wildrose. I was still a little girl at the time, so maybe you recall something more about it, Mother. Lady Ingram expressed deep interest."

Without missing a beat, her Mother took Lady Ingram's arm and led her inside. "Of course, I remember it perfectly. It was a magical summer, full of late nights and interesting conversation..."

They moved away, and Ivy couldn't hear how long the Duchess continued expanding on the topic. She was sure her mother wasn't fooled by her explanation, but she would worry about what to tell her later. For now, she would count herself lucky. Shooting a look above her shoulder at the dark alcove, she followed a sheepish Mrs Higgins, an irritated Lady Ingram, and an intrigued Duchess of Rutherford-Blythe.

Duke saved for the night, one. Headache spared for the night, none.

Chapter Four

Gabriel was sitting in his carriage on his way home from the Winters' musicale, his mood bleaker than a Whitechapel alley at night. He was looking outside, the dark streets passing by, aware that his mother and brother were sending him strange looks, unsure whether to talk to him or not. Gabriel couldn't blame them. If his face reflected even part of what he was feeling, he had to be even more forbidding than usual. He could almost feel the waves of anger and resentment radiating from him.

How dare that conniving woman think to trap him? That had clearly been her intent. He couldn't abide dishonest people. Getting involved with Lady Ingram had been a mistake from the beginning. What angered him the most was that, if not for Lady Everleigh —who somehow had realised what the scheming woman had devised—, it would have worked. He had been distracted and had not been paying attention, naïvely believing he was allowed to breathe for a moment.

Ironically, his distraction had been caused by the very same Lady who had ultimately saved him from his inauspicious fate. He thanked God for her quick thinking and acting. He even forgave her the insults she had thrown at him. No, what made the situation really unbearable was that he had been forced to hide in the dark, like a silly boy who had pilfered biscuits from the kitchen, hiding from the governess. It was absolutely unacceptable that him, Gabriel Eastham, fourteenth Duke of Blakeburne and Major of HM Army, who had faced more life-threatening situations he cared to admit, had been put in that position. He was becoming angrier by the minute, more so because he could not plan a retaliation. He had to simply act as if nothing preposterous had almost happened.

The impudence of the shameless woman!

Before his irritation reached the boiling point, he forced his thoughts to more pleasant topics. The way Lady Everleigh had looked at him when they were standing so close together. They had stared into each other's eyes for what had seemed like an eternity. For a second, before reality came crashing in, Gabriel thought she would rise on tiptoe and kiss him. And he would not have stopped her. He could well imagine him reaching for her, spanning her waist with his hands, and bringing her flush against him. He would have taken control of the kiss and, when it wouldn't have been enough anymore, fuelled by her moans, he would have tasted the alabaster column of her throat. And then…

"Blakeburne. Blakeburne! Are you listening?" Apparently, his mother was courageous enough to brave him in that mood. It surely had to do with the fact that she had brought him into the world, something that the grown men who usually cowered before his scowl could not say to have done.

"Apologies. You were saying?"

She expressed her discontent with a long-suffering sigh. "I was asking where you disappeared for so long."

"If I recall, I excused myself. No disappearance occurred."

47

"You could have fooled me. I was briefly near the balcony when that strange interaction between the Countess of Everleigh and that Baroness took place, and I haven't seen you." She narrowed her eyes at him as if trying to uncover a sinister conspiracy. Gabriel remained silent. "How do you expect to find yourself a wife if you keep acting this way? You are one of the prime catches of the season, but you have to do your part. An air of unattainability brings women buzzing around like bees on honey. That's true. So maybe it isn't all against our interests..." The remark hit too close to what happened that night, bringing Gabriel's anger back with a vengeance.

"Enough, Mother! I told you over and over again that I will marry when I deem the time is right. I won't repeat myself again."

His mother looked affronted by his outburst. "You have a duty to the Dukedom and the family name. Your father taught you their importance. You will not disrespect his memory this way."

A glacial mask came over Gabriel's face. "I know exactly what is expected of me. I allow you to talk to me like that because you are my Mother, but don't make the mistake of casting aspersions on my honour again."

His tone should have warned the Duchess to tread carefully, but she decided to ignore it. Or maybe she thought what came out of her mouth next was what Gabriel wanted to hear. "Now I recognise the Blakeburne pride. When you talk like that, I see so much of your father in you." It was the last nail in the coffin to seal the fantastic evening he had had. And *exactly* what he didn't need. The cumbersome shadow of his father always looming on him. The perfect Duke of Blakeburne, according to his mother and the entire Kingdom. The epitome of everything ducal. Always to be remembered as a severe but just man. The reality was a slightly different matter. His father had been a hard man. He had raised his children with a single all-encompassing aim. To uphold the Blakeburne name and all that came with it. The Duchy's coffers had to stay plentiful, the influence on the other peers indisputable. Those were the first lessons he remembered ever receiving from him. He had been maybe five or six years old but already aware of his many obligations as heir to the title. Gabriel had spent a large part of his childhood in his father's study, learning the ins and outs of estate management and how to deal with tenants. Those same tenants who never saw a young boy running carefree outdoor but only dignifiedly riding alongside the Duke. Many had put their hopes in the birth of a spare. Surely another young boy would have reassured the old Duke of the stability of the line. Then, he would become more lenient towards his firstborn. Unfortunately, that had not been the case. Edward's birth when Gabriel had been eight only added a new burden on those tiny shoulders. The role of older brother. Of model of conduct. He had been mostly kept apart from the untidy infant, his life almost unchanged by the new addition to the family.

Gabriel hadn't questioned his upbringing until much later. After spending the first years away at Eton, he had started to witness different kinds of interaction between fathers and sons, between siblings. Once, he had stared, flabbergasted, and kind of baffled, at the unseemly public display of the then Earl of Covington *hugging* his son, a time when he had come to take him home for the holidays. He had turned to Bellmore, who had simply shrugged, having lost his father when still a toddler. At home that Christmas —after having been retrieved from school by his father's valet— he had decided to try it as well. It had been inconceivable to hug the Duke. He had been too intimidating. That had left his younger brother. He had spent much of his time at home with him, dodging the Duke as much as possible. After Edward had broken one of his tin soldiers and Gabriel had given him one of his, he had felt two pudgy arms coming around him. He had accepted it stiffly, realising that there was something wrong with him. Because, while reciprocating the innocent hug, he could only hear his father's voice and nothing else. *Dukes don't show joy or despair; dukes don't show affection or pain.*

He had made a vow that day. Edward would not become like Gabriel. It may have been too late for him, but he would never permit that his father laid his cold, unfeeling clutches on his brother.

The same brother who, after remaining silent until that moment, decided it was wise to diffuse the situation before the thunderous look on his older brother's face became a raging storm. He had witnessed it before. He wasn't keen on repeating the experience.

"What did you think of tonight's musicale? Grace Winter is always a pleasant surprise, despite appearing on the verge of casting up her accounts at the beginning. I didn't know there would be an accompaniment, however. It was Rutherford-Blythe's gel, wasn't it?"

And they were back full circle. "Lady Ivy Kington, Countess of Everleigh, yes," answered Gabriel, looking out of the carriage window again. He felt the Duchess's eyes on him.

"Right, the unmarried Countess. She has been out for a while, hasn't she? I admit, if I think about her, nothing in particular comes to my mind." Gabriel made a noncommittal sound. Their carriage came to a halt in front of their townhouse, preventing Gabriel from voicing what came up unbidden in his mind. *Because you haven't looked close enough.*

Chapter Five

Ivy rushed down the stairs to join her family in the breakfast room. It was one of the few dictates of the house. One nobody refused to disobey. *As long as you resided under this roof, you broke your fast together with the other members of your family.* Nobody really minded. It was always a pleasant and lively moment, one when literature, politics, or the latest news published in the morning newspaper was discussed openly and without the widespread idea that women were to be sheltered from 'indelicate' topics. Other mornings, their conversation was more personal. Ivy had lost count of how many decisions had been pondered and made around that table. She could count on the fingers of one hand the number of times she had been absent. And she was not going to start that morning. She couldn't even blame the late night they had for her tardiness, for they had come home relatively early. No, it was the madness she had been part of that was to blame. She had spent the better part of two hours abed reliving the previous night's events. She had overanalysed everything that could have gone wrong, but mostly it was those few moments alone with the Duke of Blakeburne that refused to leave her mind. Thus, the undignified rush down the stairs, fortunately witnessed only by the two footmen stationed just outside the breakfast room. Ivy greeted them in passing.

"Good morning, Mother, Father!" She walked to them and pressed a kiss to each of their proffered cheeks. Her brother Gregory wasn't there, having recently acquired his own bachelor residence. He only popped in once in a while. Probably the few mornings he could extricate himself from the arms of the paramour gracing his bed.

"Good morning, dear," her mother greeted back, lifting her teacup to her mouth. Ivy thanked the footman, who immediately rushed to fill her cup. She wasn't offended that her father had yet to say a word. Years of watching him reading the perfectly pressed morning paper had shown her she only had to wait for him to finish. A few moments of reflection would follow, complemented by some frowning and humming. He would then neatly fold the paper, put it down on the table and start talking. The longer the pause between reading and talking, the more serious the discussion would be. As one of the most powerful men in the Kingdom, he was often asked for advice by the Prince Regent. Ivy was immensely pleased and proud that her father always asked for their opinions and, even more unorthodoxly, valued them by valuing their views.

Whatever was written on the front page that morning must have been of capital importance. Minutes were ticking by. Finally, the Duke raised his eyes.

"I don't like the situation in Vienna. If those at the Congress aren't aware that their squabbles are fomenting the consensus for Napoleon, they are even greater fools than I thought them to be." Well, not a light breakfast conversation today, for sure.

"Isn't Napoleon constantly watched in his exile on Elba?" her mother asked. The war with the French had been brutal. England was still trying to find a way to deal with the aftermaths of a conflict that had almost pushed the country on its knees. The idea that there might have been more to come was terrifying.

"Yes, indeed. But the air is shifting. I fear we must be prepared for the worst."

"What do you mean, the worst? You surely don't mean his return?" Ivy hoped her father was wrong, maybe for the first time ever. "Certainly, it won't come to that! If he is securely held on the island, Napoleon's attempts to free himself or to contact his Generals would be squashed."

Before her father could answer, there was a knock on the doorframe. Stevens, their butler, stood in the doorway, carrying a sumptuous flower arrangement. It wasn't rare that the Duchess received flowers as a token of appreciation for gracing one particular soirée or in the hope that an invitation would be accepted. If the Duke of Rutherford-Blythe influenced the Empire, the Duchess of Rutherford-Blythe absolutely reigned over the *beau monde*. That was why the insecurities that plagued Ivy were so difficult to understand. Why wasn't she able to shine like her mother?

Ivy wasn't at all jealous of her, however. How could she? The Duchess was an incredible mother, loving and understanding. It wasn't her fault her daughter was so…ordinary.

"Begging your pardon, Your Graces, my Lady. These were just delivered for Lady Everleigh." Ivy was spreading butter on a scone and stopped, her knife in mid-air.

"Oh, Ivy! Dear, look at these marvellous gardenias! They are quite rare and more so at this time of the year. Please, Stevens, place them here on the table. Thank you. Is there a card?" Her mother was beaming with delight.

"And from whom, pray tell, might you be receiving flowers?" Her father sounded decidedly less enthusiastic than his wife.

"I'm sure I have no idea, Father." Ivy turned towards the butler. "Stevens, are you sure they are for me?" The butler nodded solemnly, almost offended that she was questioning his efficiency.

53

"Yes, my Lady, they were delivered expressly for the Countess of Everleigh," Stevens answered with his nose in the air. Gregory always made fun of the poor butler. Ivy couldn't argue. The man was a veritably stick in the mud.

"Thank you, Stevens. Solicitous as always." Ivy tried to smooth his ruffled feathers, more interested in discovering the mysterious sender of the bouquet placed in front of her. She couldn't fathom who could have a reason to… *no*. Certainly not. Why would he? Ivy reached for the card as if she were braving a bunch of poisonous snakes and not delicate white blooms. She opened the note, aware of her parents' curious eyes on her.

Honour me with your presence for a ride in Hyde Park tomorrow. Please.
Blakeburne.

Butterflies started fluttering shamelessly in her stomach.

His handwriting was precise and without flourish, but the word *please* was written with slightly less precision, as if quickly scribbled in afterthought. As far as poetry went, it left much to be desired, but the note was so much *Blakeburne* as she had come to know him, Ivy couldn't help the small smile that tugged at her lips. A smile that didn't go undetected.

"Ooh. Did you see it, Rafael?" her mother exclaimed.

"It was impossible not to see it, my love. And I would like to know the cause of it." The Duke crossed his arms over his chest expectantly.

Oh Hell! Ivy hadn't told his parents about her conversations with the Duke of Blakeburne. They only knew they had been introduced at Lady Quindsley's ball. And certainly, they weren't aware of yesterday's bold 'rescue'.

Ivy knew she wouldn't be reprimanded. If anything, they would applaud her quick thinking. But she wasn't sure how her father would take the whole 'alone in a dark corner' part of the story. Ivy shuddered, thinking about a confrontation between the two Dukes. A sight to behold, to be sure, but not advisable. She decided to stick to an innocuous explanation, mixing truth with omissions.

"They are from the Duke of Blakeburne," she stated simply.

Silence followed. And stretched. Looking at the stunned expression on her parents' faces, she started to feel defensive.

"What? Is it so absurd that the Duke of Blakeburne would send me flowers? I know many would be surprised, but I hoped you wouldn't be left so speechless!" Ashamed of her rant, she blushed, closing her mouth.

Her mother was the first to say something.

"Of course, it isn't absurd! You know we think that any man should thank his lucky star simply for gaining your interest. Your father and I are simply surprised it was the *Duke of Blakeburne*. We didn't know you had much more than one passing conversation with him. And he seems so...*remote* all the time." The Duchess looked at her husband for confirmation.

"He certainly is a serious man. But that's not necessarily a bad trait. If his reputation is to be believed, his estates are flourishing. And his military achievements are laudable. A war hero and not yet discharged. I would have seen someone a bit more *cheerful* for you, but one would be a fool not to consider him a good prospect." He finished his reflection with a satisfied nod.

"Prospect? No one is talking about prospects! We only had a brief conversation yesterday at the musicale, before I played the pianoforte. In the note, he asks me to accompany him for a ride tomorrow. Maybe he's bored." They had clearly more to say but decided not to argue.

"Do you want to accept the invitation? If you don't want to spend time with him, you can always decline," said the Duchess reassuringly. Ivy found herself shaking her head.

"I think I will accept. I don't have any particular reason not to. Moreover, I don't think he's as cold as you say he is. He's a serious man for sure, but I saw glimpses of something else behind his seriousness. Now, if you excuse me, I will go and reply to the note. At least we'll find out his motives tomorrow." With a nod, she made a hasty retreat, realising she could have simply answered with a *Yes. I think I will gladly accept.* It wasn't necessary to run her mouth and let everyone know about her growing fascination with the Duke.

Why had he really sent her flowers? How sad was it that she was thrilled by the simple fact that he had remembered her, let alone bothered to invite her?

She left the room, puzzling over Dukes who took too much space in her mind, and she didn't notice that, back at the table, the Duchess of Rutherford-Blythe was patting the Duke's hand, half soothingly, and half as a warning for changes ahead.

Gabriel dismounted his stallion at exactly two o'clock the following day. He could appreciate why Lady Everleigh had decided to meet this early and not at a more fashionable hour. They would avoid the entire *ton* spotting them together and drawing their own unsolicited conclusions. Gabriel approved of her caution.

He had a plan. A well-structured one. He had not reached the rank of Major by not planning ahead. His invitation was not a spur-of-the-moment decision. On the contrary, after a night of sleep that had been finally able to cool down his anger, he had concluded he would risk the possibility of worsening his mother's matchmaking by asking Lady Everleigh to ride with him. A chaperoned ride in Hyde Park was a good idea for what he had in mind. Down the well-trodden paths, they would clarify what had happened on that blasted balcony. He might even thank her. They would then part ways at her house, his pride restored and his fascination with her under control. Because, yes, he had an ulterior reason for being there today. By finally being able to have a normal conversation with Lady Everleigh, Gabriel would finally dispel those irritating thoughts plaguing him. She would reveal herself to be just like any other woman he had met before, unable to keep him interested for long. What he had told his mother was the truth. He was well aware of the duty he had towards the Blakeburne line. Now wasn't the right time for marriage, though. Not because he was keen on prolonging his bachelor life, carefree, raucous, and reckless. Gabriel wasn't sure he had ever been reckless a day in his life. No, he just couldn't take a wife at the moment. The war with France seemed to be over, with Boney out of the picture, but something was changing on the Continent. He had been thinking about selling his commission for a long time, having served in his fair share of battles. But, until he was sure lasting peace reigned in Europe, he couldn't in all conscience leave the Army. Not when he still felt a duty towards his country. And not when the carnage was still what he saw when he closed his eyes. Therefore, he couldn't add the responsibility of a wife. A wife who would require his attention, his time, or, Heaven help him, his *love*. Lady Ingram's shenanigans had silenced any lingering doubt in his mind. He wasn't made for strong emotions. He was the Duke of Blakeburne. When he would finally take a wife, becoming the next Duchess of Blakeburne would have to be enough for her.

After knocking on the front door, he was led to a drawing-room by a deferential butler and left there with the assurance that the Countess would be down shortly. About five minutes later, the door opened again to let Lady Everleigh in. She was dressed in a deep green riding habit that modelled her curves to perfection. His attention was drawn to her long legs and small waist. That didn't bode well for the letting-his-fascination-go part of his plan. Gabriel had the sudden urge to span that waist with his hands and bring her body against his. He wanted to recapture the sensations he had felt in the dark alcove, where the only things that had mattered had been how their breaths had mingled, and the promise of what could have happened had they acted on their impulses.

He chased away those thoughts before his body betrayed their lustful turn. It was ironic that just a few minutes before, he had been reaffirming —even if only to himself— how he could not afford to have passion disrupt his life, and now he stood, lusting after Ivy Kington.

The Lady in question curtsied in front of him. Gabriel bowed and greeted her.

"Good afternoon, Lady Everleigh. Thank you for gracing me with your presence this afternoon. The weather is perfect for a ride." She smiled politely.

"Good afternoon to you, Your Grace. Thank you for the invitation. The weather seems indeed to be a good omen for the day ahead. Shall we?" She motioned to the door. He offered her his arm, trying not to react to the contact, so soon after regaining his control. The overzealous butler was already opening the front door.

"Thank you, Stevens," she said with a smile.

"Have a nice ride, Your Grace, my Lady. I had Empress saddled for you, as you requested. Jimmy and Henry are ready to accompany you." Gabriel looked at where he had left his horse and found not only the Countess's mount but a young woman, dressed as a lady's maid, sitting nervously on a very placid-looking brown mare, and two large, rough-looking men as well. They were sporting matching expressions of distrust on their rugged faces and, if Gabriel wasn't mistaken, firearms under their jackets. For a ride in Hyde Park? He wasn't sure if he ought to be insulted.

"I expressly requested to be chaperoned only by Poppy," she told the butler with a resigned sigh. "It'd reached Father's ears, hadn't it?" At the butler's nod, Gabriel was strangely relieved that Lady Everleigh had not been the one who had felt the need for an armed escort.

"All right, we'd better go before this veritable convoy attracts even more attention than it already has." She turned towards a groom, who helped her on the sidesaddle. They started navigating the busy streets in silence, avoiding carts and pedestrians, until they reached Hyde

Park. It was still early enough not to be forced to stop to greet and converse every few steps, but not so early to be completely alone. Well, alone as they could be chaperoned and guarded by two armed brutes.

Gabriel didn't know how to approach the subject that had brought him to her that day. It was she who finally broke the silence.

"I'm sorry for Jimmy and Henry. I know it seems slightly excessive for a ride in the Park. I'm sure my father wouldn't mind if I tell you this, but years before I was born, when the Duke and the Duchess were just married, she was kidnapped in Green Park during her usual morning ride. My father was frantic. He didn't rest until he found her. Everybody thought it was a terribly romantic gesture at the time, and luckily it all ended well, but it left my father with an overprotective side when parks and rides are concerned. I hope you didn't take it personally."

Gabriel could perfectly relate to the need to protect one's family, especially in light of such a tale. His pride was a bit bruised nevertheless. He wasn't one to boast about his skills, but he could certainly hold his own against potential assailants in a park.

"Don't worry, my Lady. I find it admirable that the Duke puts his daughter's safety above all else, more so now that I know the reason behind it. I hope you know you are safe with me." He hadn't meant to add the last bit, but it suddenly became paramount for him to know she wasn't intimidated by him like many others were. He hadn't had that impression, but Lady Everleigh was proving to be a complex young lady. He could perceive the shyness everybody talked about, but, during their brief acquaintance, she had shown him how that was only a tiny fraction of her personality.

"Rest assured, Your Grace. I don't feel in any kind of danger when I'm with you." Gabriel's shoulders relaxed. "If our past interactions are anything to go by, I'd say *you* have more to fear than me when dealing with the fairer sex." Gabriel was surprised by her blatant reference to Lady Ingram's machination. It offered the perfect opening to say what he had come to say, but he was distracted by her sharp intake of breath and her widening eyes.

"I'm so sorry. I don't know what came over me. Let's pretend I didn't say anything, please." She was obviously uncomfortable with her boldness, for she hastened to change the course of the conversation. "My, what a beautiful horse. I've never seen a coat quite so flawlessly black." Gabriel, instead, wasn't ready to let the matter drop. Looking around, he noticed that their three shadows were following them, just out of earshot. Pleased they could talk in a semi-private manner, Gabriel neared his stallion to her grey mare.

"No, no, Lady Everleigh, don't change the subject. It is, after all, the reason I invited you today."

"Oh. Of course, it is," she replied cryptically. Her face didn't betray anything, but Gabriel had a feeling those few words carried a deeper meaning.

"Right. I wanted to talk to you about the unpleasant scene on Lady Winter's balcony..."

"There isn't much to say, really."

"I beg to differ. It's not a situation I normally find myself in. Being dragged in a dark corner by an unmarried lady—"

She interrupted him, eyes suddenly aflame.

"*That* is the part that bothers you? Not the fact that Lady Ingram..." The end of her sentence was suddenly drowned by a screech coming from behind them. Both sharply turning towards its source, they saw the Countess's maid lose control of what, until that moment, had been a very biddable horse. Maybe the mount had felt the nervousness of its rider, or something had spooked it. From his point of view, Gabriel appraised it was just a matter of calming the animal down, but it needed to be done before its skittishness became dangerous.

"Oh no, poor Poppy! I knew it was too much for her to ride alone, but I let her convince me she would enjoy being on a saddle. I'll go help her before she hurt herself." Gabriel didn't dwell too much on the unusual fact that a mistress had obliged the whims of a servant. He instead saw an opening he intended to exploit. He put a hand on the Lady's arm to stop her. By the time they had noticed the commotion, the two guards had reached the distraught maid. One of them was already taking the reins from her unsure hands.

"Are you well, Miss?" Gabriel inquired. At her shaky nod, he addressed the men. "Take her to that bench. Then walk the horse for a bit to calm it down." The two seemed reluctant to leave their mistress, but, at his ducal glare, they relented and nodded. He then turned back to Lady Everleigh. "Come, my Lady. Let's wait under those trees." He could see she wanted to object to his high-handedness. In the end, she steered her grey and followed him. Once they had reached the shade provided by the canopy, Gabriel manoeuvred his stallion to stand directly beside her horse and faced her.

"Before you point out that they are *your* servants I dismissed, let me assure you I won't let anything untoward happen, especially in full view of anyone who cared to look." They *were* partially hidden from the main paths, but Gabriel wasn't going to delay their conversation any longer.

"Of that I am sure, Your Grace," she assured him with a flat voice. "What I was going to say is that I appreciate you caring for my maid. It's very...*kind* of you." Kind. Gabriel was sure many would laugh themselves silly if they heard him be defined as *kind*. He nodded graciously anyway.

"Now, for the reason I asked you here today. I'd like to hear your version of Wednesday's events."

She sighed. "I'm not sure what you'd like me to say. I thought you wouldn't appreciate being forced into a situation not of your making. I was in the right place at the right time. So, I acted." Her answer was exquisitely vague and unhelpful. She was clearly embarrassed.

"How did you know that Lady Ingram had orchestrated something? You were the one standing unseen in the dark." His tone sounded suspicious, but just talking about it sparked his anger anew.

Not at her, but at the unavoidable consequences he would have been forced into, had the Baroness's scheme worked. Only, she didn't know that. Her eyes flashed with irritation. Straightening her spine, she answered, a picture of upstanding dignity.

"If you must know, on my way to the balcony to alleviate a headache, I overheard Lady Ingram talking to Mrs Higgins about how easily the latter could 'stumble upon' you two in a compromising position. Lady Ingram was firmly convinced you would then be honour-bound to marry her. I wouldn't have given her ramblings a second thought if you didn't actually appear when she said you would. I simply reacted, driven by my morals." That confirmed the sequence of events he had reconstructed in his mind. He should thank Lady Everleigh for having spared him an unpleasant surprise. It hadn't been anything personal for her, just the demands of her sense of right and wrong. He should probably add an apology for having doubted her. He couldn't explain what came out of his mouth next.

"You thought to spare me from being found in a compromising position with Lady Ingram by putting me in a compromising position with *you*?" He immediately recognised his mistake. A big mistake. The acclaimed military man in him was asking for an immediate retreat or that he was shot for his stupidity. But it was already too late. She was openly furious now.

"I learned my lesson, Duke. Far from me to think you could have needed rescue! Especially if then I —and obviously not Lady Ingram — have to stand here to be berated for, no, accused of, the very same dishonest intents I succeeded in thwarting!" Gabriel tried to diffuse her ire. Her rightful ire.

"I apologise for implying. You are right. If you hadn't intervened, the evening would have turned really unpleasant." She raised her brows at his euphemism. "However grateful, at the same time, I don't like that you put your own reputation in jeopardy with your actions. You took a great risk."

"This is the worst thank you I have ever received. Next time, try to avoid making calf eyes across crowded rooms and spare us all the bother. It could be misinterpreted." What was she talking about? He had barely spared a few glances for Lady Ingram. He was too busy looking at, well, *her* to pay much attention to anyone else.

"I have never, and I will never, make *calf eyes* to anyone." Just thinking about it was preposterous.

"You should explain it to Lady Ingram. From what I heard, she was firmly convinced you couldn't wait to put your hands on her."

"This is not a topic befitting a gentle bred Lady! Nor is eavesdropping on others' conversations, over whose beliefs I have absolutely no control!" She couldn't possibly know Lady Ingram had been his mistress in the past. Not that it mattered anyway.

"And what I would have witnessed, had I not decided to intervene, is? Befitting, I mean. And that's hilarious! How many of *my* conversations have you eavesdropped since we met?"

"If by 'conversations' you mean hearing you talk to yourself, I have lost count."

"What are you implying, Your Grace? That I am some sort of bedlamite? How dare you, you, insufferable, arrogant—" Gabriel didn't know how the hell his well-planned conversation could have gone so wrong so quickly. He decided to do what he finally admitted he had really wanted to do. It wouldn't bring his plan back on track, but he didn't care at that point. He crashed his lips against hers.

Ivy was stunned. Never in a million years, she would have imagined that the Duke of Blakeburne would silence her with a kiss. One moment they were at each other's throats, throwing insults. The next, his firm yet soft lips were mercilessly demanding a response from her. Ivy had experienced few kisses in her life, mostly from bored country gentlemen. This had nothing in common with those gentle pecks. This was like the Duke himself: commanding and serious. At the same time, the passion behind it was as staggering as it was unexpected. Ivy again felt that something more was chained inside Blakeburne, tightly controlled. Something she had a glimpse of each time they met.

After the first moment of surprise, Ivy found herself reciprocating the kiss. She lifted a hand to his nape, drawing him near. In turn, he put his hand on her waist, deepening the pressure on her lips. He urged her mouth open with a gentle nibble to her lower lip. A guttural moan came from him when she acquiesced, and Ivy felt her body respond to his appreciation. She was utterly lost in him, their tongues duelling together, hers meeting his stroke for stroke. Her hand was now playing with his soft hair, and his was slowly rising towards the side of her breasts, the unhurried movement in deep contrast with the fierceness of the kiss. She felt drunk from those kisses, and at the same time, she was parched, a thirst that only he could quench.

In an attempt to get even nearer, Ivy leaned to the side, shifting her balance towards Blakeburne. The movement caused her to press her heel into Empress's side. All the horses in the Rutherford-Blythe's stable were skilfully trained, and hers, being no exception, reacted immediately to that pressure. Ivy felt the lower half of her body slide to the right while the upper half remained attached to the Duke. Only Blakeburne's arms, thankfully already around her, prevented an undignified fall to the ground, headfirst.

With that, reality came crashing down on her, together with a multitude of sounds and movements around her that the kiss had completely obliterated. And they weren't leaves gently moved by the wind or birds singing above their heads. No, they were voices of people and clatter of hooves. People who could have easily decided to rest under those same trees. If she had thought the events at Winter

House had had the potential of ruining them, kissing in Hyde Park would lead directly to the banns.

Still slightly panting, Ivy looked around her to make sure they had not doomed them both. As luck would have it, nobody seemed to be paying particular attention to them. Even Ivy's servants were still near the bench Blakeburne had directed them to, their backs to them. Ivy used those few moments to compose herself and find the courage to face the Duke. She was afraid of what she would see on his face. As shocking as it had been, she couldn't bring herself to regret the kiss. It had been...*glorious*. She hadn't a clue why Blakeburne had kissed her. He did not seem the type of man who went around kissing women in parks, oblivious to social convention. But she didn't know him so well to be completely sure. She didn't flatter herself that that had been some sort of earth-shattering event for him, but she couldn't bear seeing horror or panic in his eyes. Still not facing him, she was marshalling her expression while hiding her flaming cheeks. The silence was reaching an unbearable point, with Blakeburne in no hurry to break it. The only way she saw out of it was to brush the whole thing off. She was still searching for the right words when he finally said something.

"We should return. I'll see you home." Well, that was more effective than any dismissal she could have ever devised. Ivy finally mustered the will to look at him. What she found was what she should have expected from a man who most thought emotionless. Nothing. A straight face. Unreadable eyes. Ivy tried not to let him see how *that* affected her. Regret would have been difficult to bear, given that she — until a few moments before— hadn't felt one ounce of it, but at least it would have been *something*. A sign that the kiss at least had the power to unbalance him. Instead, she had to contend with a blank wall of nothing. It played right into her deep-rooted insecurities. She would have settled for a flicker of warmth in those green eyes. How pathetic was that?

"My Lady, shall we?" Blakeburne repeated. She nodded and manoeuvred Empress around. She slowly returned to the main trail, noticing that the park was getting busier by the minute. Ivy felt Blakeburne's presence behind her and the stares of the other members of the *ton*, almost assuredly wondering what they were doing together. *You and me both, ladies and lords.* She refused to meet anyone's eyes, only calling out appropriate greetings in passing. She was focused on reaching Poppy, Jimmy, and Henry, who were waiting for them, already on their horses. The two guards sent the Duke a suspicious look but didn't say anything. Ivy addressed her maid.

"Poppy, how are you feeling? Are you ready to ride home? If it scares you, you could always walk to the townhouse. Jimmy or Henry can take care of the horse." The maid looked absolutely horrified by the thought.

"Oh no, my Lady! I came here to chaperone you, and I won't slack me duties!" she said, clearly upset, letting her London accent slip through. Then, realising that the forceful words could be interpreted as disobedience, she quickly added, "You are very kind, my Lady, thank you. For makin' me rest as well. Don't worry. I only lost control for a moment. It won't happen again." At those words, Ivy felt the Duke stiffen beside her. That little telltale sign was more eloquent than any speech. Ivy suppressed a sigh and, motioning to Blakeburne that she was ready to go, took the busy street, promising herself to leave any thought of the kiss at the gates. They rode in silence, once again avoiding carts and vendors. Upon reaching Mayfair, she turned to the Duke. Years of good upbringing were stronger than the embarrassment she always seemed to feel at one point in the company of the Duke of Blakeburne.

"Are you planning to attend Lady Langton's ball tonight, Your Grace?" The Duke blinked slowly as if he had only then noticed she stood beside him. And that they had reached their destination. *My, those had to be some intense thoughts.* He cleared his throat.

"That wasn't my intention, no," was his curt answer. No excuses, no disclosure of other engagements. Nothing on which they could further a conversation.

"Oh. Well, I hope you enjoy your evening then. Thank you for today's invitation, Your Grace."

"My pleasure, my Lady." With nothing left to say, Ivy dismounted, gave the reins to the groom, and climbed the stairs to the front door, where Stevens already held the door open for her.

"I hope you had a pleasant ride, my Lady," enquired the butler. Ivy couldn't resist looking over her shoulders, but Blakeburne was already nothing more than a retreating figure. Refusing to feel rejected, Ivy plastered a smile on her face.

"It was, thank you, Stevens. I doubt we'll see more of the Duke in the future, though," she said, leaving a perplexed butler to close the door behind her.

Chapter Six

Gabriel didn't have the excuse of having been tricked by his mother this time. He had dressed, summoned the carriage, and entered Lady Langton's residence of his own volition. While the butler announced his arrival, he was still wondering why he had sacrificed another evening on the altar of society.

He could have spent it at his club, where he wasn't considered a slab of fresh —and rich— meat. Then why was he there? More precisely, for whom was he there? The answer was Lady Everleigh. If he had to be honest with himself, he had not handled the meeting with her at all well. It was embarrassing how many times he had had to admit it to himself lately. He hardly recognised the man who could be blindsided so easily and who kissed young ladies under trees. After arguing with them, if that wasn't bad enough. It was paramount that he put some distance between him and Lady Everleigh. That had been exactly his intention after leaving her that afternoon. His plan to confront her on the unfortunate incident with Lady Ingram in a civilised way had failed miserably. Nonetheless, he doubted either of them would want to rehash it once again. In the end, he had achieved his aim. That wasn't what made him search through the pile of invitations he had been only too happy to ignore, only to fish out the one she had mentioned. One of the perks of being a Duke? You could decline or ignore any invitation you wanted, but nobody would dare turn you away if you decided to suddenly appear on their front steps.

He was attracting the usual interested stares. He was still a novelty, still a bachelor, and his eligibility still beyond some mamas' wildest dreams.

He was greeted graciously by the hostess, and he immediately searched the room for the reason for his recent discombobulation. What he found instead was his mother, beaming at him, standing beside a young, familiar man. He made his way to them, cataloguing the man's light brown hair and green eyes, eerily similar to his own.

"Cousin Charles, I wasn't aware you were in Town. When did you arrive?" He came face to face with his uncle's firstborn son. Charles was a couple of years younger than him, but their slight age difference didn't become noticeable until they both assumed their sires' titles and Gabriel became the Duke of Blakeburne and Charles Lord Eastham. As children, Gabriel had always looked at Charles with curiosity, mixed with the ducal detachment that had been ingrained into him. Back then, he simply could not understand how his uncle could ever hope to raise his heir befittingly if he allowed Charles to regularly spend his day playing and not learning how to manage the lands. It was only when he had left for school that Gabriel had started to question whether his uncle had it right, after all. Now, childhood long gone, he looked at the man he hadn't seen more than a handful of times in the last ten years. Charles' lean frame had filled out, leaving behind the thinness of boyhood. If one looked closely, he and Gabriel shared almost the same height and build, traits shared by most Eastham men.

"Hello, Gabriel. What a pleasant surprise." He gestured to the Duchess. "Aunt Ophelia told me she wasn't sure you'd be able to attend. I planned to visit you tomorrow since I arrived in Town just this morning, but Aunt intercepted me and was so kind to bring me along tonight."

"Where are you staying, cousin?"

"I had my own townhouse readied before my arrival. I plan to stay in Town for a lengthy visit. That's how Aunt spotted me." Charles smiled fondly at her.

"Does it mean you too are finally in search of a bride?" His mother was really unrelenting, like the most voracious dog with a bone.

"Me too?" Charles raised a questioning brow at Gabriel. He shook his head and groaned inside. He really had to find a way to distract his mother from her obsession. Maybe, if Charles seriously wanted to fall into the parson's mousetrap, he could redirect the Duchess's attempts towards a less —for all— frustrating direction.

"It is not really for the Season's lovely ladies that I decided to spend time in London, dear Aunt."

"What is it with this generation of Eastham men? All this reticence is unbecoming."

"Ah, but I don't have the Blakeburne line to pass down to my progeny. You should introduce Gabriel here to your acquaintances, now that he's done fighting Napoleon and has decided to emerge from the country." So much for diversion.

"Lord knows I'm trying. Nonetheless, I am sure your mother would agree with me. It is high time for both of you."

"I am sure she would, Aunt Ophelia." That seemed to finally exhaust the topic, at least for the night. He and Charles started talking about the renovations Edward was planning for Blakeburne Manor and how his cousin could use some of his ideas for his own country seat. They were discussing the new developments that could lead to installing a piping system indoors when the woman who refused to leave his thoughts entered his line of vision. She was clad in a light blue gown, a sheer silver embroidered silk overlay making it sparkle in the candlelight. Gabriel wasn't an expert in female fashion by any means, but even he knew its hue and style were absolutely appropriate for an unmarried lady, few years out of the schoolroom. Then why all he was able to see was how the silver threads drew the viewer's eyes to what was *inside* that bodice? Gabriel didn't like it one bit. If *he* had to tear his eyes away from the sight, God knew how many other men without his iron control were having lustful thoughts about the woman who, just a few hours before, had been in his arms. Gabriel found himself looking around in search of those scoundrels, his insides boiling. Satisfied with what he found —or better, didn't find— he returned his gaze to Lady Everleigh. She was conversing with her Mother and Lady Victoria Gallard, a calm expression on her face, unaware of his scrutiny. The three women were soon joined by an older couple and a young woman who had to be around Lady Everleigh's age. He must have met them on a previous occasion because he was sure he had seen them before.

Realising he wasn't paying a modicum of attention to what Charles was saying, he tore his eyes away. Without his contribution, the conversation had moved on, with his mother asking Charles about something her sister-in-law had written in her latest letter. His cousin answered her, but he kept his eyes firmly on Gabriel, or rather, they focused on him after flicking briefly behind Gabriel's shoulders. Something flashed in his cousin's eyes, but it vanished as fast as it appeared.

"It's time to start mingling, my boy." The Duchess told Gabriel. The span of time between one talk of matrimony and the next was becoming alarmingly short.

"Dukes don't *mingle*, Mother. They don't need to." Gabriel counteracted haughtily.

"Oh, you sound so much like your Father when you talk like this!" Gabriel would have gritted his teeth at that, but that was something else Dukes didn't do. It wasn't the time to argue that it wasn't a compliment for Gabriel. She wouldn't have understood. She never did. The Duchess of Blakeburne couldn't see anything beyond the honour of carrying the Blakeburne name. Gabriel couldn't even fault her. She was born —and raised— to become a Duke's wife. For as long as he had been alive, Gabriel had listened to her talking to her friends about how she had reached happiness by marrying Blakeburne and giving birth to an heir and a spare within a few years of marriage. He could honestly say his mother had never called him by his given name. He had always been Addington, then Blakeburne. At least Edward had had a few years of being just Lord Edward before assuming the courtesy title of Marquess of Addington when Gabriel had inherited the Dukedom.

Deciding that maybe mingling wasn't such a bad idea, after all, he took his leave from his relatives. With plans of making a quick tour around the room to pacify the Duchess and then head towards the card room, his eyes unconsciously searched once again for the reason he had subjected himself to all that. She was now standing only with the two vaguely familiar women. But that wasn't the only notable difference. She had her back turned to him, her shoulders sagged under an invisible weight, her head slightly bent forward. He frowned. What could they possibly be saying to cause such a reaction? That wasn't at all in line with the spirit she had always unleashed on him and more with the idea the *ton* had of her.

A foreign protective instinct took over him. Before realising it, he started walking purposely in their direction. After a few steps, he forced himself to stop. *Think, Blakeburne! You can't simply march over there and pretend an explanation!* Well, actually, he could, but it would have all sorts of implications. He could only imagine how tongues would wag after witnessing it. He expelled a frustrated breath. Why did he care so much anyway? Why did he care if the woman he had just met and who had no qualms about insulting him to his face now shrank under those women's words? He had kissed her, true, but that had been an aberration.

Resolute to leave the matter alone, he resumed his walk at a slower pace. It wasn't his fault that, to exit the room, he had to walk right past Lady Everleigh. He would not be eavesdropping. *Again*. Dukes didn't eavesdrop. But if others' conversations reached his ears, what could he do?

Once upon them, Gabriel was able to hear snippets of a conversation that seemed to have been going on for a while. The older woman, who up close he was now sure he had previously met, but for the life of him couldn't remember the name, was talking, eyes fixed on Lady Everleigh, while the younger one stood silent, a bored expression on her classically pretty face.

"...my dear, are you really sure he didn't enquire about anybody else? About...I don't know, my Eleanor?" The woman's fake nonchalance in pointing at the blond girl couldn't fool anyone.

"As I've already told you, Aunt, he didn't mention anyone. I'm sure he would have, but his visit was cut short." Lady Everleigh tried to pacify the woman. He finally remembered her to be Lady Northcott, Rutherford-Blythe's sister-in-law. The younger woman beside her had to be Lady Eleanor, her daughter.

"I really don't understand what he could possibly...." Lady Northcott was saying pensively as if trying to solve the riddle of the Sphinx.

Gabriel had already walked past them, their voices out of earshot. Just before exiting the room, he couldn't help one last look over his shoulder. Whose visit were they talking about? Apart from his, that was. His eyes met Lady Everleigh's. He had been correct in his assessment before. She looked...dejected and embarrassed, even if she was doing her best to hide it. That was unacceptable. He observed her turn on her heels and walk away from the duo, heading towards the balcony. From the look on her face, she was in sore need of some peace and quiet. Given their history, he would leave her alone. Sure of the rightness of his decision, he made himself walk away and, finally, step into the hallway. He then entered the room to his right. There had to be another door leading to the bloody balcony.

❧ ❧ ❧

Damn and blast! No, Aunt, the Duke didn't invite me to the bloody Park to gather information about Eleanor! Why? Ever thought that maybe he isn't bloody interested in her? And no, we didn't talk about me asking Father to meet with him to support a bloody political bill! And you know what? He kissed me! Ah! What do you make of it, Aunt? Did he do it for Parliament or his estates? Mm?

That was what Ivy should have said. Maybe without all the 'bloodies'. But something along that line, to put her aunt in her place. Instead, like the complete ninny that she was, she had stood there for what had seemed like hours, listening to Aunt Evelyn ruminating on what could possibly have been the obscure reason why she was spotted riding in Hyde Park with the elusive Duke. Oh, she had covered all kinds of scenarios, one less flattering than the other. From simple boredom to an absurd theory of him being a foreign spy, she had come up with the same two conclusions.

One, there absolutely had to be a reason behind it. Because a young, sought-after Duke such as Blakeburne had undoubtedly better things to do than spend his time with *Ivy*. Two, even if not apparent, his final objective had to be getting to know Eleanor. In that case, it wouldn't even matter if he were a spy. The Duke of Blakeburne's interest in Eleanor trampled treason in dear Aunty's book. And Ivy had stood there, under her cousin's smug gaze. She had even apologised! Ivy knew the true reason behind the invitation, and it was hardly better than Aunt Evelyn's farfetched ideas. The Duke of

74

Blakeburne really wasn't interested in her, not that anybody would ever think he was. He was neither in desperate need of funds nor connections. And after the way they had parted, Ivy didn't need to have someone else tell her how the situation would not lead anywhere. And she was fine with that. She was the curiously unassuming daughter in an extraordinary family. Forgettable.

Ivy leaned her elbows on the balcony rail, looking at the dark night before her. If her mother were to catch her commiserating like that, there would be hell to pay. In the form of motherly love, of course. She needed the time alone, however, to bring her irritation under control. She wasn't proud of having let her aunt's words affect her so. It had been the same all her life. Victoria was convinced that Eleanor and her mother were jealous of her and the Duchess of Rutherford-Blythe. If that were the case, Ivy would trade her status for some of her cousin's confidence in a heartbeat. Actually, that wasn't true. Ivy liked being a Countess. She liked holding a title in a world where only men could boast about their power as their own, while women were only a reflection of their fathers', husbands', or brothers'. At the same time, she had always hoped that, sooner or later, she would accompany her title with a self-assurance to match. It hadn't happened yet. And each time she won the silly bet against Victoria, and she had to be reintroduced once again to someone, her hope faltered more.

This time, the matter was made worse by the subject of the conversation himself, who, with a timing she was starting to hate with a vengeance, had decided to walk past them while she was desperately trying to escape the unpleasant conversation. How much had he heard? Enough to make him stop on his path, apparently. She sighed pitifully at the sky.

"I feel another passionate speech about stars and constellations in the near future." Ivy couldn't muster the energy to be startled by the deep voice suddenly invading her quiet. *For God's sake, is it possible to wallow in self-pity in peace around here?* If Blakeburne had followed her to make sure she would not talk about the other night's events with anyone, again, she would probably scream. Or kick him. Fewer risks of attracting attention if she kicked him. Maybe, this time, he wanted to make sure she didn't breathe a word about their kiss. He didn't have to worry about that. After his behaviour that afternoon, it was already acquiring that feeling of unreality only dreams and distant memories had.

"I'm sure it won't be necessary this time. Will it, Your Grace?" Ivy said, refusing to turn and look at him. "I hate to be rude, Your Grace, but, to avoid any repetition of those enjoyable moments, maybe it would be better if you went back inside before anyone sees you." Ivy was surprised by how firm her voice sounded, not betraying the erratic beat of her heart, who had treacherously sped up simply by hearing his voice. That was good. Calm and controlled was good.

"It's only polite to look at someone when you are dismissing them, Lady Everleigh." Ivy found herself obeying his request without volition, locking her eyes with his emerald ones. His expression matched the tone of his voice and was exactly as she expected. Not a hint of a smile graced his beautiful lips to soften his words. Nothing transpired from his serious expression, those green eyes fixed on her face. Ivy should have felt intimidated, as she was sure many others were, but instead, she felt strangely comforted by his presence. He really was a formidable man. It was truly a pity that she was...well, her. Probably one of many women fascinated by his strong presence and exceptional good looks.

"Your Grace, I don't think it's wise to..."

"Stop 'your gracing' me, woman!" Blakeburne interrupted brusquely. Ivy was taken aback by his vehemence. His face wasn't emotionless anymore, his eyes ablaze. What was happening? One minute he had been the usual imperturbable self, the next, he had snapped.

"I apologise, *Your Grace*," she said, neatly enunciating his honorific. By God, the man had the power to get under her skin. And not just in a good, tingly way. Ivy's reply dripped haughtiness and sarcasm. "Last time I checked, that was the correct way to address the Duke of Blakeburne."

"I wonder where this backbone was a few minutes ago."

"I beg your pardon?"

"Yes, you should, if I am to be the only recipient of that sharp tongue of yours." He raised an eyebrow, collected once again, the earlier display of emotions a distant memory. Drat the man. That effortless movement of brows was much more effective than her scowl.

Ivy didn't know what to make of his behaviour. His earlier outburst would have been difficult to believe, had Ivy not witnessed it. Then his words registered.

"I don't have a sharp tongue!" If possible, that blasted eyebrow went even higher. There *was* a modicum of truth in what he was implying. Despite how intimidating and imposing he was, Ivy had never felt the need to retract into her shell with him. That was even more surprising given the number of times he had witnessed her in embarrassing situations. That very moment rapidly shaping into one, for instance.

"If I ever behaved in a non-impeccable way, it would be as a consequence of *your* actions." It seemed he roused her argumentative streak as well. All the other ladies swooning after the Duke would be absolutely horrified. Blakeburne emitted a sound that, from anyone else, would have been a snort. From him, it was…a regal sound of disbelief?

"Are you referring to something in particular, my Lady? Or is it my very presence that destabilises you? Please, care to elaborate?"

"Not particularly." Her curt answer was met with a slight upturn of his lips. *Yes, all very amusing, Blakeburne.* She couldn't even appreciate the rare appearance of one of his smiles. And it was all his fault.

"Then do you care to elaborate on the reason why I saw you shrink before my eyes in that room like you wanted to disappear? And on why I found you here looking so desolate?"

"Not particularly," she repeated. There wasn't a chance in hell that Ivy would talk about her conversation with her aunt with him. Not when it was very probable that he already knew he had been the topic of the conversation. That hint of a smile was swept away from his face.

"By God, woman, you are exasperating." Ivy saw the green of his eyes sparkle. She could see it clearly because, unbeknown to them both, with each retort, they had taken a step towards each other. They were almost touching. They became aware of their nearness at the same time. Their breaths mingled and became shallow, the air around them thickening.

"I am *not* exasperating," Ivy said, her voice reduced to a whisper. She tilted her head to look directly into his eyes.

His voice was hoarse when he replied, "Infuriating…."

They didn't know who closed the final distance between them. In the next breath, their lips fused together. The kiss was uncontrolled, almost wild. Their lips crashed together again and again. A struggle to gain the upper hand, a wordless continuation of their constant arguing. Blakeburne forced her lips open to his invading tongue. Ivy retaliated by pushing him against the outside wall of the house. A wise move, given that curious eyes could have easily spotted them. Not that her mind was on trivial things like being caught. Not when the Duke was currently nibbling at her lower lips, only to soothe the sting with his tongue.

"*You* are infuriating…," Ivy said once she came up for breath. Her hands were woven in his hair. She tugged at it for good measure.

"Mmm…" was the only thing he replied before taking her mouth again. Ivy was totally consumed by their kiss, but not so much as not to feel his hand gently sliding upwards from her waist to the swell of her breast. The contact sent tingles through her body. She moaned against his mouth. After one last gentle peck, he left her lips and attacked her neck. Her mind tried half-heartedly to keep the situation under control, only to be completely ignored by her body.

"Blakeburne, I think we should stop." She shivered at the wet slide of his tongue on her pulse. Her hands left his soft hair to palm the width of his shoulders and then descend to the small of his back, just above his behind, drawing him nearer to her still. It was his turn to groan when their lower bodies touched. Something hard and intriguing poked at her belly. She knew what that was. She may have been innocent, but she wasn't ignorant of the ways between men and women. All her knowledge, however, didn't prepare her for what she felt with her whole body pressed against his.

"Gabriel," he said, coming back to kiss her mouth.

"Mmm?" She was so lost in a world of pleasure she didn't understand at first.

"Call me Gabriel," he repeated, his free hand cupping her bottom, bringing them even closer, if possible. "I won't have you 'your gracing' me while your tongue is in my mouth and my hand is on your breasts." He emphasised the point by gently kneading her left breast over her gown, his warm palm stimulating the hard bud. As if she could have missed that.

"Oh..." was the only reply she could muster. She was aflame, straining towards something unknown. Her body was guided by instinct. By impulse, she moved her pelvis against the straining bulge in his breeches, making them both groan. She did it again, her core needing that friction, and Blakeburne, *Gabriel*, came back to her mouth with renewed vehemence.

"Ivy?"

That wasn't her giving him leave to call her by her Christian name. No, she was too busy exploring his body to even think about talking. Especially not when her mouth was Gabriel's willing hostage.

"Ivy, dear, are you there?" Her mother's voice finally registered in her clouded mind. She tore her mouth away. Her moan had nothing to do with pleasure and everything with the fact that, for the second time in the last few days, she found herself in danger of being discovered in the dark with the Duke of Blakeburne. At least this time, they were doing what anyone would think they were doing. Thankfully, it would be her mother who discovered them. Small mercies.

She looked at Gabriel, whose hands were still circling her waist. Unsurprisingly —or maybe a bit surprisingly, and most certainly unflatteringly— his face was expressionless. Gone was the fire that had set his eyes ablaze. Ivy mourned the loss of it more deeply than she wanted to admit. His slightly swollen and moist lips were the only indication that it hadn't all been a fragment of her imagination. Why wasn't he at least a little bit breathless?

He moved away from the wall he had been leaning against, and his front brushed against her once again. The hard ridge of his manhood was impossible to ignore. They both hissed at the contact, and, inappropriately, Ivy's spirit lifted. *Not so unaffected, are we, Blakeburne?* Despite their precarious circumstances, Ivy couldn't help the secret smile that tugged at her lips, knowing that she could stir that reaction.

"Ivy, I know you are here. I saw you walk outside after talking to Evelyn and Eleanor. Either you've jumped off the balcony, or you're hiding in the dark. Either way, I will be most displeased with you." She knew her mother was joking, but Lord knew she would really be a lot happier finding her in the arms of a man than bundled up in self-doubt in a corner. That didn't mean Ivy was ready to face the chain of events that would initiate. Her family didn't bow to conventions but wasn't *that* unconventional.

She was pondering her options —she was becoming rather good at evaluating escape plans— when he felt Gabriel's hand gently lifting her chin to meet his eyes. She didn't know what he was searching for, but he seemed to find it because he nodded. Bending his head to her ear, he whispered, "You didn't answer my question. I'll call on you tomorrow. Be at home for me."

He then turned and disappeared through the doors he had come out from. Her dazzled mind just then noticed that they stood right behind them, an easily accessible route he promptly took. Ivy had a few seconds to watch his back before her mother spoke from right behind her.

"Here you are, Ivy. Didn't you hear me calling? What are you doing here alone?" Ivy turned to face the Duchess. It was too dark to see her face clearly, but Ivy swore she could detect a subtle, sly note in her tone. Had she seen Blakeburne? Surely, she would have said something. Or maybe her mind was playing tricks on her, making up suspicions where there were none. After all, she had gone from being ignored or approached only because of her family to being thoroughly kissed —twice! — by the most sought-after bachelor of the season and concocting excuses to avoid being compromised. She wasn't cut out for subterfuges. She gladly left them to the characters in her beloved books.

"I'm sorry, Mother, I was lost in thoughts I didn't hear you. I needed some time alone." All true. The reason she had escaped the room in the first place was long forgotten, completely obliterated by a tall, austere, unpredictable Duke.

She knew what would come next, and she wasn't disappointed. "I really hope that that wasn't because of your aunt and cousin. You must stop taking everything so personally. I'm sure whatever they said wasn't meant to disparage you." Oh, it was disparaging indeed. But Ivy would rather listen to another lecture about her worth than explain the details that had led to that moment. She had always tried to shelter her parents from the animosity she felt coming from that side of the family. She absolutely wanted to avoid creating a rift among family members because of her. Not to mention, a part of her was convinced that it was her own lack of confidence that exacerbated her unease in their company.

Ivy took her mother's arm and led her inside. "Nothing to worry about. Are you ready to go home?"

"Yes, let's have the carriage bought around. Tomorrow we have that shopping expedition with Lady Winter, Grace, and Elizabeth. I need a good night sleep to keep up with Imogen," she said jokingly, smiling fondly while talking about her friend.

"You didn't answer my question. I'll call tomorrow. Be at home for me." Gabriel's whispered words resonated in Ivy's head when the Duchess mentioned their plans for the following day.

Oh, dear. That could be a problem.

Chapter Seven

"I'll have to tell them. There's no other way."

The following morning, Ivy was pacing her room, debating on how to approach the subject of the Duke of Blakeburne's impending visit.

"If we didn't have the afternoon already planned ahead, it could have passed for an impromptu decision on his part. But there's no chance in hell that I can find a believable excuse to stay home. Not when they promised me to stop at Hatchards after shopping in Bond Street. No, I must tell them to expect him. But then, I'd have to tell them *how* I know it, given that we weren't even seen talking last night." Blue eyes followed her from the stuffed chair in the corner, half curious, half bored. "I know what you're thinking, Colonel, but I don't think they'll believe I forgot to inform them of a visit we planned when we went riding in Hyde Park. Or that I forgot I had a previous engagement." The large striped cat meowed at the sound of his name. It was Gregory who had named him Colonel, after a particularly long and nerve-trying hour of incessant mewing when still a kitten, shortly after their father had brought him home as a gift. Gregory, looking at the little ball of fur finally quieted by yet another plate of milk, had been convinced that, were he human, he would have made a career in the Army, yelling orders. Nobody disputed him. Hence, Colonel.

Over the years, Ivy had always found him a valuable source of advice. "I don't see any other way around it, if not pleading forgetfulness. Oh, drat the man! What gives him leave to think I'm here at his leisure?" Another mew. "Fine. I know what gives him leave." Ivy's gaze became lost for a second before shaking herself and banning all thoughts of steamy kisses and more. "Well, you know what, Colonel? I'm neither his mistress nor his wife. I don't have to bow to his ducal demands. I will write him a note telling him I'm not at home for visitors today. Which is true. This way, I won't have to explain anything to anyone. And I'll go about my day as I should. He may be the Duke of Blakeburne, but I am the Countess of Everleigh." Colonel started to lick his front paw. "I knew you'd agree with me. You've always been a wise cat. Now I'd better go downstairs."

Ivy entered the breakfast room like any other morning, resolved to put broody Dukes and secrets out of her mind. And just like any other morning, the Duke of Rutherford-Blythe was reading. Only, that particular morning the paper was still laying neatly pressed near his plate. In his hand, a small cream-coloured card was claiming all his attention. Ivy hoped it wasn't another message sent to her mother by an admirer. His father was renowned for not dealing well with men shamelessly hoping to gain the Duchess's favour.

"Good morning, Father, Mother," Ivy said cautiously, trying to gauge the mood the two were in.

"Good morning, daughter," her father said, looking at her expectantly. "These came for you this morning. Is there something you want to tell us, par chance?"

Until then, Ivy hadn't noticed the rich bouquet of delicate camellias that stood proudly on the table. Once she did, it seemed to take up all the space in the room, ominous. Without words, he took the card from her father's hand. She weighed it in her hands, taking in its quality. One that was already familiar. Ivy turned the card to read the message.

> *Don't jump off any balcony.*
> *I will call at three.*
> *-B*

I swear that man will be the death of me, Ivy thought, even if her treacherous heart sped up in recognising Blakeburne's handwriting. Still not a poet. But there was something strangely endearing in those short sentences. Or maybe she was on her way to Bedlam if she felt warm in reading his written orders. He had obviously heard what her mother had said the night before about her launching herself from balconies. There was no way the Duchess could put two and two together. Few words out of entire conversations would surely not ring any bells…

"Isn't it a fortuitous coincidence that the Duke of Blakeburne has written the same words I said to you last night?" *Damn it!* That was one of the very few times she wished her parents were the typical *ton* couple. Frivolous, busy, and only superficially interested in their children. Instead, the Duke and Duchess of Rutherford-Blythe had always been present in their son and daughter's lives, unconcerned with the raised brows that caused. That morning, they were waiting patiently for her to answer. For a second, Ivy considered lying. But she immediately thought against it. Not only she wasn't any good at it, as history showed, but she had never lied to her parents since that time she had pilfered two biscuits for her and Gregory from the kitchen after dinner when she had been five. She had been discovered within minutes, and she had felt bad for days. Moreover, she had acted out of character enough in the last few weeks.

"First, Father, promise me not to overreact."

"Not the most auspicious of beginnings, daughter. Let me decide it after I've heard what you have to say." The Duke crossed his arms over his broad chest and waited. The Duchess nodded her head encouragingly at Ivy. So she began from the very beginning. She recounted every embarrassing moment in the Duke of Blakeburne's presence —that took quite some time—, the incident with Lady Ingram, the reason behind their ride in Hyde Park, up until the night before when the Duke had found her outside Langton House. She kept only one thing to herself. Those kisses would forever be a treasured memory close to her heart. She had found a confident, passionate woman in his arms, and simply in his presence, unafraid of going toe to toe with one of the most powerful peers of the realm. She won't allow those stolen moments to be twisted to force them both into something neither of them wanted. Coming to the end of her tale, she looked nervously at her parents, who had still to utter a word.

"So, you, see, I don't really know the reason why he should come calling today..." Ivy saw her mother opening her mouth to speak. "And before you say it, I really doubt he's interested in courtship." The Duchess closed her mouth again. "And I was about to notify him that I won't be available today. I already have plans with you and the Winters, Mother. I won't disrupt our plans for—" The Duke, notably silent until then, interrupted her.

"Oh no, dear, let him come calling. I'm sure your plans can withstand a slight delay. Fortuitously, I was planning to be in my study this afternoon. If you are pressed to leave, I'm sure I'll find a way to entertain our guest."

Oh, dear. That tone didn't bode well. *I hope your strategies are as good as they say they are, Blakeburne.*

❧ ❧ ❧

Precisely one minute after the clock struck three that afternoon, the solicitous butler announced the arrival of the Duke of Blakeburne. Gabriel entered the elegant drawing-room, where he was faced with various degrees of welcoming faces. He hadn't taken time to think about what kind of reception he would receive. Still, he certainly didn't anticipate bowing to the Duchess of Rutherford-Blythe *and* the Duke of Rutherford-Blythe, before finally bending over the Countess's hand. Ivy —he couldn't help but think of her that way— sent him a tight, apologetic smile. So, again, it hadn't been her idea to have almost her entire family present. Gabriel wouldn't be surprised if the door swung open and the Marquess of Burnam strode in to complete the picture. He was sure any other man would have felt overwhelmed by the sight, but he had been raised by the thirteenth Duke of Blakeburne and then by His Majesty's Army. The Double Duke's glacial stare didn't do anything to him, if not instil in him respect for a man caring for his family. And Gabriel wouldn't make the mistake of underestimating the female half of the family. The Duchess was more difficult to read, her beautiful face devoid of emotions to help him understand if the scale was in favour of a warm welcome. He had hoped to face Ivy in the relative privacy allowed by a chaperoning servant or companion. That did make what he had come to say more difficult.

He had spent more hours than he cared to admit debating with himself whether to follow up the words he had whispered the night before. His curiosity regarding the Countess hadn't been assuaged. What obsessed him wasn't simply her behaviour. He hadn't slept a wink, reliving, again and again, those scorching moments together. The memory of her elegant hands on him, learning the contour of his body, had been a pleasant torture he had inflicted upon himself until it had become unbearable, and he had been forced to take matters into his own hands. He had bought himself to pleasure like he hadn't done since he was a callow youth learning a woman's secrets was for the first time. It had been the inevitable peak of the crescendo he and Ivy had started together with their passionate meeting of lips and bodies. She had been so vibrant, so full of life —and irritation towards him— he had wanted to absorb it as his own. An irresistible force played with them, drawing them to one another, a pull so strong and mutual he wasn't sure who had initiated the contact. What he knew was that he had let matters get out of hand. He had let his control slip for a second to savour the pleasure she was giving him. And they had almost got caught. That would have been a disaster. Because, as much as Gabriel was drawn to the subtle allure of the Countess of Everleigh, nothing had changed. Not for him. He was still, and always will be, the Duke of Blakeburne first. Major Eastham a close second. What he constantly repeated to his mother weren't fibs to keep his bachelor status. He had responsibilities and duties that took over much of his time, leaving none of it to dedicate to the headaches that a wife would bring. Even one that he could see himself liking. Like Ivy Kington. Sometimes in the future, he would carry out his duty to the Dukedom and produce an heir, but Gabriel saw himself as a mature gentleman, retired in one of his country estates, with a younger, docile woman by his side, who didn't expect to be swept off her feet. And, for all that the *ton* inexplicably saw her as shy and unassuming, that woman won't be, couldn't be, Ivy. She already stirred feelings in him that led him to behave irresponsibly and dishonourably.

Looking at her now, poised and composed, it was difficult to reconcile her with the image that didn't leave his mind. His body, however, recognised hers at a primal level. His hands ached to span her small waist again and slide slowly upwards... He marshalled his unruly body and strengthened his resolve.

That was what he had come to do. To curtail any hope she could be harbouring for a possible courtship. It wasn't idle boast when he said he was what every woman desired: He was rich, titled, and relatively young. Nothing led him to believe that Ivy would be different. What was worse, he had already given her much more than what he had ever given any other woman, and not only physically. Yes, his mistresses, like Lady Ingram, had availed themselves of his body, but none of them had taken up so much space in his mind to become a nuisance.

He had to consign her to the role of casual acquaintance. It was as simple as that.

Taking about nuisances, as he took the offered seat in front of that formidable family and looked into a particular set of intense brown eyes, an annoying pain refused to leave the area around his heart. As if something heavy were sitting on his chest. He wondered what it was.

He cleared his voice. "Thank you so much for receiving me on such short notice. I hope I haven't inconvenienced you too much."

"Truth be told, Blakeburne, the ladies are going to be late for an important previous engagement, so if you could please state the purpose of your visit, we can all go about our day as planned." That from the Duke.

Not bad for a start, R-B.

"Oh, I'm sure Ivy and I could spare a few moments, Rafael. If you, on the other hand, dear husband, have some pressing matters to attend to, I'm sure we'll have a lovely time with our guest on our own." The Duchess fluttered her long eyelashes at her husband, who narrowed his eyes.

"Nothing that can't wait a few minutes more, my love," he replied in all seriousness, even if his eyes were various degrees warmer looking at her than they were when he was addressing Gabriel. Their love match was notorious among the *ton*, who regarded it as unbefitting their high station. Gabriel perceived the green-eyed monster behind their disapproval. For him, it was similar to when he had witnessed the late Earl of Covington hugging his son back at Eton. Unusual and foreign. The current Duchess of Blakeburne might have been deeply in love with her husband —or so she always said— but Gabriel had no idea what the late Duke had felt for his beautiful bride. If anything at all. She had been the perfect hostess, the impeccable woman who was worthy of standing at his side.

Ivy's amused voice jolted him back to the present.

"Please don't mind my parents, Your Grace. We are delighted that you have called this afternoon." She sent a pointed look at them. For his part, Gabriel was busy keeping his mind under control. Hearing her calling him 'Your Grace' like she had done the previous night was playing havoc with his body. He was in trouble if something as simple as his title caused such a reaction.

"Would you like some tea and refreshment, Your Grace?" Here she went, 'your gracing' him again. Then he saw the mischievous smile playing on her lips. She knew perfectly well what she was doing. Maybe she wasn't aware of the extent of the effect her words were having on him. Effect that, if he didn't put a stop to it, would rapidly become embarrassingly evident to all. That reinforced his conviction. Nothing had to result from their association.

He inclined his head to accept her offer while thinking of a way to broach the subject without sounding like a pompous arse. Rutherford-Blythe didn't give him the chance.

"You seem to have been patronising London's flower shops a lot lately, Blakeburne."

"Just a small token of my esteem towards the charming members of your family."

"*One* charming member, I seem to gather."

Well, if you feel so slighted, I could send a bouquet to you as well.

What Gabriel said instead was, "I had the pleasure to converse with your daughter on various occasions." He looked at Ivy when he said it. She looked at the floor, trying to hide her blush. But he had seen it. "I enjoyed the time we spent together." The two Dukes were both very apt in navigating the subtlety of high society verbal sparring. The conversation could go on for a long time, neither of them willing to concede the point.

"From what Ivy told us, your conversations don't lean towards the conventional side." That made him pause. What *had* Ivy told them? Not everything, obviously. If her father knew of the liberties he had

90

taken with his daughter, Gabriel doubted he would have been subjected only to unfriendly looks and probing questions.

"Rafael, stop badgering our guest," the Duchess said before turning to him. "You'll have to excuse my husband, Your Grace. It's not very often that our Ivy receives not one but two bouquets from a gentleman. And an invitation to a ride in Hyde Park—"

"All right, that is more than enough, from both of you." Lady Everleigh had apparently reached the end of her rope. "Please don't talk about me as if I'm not in the room." She then addressed him directly. Gabriel didn't like that her eyes didn't sparkle anymore. "I apologise for the unconventional ways of our family…." Another sharp look towards her parents. "But I have to ask you to state the reason for your visit. We really have to leave for our appointment soon."

And now Gabriel was faced with a choice. The Double Duke's pressing —and suspicious— enquiries had given him the perfect opening to set matters straight once and for all. To say what he had come to say. *There won't be anything to worry about in the future. I have no interest in marrying your daughter.* Instead, what came out of his mouth was, "I arranged a private viewing of the latest Thomas Lawrence's portraits. It would be an honour for me if you'd accompany me."

What had ever gone according to plan since he had met Ivy Kington, Countess of Everleigh?

❧ ❧ ❧

Ivy was still fuming hours after Blakeburne had left. Her father's behaviour had been appalling. He had basically verbally assaulted the younger Duke from the very first moment he had stepped into the room. And her mother! The dear woman had tried to come to her rescue, to salvage the situation, because her ninny of a daughter seemed incapable of saying anything. So, to diffuse the tension, she had decided to point out that it was new for all of them that a man would show a modicum of interest in her. That had not been mortifying at all. *Thanks, Mother.* She sighed. He couldn't blame Blakeburne for his hasty retreat after issuing that invitation to the portrait viewing. Ivy would be surprised if an actual invitation ever arrived on their doorstep.

After the Duke had left, she had read her parents the Riot act. If they ever behaved like that again, she couldn't be held accountable for her actions. She was a two-and-twenty-year-old Countess, for Goodness's sake! She was responsible for the estate that came with her title and had been running it for the past three years. She was able to manage one Duke without interference. Even if said Duke looked breathtaking in the light of day, with his unruly dark hair precisely styled back and a dark greatcoat perfectly tailored to encase his broad shoulders. She was coming to find his commanding presence irresistible and, seeing him face to face with her father, had only reinforced her conviction that she was in deep trouble. But she would dare the most uptight matron not to swoon in front of such a display of masculinity and power.

Their stolen moments continued to play in her mind, enriched by new imaginative variations that made her blush. More than once, during the afternoon out, she had to stop at the most inappropriate time and fan herself to dispel the heat. Even the cold bite of the English November air could do nothing against it. When, for the third time in the span of an hour, she was asked if she was feeling well by one of the Winter sisters, Ivy decided to concentrate on spending a pleasant time with her friends and putting all thoughts of Dukes out of her mind, before she fooled herself even more.

Chapter Eight

When two weeks went by without a single word from Blakeburne, Ivy knew he had been right. Maybe the Duke and Duchess of Rutherford-Blythe had scared him away, or perhaps that had been his intention all along.

Whatever the reason, no contact had been forthcoming. The days passing by had dulled the sting of his sudden disappearance. She couldn't even call it a rejection because, from both parts, nothing had been said to warrant certain expectations. Well, if one discarded the scorching kisses that still sent shivers down her spine. But, other than that, no words had been spoken. And that was all right. Everything went on as usual. Their lives had crossed briefly. It would become one of those memories that resurfaced at the oddest of times, without any lasting effect. But when Ivy won yet another shelling from Victoria, this time thanks to Mr Hubblecombe, it became difficult not to let it affect her.

The *ton* took the elusive Duke's absence even harder than Ivy. Everywhere she went, someone would inevitably wonder whether the Duke of Blakeburne would finally grace them with his presence. Ivy wondered if some ladies would develop a sore neck from looking around so much. She found it very amusing. Better that than facing the fact that she missed him.

That night she was sipping a glass of lukewarm lemonades the Earl of Covington, one of her brother's friends, had brought her. They had just ended a dance together and were conversing pleasingly. She liked the Earl. He was a handsome man of medium height and build but didn't have the compelling presence other men of her acquaintance had. Much like her, he didn't particularly stand out in a crowd. Being close to her brother Gregory granted him that visibility that his quieter nature didn't facilitate. And a sizeable annual income didn't hurt either. He possessed a keen intelligence that shone in his beautiful sweet dark eyes, making him one of her favourite people to converse with.

They were only minutes into the conversation when Gregory joined them. He wasn't alone. Viscount Bellmore bowed gallantly over her proffered hand, looking dashing in his evening attire. Beside him stood another gentleman to whom she had not been introduced yet. Ivy assessed him to be more or less the same age as the others. He was slightly taller than Gregory, with light brown hair. Feeling his scrutiny, Ivy looked into his eyes and was struck by the unusual emerald shade. They were undoubtedly beautiful. She felt an undeniable reaction to them.

Before she was caught staring, she forced herself to look away at her brother, willing him to rectify the lack of introduction.

"Covington! Old chap! Much more of that, and I'll be forced to welcome you in the family!"

The poor man shifted uncomfortably. Gregory's words were meant to be teasing. What the clueless nincompoop had done instead had been to put his friend in the difficult position of offending her by hastily denying any deeper interest or feigning it to spare her feelings, which was also offensive. What Ivy wanted was to bash Gregory's head with her half-filled dance card for putting the kind man on the spot. She could say to herself that it didn't matter, but she was hanging to her equanimity by a thread. A thread that had been fraying during the past two weeks. She decided to rescue the young Earl, who looked relieved when she spoke.

"Stop pestering your friend, Gregory, and introduce us to this gentleman you brought with you to witness your lack of manners."

"At your service, sister dearest. Ivy, Covington, this is Lord Charles Eastham. Eastham, let me introduce you to the Earl of Covington and my lovely sister, the Countess of Everleigh."

"A pleasure, my Lady." Lord Eastham bowed over her hand, his eyes still on her face. *Eastham?* "Had I known so many lovely ladies such as yourself were gracing London, I would have made the journey from the country sooner."

Ivy was grateful for the opening the man had provided, even if it remotely wasn't what she burned to ask. She always struggled with small talk among complete strangers.

"Do you consider the country your home then, my Lord? I'm sure I would have remembered you, had our paths crossed before." Only after saying that she realised how flirtatious her words sounded. Fortunately, Lord Eastham didn't seem to take notice.

"Yes, my Lady, I've spent a large part of the last few years in my tranquil country estate. That kind of peace it's not easy to find in Town."

"Nor that kind of dullness," interjected Gregory.

"That must be a trait you share with your cousin, for society hasn't seen you both for years," said Viscount Bellmore, who, after greeting them, had kept silent until that moment.

"Yes, well, we both prefer to keep a close eye on matters. Plus, my esteemed cousin had a war to fight." Ivy's next question really was superfluous.

"And who is your cousin, my Lord?"

"Why, the Duke of Blakeburne. I'm sure you've seen him. He's a difficult man to overlook." *Those eyes.* That explained why she felt so unsettled. The cousins shared more than a preference for rural landscapes.

"I had the pleasure of making his acquaintance, yes." Ivy sent a warning look in her brother's direction, willing him not to open his big mouth. Because he, of course, had been informed by their parents of Blakeburne's visit. It seemed having one's own lodgings didn't mean a person had to mind his own business. Ah, the blessing of a loving family.

"Good, then we already have a topic of conversation for the next dance. If you would do me the honour?" Lord Eastham extended his hand to her just as the orchestra started playing the first notes of a waltz. She really didn't have any reason to refuse the young Lord. He had been pleasant so far. Much more so than his cousin. Less sombre and intense. *Stop comparing the two men!* It wasn't his fault the green of his eyes was enough to make her heartbeat accelerate.

She accepted by placing her hand in his. They danced for a while in silence, with her constantly looking over his shoulder, too shy to look at him in the eyes at such close proximity.

"Tell me, my Lady, how did you find my cousin? He is an imposing man, isn't he?" Ivy looked directly at him then, surprised they were still talking about Blakeburne. She had thought it had been a way to ask her to dance without being too forward.

How should she answer his question without giving too much away? She finally settled for the truth. Or part of it.

"He certainly is that. I don't know him well enough to be a judge of his character, though, my Lord." That was a euphemism. Ivy hadn't come nearly close to understanding the Duke of Blakeburne.

"But certainly, you must have been impressed by him. He's young, rich and a war hero. I can honestly say that more than a lady had had her head turned by him." Ivy tried not to stiffen in his arms. Was everyone in her life trying to make her angry?

"We are lucky then that I am not like all the other ladies." He smiled at her indulgently, irking her further.

"Are you planning on remaining in Town for long?" Besides being irritated by his condescending attitude, Ivy didn't want to keep talking endlessly about Blakeburne. Her abrupt change of subject didn't go unnoticed.

"I beg your pardon, my Lady. I bored you with all my talk about Blakeburne." Bored, sure! "You see, we grew up together, and it's impossible for me not to admire all his accomplishments."

"I totally understand. I can count some impressive men and women among the members of my family as well. No apology needed." Ivy smiled, more to deluge the tension than in true forgiveness. She was glad when the dance came to an end.

"Thank you for the dance, my Lady."

"It was my pleasure, my Lord," she replied politely. He took his leave from her. Ivy watched him walk away, thinking that Blakeburne would be more difficult to ignore than she thought, especially if he didn't even have to be in the room to steal all the attention.

❧ ❧ ❧

Gabriel was sitting at White's, frowning at the news from abroad he was reading in the paper, when a smiling Bellmore joined him.

"Blakeburne, fancy seeing you here. Mind if I join you?" At his nod of assent, the Viscount took the free wing chair in front of him. "So, what has you scowling so hard this fine morning? Not that you need a particular reason." Bellmore had been teasing him for his sternness since the early days, so Gabriel didn't waste breath to argue. He folded the newspaper in half and laid it on the table in front of him.

"The Foreign Office is restless. I can't really blame them. I would be nervous too if I heard how many French are calling for Napoleon's return from Elba."

Bellmore's face sobered. "I'd hoped you would have some insight on the whole thing that dispelled this feeling in my gut that the war isn't really over. Hearing this from you, my friend, well, it makes my skin crawl."

"You could always sell your commission," Gabriel said. And he wasn't being derisory. For all his light-hearted and sometimes silly ways, Gabriel would put his life in Sebastian's hands. In and out of a battlefield. They had joined the Army together, each with a different goal in mind. Everyone expected the Viscount to come back home after a few months of life among coarse and unclean soldiers, tail between his legs. What they hadn't taken into consideration was that behind the pleasant facade hid a razor-sharp mind and bravery. And an innate way to gain others' trust.

Everybody respected Bellmore among the military ranks, and most were mystified by the fact that he was still only Captain. Gabriel instead knew it was a deliberate choice, one fully supported by Generals across the Army. Nobody could influence soldiers' mood like Captain Sinclair, making him more valuable than some higher officials. The downside of it all was that every death weighed more on him than on anyone else. He knew all their names, their stories. Gabriel had had to bring him back to his tent more than one, roaring drunk, after a particularly bloody day. The morning after was like nothing had happened, and a smiling Sebastian re-emerged like everything was right in the world. But nobody really knew the price it extorted on his soul. Gabriel wouldn't respect him any less for trying to hold on to what was left of it by selling his commission.

"Would you?" he retorted. "Didn't think so," he concluded at Gabriel's silence.

A voice fortuitously interrupted them before their minds brought them both back to darker times.

"Gentlemen. I'm sorry to interrupt what appears to be a very serious conversation, but I ran into Mr Barney here, who was champing to meet you, Blakeburne. So, Barney, Gabriel Eastham, Duke of Blakeburne. Blakeburne, Leopold Barney. Bellmore here, you know already."

"Burnam," Gabriel greeted the Marquess. He then looked at the other man. He was a portly gentleman, younger than his receding hairline and potbelly indicated. Gabriel gauged him to be at least seven years younger than himself. The man nervously straightened his waistcoat, unnerved by being the focus of Gabriel's gaze.

"Ahem...yes. A pleasure, Your Grace. I apologise for the interruption, but I couldn't pass the chance of paying my respect. My brother, William, served under you in the battle of Corunna. He speaks very highly of you, Your Grace, and we are all so grateful that, under your command, he came back home in one piece. Not many others could say the same."

"It's thanks to the bravery of soldiers like your brother that we all came home. An officer is always as good as his soldiers. Infantry, was he?"

"Indeed, Your Grace."

Gabriel didn't remember the man's brother specifically, but he knew the type of reassurance those men, and their families, needed. Especially after the bloodbath that had been Corunna. He had stopped waking up to nightmares of those horrors only years after it. The price they had all paid had been very high. Many would continue paying it until they drew their last breath.

"Your brother isn't par chance Will Barney? That man is a mean card player. He emptied my pockets more than once," added Bellmore.

"Yes, my Lord, that would be him!" Mr Barney beamed. "Makes the Christmas holidays a nightmare for old Aunt Phyllis, who hates to lose a hand at whist," he said on a laugh, joined by the Viscount. Once again, Gabriel was impressed by his friend. While he had given just a vague, albeit sincere, reply, Bellmore had, with a simple memory, made the man's brother more than one soldier among many. Those who underestimated Sebastian Sinclair were blind idiots.

"I hope he is faring well?" Bellmore enquired politely.

"Yes, my Lord, all things considered. It took time for him to feel comfortable with his civilian life, but he's happy to have all four limbs still attached to his body." Barney sobered, belying a deeper struggle, so very common in those who survived.

"I'm happy to hear that. Please, bring him my regards. And tell him I'm still waiting to win back my money."

Gabriel nodded.

Thanking them profusely, Mr Barney took his leave, his steps light. The Marquess of Burnam instead lingered, taking the one empty wing chair.

"You've made his day. Not many officers can see beyond their epaulettes."

"Many officers should find themselves fighting without infantry soldiers. See what happens," Bellmore said uncharacteristically bitter. Gabriel agreed.

"As much as I like hearing these progressive thoughts, I'm mostly relieved to see you haven't succumbed to some exotic illness, Blakeburne," Burnam said nonchalantly while summoning one of the club's liveried footmen. "Coffee, please."

"Immediately, my Lord," replied the servant, hurrying to satisfy the request.

"I don't have the faintest idea what you're talking about, Burnam. I'm perfectly well."

"So I see. Any recent blow to the head?" he prodded.

"Cut the chase, Burnam, and say what you have to say." Gabriel didn't have the patience for games.

The marquess sipped his freshly delivered drink. "Oh, nothing in particular. I just wondered what could have possibly prevented you from following up with the invitation you issued my sister a few weeks ago." Ah. Lady Everleigh's brother was on a mission to kindly remind him of his duty. As if he could ever forget it. More than two weeks had passed since he had shamefully taken the cowardly way out Rutherford-Blythe's drawing-room. Some minor issues had taken him to his estate just outside London the morning directly after. He told himself his presence was necessary to dissolve the disputes between his steward and few tenants. The surprise on his staff's faces upon seeing him told another story. One in which he had needed a few days to regroup. It was only in the quiet of the countryside that he had finally admitted to himself that he had taken the first opportunity that had come his way to put some distance between him and Ivy.

Physical miles when he appeared incapable of putting her out of his thoughts. Sooner or later, he would have to send the request for the private viewing sitting on his desk, burning a hole through the stack of various papers. He had always kept his word, and it would not start with a simple thing as an invitation to a portrait exhibition. That it tied him so tightly in knots irked him. He was the bloody Duke of Blakeburne!

"I apologise if the Countess was offended by my lack of communication. I assure you it wasn't my intention. Estate matters had brought me out of Town. I've just returned." Two days ago, but he didn't have to justify his actions.

"My sister didn't say anything, as usual. Oh no, it's the Duchess you have to worry about not disappointing." Gabriel didn't doubt it for a second. He was sure Her Grace could make her displeasure known in various ways, not least by making the *ton* an even more unpleasant place for him. But what did the Marquess mean, the Countess hadn't said anything, *as usual?*

"I'll rectify the matter immediately. I'll send a message with the time and place."

Burnam nodded, satisfied by the outcome of the conversation. The Marquess was then distracted by two young bucks, dressed impeccably in the latest fashion, who started chatting with him. Their approach was preceded by a cloud of suffocating cologne. Gabriel turned his head in search of some fresh air.

"I'm surprised you let yourself be reprimanded like that. Surely the Duchess of Rutherford-Blythe doesn't frighten you that much," Bellmore commented, his voice low not to let the son of the above-mentioned lady hear it, his ever-present smile on his lips.

"Don't you go underestimating the power of a society hostess. Moreover, I'm honour-bound to deliver what I promised. It didn't leave me much of a choice."

"Mmm, sure, that's why. Your good name is at stake," Bellmore poked him. "How could you possibly live with yourself?" He was outright smiling now, teeth and all. Before Gabriel could send him to the devil, the two youngsters took their leave, full of self-importance for having been given the time of day by the popular Marquess of Burnam. The man inhaled, taking the first real deep breath since the arrival of the two dandies. That was a miscalculation. The nauseating smell of cologne was still permeating the air. The young Lord started coughing, his face rapidly becoming a worrying shade of red. The coughs then became sneezes. Gabriel had to fight to keep his expression neutral, but it was undeniably difficult. He lost the battle against laughter when Bellmore said, "By Lord, Burnam, keep it together. You just sneezed out a Viscountcy!"

"So, you see, that's why I decided not to evict them." Ivy was saying while sipping her tea. "I don't care if Mr Wallace agrees or not. I couldn't in all conscience do it."

"I'm not at all surprised. You've always had a soft heart."

Ivy regarded Victoria, who sat elegantly on the blue chaise longue in front of her, her light blue dress and blond hair harmonising perfectly with the gold accents of the upholstery. She was drinking her tea, listening to Ivy complaining about the multiple letters she received from her steward every time she made a decision, always disputing it. She was convinced that it wouldn't take more than two lines from her father or brother to have the same result it took her pages and pages to achieve. And nobody would dare gainsay them. It was extremely frustrating.

"I'll have you know that I've considered the issue at length. I studied the ledgers, and the loss wouldn't make but a dent in this year's income. I won't throw out a family of five because the father broke a leg while working for me! And Father supports my decision." Ivy wisely put the fragile china cup down on its saucer to avoid spilling the liquid all over the place in her vehemence. She had specifically asked her father to let her administer the estate that came with the Everleigh Earldom. The Duke had been reluctant at first, not for the lack of faith in Ivy's abilities, but because of the difficulties she was sure to encounter as one of the very few women in that position. She wasn't that foolish to turn down her father's assistance, a man who had been managing estates since he was eighteen, but, ultimately, she had the last words on matters.

"You misunderstand, Ivy. I totally agree with you, and I wouldn't expect anything else from you or your family. I'm only saying that your steward, as a typical short-sighted man, likely interprets it as female weakness."

Ivy exhaled slowly. "You're right, Victoria. I'm sorry I snapped at you." Her friends waved her apology away. "Sometimes my temper gets away from me, and I come very close to sending him packing. But it has already been difficult to find someone to fill the role, knowing he would answer directly to me and not to the Duke. I only wished I were more assertive, a bit more like you." Victoria didn't own an estate like Ivy did, but she had ridden with her father so many times when he

103

went visiting his tenants it was like she did. Ivy could perfectly see her in the role, eliciting respect and awe in others.

"Don't start with that, Ivy. It's not your fault we women have to work twice as hard to be heard. I know it's not what you want to hear, but maybe you should ask your father or Gregory to deal with direct communications. It would be the easiest way, and it would spare all of you a lot of time." Ivy was already shaking her head before Victoria had finished.

"No, I want to deal with it on my own. And if it takes twice as long to reach a solution, the blame lies at Mr Wallace's door. As long as it doesn't affect the people in my employ, I won't budge."

Victoria smiled, her already beautiful face becoming really stunning. "I wouldn't want it any other way."

She took another sip of her tea. "Now, let's talk about something else."

"Agreed. I don't want to spoil your visit with my bad mood. I didn't see you last night. Did you accept another invitation that I forgot?"

"No. I pleaded stomach pains and remained home. I wanted to avoid the Earl of Sutton." Ivy conjured the image of the man in question. A pleasant-looking man, a few years past his fourth decade. A bit full of himself, but what titled man wasn't?

"And why, pray tell?" Ivy already suspected the reason why. She had seen the Earl around her friend on numerous occasions.

"He approached my father, making his intentions towards me clear."

Ivy feigned an exaggerated gasp of surprise. "Oh my God! The nerve of the man!"

It was almost a weekly occurrence for Victoria to receive a marriage proposal from one man or another. Some were young and attractive, others were… well, less young and attractive. It didn't matter since Victoria stubbornly rejected them all indiscriminately.

"Go ahead, make fun of me. I feel sorry for the man. One could do worse than the Earl of Sutton. He's good company."

"Then why did you reject him?"

"That's the thing. I didn't decline yet. He still hasn't approached me directly." She made an exasperated sound. "Of course not. He approached my father, putting me in an uncomfortable position. Anyway, I didn't want to create awkwardness. So, I stayed home." Victoria took a sip of what Ivy suspected was an empty cup. Ivy couldn't help but play devil's advocate.

"You could always accept his proposal. It seems to me you like the Earl well enough." Victoria's reticence to consider anyone's suit was a sore subject in the Gallard family. At first, her father had indulged her, ascribing it to the indecisiveness of young age. As the years progressed, the Earl's favourable disposition was waning. Ivy was convinced that a deeper reason was hidden behind her friend's refusal to marry, one she had not shared with her yet. Ivy respected Victoria too much to pry. She would stand by her even if she decided to grow an old spinster. A fate Ivy would likely share.

"I do like him. Just not enough to marry him." And with that, the topic was closed for Victoria.

Ivy was asking her what her plans for the following day were when a knock at the door preceded Stevens's entrance.

"I beg your pardon, my Ladies. This just came for you. I was asked to deliver it directly." The butler handed a sealed missive to Ivy. Since the post usually came in the morning, that had to be hand-delivered.

"Thank you, Stevens." The butler bowed and left. Ivy turned it around and broke the already familiar seal. The butterflies were back.

Dear Lady Everleigh,

It has been brought to my attention that I have been remiss in my duty. Affairs has taken me out of Town but, rest assured, I have not forgotten the promise I made to you and your family. Nonetheless, I take full responsibility for the delay. Therefore, I would ask for the pleasure of your presence, and that of your esteemed parents, tomorrow at four for a private viewing of

Master Lawrence's work. Please send a servant around with your answer as soon as you get this.

    Regards,

    Gabriel Eastham, Duke of Blakeburne

I know exactly who you are, Blakeburne, even without your full signature. Who other could pen something like that? *Send a servant around with my answer? You'll get your answer, don't you fear.* After more than two weeks, Ivy had finally been able to banish Blakeburne from her mind. Or at least not to think about their kisses and touches more than a few times a day.

She could not bring herself to regret the small amount of time she had spent with Blakeburne, even when part of it had been spent arguing. But she had brutally repressed any hope that it meant anything to him. Her pride demanded it. And now he came waltzing back, demanding her immediate attention and time.

You have a surprise coming your way, Your Grace. Ivy's heart had been beating faster since she had recognised the wax seal. Because of anger towards the high-handed Lord. What else could it be?

"Another problem from Everleigh?" Victoria asked after seeing Ivy's features darken.

"No, nothing like that. Just someone who needs to learn a few things." She pulled the cord to summon a servant while still muttering to herself.

"Who?"

"Blakeburne. The man has a nerve, I'll give him that. After everything…" Victoria was following her movements with wide eyes.

"The Duke of Blakeburne? What does he want? And what are you talking about?"

"I will not go. I refuse to be at his beck and call!"

"What…" Ivy must have a score to settle with the fates because, right that moment, her mother decided to enter the drawing-room, returning from her calls.

"Where are you not going, Ivy?" the Duchess asked, disregarding the common practice of greeting.

"Hello dear," she then said to Victoria, bending to kiss her cheek. "What got my daughter in high dudgeon?"

"Good afternoon, Georgiana. I'm not sure about the details, but, from what I gathered from her rant, it has something to do with the Duke of Blakeburne and some paintings," she ended with a shrug.

"Ah..." she said before the note was thrust unceremoniously under her nose.

"Here, read this. Can you believe it? If it isn't the most arrogant invitation I've ever seen, I don't know what it is." Georgiana scanned the note, lips twitching to suppress a smile.

"Well, I concede it is a bit presumptuous to assume we will be free tomorrow on such short notice. However, I've heard that Lawrence is planning to leave the country, so maybe he didn't have much time to work with. And we don't have anything pressing planned for tomorrow."

"You are not considering accepting, are you, Mother?"

"Unless you have a good reason not to, I don't see why not. You told me you wished to see those portraits."

Damn it. It was true. More than once, she had expressed her desire to view the portraitist's work. And she didn't really have a plausible excuse that didn't betray a deeper reason she had tried very hard to hide. To her family and herself. What could she say?

I'm sorry, but I must decline the invitation for fear that something far worse than blabbering nonsense or arguing with him would happen? Like me ravishing him? Ivy sighed.

"Fine. I'll reply immediately, letting him know we will be ready when he comes tomorrow."

"And do it graciously," Victoria added, earning a dirty look from Ivy. Victoria knew that Ivy was one of the most even-tempered people she knew, but when something really angered her, it took considerable effort to drag her back to see reason. Her answer wasn't comforting.

"When am I anything if not gracious?"

Chapter Nine

The paintings were everything Ivy thought them to be. Lawrence was an absolute master in reproducing more than his subjects' outward appearance. He was able to convey those character traits they wanted the world to see.

They weren't at the artist's home, but Blakeburne had managed to gain access to one of the biggest collections in London. Ivy was examining a particularly flattering portrait of the Prince Regent while, a few steps ahead, the Duke of Rutherford-Blythe was debating with his wife the merit of commissioning a family portrait. A silent Duke of Blakeburne stood beside her, not having uttered more than a few words after the polite greetings back at her residence. It was a bit disconcerting for Ivy to have that looming presence following her around, watching her.

The Duke would surely be a favourite among painters. Imposing and oh-so-very handsome, it would be a challenge to capture Gabriel

Eastham's essence with the strokes of a brush. The days without seeing him had almost made her forget the impact that his emerald eyes and strong figure had on her. She had been remembered of it all too well upon spotting him alighting his carriage. His dark brown greatcoat perfectly complemented his equally dark hair, and its precise cut emphasised the set of his shoulders and narrow waist. Even now, she couldn't help observing him furtively.

"Are you enjoying the art, my Lady?" he finally said, clearly having come to terms with the fact that he wasn't a statue but a living —and talking— being. He had to do it by letting her know he was aware of her scrutiny, the exasperating man. Lord knew what she found so fascinating in him.

"Very much, Your Grace. Much more than you, it would seem," she couldn't refrain from adding.

"Why do you think that?"

"You haven't said more than two sentences since we arrived. Either you are overwhelmed by Lawrence's talent, or you'd rather be somewhere else." Ivy recalled the opening of his note. *It has been brought to my attention that I have been remiss in my duty.*

"What made you decide to arrange this afternoon in the end?" she asked, narrowing her eyes at him, who wisely immediately picked up the change in her disposition.

"I'm sure I don't know what you are talking about. I had promised you and your parents this private viewing. Estate matters got in the way, as I wrote you. Your brother only reminded me you were awaiting a word from me." *Gregory.* She should have known. Nothing remained private in her family. Ivy felt anger enveloping her like a mantel. She wasn't sure at whom she was angrier. At Gregory for believing she wanted someone to be coerced into inviting her; at Blakeburne for not making the minimal effort to pretend he wanted to be there; or at herself for being blinded by him for a moment. Given that the first wasn't presently available for a tongue-lashing, and she would kick herself for her stupidity alone later, all it was left was Blakeburne. She smiled at him and spoke in an exaggerated saccharine tone.

"I am really sorry."

"What are you apologising about?" Evidently, the Duke's earlier perceptiveness didn't extend that far.

"It must have been a nuisance having my brother approach you and insist on the trivial matter of an all but forgotten invitation." Ivy underlined how sorry she was by putting a comforting hand on his forearm. Inside, she was seething. Rage was way better than thinking that her own brother pitied her to such an extent as to force a gentleman to issue an invitation.

It was the Duke's turn to narrow his eyes. "I assure you it isn't a hardship being here with you, my Lady. Truth is, portraits or not, I wanted to talk to you." Well, that changed things. She looked at him, waiting. The Duke's eyes darted to where the other couple was still deep in conversation.

"The reason behind my last visit to your residence wasn't to invite you today." *Surprise surprise.* "I had hoped to have a few private moments with you to discuss our..." he hesitated slightly over the last word. "Acquaintanceship." His face remained emotionless. "First, I'd like to apologise for my behaviour towards you." That was surprising, for real. Ivy had the impression apologies didn't come easy for the Duke of Blakeburne.

"You have been provoked more than once, Your Grace. Arguing, repeatedly, with a gentleman isn't my usual behaviour, either. Not my finest moments. However—"

"I don't care about that. I should never have kissed and touched you, damn it!" he finished with an angry whisper.

She was struck speechless by his brutal honesty. If she had slapped her, he would have had the same result. And he wasn't finished.

"I find your company preferable to that of many other members of the *ton*. Even if we don't spend much time together, you make balls and soirées infinitely more bearable. I just don't want you to harbour

111

any hope that it would lead to courtship. Because it won't. I find it fair to warn you, in the event you started to feel what you think is affection for me."

Ivy was so stunned she didn't know where to start to address what he had just said.

"Well, Your Grace—"

"You know I dislike you addressing me like that."

"Honestly, *Your Grace*, I don't really care if you dislike it or not at the moment."

"I apologise if my words offend you. My intention is not to mislead you."

"You misunderstand. I'm not offended in the least. I only find it incredibly conceited and arrogant of you to think that a couple of kisses would lead me to throw myself at your feet and start planning our wedding."

"Other ladies had presumed more based on far less than what you and I shared."

"You'll see, Your...mmm, Blakeburne, I don't have much in common with all the other ladies," she echoed what she had said to his cousin a few nights before.

"I'm starting to appreciate that," he said in all seriousness.

"Moreover, you said it yourself. What happened in the park and again at Lady Langton's ball shouldn't have happened. It was a meaningless lapse of judgment. Not worthy of being mentioned again." Lights played tricks in his eyes because Ivy could have sworn something dangerous passed over them. But it was impossible. She had just agreed with him, so what could he possibly be angry about? Ivy had put all her pride behind her words. It had cost her to belittle what she had felt in his arms. Even when she denied it to herself, she knew that deep down, she wanted to find again the woman she had been with him. Instead, she had been put back in her rightful place.

Behind all the hurt, she could appreciate the meaning of his warning. It was not his fault there was more than a grain of truth in his words.

Tearing her gaze away, she searched for her parents, to put an end to that unbearable conversation. She was relieved when she saw them approaching. With his back to them, Blakeburne said, "I'm glad we are on the same page. I would have hated to severe all contacts with you, for I fell only the utmost respect for you."

"And so you should." Ivy managed to have the last words. A small, bittersweet victory. Hearing her parents' approach, Blakeburne turned to face them. Her father was assessing the air between them.

"Your conversation seemed serious. Did one particular painting inspire it?" intervened the Duchess. Ivy took her father's arm and steered him towards the exit, leaving Blakeburne to escort her mother.

"The portraits are real masterpieces. No, the Duke and I were just discussing our new friendship." She looked over her shoulder.

Not at the Duke, but at the piece of her heart that would smear the elegant marble floor after being crushed under one man's polished boots.

Chapter Ten

The dratted man was everywhere. Or so it seemed to Ivy. She had heard many comments on how the private Duke of Blakeburne attended only a few selected events, pushing the *ton* hostesses as far as to try to bribe servants to discover which ones. Well, they could have saved their efforts. And money. She could have told them. Everywhere she went, the frustrating man was there. He attended the Aston ball, the Featherstone card party, rode in Hyde Park, and even strolled down Bond Street.

To be honest, he wasn't really *everywhere*. She was starting to suspect Blakeburne had elaborated a strategy that pleased everyone around him. She had observed that he could be found at one soirée every three days. That made an average of two big events a week.

Not that she was looking that closely.

Added to some unpredictable encounters outside ballrooms and townhouses, it was enough to make it impossible for her to escape him.

To make matters worse, the Duke always took care to exchange pleasantries with her and her family whenever they ran into each other. But there hadn't been any other visit. Without the cumbersome weight of fending off Ivy's romantic interest —she was still fuming thinking about his belief that she couldn't help herself but fall in love with him—, Blakeburne was visibly more at ease with the Kingtons. Soon, simple pleasantries became lively discussions, and even her father had to admit that he started looking forward to them. Meanwhile, Ivy had been forced to shove her hurt deep. There was no way in heaven she would let him see how his words still affected her. And sure as hell she won't admit that more time she spent with Blakeburne, more her fascination with him grew, including his sharp mind to the list of things she could not let herself like about him. Or the fact that he didn't find it inappropriate for a lady to discuss matters like Parliament bills or the price of that year's harvest. More likely, he found her a tolerable oddity that came with the Kingtons, as shown by the fact that Ivy had felt his eyes on her person many times. Her role of being 'somehow part of things' had been completely re-established. *Lucky her.*

That night, she was explaining to the Earl of Covington what changes she wanted to make in her estate, her brother beside her corroborating her ideas, when the Duke made his appearance.

"Good evening Burnam, Covington. Lady Everleigh." He bent over her hand, and Ivy was annoyed that she once again noticed his handsomeness. That evening's attire was completely black, the only concession to colour, if you could call it that, was his starched white cravat. And the emerald green of his eyes. He seemed unaware of all the longing looks that followed him. Not many ladies shared Ivy's unwillingness to throw herself at his feet. Not many ladies had been warned against it by the Duke himself either. *Not that again, Ivy.*

"Blakeburne! Just the man I was hoping to see." Ivy internally rolled her eyes. She must have made some sort of sound because the Duke's gaze shot to her. Fortunately, he didn't say anything before her brother continued, "I was hoping to get your opinion on the new developments in field irrigation. Ivy and I agree on the merit of it, while traditional Covington here argues that it's unnecessary to change something that already works. What do you think?"

"I'm not *traditional*. I only believe that the costs of putting a new system into place far surpass the benefits it would bring. If you had lands that suffered from a lack of water due to an inefficient system, then I'd say it could be a possible solution. Otherwise, why risk it?" objected Covington.

"The Earl has a point." Blakeburne's deep voice carried a sense of authority that belied his relatively young age. "It's an investment that would tie capitals to the land for a long time." He looked briefly at Ivy. "However, I have been reading much about this new system myself, and it could really turn unprofitable land into fertile soil." *Damn it.* It was very difficult to remember where they stood when her new *friend* talked so serious and ducal. It made her want to go to him, tousle his ruthlessly combed hair, ruin his perfect cravat with her hands by pulling him to her and kiss him senseless. She knew how those firm yet full lips felt on hers, how softly his dark locks curled around her fingers. She jolted out of her inappropriate thoughts to contribute to the discussion.

"No progress has ever been made in history without risks. Don't you agree?"

Blakeburne was once again looking at her.

Their gaze met and held. Their connection uncaring of their reasoning and excuses.

Undoubtedly someone would soon remark upon it. It was impossible that those kinds of stares would go unnoticed. Ivy felt the warmth she now associated with his proximity engulfing her. His eyes, unwaveringly fixed on her face, darkened, the pupils slowly swallowing the green of the irises. It was all very confusing. She didn't have much experience with gentlemen's romantic attention, but that seemed a lot of heat for someone who tolerated her for the sake of alleviating boredom at social functions. Not that she would ever ask about that fire in eyes. She wasn't sure she could bear another speech about how inconvenient her feelings for him would be. At best, she would bloody his nose.

"Oh, dear me, don't tell me you are boring these fine gentlemen with talk of your quaint little estate, dear cousin!" Ivy turned and found herself facing the most unlikely pair. Cousin Eleanor, petite and delicate in her lilac gown that enhanced the blond of her hair, was accompanied by Lady Ingram, with matching blond hair and a deep burgundy dress that displayed her slender yet curvaceous frame, cleavage, and all.

Ivy refrained from pointing out that her 'quaint little estate' was more extensive and employed more tenants than Uncle George's one. Well-bred ladies didn't boast. How much of a well-bred lady she really was was soon put to the test when Lady Ingram had the audacity to say, "Lady Everleigh is a greedy girl, keeping all these handsome men all to herself." Her tone was meant to be jesting, if not for the malicious glint in her eyes and subtle smirk. Smirk that was mirrored on Eleanor's face. Ivy gathered all her rightful irritation to form a fitting reply, fighting against her innate shyness that abhorred that kind of confrontation. She was sure that part of their cattiness was caused by the Duke of Blakeburne's presence. She was used to Eleanor's pettiness, but a coalition with the woman whom Ivy had witnessed trying to trap the Duke was new. Channelling the Kington in her, she looked down her nose at the two.

"It's very fortunate that you joined us. I wouldn't dream of *trapping* anyone in conversation against their will. It would really be bad taste." She looked pointedly at Imogen Ingram, pleased to see her smile disappear. She felt the men's confused eyes on her. All except one, who was aware of what she was implying. Again, it was all his fault.

The small orchestra chose that exact moment to start playing. None of the men had said anything yet, until Gregory, either aware of the mounting tension or completely oblivious, extended his upturned hand towards Lady Shrew Ingram.

"Would you do me the honour of this dance, my Lady?" His grin was difficult to resist, and Lady Ingram nodded her assent, her face pleasantly angelic. Oh, she was good at playing the game. But so was Gregory, so Ivy didn't worry about him falling into her clutches.

"And you, Lady Eleanor, would you be so kind as to partner me for the next set?" Eleanor shot a hopeful look in Blakeburne's direction, probably fantasising about a battle for her hand worthy of the knights of old. When it became clear that none was forthcoming, she was left with no plausible reason to refuse the Earl of Covington. With a regal nod, she let the Earl lead her onto the dance floor. Ivy watched the couple fall into their respective positions, ready for the quadrille. Once again, she had been left standing alone beside the Duke of Blakeburne. And once again, he didn't seem even slightly inclined to ask her to dance. If last time he could have pleaded their fresh acquaintance as a motive, this time nobody would find it strange to see them dance together. If anything, everyone would wonder why they didn't. Her parents had taught her not to care about these inanities, but it wasn't easy not to feel humiliated by his lack of social graces. Come to think about it, since meeting him, Ivy had never seen the Duke dance. She was dying to ask him if he had some aversion to it, but she bit her tongue.

That was the first time they had found themselves relatively alone since that catastrophic afternoon. Nothing had changed for her; his nearness still had the same effect.

Scrambling to find something to say, she decided to test her theory.

"Tell me, Your Grace, will I see you tomorrow night at the Emerson card party?"

"Unfortunately, my Lady, you won't. I don't plan to attend."

"That's a shame. I was looking forward to partnering you in a game of whist. And what about Lady Morton's ball three days hence?"

"I believe I have accepted that particular invitation. Will we be graced by your presence as well?" Pleased that her theory had been confirmed, she smiled cunningly.

"Of course. Just as we will be blessed by yours at whichever soirée will take place three days after the ball."

"I don't know what you are talking about. I can't possibly say what my plans are without looking at the invitations."

"It's just that I noticed a certain pattern in your social calendar. One evening every three days, plus miscellaneous obligations. That's how much the *ton* has been seeing the unapproachable Duke of Blakeburne."

He blinked at her. She gifted him a self-satisfied smile.

"Bravo, Lady Everleigh. I thought my methods would remain undetected a bit longer. You should know they have been satisfactory for everyone so far. My mother stopped hounding me about taking more interest in the *beau monde*; the *ton* has its pound of my flesh to feast on; and, more importantly, I got to keep my sanity intact by not being subjected to more talk of the weather and *on dits* I can stand." Ivy could see his point. She had seen with her own eyes how, whenever he entered a room, he was besieged by people —mostly women— vying for his attention.

"Don't worry, Blakeburne, your secret is safe with me." This time her smile was genuine. She liked thinking he had let her under the façade he showed the world.

"Why this intense interest in my movements, my Lady? I thought we agreed...." And the happy bubble burst. Ivy should have known he would conclude that only a deeply infatuated person would scrutinise his behaviour so closely to discern a pattern.

Isn't he right, though? No, he isn't. She straightened her back in a defensive stance.

"Oh, don't look so worried, Your Grace. Anyone who cares to look can understand what you are doing. Fortunately for you, aristocracy is famous for seeing only what it wants to see. Believe me, I should know." She looked away from him, her eyes set on the couples harmoniously parting and coming together. "Don't insult my intelligence. I perfectly understood your speech the other day. I beg you to spare us both the pleasure of warning me again against becoming one of the many women that fall hopelessly in love with you. It's becoming tiresome. And unnecessary, I might add." She couldn't refrain from adding. Her pride dictated it.

His jaw flexed in annoyance. "That is not what I was implying." Before the conversation became even more unpleasant for them both, Ivy decided to satisfy her curiosity about that other matter.

"Do you ever dance?" If Blakeburne was taken aback by the sudden change in topic, he didn't show it. Not that Ivy expected him to. She had seen him remain impassive in much more flummoxing situations.

"No, not usually," was his simple reply, as if it were pretty obvious, which, indeed, it was. It surely was very uninformative.

"Why not?" she prodded. She envisaged an answer on the line of 'I don't like to dance' or even 'I have two left feet', which seemed improbable given the elegance of his gait, but one never knew. What she got instead was, "Why do *you* almost never dance?"

Oh, low blow, Blakeburne. You really are an arse. Ivy decided to hit him with brutal honesty.

"Like many of your fellow peers, you are not very observant, Your Grace, or you would have noticed that gentlemen don't champ at the bit to ask me to dance. And it is pretty important that someone asks, in order to dance, you know? And, as a woman —I hope you at least have noticed that—, I can't do much more than wait for men's whims." When she was finished, he was back at looking at her as if trying to solve a complex equation.

"That is what I don't understand," he began, looking at her and frowning. "Why *aren't* they? You come from an illustrious family, have powerful connections, and are a perfect Lady. Many matches have been made based on much less auspicious circumstances. Nor there is anything wrong with your appearance or a particular scandal linked to your name. On the contrary, nothing is ever said about you." *Gut me with a blunt knife, will you?* She had unwisely opened that particular pandora's box. Short of waking away, now she had to face the consequences. She had started with the truth; she would finish with the truth as well.

"They forget about me, all right? There is nothing in me that leaves them longing for more. It's kind of sad if you think about it. For all my wealth and social standing, they struggle to remember my name." There, she had said it. The sad, pathetic truth.

She waited for Blakeburne to acknowledge the accuracy of her words. Silence thickened the air, and she turned to look at him. Surely, baring the festering pain she usually kept well buried in the deepest recess of her soul warranted some sort of reaction. His face seemed to be carved in stone, each feature starkly accentuated. His jaw was clenched so tight, Ivy fancied she could hear his teeth grinding. His eyes were flashing brilliant green. Around them, the music changed, signalling the end of the set. People changed partners or went to stand along the walls. Blakeburne took advantage of the temporary disorder they created and grabbed her arm, pulling her gently but firmly with him. Ivy had no choice but to follow him, her resistance drawing more attention than her compliance. He led her behind a big potted plant. They were just out of sight, but anyone could easily spot them. And given the fact that the Duke had rendered the female half of the *ton* like street urchins salivating at the sight of gingerbread, Ivy doubted eyes didn't follow him. What was the oh-so-proper peer thinking, behaving that way? And why was he looking angrily at *her?* She didn't know what to do with the intensity of his gaze. So, she forced herself to speak.

"Listen, Blakeburne. I don't know what you think you're doing, but —"

"It's impossible," he interrupted, the short sentence sharp and final as a royal verdict.

"What is?" She blinked.

"I don't know what you are playing at, but spinning patently false tales like that won't lead you anywhere."

Ivy regarded him like he had lost his mind. Which she suspected he had. "I beg your pardon?"

"And so you should. Fishing for compliments is all right and well, but such a pitiful story isn't only untrue, but also very unbecoming." She couldn't believe her ears. As if it wasn't humiliating enough that she had spoken about it, the fact that he had reduced it all to vapid lies only to be complimented was beyond hurtful.

"Do you know how many times I had to be introduced to Baron Whintrope? Four! And I've lost count of how many times someone has called me Miss before they realised who I was. Oh, and let's not forget the time when an Earl talked with Victoria and me about how to approach the elusive Countess of Everleigh. Now that I think about it, it happened twice."

"What's his name?" Blakeburne's fists clenched, his knuckles turning white. His expression was so forbidding that she almost stopped talking. But the dam had broken. So, she continued.

"Whose name? That Earl's? It doesn't matter. My point is, I'm shy and unassuming, and I will never shine as brightly as the rest of my family. I accepted it. I don't need it. I am not waiting for a man to fall madly in love with me."

"You should." Those two words were the last straw. He didn't get to kiss her, touch her, insinuate under her skin, to then distance himself and keep her at arm's length. And now, he was looking at her with eyes that were almost... compassionate.

"Stop, Blakeburne. Just stop. I knew you could be arrogant and brusque, but I didn't think you were cruel."

"Cruel? How in heaven am I—"

She left him there, wishing he was as easy to forget as she was.

Chapter Eleven

"Unbelievable," Gabriel murmured to himself, eyes following one particular lady.

"What's unbelievable?" enquired Bellmore, who was standing beside him, a glass of champagne in his long-fingered hand.

Two nights had passed since he had made a mess of things with Ivy. *Lady Everleigh.* He shouldn't have attended the Whiteridge ball — held by the fierce Dowager Marchioness's son. According to his method, which Lady Everleigh had correctly surmised, he should have forgone that night's ball for a more moderately sized dinner the following evening. Only, merely for the sake of not being considered so predictable, he had decided to change things around a little. A significant part in his decision was played by his newfound interest in disproving the Countess's dejected statements. Not because he wanted to prove a point, but because it was impossible for him to believe that a woman like Ivy Kington could be overlooked. She was beautiful, kind, sharp as a whip, and the daughter of one of the most powerful men in the realm. As he had told her, ladies with fewer desirable qualities were sought after and married off all the time.

Much later that night, alone in his study, he had acknowledged the fact that, maybe, accusing her of inventing that pitiful tale hadn't been the best course of action. And maybe —and that was so ridiculous he would deny it through his teeth— he hadn't wanted to believe it. Because how could anyone fail to notice her when he wasn't able to stick to his own decision and stay away from her? He had meant to. After finally explaining why nothing could ever happen between them in a very reasonable way, he had intended to resume his life and forget about her. Instead, he had scheduled his social appearances —with the added benefit that his mother wasn't tricking him into agreeing to attend anymore— and had made sure to stop and converse with her each time. Oh, from the outside, he had made it seem like he was furthering his connection with Rutherford-Blythe and other influential Lords. In reality, he had spent that time observing and getting to know Ivy Kington. And becoming more and more captivated by her. By how she could effortlessly carry out a conversation about topics that would be completely obscure to most. And by how her pretty face became blindly beautiful when she smiled and talked fervently about Everleigh. At the same time, he saw that, despite her vast knowledge, she wasn't comfortable among many people. That shyness that was recurrently linked with her was always just under the surface. A keen eye could see the constant effort she made to overcome it. And to him, it was a sign of great strength. Another thing to admire about her. It didn't change anything, however. He stood firm in his belief that he could not consider her as a possible bride. She may have been constantly changing before his eyes —from a typical well-bred Lady to an intelligent, witty, and deeply passionate woman who could set his blood on fire—, but he was still the same.

His reaction two nights before had been sparked by her question about dancing. Instead of giving a vague excuse, he had retaliated out of irritation. Immediately, he had wanted to apologise but, as typically when Lady Everleigh was concerned, he had been taken by surprise. He still didn't believe the picture she had painted for herself, but the look on her face, the old pain that dimmed the light in her brown eyes, had made him want to break something. Possibly some halfwit's nose.

Upon arriving at the ball that night, he had constantly watched the Countess's interactions. He had observed her many times before, but he focused now on a broader picture than the Lady herself. And his desire to pummel someone had intensified tenfold. It was all very subtle. Nobody gave her the cut or was outright rude. People came and went, paying their respects, some chatting about inanities. Their attention, however, was always more on the Duchess of Rutherford-Blythe or Lady Victoria. Ivy simply stood there, a pleasant smile on her face, none of the vibrant life he had witnessed in her to be seen.

Gabriel suddenly remembered her curved shoulders the night they had kissed on Langton's balcony. At the time, it had seemed crucial for him to understand the cause behind it. But then he had been too affected by the fire that burned between them, and how to distance himself from it, that it had slipped his mind. Now it came all back, the pieces clicking into place. And, watching a confused Baron Whintrope looking up at Lady Everleigh like he had never seen her before, Gabriel came to three realisations.

One, Ivy had told the truth.

Two, he wanted to march over there and shake some sense into her. Because, for how much these shallow people deserved a collective horsewhipping, what was really unbearable was seeing her fading into the background, accepting the place someone else had carelessly chosen for her, without putting up a fight. That was completely unacceptable.

"Blakeburne? You are woolgathering again. What is unbelievable?" Bellmore's voice penetrated the curtain of anger and frustration that was inexorably coating his mind. He had almost forgotten that his friend was standing beside him. He turned towards the Viscount.

Bellmore's brows shot up. "Dear Lord. What is that glower for? We are lucky there are no children around, or you would scar them for life."

Gabriel ignored his remark. "Did you notice that? How could they behave that way towards *her*?" He waved in the Countess's general direction.

"Notice what? Where? Who?"

"Lady Everleigh! Burnam's sister! If you have forgotten her, I swear to God...."

"Calm down, Blakeburne. What has got into you? Christ. I know perfectly well who Lady Everleigh is. Have known her for years." That calmed Gabriel down a fraction. He immediately regretted his outburst. Mainly because he now owed Bellmore an explanation. Gabriel was sure Ivy wouldn't appreciate him betraying her confidence.

"What do you think of Lady Everleigh?"

Bellmore stroked his chin, pensive. He had rightly gauged that Gabriel's question required a serious, and not his usual flippant, answer. He probably wanted to avoid that Gabriel bit his head off.

"She's a fine Lady. Interesting conversation. Although I have to admit, I've spoken to her only a few times since I've known her. Don't really know why. Before you came back and started spending more time with the Double Duke and Burnam, I haven't really spared much thought for R-B's daughter."

Satisfied by his honest answer, Bellmore glanced at Gabriel. His jaw slacked when he turned on his heels and began striding across the room.

"Where are you going? Blakeburne!" He followed, hot on his heels, obviously curious about what was happening. Gabriel didn't really know himself. He only knew one thing: the third realisation he had? He was as guilty as all the other careless idiots of the *ton*. Only, he hadn't unconsciously made her feel small and inconsequential. He had wanted to do it. To protect himself. Which was way worse.

The first sign that something was happening was Victoria's voice breaking off in mid-sentence. The second, her eyes widening. The third was her saying, "The cavalry is approaching," without taking her gaze away from something behind Ivy. Turning, she could see what her friend meant. There, amid people trying in vain to engage him, the Duke of Blakeburne was making his way towards them, Viscount Bellmore following closely. She briefly considered running away or at least hiding behind something. Ivy had been the recipient of various of Blakeburne's less than affable expressions, but now his eyes weren't shooting only daggers, but swords and sabres as well. He was oozing dark determination, and all around him, others started to perceive it, deciding it was safer to jump out of his way. Ivy was soon captured by that intensity, the instinct to flight forgotten, replaced by shivers that infused her body in front of such an air of command, which had nothing to do with fear. She dreaded what he would do once he had reached her, but she wasn't afraid of his scowl. Or of him. Which was insane because he was the most dangerous threat she ever had to protect her heart from.

After what seemed like hours, but couldn't have been more than a few minutes, the Duke and his frowning face stopped right in front of Ivy.

"Dance with me." *What?* Ivy looked at his proffered gloved hand as if she had never seen that particular human extremity before. His request —or, rather, order— came completely out of the blue, especially after he had categorically refused to dance before. *Say something, you ninny!*

"You want to dance. With me." *Excellent, Ivy. All those years with tutors, and this is the result.*

127

The nerves of Blakeburne's jaw throbbed, the only visible sign of impatience.

"That's what I said. Would you do me the honour to dance with me, *please?*"

"With pleasure, Your Grace." Ivy let Blakeburne lead her in the middle of the dance floor, leaving behind a bewildered Viscount Bellmore, who said to an equally bewildered Victoria, "We might as well follow their example. What do you think, my Lady? We can at least keep an eye on those two." They were already too far to hear Victoria's answer, but she saw her and the Viscount join the dancing couples. She soon forgot about them when she felt Blakeburne's hand span her waist in a caress. She looked up at his face and was immediately captured by the fierceness of his gaze. Some of the anger she had felt coming from him had cooled down, but it was like a blacksmith was hammering on his anvil in the recess of his eyes because sparks were flashing in his green orbs.

She was able to look away only when he took the first step, leading her. It didn't really come as a surprise that he put the same seriousness in dancing that he put in everything else. His steps were precise, steady, and elegant, yet they lacked the easiness that came from engaging in it often. Or enjoying it. Nonetheless, the Duke of Blakeburne was undisputedly a proficient dancer.

"I thought you didn't know how to dance…." Ivy said while he executed a perfectly controlled turn.

"I said I don't usually dance, not that I didn't know how. Dancing is part of every gentleman's education, whether he's agreeable to it or not."

"That's true. But waltzing? I doubt it was part of the dancing lessons you had when you were younger." It was too new an addition to the dancing repertoire.

"A Duke had to master everything that's required to keep his place at the top of the social ladder." Ivy couldn't stifle the chuckle that burst out of her. That had to be the most ducal remark that had ever come from him. He raised an eyebrow, adding to the effect, his face impassive. He really believed it. That only fuelled her laughter.

"I'm sorry, but that was the most supercilious thing I have ever heard. I hate to be the bearer of bad news, Your Grace, but no one could be perfect at everything." That arrogant eyebrow raised a bit more, if possible. Ivy found that strangely endearing. Irritating as hell, but also endearing.

"Will you ever tell me the real reason why you don't dance?" Ivy risked another rebuttal, just like when she had previously asked, but there, within the circle of his arms, gloved palms touching, she didn't care. She couldn't find the strength to keep the distance he demanded.

"Society makes too much fuss about a trivial thing like dancing. It's enough for me to be seen partnering a particular lady once, and speculation would start flying whether by the end of the night she would be the future Duchess of Blakeburne. I won't have my hand forced for a couple of twirls and a few steps. And, honestly, I have never cared to dance before." Having been raised among the same gossipmongers, Ivy understood his reasoning.

"Why are you dancing with me now, then?" Anyone could have predicted her next question.

Ivy held her breath, feeling her heart beating faster. If what he said were true —and she had no reason to doubt it— this meant more to him than a filled place in a dance card.

"Can we not simply enjoy this waltz?" he countered. It was Ivy's turn to raise an eyebrow.

"Of course not." He sighed. "As you wish, my Lady. After our conversation two nights ago, I have been observing you closely." Ivy stiffened. "Rather, I have been observing how others behave around you. I don't understand how it's possible, but you were right. You don't attract the attention you deserve."

"Well, thank you, Your Grace, for pointing out what has been obvious to me since my coming out," she replied sarcastically. "What I fail to understand is what all that have to do with asking me to dance."

"If you could kindly control your sarcasm, what I was trying to say was that had I noticed it before, I would have handled some of our interactions differently. So, in light of my newfound knowledge, I've decided to make amend by using my blasted visibility for something good." It was like waiting for a carriage wreck to happen. With growing horror, Ivy seriously thought about slapping her hands over his mouth to hush him. He had already said enough for her to draw a fairly good picture of the situation. She now knew it really would have been better if they had just enjoyed the dance.

"After the entire *ton* sees you catching the attention of the highly eligible Duke of Blakeburne, every bachelor across Town will start wondering how he could have been so blind as to fail to notice you. They will buzz around you like bees with honey." Ivy was completely, utterly, at a loss for words. She had always been able to muster a smart retort to counter the Duke. It had been one of the things she had mostly liked about him. The courage he drew from her to stand toe to toe with him. Looking at his pleased expression, her mind was blank, any thought drowned under the noise of that wreck. Only it wasn't the cacophony of the spidering wood of a carriage. Once again, Blakeburne had taken a piece of her and callously shattered it.

"You…" She cleared her throat. "I really don't know how to respond to that."

"There's nothing to say. Let's enjoy the rest of the dance, shall we? And then you can reap all the benefits. Even if someone starts gossiping about us, it's a risk I'm willing to take. I'd gladly do it for you." Looking around, Ivy noticed with abject consternation that many pairs of eyes were already on them. However, that didn't stop her from trying to break free from his hold. There wasn't much left to the dance, and she needed to get away from the Duke. Immediately. Despite what he thought to have understood, Ivy didn't want, or needed, that kind of help. Especially not out of pity.

His hand tightened on her waist, and his strong fingers squeezed hers, stopping her from going anywhere.

"What do you think you are doing? Attracting attention is one thing, but I won't countenance the spectacle of you causing a scene." His face had now lost all traces of smugness. His eyes were boring intensely into her. She straightened her spine, but her voice came out more like a whisper.

"Let me go, Blakeburne. The dance is almost over. Nobody will object if we part here."

"I would. Explain why you look like that. You should be elated that I helped you solve some of your problems. Now, if you just would let others see the fire you show when you argue with me…."

The voice she had lost came back in full force.

"You know what, Your Grace? Sometimes I really, really hate you." Ivy realised it was true. She hated him for thinking she was so shallow that she would be happy to attract men because she had been seen in the company of the high-and-mighty Duke of Blakeburne. That the time they had spent together, both within and outside the boundaries of propriety, had meant so little to him, he was happy to parade her in front of every available man. Most of all, she hated that, since the night they met, his actions had the power to hurt her with so little effort.

She had delivered those spiteful words looking directly into his beautiful green eyes, and she could have sworn a flash of hurt passed over them. Fortuitously, right then, the last notes of the waltz resonated in the air. Even more fortuitously, they came to a halt directly in front of the doors leading to the garden. Ivy curtsied and murmured, "Thank you for the dance, Your Grace," before fleeing across the open doors. She was almost running, more to escape her thoughts than for fear of being followed. There was no danger that the mystified man she had left behind would come after her. It would be too undignified.

She stopped only when the lights from the house were too far away to illuminate her and her surroundings. Her breath was laboured, but it wasn't her physical effort that had caused it. It was her pounding heart, her knotted stomach that threatened to rebel. She forced herself to inhale long and slowly, aware that all the tension would soon morph into a splitting headache. After a few deep breaths, she was able to control herself. Only then she heard the sound of nearing footsteps. The figure approaching was big and menacing, obviously male. The lights at his back were enough to show only half of his face. She had been wrong once again. Blakeburne could follow her, and he had. And he was furious. If that was what his enemies saw in battle, it was almost scarier than the slashing of his blade. *Retreat, Ivy! Retreat!* Her feet refused to follow the wise advice of her brain, anchoring her on the spot.

His long legs soon brought him in front of her. He stood so near that Ivy could feel the warmth radiating from him. Fists clenched, he looked at her like he wanted to throttle her. Strangely enough, Ivy was certain that, as angry as he appeared, he would never hurt her. Physically at least. Emotionally, she felt like a shooting target.

"What the hell was that?" he spat. Ivy had never heard the Duke curse. That was a clear indication of his barely contained rage. She mustered all the anger that simmered inside *her*. What right did *he* have to be incensed?

"First of all, *Your Grace,*" Ivy purposely used his title mockingly, knowing how it vexed him to hear her say it that way. "You don't get to follow me and throw words at me."

"And you don't get to tell me you hate me and walk away from me like I've done something reprehensible, when all I did was dance with you. For you!"

"For such an intelligent man, you really are dense sometimes, you know that, Blakeburne?"

"You must be right because I still haven't got a clue why you are so angry with me. For fu...for heaven's sake!" Blakeburne made a considerable effort to rein in his temper. Ivy realised he really didn't understand. Behind his fury, confusion shone in his eyes. He wasn't used to being in the dark and didn't like the feeling. Ivy exhaled deeply and tried again to be reasonable.

"I appreciate the gesture. I really do. Your intentions were honourable. But it really wouldn't change anything for me."

"I beg to differ, my Lady. I've seen it happen before. A woman sometimes only needs a little help to be noticed. I felt sorry for not realising it sooner. It is hard for me to fathom how you could ever fade into the background." Ivy knew she should focus on the backhanded compliment, but she couldn't get past '*I felt sorry*'. He had expressed the sentiment more times she cared to count, that night and before, and Ivy was tired of it. Bone tired of how her stomach dropped each time. Of how she was always disappointed. Her effort to be reasonable flew right out of the window. Metaphorically, since they were already outside.

"You can take your pity and choke on it, Blakeburne!" The Duke was so taken aback by her outburst that he took a step back in surprise.

"Pity? Woman, are you insane?" Maybe she was, hearing what came out of her mouth next.

"I must be insane! What other explanation there would be otherwise for foolishly hoping you would invite me to dance because... oh, I don't know...you wanted to?" She mimed an expression of utter horror. "Or that, between talks of stewards and political bills, you maybe, *maybe*, appreciated my presence. And if you open your mouth and repeat again how I should refrain from falling in love with you, I'm slapping you."

"Are you finished? That's quite a fishwife's speech for a Duke's daughter." His collectedness did nothing to calm her down. That added to the realisation that she had basically admitted being like all the other pathetic women, waiting for a scrap of attention from him.

"Yes, well, since I met you, I am not acting like myself!" Another embarrassing admission.

"That makes the two of us, Ivy!" Her traitorous heart jumped at his use of her given name. "You are a madness! You are a mystery I am unable to solve. You are tempest and still waters. You are an unmovable oak and a fragile bloom. You've taken residence in my mind, and no matter how much I will you to, you won't leave. That is why I can't understand how so many idiots don't see you! Because if it's impossible for me —and believe me, I've tried—, how could *they* overlook you?"

Ivy had never seen Blakeburne like that. He was waving his hands around madly, the dim light not enough to conceal the flame that made his eyes flashing like the gem from which their colour took its name. She had been right from the very beginning. Under the severe and unmovable part of him he showed the world, his passion ran deep, scorching in its intensity. And Ivy, shy and insecure Ivy, had unleashed it. As it had happened when she had heard him laugh the night they first met, she wanted to draw this reaction from him. Like a moth to a flame, conscious that it would not end well, she wanted to get burned.

"So, it's true. I didn't want to dance with you!" He took a step towards her. Then another. "Not when what I really want to do is this!" If ever a kiss could be described as an explosion, it was that one. His hands immediately went to her waist, and Ivy could feel the heat ever through her gown. It was like during the waltz, only ten times more intense. But it was nothing compared to the furnace that awaited her when the hard planes of his chest pressed unforgivably upon her softer curves. Her mind finally caught up with what was happening, just enough to will both of her hands to palm his neck, rising on tiptoe. She kissed him back with all her pent-up frustration. It was a kiss of retaliation, for all the times he had carelessly hurt her.

After a few strokes of his tongue, however, all that ceased to matter. What mattered was how he was making her feel. How *she* was making *him* feel. He groaned deep in his throat, a sound that was both of surrender and satisfaction. His lips left hers to trail small kisses along her jaw until it reached its destination at the beating pulse of her neck.

"Blakeburne, we should stop…." *Stop?* How could she say such a thing aloud was a mystery, when inside she was screaming for more. Much more.

"Mmm…yes, we should," he agreed, gently sucking on her collarbone. It elicited a needy moan from her. He followed it by caressing her breasts, making her hiss the last air she had in her lungs. *Who decided you needed air to breathe?*

She tried again. "This is most improper." Not that she was doing anything to put an end to it. On the contrary, she had one hand in his hair, the other slowly perusing his muscled back, until it reached the firm curve of his behind, tentatively squeezing it. Did she dare move to the front?

"What, Ivy?" he said, leaving her neck to stare in deep concentration at her breasts where his hands were now kneading, like his sole mission in life was to make the tips into two hard points.

"What what?" She was so lost in the pleasure of his caresses, she had completely forgotten what they were talking —well, moaning— about.

"You were saying something about stopping…."

"NO!" she exclaimed. He chuckled. "I mean, yes, we have to stop kissing in anger. That's not a way to end discussions."

"Does it feel like anger to you?" Blakeburne pressed that hard part of his body to her core. That hard part of him she was developing an overwhelming desire to touch. To stroke. To feel without any barrier between them. And she had said his kisses were improper.

"It doesn't mean anything…."

"Like hell, it doesn't! Feel what you do to me." He took Ivy's hand and put it on the front of his breeches, where it was met with a significant bulge. He groaned again at the contact, more so when she started moving her hand, gently stroking him through his clothes. She was acting by instinct. She had once seen the act in one of Gregory's prints he thought he had so cleverly hidden, but never in her wildest dreams had Ivy thought it would feel that way. She must have been doing something right because his hands stilled their caress, and he looked up at the sky. From his expression, he seemed almost in pain, but when he murmured, "Oh God, yes!" it was apparent pain wasn't what he was feeling. His eyes came back to her, so dark and intense she was unable to look away from them. He drew her ever nearer, his hands resuming their study of her body. When they reached the swell of her bottom, Ivy thought he would hug her. Instead, he ventured under her skirt, the sudden fresh air on places that usually didn't feel any shocking her.

"Gabriel!" she cried, those skilful fingers leaving a tingling trail along her leg, inexorably nearing the apex of her thighs, the spot where she was throbbing with need. She couldn't fathom how she could have lived so far without experiencing that kind of pleasure. Not when it now consumed her completely. He was moving so slowly she was one second away from taking his hand and putting it where she wanted it. She had lost all restraint, her fingers fumbling with the fall of his breeches on their own volition.

"I love hearing my name on your lips," he said, caressing the skin just above the edge of her stockings.

"Really, Your Grace?" She smiled, pressing her lips against his for a swift kiss. Her fingers were trembling, making it hard to free the blasted buttons. But she was nothing if not determined. Finally, she freed him. Hard and heavy in her hand, she was momentarily distracted from the slow ascent of his fingers on her. Ivy found herself staring. She had nothing to measure it up against, but she was sure it was more than…*adequate*. When looking wasn't enough anymore, Ivy circled his length with her hand, gently brushing the moist head. The groan that rumbled in his chest was deeply satisfying, encouraging her to continue. Not to be outdone, he finally reached the destination of his overlong journey. He caressed her folds open, finding her embarrassingly ready to meet his touch. He took it as an invitation to proceed. He entered her with a finger, the foreign invasion making her whimper. He stopped to make her adjust, eyes on her face, waiting for any sign from her. She answered by stroking him. He closed his eyes briefly, swallowing hard. When he opened them again, the green was almost entirely eclipsed by the black centre. His eyes never left hers as he started moving his finger inside her. They were both panting heavily, their breath mingling, their strokes synchronised.

He suddenly deprived her of his body, much to her dismay. Embarrassedly, she even let out a needy sound of protest.

She wasn't left bereft of his touch for long, though. With a wicked smile, he passed his hand over her breast, making her shiver, while the other gently rested between her shoulder blades. After a few tweaks on her distended nipples, he once again raised her skirt, this time from the front. The few seconds of respite between his touches allowed her to regain partial use of her brain. With that, she was assaulted by a sliver of rationality. *What are we doing? If we were to be discovered, there would be no coming back. Deep down, nothing has really changed, even if I'm changing forever under his touch.*

Gabriel must have felt her subtle withdrawal because he redoubled his efforts to recreate their bubble of desire.

"Don't think, Ivy. Not yet," he whispered into her ear while re-entering her. His thumb pressed against the nerve on top of her warmth, triggering a pleasure so intense she had to press her forehead against his coat to stay upright. With that feeling came an overwhelming need to make him feel the same. She willed herself not to be only at the receiving end of his caresses but to give him as much. She matched him stroke for stroke, her head still burrowed into the rich fabric of his coat. She felt him resting his chin on her hair. From the outside, it would appear they were just embracing. It was enough to compromise her, but observers wouldn't even begin to imagine what they were really doing. That she was holding the Duke of Blakeburne's manhood in her hand and that the sombre, cold Duke was driving her wild with his strong fingers. The rhythm of their movements increased, just like their breathing, which was becoming more and more ragged. Her heartbeat was erratic, and she could hear Gabriel's own pulsations clearly through his clothes. She felt on the brink of something. Something she had only read about so far. Something she was sure she wasn't meant to be experienced like that.

"Oh, fuck." Gabriel's strangled groan accompanied a few drops of liquid that coated her hand. With a sense of urgency, he pushed his finger deeper inside her. She gasped. That, together with his clever stimulation of her bud, brought her over that elusive edge. She planted her face into his chest, biting the fabric to stifle the cry she wasn't able to suppress. He stiffened and let out a sound similar to a grunt, reaching his own release.

Leaving the deep recesses of her body while cradling her head with the other hand to keep her against his chest, he hastily reached for his breast pocket. Hot spurts of liquid covered her hand, soaking the handkerchief he used to cover him and her both. Shudders ran through him. He brought her flush against him while waves of pleasure kept travelling through her body, a sense of peace and contentment infusing into her. They stood there, in silence, trying to bring their breathing under control. Her ear was pressed on his heart, listening to its rhythm slowing down. She smiled when she felt his lips against the top of her head.

He was holding her tightly, stealing a few moments more from reality, before the inevitable intruded, bringing back all the reasons they shouldn't have let their control burst into flame.

"Tell me you don't hate me," he said softly, his voice a little hoarse. The quietly spoken order had a pleading note that was so foreign for the Duke it was like the sun at midnight. A hint of vulnerability from a man who could make grown men cower with only a dark look. *My poor stubborn, broody, dear, man.*

Wait, no. Blakeburne isn't yours.

But there, in the dark, in the aftermath of that extraordinary experience, she could admit to herself she longed for him to be.

Ivy raised her head and leaned back just enough to look directly into his eyes. They were soft, yet no less intense. The Duke was nowhere to be seen. Gabriel was expectantly waiting.

"I wish it were possible to feel nothing for you." She was being more honest she had ever thought she would be with him. Under normal circumstances, her pride wouldn't have allowed her to bare her soul without putting up a fight. There, however, within the circle of his strong arms, she felt safe. "It would be a lot easier."

She suddenly found the embossed buttons on his waistcoat very interesting. As the glow started to recede, Ivy realised she should have listened to what her brain had been trying in vain to tell her. "I don't expect that this has altered any of our convictions. I will cherish these stolen moments with you, Gabriel, but I believe we should try to restore distance between us."

"Don't I get a say in the matter, Ivy?" He was still so close she could physically feel how, heartbeat after heartbeat, he was becoming the Duke of Blakeburne again. As much as she was attracted to the powerful and commanding peer, she mourned the loss of the man who asked her not to hate him.

"Of course you do. But I'm aware that your honour right now is probably demanding to go ask my father for my hand." He didn't react to her words, wordlessly acknowledging them. "I save you the trouble. I wouldn't accept your proposal anyway." Ivy tried to soothe the sting of her words with a small smile. "I haven't forgotten all you've been telling me. It's better for us both if we leave everything the way it is. You know I'm right." Gabriel studied her face, trying to read her. If he based his judgment on women like Lady Ingram, she couldn't even fault him for doubting her. After long moments of reflection, he nodded.

Ivy took a step back, his arms still around her, as if reluctant to let go. She shared the feeling. The moment they parted, masks would fall into place. She brushed her dress down to remove any crease he had made. She then patted her head to feel if her coiffure was still intact.

Everything was still in place, but barely. The heavy mass of her hair was threatening to fall. Her hairstyle was unstable at the best of times. His fingers had done the rest. The night was over for her —not that she had any desire to prolong it—, but she had to go inside to retrieve her cloak and her mother.

"How do I look? Am I fit to go back inside?" Gabriel's intense eyes perused her, taking the question very seriously.

"You'll do," he said with a sharp nod of his head. It was such a typical answer coming from him that she didn't take offence. Instead, she burst into laughter.

"Thank you, Your Grace." She left the warmth of his body, the effort greater than she had imagined. "It's better if I go now. Wait a few minutes before following me." She walked away from him then, her steps slow as if delaying reality as much as possible.

She was barely within earshot when Gabriel said, "You look beautiful. You looked perfect in my arms."

She turned, smiling so wide her cheek started to hurt.

"Goodnight, Gabriel."

She went without turning again.

Chapter Twelve

Gabriel was once again in his study, the Duchess of Blakeburne gracefully sitting on the wing chair in front of his desk. For once, he welcomed her presence invading his sanctuary. It gave him an excuse not to focus on his duties in the form of unread reports and letters that were looking at him disapprovingly. It had been foolish even thinking about concentrating that morning. Not after the night before. He went against everything he believed in and everything his father had inculcated in him since his birth. *Dukes are never to be found in compromising positions. They are not monarchs. Dukes are much more powerful. They influence monarchs.* His father had been the last thing on his mind while he was shamelessly ravishing Ivy Kington. Countess of Everleigh. Daughter of the double Duke of Rutherford-Blythe.

Well, when he decided to act inappropriately, he did it rather spectacularly.

He should never have followed her outside. That had been his first mistake. If he had to be honest with himself —and it was something he always prided himself of— that had not been his first mistake. But when she had looked directly at him with eyes full of hurt and disappointment and told him she hated him, no ducal precept could have stopped him. Each step he had taken was one nearer to disaster, but his stride hadn't faltered once. And like a bottle of champagne after being shaken, they came together with the same momentum, unstoppable and chaotic. She had almost brought him to his knees with her soft and untried touch alone.

The strength of his need for her frightened him. It gave her too much power over him. He who was used to inspire obedience. That had not been an issue with his past mistresses. The physical pleasure he had shared with them hadn't come even close to occupying his mind or everyday life. Just how he liked it.

However, even after the extreme pleasure they had shared, Ivy still represented everything he had tried to avoid. She would not be ignored. She was too intelligent and educated to accept the role of a meek wife. And he may have been heartless, usually, but he would not be responsible for stifling her spirit.

That didn't mean he hadn't spent the greater part of the night — and morning— relieving each stroke of hands, each sound, each kiss, until the need to feel her hands on him became almost unbearable. He felt warmth infuse his body and crawl up his neck for the umpteenth time in the last few hours. It really was not to be borne.

Hence, his willingness to focus his attention entirely on the Duchess. His mother would cool his ardour for sure. As it turned out, it was fortunate he had decided to listen when he did.

"A ball? Here at Blakeburne House?" he blurted, appalled.

"Don't you agree it's a splendid idea, Blakeburne?" No, he didn't. "It's been more than a decade since we hosted a ball." His mother's eyes lit up with enthusiasm. Gabriel could already hear the hustle of servants and suppliers running around his house for days to prepare for the evening. Not to talk about the disruption to his life. Furniture moving around to make space for the dance floor and card tables; musicians endlessly strumming, trying to get hired for the night. He visibly shuddered.

"And with good reason."

"Which is?"

"I didn't want to host one." The Duchess huffed at his simple, yet indisputable logic.

"Well, I think it's high time you do. You are starting to get a bit of a reputation as a recluse."

"I am not a *recluse*. A recluse is someone who spends all his time holed up in a dark room hating other people." That was met by a raised brow and a long silence.

"*I*, on the other hand, don't hate people. I only find most of them a waste of space." Why was he even feeling the need to defend himself and his choices? "I have been taking part in the Season's entertainments, have I not?" He raised an eyebrow to match. It seemed that particular trait didn't come from his father.

"That you did, dear. Speaking of which, I've seen you are expanding your circle of acquaintances to include the Kingtons. I applaud your choice. Why waste time with lower members of Society when you have access to the very top? You stand on that top, after all. And Rutherford-Blythe is one of the few peers who could say to equal your standing." Inevitably, talks of the Double Duke brought Ivy's image to the forefront of his mind. Ivy kissing him, Ivy coming apart in his arms...*damn it!* Gabriel focused on the Duchess, who was carrying on.

"And colour me surprised when I saw you dance with R-B's daughter. You surely made the young lady's night." Gabriel scoffed in thinking back at Ivy's reaction to the dance. *Made her night indeed.* "She had finally gained some attention from the male half of the ton, thanks to you. It was really a sin than a Countess of such a powerful family didn't occupy her rightful place in Society." Was it hypocritical that he was irked by that comment when he had thought the same just the night before?

"And what place is that?" Gabriel found himself viscerally disliking the notion of Ivy fending off the clumsy attempts at flirtation of those halfwits. It was deeply egotistical of him, but he wanted to be the only one to see what shone under the surface. A connection only they seemed to share that he felt even across ballrooms. If others discovered that same connection, where would it leave Gabriel? As one of many admiring men. One who could offer her less than she deserved. Hypocrisy abounded.

"Why, the place where she could be admired for her beauty and accomplishments. Surely her family wants her to get married. She left the schoolroom some years ago now. I spoke to her recently, and she is charming and kind. Surely—"

"Fine! When?" Gabriel had had enough of hearing his mother sing the Countess of Everleigh's praises. Not when he was trying not to think about her.

"When what, dear?" The Duchess appeared confused at his outburst, but a worrying glint lit up her hazel eyes.

"When do you plan to have this ball?"

The crisp morning air was helping Ivy to wake up fully. The timid sun shining above wasn't doing much to raise the temperature, but she didn't mind. It wasn't a particularly early hour, as shown by the number of riders and pedestrians leisurely promenading around the park. Those people were too cheerful and lively for her liking.

"Ivy, are you listening to me?"

"I'm sorry, Mother, but no, I wasn't."

144

"It's not like you to struggle to wake up in the morning. Are you sure you are feeling well?"

"I'm fine, really. No need to worry." In truth, she hadn't been sleeping well lately. And the blame laid, once again, at the Duke of Blakeburne's feet. *The darn man!* While she was able to keep her thoughts under control during the day, her mind had devised a nefarious plan to make her dreams different and sizzling variations of their encounters. The only constant was the leading role played by the Duke of Blakeburne. Or Gabriel, like she usually called him in her dreams. She always woke up sweating, in need of *something*. She was rather sure it was *someone* she really needed. And that she couldn't tell her mother. They were close, but some things were not meant to be shared. She felt herself blushing under the Duchess's scrutiny all the same.

Ivy tilted her head up to busk in what little sunlight they were granted that morning. She had promised herself to ban all thoughts of Gabriel from her mind. Four days of not having set eyes on the bloody Duke had achieved close to nothing. She was feeling positive, though.

Resolve in place, she opened her eyes and looked around, finding many familiar faces. Lady Quindsley was talking poor Lord Quindsley's ears off; the Earl of Covington was accompanying the Dowager Marchioness of Whiteridge, whom Ivy remembered to be his Godmother; there were Mrs Higgins and her companion, the Duke of Blakeburne and Viscount Bellmore on horseback...*Oh, for God's sake!* Farewell, promise. Another time perhaps.

Ivy couldn't help but stare at the approaching duo. The men rode with purpose in their direction. As they neared, Ivy noticed that Blakeburne was preceding his friend, who was following with an amused expression on his handsome face.

"Good morning, Your Grace, Lady Everleigh." The Duke bowed elegantly from the saddle, imitated a few seconds later by his friend.

"A sight for sore eyes! This abysmal weather could only be brightened by the beauty of two Ladies like you." That extravagant compliment could come from none other than flamboyant Viscount Bellmore.

"If only flattery could control the weather, my Lord," the Duchess promptly replied with a gentle smile. Fortunately, her mother and the Viscount were present. Otherwise, the encounter would have been reduced to a silent exchange of heated looks between Ivy and Gabriel. The Duke, in fact, was too busy scorching her with his intense stare, making her squirm on her saddle, to contribute to the conversation. To escape the heat, she turned to the Duchess.

"Mother, would you like to walk for a bit down the path? I feel like stretching my legs."

"As you wish, my dear." The Duchess summoned the servants to take their mounts' reins. The two gentlemen immediately followed suit, skilfully dismounting their own horses. Before she could do anything else, strong hands were gripping her waist, gently helping her to the ground. She should have predicted that Blakeburne would not have let servants let her down to the ground. Now, the heat of his eyes was amplified tenfold by the touch of his hands. Ivy was aware she was starting to shake, and surely, he could feel it. He didn't say anything, though. He simply continued holding her captive with his emerald windows to his inferno, but he seemed otherwise unperturbed. If not for the fact that he still hadn't let her go, even though her feet were firmly on the ground. She cleared her throat, much for her benefit as for his.

"Thank you, Your Grace," she said, her voice reduced to a whisper.

"My pleasure, my Lady." His voice was deep and husky, and his words contained a world of meaning behind them. Ivy looked around her for fear they were being noticed. Instead, she found that, despite its intensity, it had all lasted only a few seconds. Viscount Bellmore was still helping her mother down, and the servants were taking care of the horses. She was relieved nobody had noticed anything, but, irrationally, she wondered how it was possible that something so strong could go unnoticed. Was it all in her head?

"Please, let me escort you on your walk," Gabriel said, offering his arm to Ivy. She put her hand on it, trying —and failing— not to notice how strong he was under his perfectly tailored wool coat.

The path was wide enough for the four of them to walk side by side, making it easy to converse. Ivy was glad for it because she was suddenly at a loss for what she could say to the Duke. Not when all she wanted was to pull him behind that big tree and ask for a repeat performance of the other night. She really was a lost cause. So, she focused on the topic of the friendly chat —a new play at Drury Lane — and she soon found herself enjoying herself very much. Part of her mind was always focused on the man beside her, but she couldn't help but become engrossed in such stimulating company. The Viscount often took the most outrageous positions, while the Duke was his usual serious self, even if Ivy detected he was more relaxed in their company. She saw glimpses of that sense of humour she had first experienced the night when mice had entertained guests at Lady Quindsley's house.

They were debating the merit of royal patronage for artists when two older men stepped on their path. Both carried walking sticks that were surreptitiously used more for support than for fashion. She was sure she had seen them around before. One was tall and rail-thin; the other was slightly shorter but with a belly that made his waistcoat's job pretty difficult. Besides their age —Ivy estimated they could easily have reached their seventh decade— they both shared an unfriendly and snobbish expression on their wrinkled face. She gave them the benefit of the doubt nonetheless. Not everyone aged well, after all.

Blakeburne and Bellmore didn't seem too happy to have run into the old duo either, strengthening her first impression of dislike. The Viscount spoke first, ever the congenial one.

"Fine morning for a stroll, isn't it?" His polite words weren't met with equally welcoming greetings.

"Good morning. Your Grace, Blakeburne, Bellmore and Miss…" The shorter one barely managed to come up with the measly address. Ivy opened her mouth to fill the gap, but Gabriel preceded her.

"Lady Ivy Kington, Countess of Everleigh, Markham," he said through clenched teeth as if it were a personal insult to him that he had to tell him her name. Warmth spread through her body.

"Of course, of course. I should have guessed seeing Her Grace the Duchess." He didn't exactly sound apologetic. Not that Ivy cared one iota about an old cantankerous man's apology. She waited for the usual pleasantries to be exchanged. Instead, the next words out of the other old man's mouth were, "I see the country had finally spat you out. It was starting to cause some perplexities among the higher circles." The tall men's words were clearly direct at the Duke. Ivy was flummoxed that someone had the temerity to sound so patronising with Blakeburne. It was probably to ascribe to the advanced age.

"As you well know, I was a good friend of your father, the late Duke. Upstanding chap. And of yours too, Bellmore. Taken from us too soon." Ivy looked back and forth between the men, waiting to understand where all that was going.

"We are aware of that. I lost count of the number of times you've told the tale of how you took the young nobles under your wings, even not being much older yourself, my Lord Thomson," confirmed the Viscount. Finally, Ivy was able to place the two men. Lords Markham and Thomson had been a constant fixture in Society since well before she was born. Her family didn't have much interaction with them beyond passing greetings because they incarnated the staunchest conservative views, something you couldn't say for the Kingtons.

"And a fine job we did too. Shaped them the right way, didn't we?" The portly one nudged the perilously thin man, making Ivy fear for the integrity of his ribs. "Not a fanciful thought in their heads." Ivy was starting to lose her patience. Those two men were poisoning what had so far been a really enjoyable morning. On top of that, implying Gabriel Eastham was 'fanciful' was just outside of ridiculous.

"You sure did a wonderful job, my Lords. You are surely bursting with pride at seeing it passed down to the next generation of honourable men." Two sets of senile, yet sharp, eyes jumped to her as if surprised she was capable of speaking or affronted by her impudence. She was surprised herself. She didn't usually throw herself in those tense situations, but she was feeling protective. She felt her mother's and Gabriel's eyes on her too. She could feel their brows rising. She didn't care.

"That shows how much you know, young Lady." Markham's tone was so condescending, Ivy imagined taking his walking stick from his arthritic hand and brain him with it, old man or not. "Old Blakeburne and Bellmore would have never done something so foolish and reckless as to enlist to fight those French, putting two venerable lineages at risk to go play with rifles." Ivy felt Gabriel stiffen beside her, the muscle of his arm becoming harder than steel. She was sure her mouth was open in shock for the insult Lord Markham had thrown at two decorated war heroes. She shot a look at Gabriel, and what she saw didn't look reassuring. His jaw was so tightly set she could see his teeth grinding. Only the public setting and the very respect for the elders the old fools were putting into question were saving them. She had to find a way to pull the men away. Her mother must have thought the same because she saw the Duchess trying to speak. Lord Thomson had another plan. Looking at Bellmore, he said, "At least Blakeburne had the good sense of raising through the ranks and becoming a Major. You, on the other hand, Bellmore, are still a Captain." He spat the word *Captain* as if it were worse than being a spy for the enemy. At that, nothing could have kept Gabriel silent. And, personally, Ivy didn't want to stop him.

"That's enough." His tone was so glacial that Ivy felt goose pimples on her wool-covered skin. His expression was completely emotionless, which Ivy had learnt meant he was beyond furious. To be honest, she would have been slightly frightened if that tone were directed at her. "You can walk around gracing the world with your unsolicited opinions because of the sacrifice of men like Bellmore. Show some respect for them and yourself. You surely don't want your influence on the Parliament to be jeopardised by your views on the war. I happen to know the vote on the bill you support is nearing. It would be a shame if something thwarted it."

"You wouldn't dare Blakeburne," sputtered Thomson.

"Oh, I don't know. It wouldn't be the first *foolish* decision I make, apparently. Now, if you excuse us, let's not bore the Ladies more than we already have."

"I pleasure, my Lords, as usual." Bellmore touched his hat mockingly. He had wisely decided not to intervene for the sake of ending the unpleasantness. It must not have been easy for him.

They turned to walk away, leaving two sputtering Lords behind.

"What detestable individuals. Now I see why my husband doesn't give them the time of day."

"The Duke is a wiser man than us, Your Grace. Unfortunately, we do share a bond through our fathers. The years have not agreed with them." Viscount Bellmore was back to his charming self. Ivy would have liked to know what was really going through his mind. She had been too engrossed in the Duke to notice the Viscount's reaction to Lord Thomson's cruel words, but she doubted they had not affected him, even if he pretended otherwise. Speaking of inscrutability, Gabriel was every inch the powerful Duke at the moment, but Ivy could feel the fury still coming from him in unstoppable waves. She couldn't blame him one bit. She would have done the same. On the contrary, she was impressed by him. Never losing his composure yet making his opponents feel inferior. The Duke of Blakeburne at his finest. And she would be lying if she said she didn't find his rightful anger and his defence of his friend and soldiers...stirring. His seriousness was quickly becoming one of his most attractive traits. The big tree behind which she wanted to pull him? They were passing by it again, and the urge to have his hands on her person and all his passion unleashed upon her was even stronger than before. She was becoming a real wanton when he was concerned.

The sky clearly thought she had to cool down her ardour when a drizzle started to fall on them. It wasn't really that effective, but it effectively put an end to their walk. Fortunately, their servants weren't far away.

"I'm sorry you had to witness that, my Lady, Your Grace," the Duke said, looking straight ahead. As if it were his fault those two embittered old men felt threatened by anything that didn't fall into their immovable beliefs of what a nobleman should be.

"Oh, no apology needed, Your Grace. I applaud your ways. I was minutes away from sending them both to hell," Ivy's mother said. And because she was the Duchess of Rutherford-Blythe and mother of two, she could get away with swearing in public. Ivy didn't swear but did something more scandalous. She furtively reached for his hand and interlaced her index finger with his. She was hidden behind the folds of her skirts, so nobody noticed the gesture. Or the fact that, before releasing her and helping her on her horse, he squeezed her finger back.

❧ ❧ ❧

What should have been a simple ball had quickly escalated beyond anything Gabriel could have ever imagined. He had thought he had been clever letting the Duchess plan everything. Not that he had ever had any intention of offering his opinion on something so beyond his expertise. How to manage estates and hundreds of tenants without putting a foot on the land for years? He wouldn't break a sweat. Choosing the right linen for tablecloths from two seemingly identical pieces of fabric? He couldn't run for his club fast enough.

Then, more or less three days after he had agreed to host the blasted ball, after returning home from the park in a dark mood, he heard two words that sent shivers down his spine. And not in a good way.

"Christmas ball."

Gabriel regarded the woman who had birthed him as if she had spurred a second head. He had thought he would have *months* of small doses of planning ahead of him. With December halfway gone, he would have to face days of delirium. If it was even feasible in such a short time.

"Don't you think it's a great idea?" No, Gabriel didn't think it was. "Moreover, Blakeburne, all those who matter will be leaving for the country for the holidays. Winter weather and nothing to do in the middle of nowhere if not talking about how magnificent the Blakeburne ball had been and how they could get away with copying my style." The Duchess wrung her hands in glee at the thought. Gabriel, worried by the dangerous glint in his mother's eyes, tried to reason with her.

"But Mother," His voice didn't come out as petulant as it sounded, did it? "Christmas parties are notoriously difficult. People always expect holiday extravaganza, elegance, and merriment all in one. There isn't much time to put it all together."

"And you think I'm not capable of hosting a Christmas party?" Damn it. She sounded hurt, her beautiful face disapproving.

"Of course, I don't think that. If there is a hostess up to the task, it's you."

"I knew you'd agree with me!" Before Gabriel could point out he didn't at all agree with her, Jenkins arrived carrying an overflowing silver tray.

"Your Grace, my Lady, the first replies are already arriving."

"Replies to what?" asked Gabriel suspiciously, looking at the blond head of his mother, already bent over the correspondence.

"To the invitations to the ball, Your Grace." It was Jenkins who replied as if it should have been obvious. The butler then turned to the sly Duchess. "The modiste is waiting for you in the blue drawing-room with the samples you asked, Your Grace. And Cook is convincing the supplier to prioritise his order. Christmas is a busy time of the year, but I don't foresee any problem on that front."

"What order?" The butler was too experienced to let any emotion show, but it was clear he thought the Duke was useless in that particular conversation.

"For the ball, Your Grace," he said, his patience endless.

Gabriel narrowed his eyes, putting all pieces together.

It seemed the Duchess had failed to inform Gabriel of one thing or two.

Given the futility of arguing against a *fait accompli*, Gabriel accepted his fate as the host of a Christmas ball. He sighed.

"Do you need my help for anything, Mother? Seeing that my thoughts on the matter carry so much weight."

"Don't be like that, Blakeburne." She waved his sarcasm away with an elegant hand. "Go on with your day, dear. I have everything under control. Unless you really want to discuss the colours of the flower arrangements...."

"I bow to your supreme taste. I am sure it will be unparalleled." And Gabriel didn't say it only to escape. Few would be able to surpass the Duchess of Blakeburne in putting together a fête for the centuries. Maybe a few Marchionesses could try to emulate her style, but nobody could outdo her. The Duchess of Rutherford-Blythe was rumoured to be an impeccable hostess, exploiting the exuberance that characterised her family. Well, not everyone in her family.

Ah, here he was again thinking about Ivy Kington. The worrying news of the upcoming ball he was to host had allowed him a temporary reprieve from the sequence of images that played endlessly in his mind. He and Ivy alone in the dark garden. Ivy coming apart under his touch. Ivy in all her magnificence on her horse in the park.

Her silent show of support after coming across Markham and Thomson. His desire to take her in his arms again. And repeat. It was madness. Like he had told Ivy before. But, after too many sleepless nights, he had come to a conclusion. He was done fighting it. He was done fighting his attraction to Ivy Kington, Countess of Everleigh. As long as it allowed him to carry on with his life without disrupting it too much, he would start spending time with her, as his heart desired. He would do what he had never imagined himself doing. He would take it one day at a time without planning it all. It could seem like a herculean effort for a man like him, but the alternative, so far, had been a total failure.

He only hoped it wouldn't end in disaster.

Chapter Thirteen

Later that night, Gabriel was purposefully making his way through the throng of people chatting in the theatre foyer during intermission. He would be surprised if even one of the small groups gathered there was talking about the opera they had supposedly come to see. He wasn't an opera enthusiast by any means, but he had at least listened to it the few times he had brought himself to attend. That night, the talented soprano wasn't able to breach through him, not after he had noticed that, from his seat, he had a perfect view of the Rutherford-Blythe's box. The *full* R-B's box. Where a light green-dressed Lady Everleigh was looking beautiful and resplendent. Since he had given himself leave to stop fighting the pull that constantly drew him to Ivy, the madness would have receded into something calmer. Or at least become less time-consuming. All it had managed to do, instead, had been opening a crack in his masterfully built walls, through which a new impatience was trying to find its way out. Much like what Gabriel himself was doing among all those theatregoers, having left his mother back in the ducal box, entertaining friends. He was still warring with his honour demanding he immediately married the Countess, but, for once in his life, he was contemplating ignoring its demands. See, that was the level of madness he had descended into.

When he had seen her rise and leave her box, Gabriel had decided that a trip to get some refreshments was sorely needed.

She was standing with her parents, the Earl of Covington, and his cousin Charles. Gabriel wasn't even aware his cousin was in attendance. Or that he was acquainted with the Kingtons. The group laughed at something Covington said. The smile on Ivy's face was riveting. Something the other men had surely noticed. *Oh, hell no.*

The Double Duke acknowledged him first.

"Good evening, Blakeburne," he greeted with a nod.

"Good evening, Your Graces." He bowed over the Duchess's proffered hand and, finally, turned to Lady Everleigh. "My Lady." The smile Ivy had in store for him wasn't the bright one she had gifted Covington. It was different, more reserved, but more intimate. He felt slightly calmer.

"Your Grace. How are you enjoying the opera? I saw you with a rapt look on your face." He surely wasn't looking at the stage raptly, and she knew it.

Her comment made it clear things had changed for her as well. Did she come to the same conclusion as him? All that fighting against their bond was not only exhausting but pointless, as history showed. Whatever the case, the new air around her drew him in even more, if possible. His hands were itching to touch her skin, to learn again, and more deeply, the contours of her body. He cleared his throat.

"Yes, I was fascinated by what was in front of me."

"Well, good evening to you too, cousin." Gabriel was distracted from observing the becoming blush spreading on the Countess's cheeks by his annoying relative. That he had failed to finish the round of greetings to keep staring at Ivy was inconsequential.

"Cousin Charles. Covington. Nice evening, isn't it?" There, politeness performed. Now, back to the arousing banter with Lady Everleigh. Only, blasted Charles had other ideas.

"Really pleasant indeed. I was just having a diverting conversation with Lady Everleigh on whether it's important to understand the words of an aria or if the music is enough to appreciate an opera. I believe in the power of music. Lady Everleigh, instead, is a staunch supporter of the libretto."

"I don't dispute the power of music. What I believe is that the poetry of the words adds something precious to the notes. But maybe it's easy for me to say, given that I understand Italian. So does dear Covington, or he is simply too polite to disagree with me." *Dear Covington? Dear?* Ivy smiled fondly at the oh-so-polite young Earl, who replied with a lecherous smile. The cad. Why wasn't R-B intervening to put a stop to it?

"It's true. But even if I didn't, you made the most compelling argument, I'd agree with you anyway. Apologies, Eastham." How could everyone overlook the Earl's forwardness? His hands itched to grab the pup by the collar and toss him on the street. Now that was a satisfying fantasy.

"I'm not expert enough for my opinion to carry any weight. It is my greatest belief, however, that beautiful things must be appreciated for what they are, without too many hows and whys." Despite addressing the whole group, his eyes were once again on Ivy, who, understandably, regarded him as if he had lost his ever-loving mind.

"That is very well said, Your Grace," said the Duchess of Rutherford-Blythe.

The bell alerted them it was time to return to their respective boxes. Among the people that started moving like one giant body, Gabriel surreptitiously brushed against Ivy and grabbed her hand. Surprised eyes met his.

He bent slightly and whispered so low only she could hear, "Excuse yourself halfway through the act. I'll be waiting for you." Gabriel walked past her as if he hadn't just proposed something scandalous. Was he certain she would meet him? Absolutely not. After all, all the different directions in which he was pulling her were surely making her dizzy. However, he had felt her shivers and the sharp intake of her breath. Gabriel felt pretty good about his odds.

❉ ❉ ❉

She was out of her mind. *He* was out of his mind. It must have been the hundredth time Ivy had repeated that since the irreproachable, honourable Duke of Blakeburne had asked her to meet him. Alone. At the theatre.

She had briefly contemplated the idea of not complying with his request. Would it kill the man to ask? Was he even able to formulate a request?

Whom was she trying to fool? When she had looked into those brilliant green eyes, flashing with suppressed emotions, she had known how futile her inner struggle would be. She was curious. And more than that, she was excited at the thought of being alone with Gabriel again.

Something had changed in Gabriel's behaviour. She had felt something lighter in him, as if a weight had been lifted from his shoulders. Not that it lessened his intensity. On the contrary, it seemed like all his focus was on her. She wouldn't dwell on it for the moment. Because she was also certain their respective views on the greater scheme of things remained unchanged. So, what was she doing, risking ruination like that?

Marble statues were casting long shadows on the deep burgundy curtains. Her parents hadn't batted an eyelid when she had whispered that she was going to the lady's room. Why would they? She had never even thought about causing scandals. Not her, boring, invisible, Ivy.

Maybe it was the vibrant colours surrounding her or the play of shadows that made the hall a fit place for the mysterious and daring, but upon spying the black superfine coat of the man leaning against the wall, her steps quickened, matching the pounding of her heart. In two strides, she was in front of him, opening the door that was fortuitously right beside him and pulling the Duke, who didn't offer any kind of resistance, with her by his sleeve. Inside what revealed itself to be a small dark room, her frenzy calmed down only when, finally, she put her hands around his neck and pulled his mouth down to hers. Her mind may have calmed down, but her body hadn't. She was kissing him with fervour, only coming up for air when absolutely necessary. Ivy was relieved that Gabriel almost immediately started responding with equal enthusiasm.

"If you asked me to meet you for something else other than this, I'd be mortified," Ivy said in between kisses, her breath laboured. Her whole body tingled. She had begun to associate that particular state with his presence. She wasn't sure it was healthy in the long run.

Being in his arms felt right. Tongues duelling, hands roaming. Ivy was ruffling his perfect hair, his perfect cravat and creasing his perfectly pressed coat. It was only fair, seeing he was constantly tangling up her mind and heart. Together with her hair. She was certain she heard the ping of a hairpin clinking on the floor. Goodbye hairpin. She added it to the list of things she should have cared about and about which she would undoubtedly start to care again in a moment. In a few moments…

The small room was filled with the noises they were both making, the air warm around them. After who knew how long, Gabriel tore his mouth away from hers with a groan.

"Actually, there was another reason." His voice was the deepest she had yet heard, and he was as out of breath as she was. She couldn't see his eyes, but she felt them focused on her like a caress.

159

"Dear Covington?"

She was confused. What had the Earl to do with anything?

"Why is he 'dear Covington'?" he elaborated. Ivy could see with her mind's eyes a ducal eyebrow raising. Finally, she understood he was talking about the conversation they had had before in the foyer when Gabriel had appeared like she had conjured him after she had spent the majority of the first act trying not to look at him too much from across the theatre. She was having some difficulties in carrying on the conversation with Lord Eastham, who was unintentionally unnerving her simply by looking at her with eyes almost the exact same shade of green as the ones that constantly haunted her. When Covington had joined them, she had been grateful for the reprieve, and the endearment had slipped out without anyone noticing. Or so she had thought.

He wasn't owed any particular explanation for something so trivial, and she would much prefer spending the moments they still had together doing something other than talking about Covington. To make the point clear, she put her hands that were resting lightly on his hips back on his nape and pulled him to her again.

"Shut up, Gabriel."

Chapter Fourteen

The night at the theatre marked the beginning of the most thrilling days of Ivy's life. And the most dangerous to her reputation. If anyone among the members of Society were asked to point out two individuals whose morals and virtue were as fragile as an iced lake in April, the list would be miles long before the names of the Duke of Blakeburne and the Countess of Everleigh would be brought up. Yet, if one looked closely at dark alcoves and behind big plants, it was exactly who they would find.

Sometimes they were more or less innocently talking, and Ivy loved their conversations. Loved to taunt him, playing devil's advocate in many of their discussions, making him shed that sense of self-importance that accompanied him everywhere. Or at least some of it. She would miss it if he ever became humble. But she would never tell him that. And Ivy loved even more that he sparked that side of her, something that only her family and few friends had been able to do so far. No topic was deemed 'not for a young lady's ears', so much so that Ivy started to feel at ease in asking for Gabriel's opinions in her estate's matters and in giving some in return. Other times their mouths —and hands— were busy in more pleasurable ways. They hadn't gone as far as they did that night in Lord Whiteridge's garden, always mindful they were a few steps away from discovery, always secretly excited by it. They often promised one another that that would be the last time they met that way, but the following ball, dinner party, or musicale —to which Gabriel had started to take part with more enthusiasm— one look was enough to send all those promises to hell. Without fail, one or the other was pulled in one of the above-mentioned dark corners. Let's say, Ivy would have to order new hairpins soon.

Some promises were disregarded, others weren't even spoken. They were sharing things that only married couples should share, yet neither of them had uttered a word that hinted at a future together. When Ivy was far away from the ever-but-not-quite-so-serious Duke, Ivy asked herself what they were doing. Just the week before, Miss Margaret Nigel's parents had announced the daughter's betrothal to one of the worst scoundrels of their time. Why? Because she was found alone with him in the hall during a card party. If one multiplied that risk for every · time Ivy and Gabriel had found themselves in the same situation, well...You had a foolishness level that belied how intelligent they were both supposed to be. Ivy knew her family would not abandon her if they were discovered —God knew it wouldn't be the first scandal her family had to weather— but they would surely be disappointed in her.

At night, alone in her bed, she wondered if the lack of any promises between her and the Duke was a warning bell to which she had to pay heed. Then, across a room, his frown would ease upon spotting her, and each time Ivy decided to put her fears and self-doubts to rest. Her heart was on the line but, for the first time in her life, it beat strongly with a certainty. She was seen.

That night was the night of the Blakeburne Christmas ball. The event of the Season so far. The last chance to shine before the *ton*'s retreat for the holidays. Most, including Ivy's family, would remain in Town for only a few more days. Usually, almost nobody would still be in Town that late in the month. But the rarity of the event and the expectations surrounding it made it so that only a few were unwilling to change their plans to attend. Even Ivy's mother, who was renowned for hosting the most opulent —and sometimes extravagant— balls, couldn't hide the reaction to the magnificence of the Blakeburne residence. It was like entering a fairy village. Where magic was at the service of elegance. Candlelight was casting a golden hue on the ice sculptures of swans and dancers. White tablecloths and upholstery added to the idea of a snowy atmosphere. Mistletoe was strategically placed to avoid vulgar customs without forgoing tradition.

"Her Grace really outdid herself this time," Ivy's mother said while she, her husband, Ivy, and Gregory were waiting in line to greet their hosts. She had indeed. And resplendent like the room itself was the night's hostess. Dressed in a deep bronze gown with some gold touches, the Duchess of Blakeburne wouldn't have been out of place among fairy royalties. Her blond hair was elaborately styled, and her hazel eyes were alight with pleasure, and more than a hint of smugness, while she looked at her guests' awed faces. And speaking of magnificence, the opulent Christmas wonderland faded away when Ivy's gaze fell on the man standing near the Duchess. He was the furthest thing from a fairy creature you could find. Uncompromisingly dressed in black evening attire, Gabriel greeted the newcomers with his unfailing politeness. No one could mistake him for an enthusiastic host, but few really knew how far away from there he really wanted to be. Ivy was privy to it just because, a few days before, she had casually asked him if he was looking forward to the ball, and the answer she got had been, "How good a shot are you, my Lady?" So no, he wasn't looking forward to it.

Their turn came to greet the hosts. Only then did Ivy notice that Lord Addington, Gabriel's younger brother, was lined up with the rest of the family. It was quite the gathering of titles.

"Good evening, Your Grace," Ivy's father greeted the Duchess first. "Thank you for the invitation. I can already say this evening will be talked about for years to come." The Duchess beamed under the Duke's praise.

"You are too kind, Your Grace. Welcome to our home," she thanked him.

"People would be hard-pressed not to be blinded by all this Christmas splendour," intervened Gabriel. If his words had been uttered with less affection, one could have thought they were meant as an insult. Instead, Ivy saw the feign —or almost feign— long-suffering looks Gabriel sent his mother, who swatted his arm elegantly.

"The Duke simply has an eye for beautiful things, my dear. Now, let's not keep our guests from experiencing all this *Christmas splendour.*" She pointedly looked at her son. "I am sure you will have many more opportunities to sing your dear mother's praises during the night." Ivy heard stifled laughter coming from the younger son, who wisely kept silent and composed himself at the Duchess' warning look. The greetings proceeded smoothly from there, the only hitch being when Gabriel bowed over Ivy's hand. She covered her sharp intake of breath with a light cough, which fortunately remained unnoticed by all except the man who had caused it. His lips curved in the slightest of smiles. At that arrogant display, Ivy silently promised him retaliation before finally leaving the place to the next in line, waiting to be welcomed by the Easthams.

Her time came a good two hours later. She was sipping a very refreshing glass of lemonade, observing the couples dancing, listening only distractedly to Gregory going on about a horse he wanted to purchase at Tattersalls when Gabriel joined them. It was their turn for a moment of the Duke's time before he went on to another chatting group. It must be killing him. Poor soul. She decided to refrain from petty revenge. Well, after this.

"Your Grace! Your ball is really wonderful. Have you talked to Mrs Higgins and Lady Camden yet?" she asked, purposely mentioning two of the *ton*'s worst gossips, famous for their *lengthy* conversation. "I see them over there."

Ivy raised her hands to point in their direction when the Duke blurted, "Dance with me."

"Why, thank you, Your Grace. With pleasure. Thanks for asking so kindly." Ivy took his proffered arm, trying not to laugh at the horrified expression he wasn't able to completely hide at the prospect of facing the two matrons.

"I'm relieved to see the colour come back to your face. You were looking slightly green for a moment." Oh, she was terrible, but she loved his glower. They gravitated towards one another, their bodies more familiar than they were supposed to be.

"Are you enjoying yourself, my Lady? You weren't lacking dance partners tonight." It was true; she hadn't seated one dance since the orchestra had started playing. It must have been the evening's merriment. Everybody was laughing and dancing. She had been secretly hoping for a dance with a particular man, but she hadn't been sure if that fell into the 'something-that-now-the Duke of Blakeburne-allowed-himself-to-do' category.

"Yes, I am, thank you. The ball is really lovely."

He nodded courtly at her answer.

"As I predicted, me spending time with you and your family had the desired effect of making you more desirable." Ivy stiffened and almost stumbled. That was uncalled for. Irritatingly accurate, but unnecessarily. If he had wanted to tease her back, that wasn't the way to do it.

"You, Your Grace, are an arse. Please, lead me back to my brother." Ivy said with all the dignity of a Countess. The arm on her waist tightened.

"No, I won't." Was this man serious? "I apologise. That wasn't well done of me."

"No, it really wasn't, Your Grace." Ivy then sighed. "I suppose I should apologise for teasing you before. If I had thought it would be so badly received, I'd have kept my mouth shut. I repeat, please, lead me back to my brother." She couldn't look him in the eyes, embarrassed by her actions and her reaction to his words. She was really disappointed in herself for making her confidence so dependent on one man's attentions.

Gabriel led her away from the other dancing couples. But, instead of leaving her with Gregory, she found herself on yet another dark balcony.

"Please don't look so forlorn, Ivy. I can't stand to be the cause of it."

"Then stop saying horrible things gratuitously. I'm really sorry if I offended you. It won't happen again. No more teasing if it meant for me to be subjected to your hardheartedness."

"I don't care a fig about the teasing. I like it. Listening to you is the highlight of my evenings…." He paused, and Ivy crossed her arms under her breasts, looking at him and waiting for him to go on. He would not get away with it so easily. Even if she mellowed a little inside.

"I…I don't like seeing all those men dance with you. Although I love how happy you looked, and I would squash everything that took it away from you, I hate that it wasn't me that put that look on your face. It turns out, it's me who took it away. There, are you happy?"

There was a lot of 'like', 'love' and 'hate' in the speech of a reputedly cold and unfeeling man. And he looked miserable while saying it.

"I'm not happy. But I'm slightly less irritated with you. What you just said is— "

"Irrational, I know!" he interrupted.

"I was saying 'oddly sweet', but I suppose 'irrational' fits too."

"It's been that way since I met you." He looked so wretched. *Let's put this man out of his misery.* Ivy gently touched his face and stood on tiptoes to whisper against his lips.

"I tell you a little secret, Your Grace. I feel irrational too. On the verge of madness sometimes." She gave his mouth a light peck before putting some space between them.

She promised herself sooner or later she would meet him like that in the sunlight. She yearned to clearly see his emerald eyes blazing with fire, discarding the veil of detachment he put between himself and the world.

"Now, let's go back inside before our absence is noticed."

She took two steps before he stopped her.

"You are *my* madness. I've grown rather fond of it."

Gabriel entered his study, leaving the door ajar.

"What may I do for you, Charles? If you haven't noticed, I have guests. And you know how it upsets Mother if I shrink from my duties as host."

Gabriel observed his cousin, waiting for him to explain the reason why he had asked to talk to him alone. He had just left Ivy to the waiting arms of another insipid Lord when his cousin had cornered him and asked to have a word. He didn't seem to have something weighing on his mind, but Gabriel thought it better to get it over with.

Charles made his way to the cart and poured himself a glass of brandy, warming it between his hands. "Cannot a man inquire about how his cousin is faring? After all, it's been a while since we spent some time together."

"Of course, he can. I don't see why you couldn't do it among others, though. I am well, thank you for your interest. Now, if you excuse me, I've been away too long." If one counted the time spent with Ivy…

"I was wondering..." *Ah, here we go,* thought Gabriel. Growing up, Charles had always been a thorn in his side, irritatingly following him around everywhere, aping him. Gabriel had tolerated his presence at his father's insistence and because he was fairly innocuous. Charles apparently drew the line in mimicking him at joining the military. In the years after buying his commission, Gabriel had rarely spoken with his cousin until recently.

"What were you wondering, cousin?"

"I was wondering if we'll be hearing wedding bells soon."

"What are you talking about?"

"Oh, nothing in particular. Rumours are circulating that you've been spending a lot of time with a daughter of a certain Duke." Gabriel didn't like the tone Charles was using. His instinct told him not to give away his relationship with Ivy. Well, apart from the fact that it would compromise them both.

"You mean Lady Everleigh?"

"Exactly. The Countess of Everleigh. Good choice. She's pretty, I have to admit. Not whom I would have expected from you, but there is hardly a better connection to make than Rutherford-Blythe, so there's that."

Gabriel ground his teeth. It was absurd to have his relationship with Ivy reduced to profitable family ties but decided not to correct him. Having had enough of that pointless conversation, he pushed him to get to the point.

"And if it were true? Afraid to lose the position as the second in line to the Blakeburne fortune? I'm not sure Edward would appreciate you making plans on his inheritance."

"You wound me, cousin. Of course not. You know I do not need your fortune." That was true. Unlike many other younger sons and minor family branches within the aristocracy, Charles's finances weren't dependent on allowances from the head of the family. The Eastham's coffers were full thanks to Charles's shrew mind in matters of investments.

"Really, Gabriel, I only wanted to confirm or deny the rumours." He seemed sincere. Gabriel started to relax. Until... "If there's no truth in what's being said, I might try to further my acquaintance with Lady Everleigh myself. I don't know how I could have overlooked her so far, even if I do have the excuse of having been away a lot. This is not her first season. She will be grateful for the attention." Ire began to mount, but Gabriel remembered another trait of his cousin's character. Since Gabriel could remember, Charles had always wanted what others had. A toy, a horse, or attention. Once he obtained his prize, it would lose its value in his cousin's eyes, to be discarded for something new. It wasn't fair to Ivy to be made the unknowing target of Charles's games. So, he lied through his teeth.

"Thank you, cousin, for thinking about coming directly to me. Rest assured, I have no lasting interest in Lady Everleigh. You are right. Esteemed family or not, she isn't one to keep a Duke's interest for long." His words left a sour taste in his mouth, but he continued, to remove any doubt. "It's true that I've been spending some time with her, but only because she isn't as vapid as many other simpering misses and makes social obligations bearable. And it's always good to one's ego to have an intelligent woman eat from the palm of your hand." His face wasn't betraying any emotion, a cruel smirk on his lips, but an ache spread in his chest at the mountain of falsehoods he was spouting. He barely refrained from rubbing the spot where his heart was supposed to be.

"She gave me leave to use her Christian name, but I sometimes have problems remembering it. Let's hope her personality doesn't mirror her clingy herbal namesake. The drama would be a nuisance." The thud of something hitting the floor just outside the room made both men turn. Gabriel went to open the door and looked over the threshold, but the corridor was empty and silent.

"A servant must have dropped something before scurrying away. Now, if your curiosity has been appraised, let's go back to my guests."

❖ ❖ ❖

Not what I would have expected from you, but there is hardly a better connection to make than Rutherford-Blythe…

…she will be grateful for the attention…

…she isn't one to keep a Duke's interest for long…

…it's always good to one's ego to have an intelligent woman eat from the palm of your hand…

…I sometimes have problems remembering her name…

…clingy…

…problems remembering her name…

Ivy couldn't do much more than put one foot in front of the other. Her eyes were full of tears that blurred her vision, making it difficult to see where she was going. She had left the ballroom in search of a restroom. After thanking the servant that had accompanied her, she had given a quick look at herself in the mirror and made her way back. Nobody was in sight, the hall silent. That was why she had heard the muffled voices coming from her left. She hadn't really been interested in finding out who was conversing behind the half-closed door until she had heard her name. Curiosity had got the better of her. She had peeked inside what revealed itself to be a study and saw Gabriel calmly conversing with Charles Eastham, who was nursing a full tumbler of brandy. She was starting to turn away and leave when Lord Eastham's words stopped her in her tracks.

170

"The Countess of Everleigh. Good choice. She's pretty, I have to admit. Not whom I would have expected from you, but there is hardly a better connection to make than Rutherford-Blythe, so there's that."

Annoyed by Lord Eastham's unsolicited opinions, she had waited for Gabriel to dispel his cousin's notion. After spending so much time with him, and after their recent conversation, she had been sure he would be displeased by the cynical words. She didn't care a wit about what Eastham thought of her, but she had meanly delighted at the idea of Gabriel putting the other man in his place. Therefore, she had been absolutely unprepared for what came out of Blakeburne's mouth next. With few well-placed sentences, he had exposed all her deepest insecurities, twisting them into contempt and destroying everything. Destroying *her*. The worst of it was, she had given him the ammunition he needed. Suppressing a sob —God forbid she was discovered bawling like a ninny by those who were the cause of it— she had run away. In her haste, she had tripped over the small table near the door. She had managed to catch the decorative vase that stood on it before it crashed to the floor, but the noise had surely carried inside the study, alerting its occupants. So, she had fled. Ivy would never give Blakeburne the satisfaction of seeing her cry. She had to leave the ball altogether. She wasn't sure she could face Blakeburne without betraying the hurt and anger she was feeling. Wouldn't it be spectacular if she made a scene among the most prominent members of society by punching him? She may have been a naïve fool, but she had her pride.

Ivy stopped just outside the ballroom doors. Taking a fortifying breath, she tried to school her features, praying that nobody noticed her red eyes. If she could just reach her mother without being stopped by anyone, Ivy could plead a migraine, which wasn't far from the truth, and go home, where she could lick her wounds in the solitude of her room.

She seriously needed to revise her judgement on others' character.

Ivy finally spotted her mother and made her way to her, keeping her eyes downcast. Just when she started to feel victorious, a woman stepped in front of her, effectively blocking Ivy's escape plan. Raising her eyes to excuse herself, Ivy met brilliant hazel eyes. The Duchess of Blakeburne regarded her with concerned eyes.

"Are you well, my dear? Has something happened?" Of all people who could have intercepted her path, it had to be Blakeburne's mother. Just her luck. "Oh no, Your Grace, everything is fine. I just had to step out for a moment. It seems I stood too long near that mistletoe. Foolish of me. It makes my eyes water terribly. I should have known better." Ivy sincerely hoped that was enough for the Duchess. She didn't even know if it was possible to have such a reaction to mistletoes.

The Duchess regarded her closely for a moment longer before saying, "I'm sorry to hear that. I hope it passes soon. I wouldn't want to make people ill at my own ball. You let me know if you need anything."

"You are too kind, Your Grace." Ivy was gratefully taking a step around the woman when the Duchess asked, "Have you seen my son, Lady Everleigh? It seems I can't find him anywhere."

"I can't say I have, Your Grace. Now, if you excuse me, I see my mother..." The Dowager Duchess stopped her retreat again.

"I would like to ask you something, Lady Everleigh. It's no secret I hope the Duke would soon take a wife. Blakeburne thinks very highly of you." She would have laughed in the Duchess' face if it weren't highly improper. If she had had the strength for it, maybe she would have done it regardless. It seemed Blakeburne had fooled not only her but his mother as well. This conversation was taking every ounce of pride Ivy had left.

"What do you think of Miss Davenport as a possible future Duchess? She surely is the toast of the season." Ah, the beautiful, poised, much admired Miss Augusta Davenport. The niece of the Marchioness of Whiteridge, but without her wit and sharp tongue.

Not carrying a title like Ivy, but a perfect ornament for a powerful man's arm. And that was the only thing women could aspire to be among their circle.

That sealed it. She was stepping away. From Blakeburne. From everything. But for now, she was simply going home. "Miss Davenport is a lovely young lady and would make any man very happy. I don't think I can influence your son's opinion, however. I am barely an acquaintance," she said with a sad smile. "I beg your pardon, Your Grace. I see my mother waving at me. Enjoy the rest of the evening." Ivy left the very puzzled Duchess and finally approached her mother. Taking a look at her daughter, she excused herself and gently led her away.

"Ivy, what's the matter? Is it one of your headaches? Do you need to go home?"

"Yes, please. I feel a migraine coming up. But I don't want to spoil your evening. I'll just take the carriage and send it back for you."

"Nonsense." Her mother stopped a passing footman. "Find His Grace, the Duke of Rutherford-Blythe and send him to us. And have someone summon the carriage, please." The man nodded and hasted to do her bidding. "We'll go retrieve our greatcoats."

"What's wrong?" Her father appeared scarcely two minutes later. Apparently, Rutherford-Blythe's influence extended to servants in other households as well.

"Nothing, Father. Just a headache. I told Mother you could stay here and enjoy the rest of the ball."

"Your carriage is ready, Your Graces, my Lady." Blakeburne's butler put a stop to Ivy's protests.

"Let's go," her father said, putting a hand on her elbow. Once in the hall, from the corner of her eyes, she saw the Duke of Blakeburne, who stopped upon seeing them, tilting his head questioningly. He opened his mouth to say something, but Ivy turned her back to him before he could. Back straight, she left the house, the efficient butler closing the door behind them.

The ride home was uneventful and silent. Her parents sent many worried looks her way, not talking, careful not to worsen the headache that was already pulsing inside Ivy's head. She felt bone tired and was looking forward to going to sleep, to at least try to hush the questions resonating deep inside her.

Why? What did Blakeburne hope to gain by misleading her to that extent? And, most worryingly of all, *how could I have fooled myself so much?*

Chapter Fifteen

After a night spent admiring the beauty of her room's ceiling, Ivy entered the breakfast room to find her parents already at the table. Through puffy eyes, she saw they were both reading the morning paper, like any other morning. Hearing Ivy's approach, they looked up at the same time.

"Good morning, dear. How are you feeling?" The Duchess studied her closely. "You look tired. You didn't have to come down so early." Ivy knew her appearance betrayed a less than restful night. Her mother was being tactful in saying she looked 'tired'. Tossing and turning, she had finally fallen asleep when the sun was already peeking through the heavy curtains. She couldn't stop thinking about what had happened the night before and how she should behave from then on. Could she pretend she hadn't overheard those hurtful words? She certainly couldn't let it go and turn a blind eye, but could she ignore him? Or should she confront the Duke directly? All those thoughts swirling inside her head hadn't helped her headache either, which hadn't disappeared like it usually did after a night's sleep. Taking control over the chaos in her mind, Ivy answered her mother's question. "I'm feeling better, thank you. Even though sleep couldn't cure my headache completely, I am sure a good breakfast will do the trick."

"Oh, are we still pretending there is nothing more than a headache afoot? Very well," her father said, picking up the newspaper again, unfolding it theatrically and patently not reading it.

"Rafael!" reprimanded his wife. "Give it some time. I'm sure Ivy will come to talk to us when she's ready." Ivy sighed. She hadn't fooled anyone, apparently. Only herself.

"If Ivy says she's fine, she's fine. Now, given that you will be right as rain in no time, tonight is Lady Covington's musicale."

Her shrewd mother presented her with a conundrum she had elegantly created. If she said she didn't want to go, she could very well admit that she was trying to avoid something. Going, on the other hand, meant putting a happy face in front of the *ton*, which Ivy wasn't sure she could do. Pleading a lingering headache or any other ailment would worry her parents needlessly and could lead to the summon of the family's physician. Swearing under her breath, Ivy chose what she hoped would be the lesser of the two evils.

"I'll be ready."

❧ ❧ ❧

After breakfast, Ivy was in the library, pacing a hole in the Aubusson rug. Fortunately, her headache had indeed improved after putting something in her stomach. The downside of it was, she couldn't use it as an excuse to stay home. Now clear-minded, she was able to lock away her emotions and face her problem rationally. An over-six-foot-tall, dark-haired, green-eyed, deceitful problem. It hurt too much to think about the Duke of Blakeburne as the man she had shared those passionate moments with, who had spent so many stolen moments deep into conversation with her. No, no more. Gabriel Eastham, fourteenth Duke of Blakeburne, had to become nothing more than a Debrett's entry. A few lines in an endless, arid book. Not a flesh and blood man who could make her forget everything she knew about propriety, society, and scoundrels. Not a man who made her think she could shine beyond the tidy little box she had created for herself, and the *ton* had closed her into with a tightly knotted silken ribbon.

After what had to be the fifth turn around the library, even Colonel had had enough. He jumped down his cushion on the window seat and meowed loudly, looking at her with narrowed feline eyes.

"You are right, Colonel. I can walk the distance from here to India in this library, but it still doesn't change the fact that I'm not sure what will happen once I have Blakeburne in front of me. I won't be made a fool in front of the entire *ton*." Ivy stopped pacing in front of the window, staring at the back garden. "What can I do to eliminate the problem?"

She was so engrossed in her preoccupations that she didn't hear someone enter the library until he spoke.

"Who are you going to eliminate? Oh, hello there, Colonel. Somewhere pressing to be?" Ivy turned towards her brother, seeing Colonel slipping between his legs, probably heading for the kitchen. *Even my cat had had enough of me,* she thought morosely.

"Good afternoon, Gregory. What brings you here at this early hour?"

Gregory reclined languidly on the *chaise longue* near the fireplace, closing his eyes.

"Did Mother send for you?" Ivy asked suspiciously.

"No, she didn't. I simply fancied a good meal from dear old Cook. Why? Is there a cause for me to be summoned?" He sounded sincere. Ivy decided to believe him.

"No, none. Never mind."

Keeping his eyes closed, Gregory shifted and made himself even more comfortable.

"How did you like the ball last light? I was there only for about an hour, but it seemed to me that nobody dared refuse Her Grace's invitation." Ivy did not doubt that the ball could be considered a smashing success. It was unfortunate that something else had been smashed the previous night. And it hadn't been a vase. Gregory prattled on, oblivious to the effect of his words on Ivy's already scattered thoughts and aching heart.

"She must be ecstatic to have so many young eligible ladies craving for Blakeburne. Poor chap, can't say I envy him. Even that fierce scowl of his can't keep marriage-minded ladies at bay. He is bound to succumb sooner or later." He opened his eyes slightly and looked at her sister. "You are eerily quiet. Mother said something about you not feeling well. Is everything all right?"

Ivy's mind was racing. Maybe the solution to her problem was simple. Instead of beating herself up for believing in a fantasy of her own making or, worse, subjecting herself again to Blakeburne's lies, she would remove the very reason for her idiotic fanciness.

"I will marry Blakeburne off," Ivy said under her breath, a new resolve in place.

"Sorry, you *what?*" her brother exclaimed, snapping his eyes open. He sat up straight. "Did you just say you will marry the Duke of Blakeburne off?" *Damn it.* There she went again, saying things aloud that sounded better in her head.

"What I meant is that maybe I could help the Duchess. She has always been kind to me, but being closer in age to a Duke's prospective bride, maybe I could offer my perspective."

"But I thought that you…." Gregory was clearly struggling to understand Ivy's sudden interest in matchmaking.

This is not going to end well, he thought.

"I, what?" Ivy urged defiantly.

Gregory decided to proceed with caution. "Nothing, apparently. What are you doing now?"

Ivy had opened a desk drawer and taken out a piece of paper.

"I'm making a list. First, Miss Davenport. Her Grace mentioned her last night, so it's safe to say that she meets her approval. Who else? There are Miss Ashton and Lady Coperland. Even Victoria and Eleanor fit all the criteria to become Blakeburne's bride."

Gregory spoke up hearing that. "I don't understand your sudden interest in Blakeburne's marital status but, hypothetically speaking, and since we are putting down names, yours should also be on that list." He was half joking and half testing the waters to get to the bottom of her strange behaviour. He didn't anticipate her reaction.

"No! I am *never* writing my name on this list!" Ivy said vehemently, looking up straight at him. He didn't like what he was seeing in her eyes. There was determination there but, hidden beneath it, pain. A lot of pain. *What in the everlasting hell?*

He raised his arms in surrender.

"All right. I was just trying to be helpful. So, what's your next step? Visit each lady on your little list and ask them if they are amenable to marrying Blakeburne? Has the man no say in the matter?"

"Of course, I'm not going to do that, Gregory. Even though you might have a point…."

"I wasn't trying to suggest anything. I was pointing just out how…."

But Ivy wasn't listening.

"I could call on a couple of ladies and see if any of them is interested in furthering her acquaintance with Blakeburne. Oh, what am I saying? Of course, they are interested. It's *Blakeburne* we are talking about. I have to go change." She stormed out of the library, leaving a speechless Gregory behind.

"What in hell just happened? I feel like I should warn Blakeburne."
He stood and shrugged. "But first, I need a drink."

❈ ❈ ❈

"So, Blakeburne, should we head for White's afterwards? Or I hear
Prinny has hired acrobats. I wouldn't be opposed to being graced with
such flexibility." After hosting the ball the night before, Gabriel would
have rather stayed home than attend a musicale. Apparently, however,
that was another of those invitations he had magically accepted
without realising it. He had thought those days were behind him.

At least, that night, it was a small gathering of around thirty people
at Lord Covington's townhouse.

Blasted Covington, always a nuisance.

Gabriel wanted nothing more than accept Bellmore's suggestion —
maybe not the one about the Regent's party—, but he had promised
his mother to stay for more than a couple of hours. He also had
another reason for being there that night. Gabriel hadn't had the
opportunity to talk to Ivy after her hasty departure from his ball.

Inspecting the room, his eyes eventually found her. Clad in a green
gown embellished with gold leaves sewn in the neckline and down near
the hem of the skirt, she was simply beautiful. Her hair was up in her
usual elegant yet simple style. She was conversing with... Lady
Coperland? Gabriel frowned. He didn't know Ivy was friends with the
Lady. Lady Coperland was one of the diamonds of the Season.
Beautiful but, from the few times he had been in her company, he
couldn't recall anything they had said to each other. Aside from her
looks, Gabriel couldn't honestly tell her apart from any other young
woman he has been introduced to since his re-entry into society.

Sensing his eyes on her, Lady Coperland looked up and smiled at him. Gabriel nodded politely in return, hoping few people noticed it. God forbid something came out of him looking at a woman while thinking about another.

"Lady Coperland looks particularly fetching tonight. Maybe her looks are enhanced by the contrast with the Countess."

Gabriel snapped at Bellmore's comment. "What the hell is that supposed to mean? Lady Everleigh is just as beautiful as Lady Coperland. And her inner beauty outshines even her looks." Silence followed. Bellmore now looked at him as if he had said he was moving to France.

"I didn't mean anything by it. It's only that they have opposite colouring, and Lady Coperland's light pink gown contrast with the dark green one of the Countess. If I knew talks about colours would bring such a visceral reaction, I would have stayed clear of it. I pity your tailor." Gabriel frowned at him. "I didn't mean any offence. I know you are friendly with the Lady." *Friendly*. If only Bellmore knew. Looking again at the two Ladies, Blakeburne had to begrudgingly admit his friend was right. One blonde, one dark-haired. One petite, the other tall, the two Ladies couldn't be more different. One was a young girlish beauty. The other was Ivy. He couldn't find better words to define her. His Ivy.

"It seems the Ladies are coming this way. How do you want to play it, Blakeburne?" Bellmore asked, amused. Before Gabriel could ask what he meant, the two women were upon them.

"Lovely evening, isn't it, Ladies? You both look ravishing tonight," Bellmore greeted with his signature grin. Lady Coperland immediately giggled, clearly used to compliments.

"Why, thank you, my Lord. It is indeed a pleasurable evening in the company of so many illustrious guests." Turning towards Gabriel, she continued, "Lady Everleigh was just telling me you wish to visit the new exhibition at the British Museum with a group of friends. It is my deepest wish to see it. I hope you don't think I'm too forward, but I was hoping you'll include me among your friends." *What the devil?*

Marshalling his facial expression to hide his shock, he glared at Ivy. She knew perfectly well they had talked about going together, just the two of them. And a chaperone, of course. Now, if he couldn't find a valid excuse, he has to extend an invitation.

Addressing her, he was met by expressionless eyes. "Is that right, Lady Everleigh? How kind of you to help plan my visit." She smiled, even though it didn't reach her eyes.

"Oh yes, Your Grace! I just thought it would be nice to include some lovely people like Lady Coperland. And Lady Victoria, and my cousin as well. These are people to warrant *lasting* interest, don't you agree? You too, of course, Lord Bellmore. The more, the merrier, I always say." Since when? Ivy wasn't one to always crave people's company. On the contrary. And to trade the few private moments they could spend together for the company of Lady Coperland? Gabriel was officially confused.

Meanwhile, that sneaky Bellmore was answering enthusiastically, "I gladly accept the invitation you extended on behalf of my friend here. It sounds interesting." Idiotic grin in place, Bellmore addressed the younger woman, "Lady Coperland, would you be so kind as to take a stroll with me around the room and enlighten me on the marvel of this exhibition we are going to see?"

The young lady seemed reluctant at first, but the Viscount's charm won again. "It would be my pleasure, my Lord. If you would excuse us, Your Grace, my Lady."

"Lady Coperland, wait!" Ivy protested, weakly and futilely, since the two were already walking away.

"Care to explain this change of plans, my Lady?" asked Gabriel, pleased by his neutral tone.

"I only thought it'd be better for you to spend some time with interesting people. After all, I am *grateful*, but it isn't fair to monopolise your time. What do you think of Lady Victoria? She is one of my best friends and a smart, lovely lady. Ah, I see her. Care to accompany me to her?"

"What has got into you?" Gabriel blurted out while still offering his arm, probably to avoid being dragged. Ivy led him where Lady Victoria Gallard conversed amiably with Elizabeth and Grace Winter and his cousin Charles.

"Good evening, Lord Eastham. What a happy coincidence. I brought your cousin, see."

Turning to Gabriel, she said, "I reckon you've all met before. Lady Victoria is a wonderful rider, and I know you enjoy the sport as well. Isn't it right, Your Grace?"

Bemused, Gabriel shifted his attention to the daughter of the Earl of Gallard, who gave him a kind smile. They entered an unexpectedly stimulating conversation about the latest horses to be purchased at Tattersalls, and he found himself smiling at her colourful description of some of the regular buyers. Ending their discussion by agreeing on the ridiculousness of some recently published breeding theories, he turned back to Ivy. Bafflingly, he discovered that, while he thought she was conversing with Charles and the Winter sisters, at some point, she had left. Irritated by what he considered a very rude behaviour but more confused than ever, he let his eyes search for her, finally finding her standing alone near a plant, watching him with the saddest smile he had ever seen on a human face. He felt it like a physical blow to his midsection. Taken aback by it and before realising what he was doing, he excused himself and strode towards her.

He came up to her nonchalantly, as if that was any other evening, and not the oddest one since meeting her. He hated when things didn't go as they should. And Ivy's behaviour certainly was unusual.

Before he could point it out, Ivy started talking, not bothering to look directly at him. "I knew you would get along with Victoria. She's extraordinary. She's so much more than her family. And Lady Coperland as well. She is a very...ahem fine Lady. You'll see when you'll get to know them better, Your Grace."

"Why are you so keen for me to further my acquaintance with Lady Victoria or Lady Coperland? Are you trying your hand at matchmaking?" he joked, but she simply shrugged.

"If you are so interested in me getting married, why don't you state your intention? Why don't you propose yourself for the spot while you are at it? Seeing that you seem to know my tastes so well." His voice came out harsher than he intended, laced with sarcasm. He was fuelled by irritation, puzzlement, and, yes, hurt. Have the past weeks been so meaningless to her? The thought had made his words lash out like a whip, mocking.

He readied himself for a well-deserved set down, but, like everything else that damn night, it didn't go as he expected.

Ivy finally turned to him. Without raising her eyes, she whispered, "Don't. I beg of you, just don't."

Nothing else.

She walked away hastily, but not before Gabriel could see the tears threatening to spill from her eyes.

"Lady Everleigh, wait! What..." He gathered his posture. It wouldn't do any good to cause a scene. So, he let her go, even if it went against everything he was feeling. He had to get to the bottom of it, and he would. Her behaviour was too bizarre not to be caused by something. That, and her hastily leaving his ball, meant something had to be wrong. But what? He would demand an explanation the next time he saw her. He was the Duke of Blakeburne. If something was bothering her so much, surely it was in his power to make it better. And something certainly was, to make her talk in such a preposterous manner to him.

"My, isn't it a fierce look you have on your face, Your Grace. Did someone dare contradict you?" A delicate hand landed on his arm. Looking down, he saw Lady Ingram regarding him with a sultry smile. "I can cheer you up. Just like old times." His former mistress whispered those provocative words directly in his ear, putting her free hand on his chest. Fortunately, they were standing slightly apart from the rest of the guests, so nobody seemed to be witnessing her forward behaviour. Gabriel looked around to make sure they weren't observed. His eyes met Ivy's from the other side of the room. She was just re-entering after having stepped outside. Her steps faltered, then she resumed walking, joining her mother, who was deep in conversation with Lady Whiteridge. He was so focused on following her every step that he hadn't realised Arabella was still touching him. Not taking well to being ignored, Lady Ingram tried to draw Gabriel's attention back to her by moving the hand on his chest in a light caress.

"Darling, who are you staring at?" Following his line of sight, she said, pouting, "Ah, the Countess of Everleigh. Poor thing. If her blood weren't bluer than the King's, she would be a hopeless wallflower." She shook her head in patently false sorrow. It was twice in a short time that he had to listen to people belittle Ivy. First, his cousin the night before and now...everything in him froze. No, it couldn't be. Conversations came rushing back to him. Charles, goading him into admitting his interest in Ivy. He, lying through clenched teeth, denying even the slightest connection. Then, snippets of what Ivy had said earlier tonight about people being 'worthy of his attention' and 'being grateful'. And, final nail in his coffin, his cruel, admittedly unwarranted comments about her becoming his wife. It all fell into place, but the picture it created filled Gabriel with a horrifying certainty. Ivy had overheard him talking with his cousin Charles. It had not been a servant who had made that noise outside the door. She had heard all the terrible, untrue things he said last night. He remembered every word, and, with them, the foul taste they had left in his mouth came back.

His eyes frantically searched again for her, his mind spinning for a way to solve the mess he had created while trying to protect her from something he wasn't even sure his cousin would do. What was certain was the pain in her eyes. After hearing him mocking her and her fears, Ivy had stood there, facing him, head held high.

Finally, Gabriel spotted her, politely taking her leave from their host. She headed towards the front door and, believing she was out of sight, let her shoulders drop in defeat after a long exhale. And Gabriel Eastham, fourteenth Duke of Blakeburne, Major of His Majesty's Army, was brought to his knees by a pair of sad brown eyes.

Oh, Ivy. What have I done?

Chapter Sixteen

Christmas came and went. Ivy had a pleasant time with her family at Wildrose Manor. The Kingtons had spent their time leisurely enjoying the country air, taking part in the festivities in the nearby village. The villagers, used by then to the ducal family's presence, had welcomed them warmly, just like they did every year. A few tankards of local ale and more than a few glasses of mulled wine —all in the name of chasing away the cold— had washed away ranks and status. Even Ivy's shyness had been left behind in London's stuffy ballrooms. It was her favourite time of the year, and she did her utmost not to let a certain Duke spoil that for her too. It had not been an easy feat but, if anyone had noticed that her laughter was a bit less carefree and her smile a bit more forced, they didn't remark upon it. Her heart still felt heavy, the wound fresh and bleeding each time she perversely relived the moments that had led to that point. Which was almost daily.

Back in London, Ivy was perusing the shelves of her favourite place in Town. The dark atmosphere and musty smell of the little bookstore were always a balm for her soul. That day was no exception. After crying herself to sleep again the night before —apparently, she had not run out of tears and self-pity yet— she had woken that morning not liking the person she saw in the mirror.

Observing herself, she had had enough of the questions that still plagued her after more than a fortnight. What was she thinking, believing that Blakeburne would really be interested in her? *Her*? With her shy personality and unassuming appearance? Could she really fault Blakeburne's behaviour? Her thoughts had come to a screeching halt. She had almost slapped herself. Of course, it was Blakeburne's fault! She deserved at least respect, lack of allure or not.

Pulling herself together, she did what she always did when the feeling of loneliness emerged and threatened to pull her under. Unable to eat, she summoned her carriage and gave the coachman her friends' addresses. Ivy didn't give Victoria, Grace, and Elizabeth a chance to refuse a stroll down Bond Street. Not that they had tried to argue.

After a pleasant walk, Ivy had felt marginally better. She was getting better at hiding what was troubling her, and she had to thank Blakeburne for that. None of her friends asked the reason for the impromptu promenade. She was grateful for them. And even more grateful when Grace proposed to head for The Turning Page. Located just a few streets away from Bond Street, the bookstore was an often-overlooked gem. When they entered, it was empty, except for the owner, who greeted them warmly.

"Lady Everleigh, Lady Gallard, Miss Winter and Miss Winter! What brings you to our fine establishment today?"

"Good afternoon, Mr Davies. We were passing by and couldn't in all conscience not enter," replied Victoria.

The man smiled and bowed to some of his best customers. "I'm deeply honoured, my ladies. Please, feel free to peruse our collections at leisure. Would you care for some refreshments?"

"Oh no, thank you, Mr Davies. We plan to stop at Gunter's on our way home." This time it was Elizabeth who answered.

"Very good. Let me know if you need anything." Mr Davies motioned for them to enter the area where the books were shelved. Feeling right at home, Ivy started reading the titles alongside her friends. They sometimes exchanged comments on a volume one of them had found, but mostly they looked around in silence.

"I think I'll go upstairs to search for a book about India that Gregory mentioned. I could always bribe him with it. One never knows when one might need it." Ivy was met with nods, but nobody moved to follow her. Thick carpets covered the whole floor, muffling any sound from downstairs. She usually loved that kind of peace, but lately, she didn't appreciate being left alone with her thoughts. She decided to concentrate on finding the book her brother coveted.

She didn't know how much time had passed when she heard footsteps. Someone was coming from the stairs. Thinking it was one of her friends, she spoke without looking in the newcomer's direction.

"I didn't find what I was looking for. Do you think he would like a book on the history of India?"

"And who might *he* be?" Ivy closed her eyes at the sound of that deep voice and brought her hand to the bridge of her nose. How could she have thought those heavy footfalls belonged to one of her female friends? She didn't turn towards the intruder, who, with a question, had shattered what little sense of peace she had been able to create.

"Not that is any of your business, Your Grace, but for honesty's sake —something I know you value above everything else—," she added ironically, "I was searching for a specific tome for my brother." The *ton* would be horrified if they heard her addressing a Duke with such a lack of deference, but the *ton* hadn't been subjected to what she had been at the Duke's hand. She heard a long breath leave him. She was still pretending to peruse the shelves intently, as if her life depended on it, looking for strength rather than books.

"Ivy, look at me." *Oh, look how masterfully this title is carved.* "Look at me, please." It was the *please* and the soft tone, coming from such an authoritative man, that made her relent. She turned slowly, hardening her heart to what she was going to see. He was perfectly dressed and without a hair out of place. Still too handsome. His expression was guarded, but Ivy believed she could glimpse remorse underneath.

"What do you want, Your Grace?"

"I know you heard me talking to Charles the night of my mother's ball." Her eyes widened in shock. How could he know it? She hadn't told a soul. Many suspected something had happened, but nobody knew for sure what.

"Again, I ask you. What do you want from me? Have you something to add to your praises? Do you want my gratitude for putting up with me? It must have taken a great effort for your part." Ivy saw him flinch at her coldness. Good. Some uncharitable part of her wanted to hurt him like he had hurt her. Like he had been doing time and time again.

"No, Ivy. Listen to me. It's true. I said all those horrible things to my cousin." Ivy closed her eyes to stem the new wave of pain crashing into her.

"Thank you for the confirmation. Now, if you'd excuse me—"

"When we were young, Charles had this kind of twisted idea of jokes. It was mostly harmless. Until one day, he made my father believe I was having an affair with an upstairs maid, something the Duke had instilled in me from the cradle was beneath the heir to the Blakeburne name. I was trying not to make you a target of some kind of game by exposing our…acquaintance." Ivy had been shaking her head during his speech.

"Even if it were true, you could have diverted him without throwing everything I ever told you about me like wash water. You could have deflected, changed the subject. You didn't need to be so cruel, so heartless. If I had ever thought you would exploit it as a weapon, I wouldn't have told you anything you could use as ammunition."

Gabriel looked crestfallen, his head hanging low. For such a proud man, it was a testimony of how much her words were affecting him. Too bad that her granted wish to hurt him wasn't bringing her any pleasure.

"You don't know how sorry I am for hurting you. Please believe me."

"The worst part of it all is, I secretly agreed with you. I stood there, listening to you belittling me, and thought, 'well, he isn't wrong'." Ivy's voice wasn't more than a whisper. Gabriel heard it all the same. His head snapped up, the contrite expression trading place with a vexed one.

"What I said isn't true, and you know it."

"Do I?"

"For God's sake, Ivy! How can you even think that?" Gabriel's almost bellowed. He quickly scanned their surroundings. Her friends downstairs were fiercely protective of her and wouldn't hesitate to climb the stairs to ascertain Ivy's wellbeing.

When she didn't reply, Gabriel decided that words weren't enough. Looking around one more time and not hearing anything, he gently, but urgently, pushed Ivy against the shelf on the far end of the room. Ivy emitted a surprised gasp but didn't resist. Lifting her head to shoot him a surprised gaze, she could only see a flash of heat in his green eyes before his mouth came down on hers. His kiss was deep, passionate, and it was impossible for Ivy not to respond. They poured everything into it. Sadness, guilt, anger, hopelessness, lust, and any other feeling they weren't ready to acknowledge, even to themselves. Their kiss became desperate. Ivy opened her mouth to his tongue, lifting her hands to his neck, bringing him even closer. Gabriel caged her with his body, his urgency growing with every contact. His hands seemed to be everywhere at once, finally setting on her bottom, bringing her flush against him. Ivy moaned against his lips, feeling the hardness inside his breeches. Nothing mattered, only getting even closer to him. That moment she felt powerful, able to bring this man to his knees. Her hands travelled to his broad shoulders, sensing his muscles tense. She didn't know how long they stayed like that, but it was quickly becoming clear that kissing wasn't going to be enough. She saw the same desire reflected in his eyes when they finally came up for air. They stared at each other for a while, without saying anything. Then Gabriel groaned and took her lips again, this time bringing his arms to each side of her head, clutching the shelf behind her.

Ivy was rapidly becoming lost in him again when voices intruded the fog of desire in her mind. Sensing her distraction, Gabriel quickly stole a few kisses along the column of her neck. Ivy had to suppress a sigh. Reluctantly, she put her hands on his chest to still him. He touched his forehead to hers, regarding her earnestly. "I wish this would obliterate every false word I said that night."

People were climbing the stairs. Reality slowly came back.

"I really wish to believe you."

"I swear to you, you can," he said, straightening to his full height. The Duke of Blakeburne stood proud in front of her, his words a vow.

"Ivy? Are you here?" Victoria's voice was getting nearer.

Ivy stepped out of Gabriel's arms. She had almost managed to regain her composure, but it all went to hell when Gabriel whispered in her ear, "You better step in front of me now, my Lady, otherwise your friends will see more than they have bargained for." Understanding his meaning, but forcing herself not to look down at the incriminating part of his body, she blushed a deep shade of red. She didn't know what to do with this playful, sensual side of him.

"Ah, here you are, dear, didn't you hear us calling?" Victoria stopped short in front of the scene. "Oh, Your Grace, what a... ahem surprise seeing you here." Ivy jumped at her friend's word, turning around at the same time. The two actions didn't go well together, and she lost her balance in her haste to face Victoria. Gabriel steadied her, then slid his hand down her arm, light as a feather. Reaching for her hand, he pulled it slightly back, hidden by her skirts, and interlocked their fingers together. All while looking directly at Victoria, who was observing them, a knowing look on her face.

Gabriel nodded his head in greetings, answering her with his customary calm tone, "Lady Victoria. I apologise for not coming to greet you immediately downstairs once I first entered the shop. I spied Lady Everleigh from a window and had some pressing matters to discuss with her." He had the cheek to grin. It was so out of character for him that even Victoria was clearly stunned by it.

The cad was slowly circling his thumb against her palm, making her shiver. Struggling to find the words, Ivy finally croaked out, "Yes, indeed. Pressing matters." *Perfect, Ivy. You and parrots share the same eloquence.*

Her lacklustre contribution didn't go unnoticed by Victoria, either. "So, if the business with His Grace has come to a satisfactory conclusion, we are ready to go." Ivy's mind had to be still addled. Victoria could not have intentionally put so many innuendos in one sentence.

Cheeks still red, she opened her mouth to agree, taking a step forward, but Gabriel stopped her with his next words. And by not releasing her hand. "If you would be so kind, Lady Victoria, to precede us, Lady Everleigh will be down in a minute." Victoria's answer was to look at Ivy, who nodded slowly.

"We'll be downstairs."

Once Victoria was out of sight, Ivy turned and buried her flaming face in Gabriel's coat. "That was so embarrassing. I think she knew what we were doing." At her muffled words, a low rumble started in Gabriel's chest. "Don't you dare laugh, you horrible man," she reprimanded from her hiding place. His only answer was to kiss her head. Ivy didn't really want to move from the haven that was his arms. However, she knew one —or all— of her friends would be back if she didn't appear soon. Not to think about the possibility of other patrons stumbling upon them. They could not be caught kissing in a bookstore! She lifted her head and, forcing herself not to fall prey to those brilliant green eyes, reluctantly said, "Blakeburne, I need to go. They are bound to come for me again. You don't want to risk being caught with me here." He sighed but released her.

"One day, you will stop saying things like that. For now, I'll make my mission to erase what you heard that night from your memory." He gently pushed her towards the staircase. Ivy was prevented from adding anything else by the sight of her friends waiting for her at the bottom.

"I'll take my leave now. Lady Victoria, Miss Winter, Miss Winter, have a wonderful day." Flashing that uncharacteristic grin again, he stepped outside, leaving four speechless women inside. Ivy regarded his retreating back, diverting her gaze only when she heard Grace say, "My, Ivy! What on Earth have you done to Blakeburne?"

The carriage ride home represented a challenge for all parties involved. Victoria and Elizabeth fired endless questions on the events they had —fortunately for Ivy— only partially witnessed, while Grace was silent, a frown marring her forehead.

"What did you and Blakeburne talk about, alone on the upper floor? You did appear quite cosy."

"Why didn't we know you were in such familiar terms with him?"

"Did you arrange to meet with him today?" That from Victoria, eyes twinkling.

Blinking rapidly, she tried to focus on her friends' not so subtle interrogation. "No, of course, I didn't know he would be at the bookstore. On the contrary, I would have preferred not to see him at all."

"Did he corner you without your consent?" That was the first time Grace had spoken since entering the carriage. Startled by her friend's conclusion, Ivy immediately shook her head and answered, looking directly into her worried eyes.

"No, no, nothing like that. Blakeburne is one of the most honourable gentlemen I've ever met." Seemingly pacified, Grace crossed her arms under her bosom and looked at her expectantly.

"Good. You have some explaining to do, then, Lady Everleigh. What we saw wasn't a normal occurrence, especially when the frosty Duke of Blakeburne is concerned. Start talking."

Looking at her closest friends, Ivy couldn't do anything else except capitulate. She exhaled slowly. "Very well. First of all, you must know that I didn't purposely keep something from you. It's only that I didn't know what to think of it myself. As you know, we all first met the Duke of Blakeburne the night of Lady Quindsley's ball." At their nod of assent, she continued, relating the first embarrassing exchanges at the beginning of their acquaintance. They cringed with her at the right moments. She then told them about the late-night talks and chance encounters, omitting only the most private moments.

"So, you see, we formed this kind of friendship." An unladylike snort coming from Victoria's direction interrupted her stream of words.

"Friendship, right. From the colour of your cheeks, I don't think friendship is the right term." Ivy hadn't realised she was blushing, but again, Victoria had always been able to read her better than most. She wasn't ready to divulge the intimate parts of her relationship with the Duke, however.

For all the talk he had been doing about forgiveness, Ivy wasn't ready to let her anger go. A little tear could easily reopen the wound that was just starting to heal. No, she couldn't trust him completely.

Her thoughts were scrambling one upon the other, but she forced herself to keep them on track, to end her tale.

"Yes, friendship. Anyhow, whichever way you'd want to name it—" Ivy ignored Victoria's obviously fake cough, who strongly resembled the word *courtship*, and continued.

"I started looking forward to meeting him more and more, and I thought the feeling was mutual. Until the night of the Christmas ball." Ivy unconsciously rubbed a spot just above her heart, where she could still feel the phantom pain of what she had felt that night. "To make the story short, I overheard him talking to his cousin, Lord Eastham. It wasn't my intention to eavesdrop, mind you. I was making my way back from the restroom when I heard my name being spoken. I couldn't walk away from my curiosity. How dearly did I pay for my weakness." She paused.

"I guess what you heard wasn't complimentary," commented Victoria, sensing the story wasn't going to end well. A mirthless laugh escaped Ivy.

"You can say that. I don't much care to repeat it. Let's just say, the most gracious thing was that the only thing I have to recommend me is my family." Ivy cast her eyes downwards.

"The cad!"

"The worthless scoundrel! Who does he think he is?" Her friends jumped to her defence, talking one over the other in their indignation. Once again, it was Grace who restored the calm. "This isn't the end of the story, I gather, if he was at The Turning Page today."

Ivy sighed. "No, it isn't. His betrayal shattered me, but I was even angrier at myself for believing that a man like Blakeburne could spare more than a thought for a woman like me." She raised her hand to stop the protests already forming on their tongues. "Believe me, I know what you are going to say. That doesn't change the way I felt. I felt used, rejected. Once again, inconsequential. I wasn't sure I could face him again without crumbling. Or throwing something at his head." Hums of agreement and sympathy.

"The following morning, I woke up with a new resolution. I thought that, if Blakeburne were to find a wife, he would be occupied

196

elsewhere, and I wouldn't have to deal with him anymore. So, I took upon myself to help him, without informing him."

"But why did you not tell us?" Grace's face was full of compassion. Her friend had probably realised that it hadn't been 'friendship' that had guided her actions. Friendship wouldn't have hurt so much. She could see in Ivy's eyes what that endeavour had cost her. She couldn't imagine pushing the man she cared for —because obviously Ivy cared deeply for Blakeburne— in another woman's arms.

"Firstly, I was embarrassed. I didn't want what to be pitied by you."

"We would never have pitied you! We would have comforted you."

"Or we could have run Blakeburne over with my phaeton." Victoria's bloodthirsty tendencies sometimes worried Ivy.

"Thank you, but I wasn't ready to talk about it with anyone. I think my family suspected something was off, but they gave me space."

"You said 'firstly'. What happened then?"

A new wave of embarrassment crashed into Ivy. "Then I thought one of you could become Blakeburne's wife." She refused to look at them.

"*What?*" Their simultaneous exclamations managed to put a smile on Ivy's face.

"I apologise in advance for what I'm going to say, but, Ivy, this is one of the silliest ideas I have ever heard." Victoria voiced what they were all thinking.

"Believe me, I know now. It seemed like a sensible idea at the time. Each one of you could have made him a fine wife. Especially you, Victoria. You have much more in common with him than me."

"This is ridiculous!" countered Victoria. "Apart from the fact that we would never suit, if he hurt you so much, how do you think you could have borne seeing me with him for years to come? Because I would never lose a friend over a husband."

"That's why you fled that night. You couldn't go through with it, could you?" asked Grace in a soft voice.

"I wouldn't call it fleeing—" Ivy protested, only to be interrupted by Victoria.

"Listen, I would like nothing better than continue this discussion and find a painful way to maim Blakeburne, but we only have a few minutes before we arrive at my house, and I would like to know what happened today at the bookstore. You didn't seem so angry with him when he left."

Ivy, blushing furiously, knew this time she couldn't hide anything. "I don't know how Blakeburne came to know where I was today, but he wanted to explain his behaviour. Somehow he discovered I overheard him."

"And how did he try to justify it?" If they didn't stop interrupting her, it would take a trip to Scotland to finish her story. Ivy couldn't blame them. If the role were reversed, she wouldn't be able to contain her curiosity either.

"He said they were all lies to protect me from being targeted by his cousin. And before you start thinking it's all balderdash, let me assure you that he only did it because he is convinced his cousin's only interest would be in besting him by winning the favour of the woman who caught his attention." She hadn't yet had time to muse on the meaning behind his words. Sadness and anger rushed upon her anew when she reflected that even Blakeburne didn't believe someone else could develop feelings for her but had to have ulterior motives.

"Ivy? Are you well? What did you say to him?"

Shaking off those pointless thoughts, she continued, "Yes, sorry. I was woolgathering. Let's just say that the conversation got a bit incensed and then...distracted. He kissed me. Passionately. If Victoria hadn't appeared, I don't think we would have stopped only at kissing. In a bookstore." She groaned in her hands while silence reigned in the carriage. She had finally succeeded in rendering them speechless. Not a small feat in her book.

Blinking rapidly, Grace was the first to speak. "So, all is forgiven?"

Therein lay the problem. Ivy didn't know what to think. When outside the circle of his arms, when his intoxicating presence didn't obfuscate her mind, she had to admit that she wasn't ready to let it go.

More than his cruelty, fake or not, it was his blatant disregard of her feelings that worried her. If he could so carelessly use her insecurities for his own aim, did she really know him at all? She wasn't even sure he was telling the truth. She didn't know what to believe anymore. She regarded her friends, every one of them patiently waiting for her answer. They could be noisy at times, but, looking into their kind eyes, she could appreciate their steady presence and answer honestly.

"I don't know."

Chapter Seventeen

It seemed all Gabriel did lately was scan rooms in search of Ivy. She had better be there somewhere, so he could wring her beautiful neck. He had to give it to her. She had been thoroughly efficient. He had just escaped a horde of matrons who, with the finesse of a pirate crew boarding ship, had enquired about whether he really would select a wife by the end of the Season. At least he had come away with one certainty. Dear Lady Everleigh had a plan in store for him. It had become clear when four —sorry, five!— of said ladies had mentioned Ivy as the one who had encouraged them.

Ivy had put many marriageable ladies on his path, with all the subtlety one had when trying to push someone under the wheels of a moving carriage. In her brief quest for a bride for him, she had succeeded in luring the interest of the entire female half of the *ton*, and a fair share of the male one. Or so was Gabriel's impression while extricating himself from yet another tiresome conversation with a hopeful father, who was filling his ears with all his daughter's exceptional accomplishments. Which weren't exceptional by a long shot. If he had to listen to them droning about how well Lady Margaret played the piano, or how splendiferous —yes, splendiferous — Miss Hastings's drawings were for another minute, so help him God...

The situation was even direr than before because, now that his initial bewilderment had worn off, he could see a pattern in all those who tried to view for his attention. Somebody had clearly educated them about his supposed 'interests' and 'favourite topics', and they had latched onto it like starving puppies, with single-minded focus. The culprit who had unleashed the *ton* on him was notably absent, more to Gabriel's annoyance. Nobody knew how close he was to losing his mind. He was sporting his usual detached expression, while inside he was plotting his escape. Which was preposterous. Dukes didn't flee. And he couldn't leave without talking to Ivy. Apart from letting her know what he thought of her little plan, he wanted to ascertain where he stood. He was sure progress had been made in clearing the air from wrongdoings and misunderstandings yesterday at that little bookstore. A small smile tugged at his lips when he remembered how she had reacted to his kisses, despite being justifiably angry. He had meant for them to be quick pecks, reassurances, maybe even for himself. But, as it usually was with Ivy, the situation had escalated out of control like a spark near dry straw. What he wasn't sure of, however, was that she had forgiven him. Gabriel couldn't blame her if she still harboured mistrust towards him. He felt acid in his gut every time he thought about the hurt he had inflicted on her. Hence, the need to see her. He was ready to face everything she was going to throw at him, metaphorically and physically —if it came to that—, but he couldn't let her doubt her self-worth ever again. His feelings for her ran too deep to leave it alone. He was finally ready to admit it.

That didn't mean they didn't confuse him. Because they did.

His eyes swept Lord Sutton's ballroom one more time, this time finally setting on Ivy, standing by her parents. She looked stunning, cladded in a light blue gown with darker embroidery. Hanging to his patience by a tread, he quickly took his leave from the matron currently at his side, Lady Covington, mother of the thorn in his side that was the Earl of Covington, who had a younger sister to marry off too. He crossed the room with intent focus. It didn't take more than a few strides, but it was enough to bring his annoyance under control. He bowed politely to the Duchess.

"Your Grace, a picture of beauty, as always."

"You are very kind, Your Grace."

"I see you have finally extricated yourself from Lady Covington, Blakeburne," said the Duke of Rutherford-Blythe, a smirk on his face.

"Indeed, I have. A man can muster only so much interest in the weather. Before the Lady summons the rain inside her ballroom by the sheer number of times she mentioned it in the span of a brief conversation, I would be honoured if Lady Everleigh would partner me for the next dance." He finally turned to Ivy. Once upon a time, Gabriel refused to dance. Now, he seemed to always find a reason to ask Ivy. Fancy that. This time, it would keep people at bay, at least for the duration of the dance. And it would give him the possibility to explain why Ivy's plan was nonsensical. Thirdly, and most importantly, it was a society-approved way to take her into his arms. The interlude two days prior had been far too short, but long enough to make something inside him shift. All those emotions, bottled down by his very nature, had turned into something incandescent that nobody could touch if they didn't want to get burned. Nobody except Ivy, who could grab that part inside him with her elegant hands and cherish it.

Taking her gloved hand in his own, he led Ivy to the centre of the room as the musicians started playing the first note of a country dance. She still hadn't said anything, but when she placed her hand in his, she looked directly into his eyes. Her expression was guarded. He realised he had been right in thinking it would take more than a hurried meeting and a few kisses to put her doubts to rest. However, he was heartened by what he saw behind the veil of reluctance. A heat that matched his own, too strong to be buried and ignored.

"Are you having a pleasant evening, my Lady?" he asked politely. To any observer, his words would seem perfunctory.

"Thank you, Your Grace. I have to say it has been a pretty unremarkable evening so far. I saw that yours, on the contrary, has been vivacious."

"Vivacious, you say? You should have looked closer, my dear, for I have never been more bored in my life." They moved together flawlessly, adapting to one another's pace, the fit perfect. The step of the dance separated them momentarily, and when they came back one to the other, the slight touch of their hands was enough to make her breath catch even through the gloves.

"Gabriel..." she whispered. The fire was blazing, travelling down his spine, making it difficult to continue the modest dance with decorum.

"I have spent the last hour listening to people endlessly raving about horses, military literature and other topics that would have interested me if spoken about with any knowledge whatsoever. Why do you think is that?" His tone dripped irony, but he couldn't help it. "I couldn't take a step, grab a glass of champagne, without someone not so subtly informing me that their daughter came from a healthy, prolific stock. I commend your efficiency, my Lady."

"I am sure I don't know what you're talking about."

"Oh, I'm sure you do." His intense gaze bore into her, waiting.

"Very well. I could possibly have told someone you were actively seeking a wife."

"And why would you do such a thing?"

"I was trying to help the Duchess." She raised her chin high. "And it really was in your interest."

That spiked his irritation. Really, this woman could take him from burning with need to burning with anger in a heartbeat, incensing him into forgetting decades of practised detachment.

"In *my* interest? Or do you mean *your* interest? You wanted me to pay for slighting you, so you unleashed the entire power of the *ton* on me. Confess it." Throwing accusations around really wasn't the best way to return in her good graces. It was useful to draw the truth out of her, however.

"You are right. I did it for myself. But not for the reason you think."

"Explain then, my Lady, because I can't think of any other plausible reason for your silly plan."

She met his gaze unflinchingly, brave, and proud.

"I wanted to deprive myself of any reason to hope." He stopped so suddenly, she stumbled. Gabriel caught her by sliding both hands to her waist and bringing her to his chest. He had to take her out of there. How to do it without drawing even more attention was another matter entirely. The Duke of Blakeburne dancing was a rare occurrence. The Duke of Blakeburne absconding with the Countess of Everleigh was begging for a scandal. And the Duke of Blakeburne didn't do scandals. Which, come to think of it, wasn't true anymore. Not since he had met the woman currently in his arms.

Gabriel could already feel multiple pairs of curious eyes fixed on them. Scanning the room, he saw Bellmore looking at him speculatively. Then, with a nod of understanding, he suddenly and with uncharacteristic clumsiness turned to his left, knocking over the turban on the much shorter Dowager Marchioness of Whiteridge's head.

"I humbly beg your pardon, my Lady! Here, let me help you right yourself." Bellmore's voice boomed across the room, the volume high enough to wake the dead. His hands pawed the confection like a caveman who had never used hands before, constantly repeating, "Oh, I'm so sorry," "I don't know what has come over me tonight."

The old Lady finally had enough and shooed the Viscount away. "Enough, you scapegrace! Stop molesting my turban! What would your Mother say of your disgraceful behaviour?" She shot him one last disgusted look before righting her appearance on her own. The commotion had been enough to draw the attention away from Gabriel and Ivy. He owed Bellmore a bottle of his finest brandy. Make it two, seeing that he was still the object of Lady Whiteridge's tirade on the sad future of the Empire if the new generation of men couldn't even be trusted to take a step without causing disasters. Averse to letting his friend's sacrifice go to waste, he took Ivy's hand and led her through the door without giving her chance to protest.

"Blakeburne, where are we going?"

Gabriel's grip on Ivy's hand was firm, but not crushing. She knew with absolute certainty that if she tried to free herself from his hold, he would release her immediately. She didn't want to be freed, though, so she let him drag through a series of doors. For propriety's sake, she felt the need to offer a feeble reminder of the impropriety of the situation. "You are aware that you sprinted me away from a crowded ballroom, I gather?" His answer was intelligible, intent on his march. "Ah well, as long as you are aware that no less than twenty people could have seen us…."

Gabriel opened and closed a series of doors, then he finally reached his destination, leading them inside a library. He turned, gently manoeuvring her so that they stood one in front of the other. Taking her other hand in his, he looked intently into her eyes.

"What did you mean, 'to deprive yourself of any reason to hope'?" Realising she had fully betrayed herself by revealing the last, most fragile part of her heart, Ivy squared her shoulders and met his gaze head-on.

"You hurt me, Gabriel, deeply." Remorse coloured his green eyes. "Please, let me finish," Ivy stopped him when he opened his mouth to speak.

"I tried to shove the pain you caused in a box that I would have labelled 'silly Ivy's fanciful thoughts'. But a part of me couldn't let the memories of the time we spent together go. I knew that, if I ever wanted to eradicate those ridiculous feelings for good, I needed to eliminate their source." He raised his brows at that. Seeing his surprised expression, she let out a chuckle. "Don't look at me like that. I didn't think about literally eliminating you." She sighed. How could she explain her actions without appearing like a desperate ninny? "I thought I could stand seeing you married to some perfect lady if it meant that you would return to the country, and I could finally stop wishing…." Her voice stuck in her throat, making it impossible for her to finish.

"Stop wishing what, Ivy?" Gabriel prodded. "Tell me, love."

"That you really saw me! That you cared for me!" The words bust out louder than she intended.

She raised her chin defiantly. Her pride stood on the line beside her heart, ready to face the firing squad that would be Blakeburne's next words.

"Oh, Ivy." He cupped her cheek gently. He had really done great damage, hitting where she was the most vulnerable. Guilt was an unfamiliar feeling for him. He had always lived his life trying to make the right decisions, but knowing that deep down, Dukes could do no wrong. His father had taken care of instilling it in his mind from the moment he was born, and Society hadn't disambiguated him of the notion. It wasn't true, obviously. The Countess of Everleigh had shown him without a speck of doubt that he could go more than wrong.

And looking in the eyes of the woman who constantly put everything he knew into question, he traced back in his mind every interaction, every conversation. And he came to a conclusion. He would marry her. Not because he felt guilty. Or because they had been flirting with scandal many times. And not because she embodied everything he searched for in a wife. She didn't.

He would marry her because she was intelligent, witty, and beautiful. Because he wanted her with a passion he didn't think he was capable of. Because he couldn't go on glaring at the Earl of Covington for standing next to her and making her laugh. And he couldn't bear seeing her hurt by the thoughtlessness of Society.

Dukes always made the right decisions. And, with a sense of calm settling over him, Gabriel knew that was one of those. After they married, it would be his right to touch her, kiss her, have her. And crush under his perfectly polished Hessian boots everyone who dared make her feel small. Hopefully, he would stop acting like a fool and make a mess of things. He would spend the rest of his days making sure she would never doubt herself again.

As focused as he was on the feeling it infused in his body, he didn't even notice the sudden draught that made the door close with a click.

He would not ask her now. She could think it was out of obligation after the way he had unwillingly treated her. But he would. So, instead of voicing the revelation that would change his life forever, he simply tried to right his wrongs.

"I have used innumerable words in my life. Some kinds, some less so. Some had launched troops, and others had made Generals change their minds. But never have I regretted saying something like I do those words I carelessly said to my cousin. And any other that had made you feel less than the extraordinary woman you are. Please, forgive me." He drew her near, and she let him. He touched his forehead to hers, and he willed her to believe the truth behind his words.

She exhaled slowly, and with that, part of the tension left her body. She circled his waist with her arms and pressed herself fully to his chest without saying anything. A small victory for Gabriel. Maybe, at that moment, he could have obtained a bigger one. But not yet. Soon.

Ivy left Gabriel in the library after he had sweetly kissed her forehead and told her he would join her shortly. Something had shifted again in their relationship. She wasn't exactly sure what it was for Gabriel. For her part, she was feeling lighter than she had for weeks. And it was all thanks to the determined light she saw shining in his eyes. She decided to believe him and his remorseful words. Was it wise? Maybe not. Would she be hurt again? Most certainly. But she decided to have faith in him. And in herself.

Her good humour could not be dimmed even when Baron Whintrope accidentally bumped into her and apologised with "I beg your pardon, Miss ahem...."

Back in the ballroom, she smiled widely at the sight of almost all the people she loved chatting amicably together. A smile that didn't go unnoticed.

"Someone is feeling cheerful," said the Duchess of Rutherford-Blythe.

"Well, we are having a pleasant evening. And I am simply happy to see many people I care about enjoying each other's company." There were Duke and Duchess of Rutherford-Blythe —who could never be found far apart in this kind of public setting— Gregory, Victoria,

Grace, and the welcomed addition of Viscount Bellmore. It wasn't rare seeing them all together, and it always guaranteed the most stimulating discussions. No talks of the weather with this group. Or, at least, if it wasn't related to harvest predictions or astronomy.

"I'm sure it is us here doing nothing that put that look on your face," Victoria remarked cheekily.

"I didn't notice where you went, sister dearest. You weren't dancing right now, were you?"

Ivy scrambled to put together an answer that wasn't an outright lie, but she was spared when Victoria countered, "You don't notice much, do you?" Her tone was like a scalpel scraping an ice block. Ivy's happy fog lifted for a moment, allowing her to see that, while the general atmosphere was congenial, her friend was standing rather rigidly beside her brother, who looked bewildered by the sudden attack.

"What do you mean, Victoria? What should I notice?"

"Nothing, Gregory. Nothing at all." Ivy looked at her other friend, Grace, for a clue as to whether something had happened while she was ensconced in the library with Gabriel. She simply shrugged. Not for the first time, Ivy noticed that the easy camaraderie she had assumed extended to Victoria and Gregory was absent. In its place, a strange undercurrent passed between her brother and her friend. *Could it be?* No, she surely would have noticed. The conversation thankfully steered away from the odd exchange and resumed its easiness. At least until...

"I'd say, R-B, I haven't talked to you for a while now. Shunning the right discussions, are we?" Well, those two sentences were really a masterpiece of rudeness. Ivy had to give it to the old man, it must not have been easy enclosing a lack of courtesy, a patent disregard for the assembled company, a groundless familiarity, and a reprimand, all in what should have been a greeting. Some talents were difficult to teach.

Everyone turned towards the bulky presence of Lord Markham, who, as always accompanied by Lord Thomson, didn't acknowledge anyone else, his rheumy eyes fixed on Ivy's father. The Duke, usually an affable sort, could be very fearsome if the situations warranted it.

"Indeed, we could discuss what constitutes a 'right discussion', my Lord. And you surely see that I am delighted by the company of my beautiful wife the Duchess, my lovely daughter, Lady Everleigh, my son, Lord Burnam, and our friends Lady Victoria and Miss Winter. Viscount Bellmore, you surely know. I'm sure they reciprocate your warm greetings." He pinned the men with a look so full of disdain, lesser men would have run for cover. Either the decrepit lords were too short-sighted to see it, or they were made of sterner stuff.

"Yes, yes. Esteemed company. Well, with some contamination." The not-so-subtle look of disgust Lord Markham sent Bellmore wasn't lost to anyone. Ivy's jaw would have gone slack if she wasn't bristling with fury. She had met the old men twice, and each time they had attacked the Viscount directly and without any apparent reason. Bellmore smiled sardonically, wisely giving the jab the weight it deserved, which was none. Someone, however, had other ideas.

"Oh, there you are, my Lords Markham and Thomson. I wanted to express my sympathy for your failed bill. All that work gone to waste." The deep voice that never failed to send shivers down Ivy's body was filled with false commiseration.

"Are you addled-brained, Blakeburne? Parliament's vote is in two weeks," snapped the always-so-charming Lord Thomson.

"I'm aware," was all he said. A pregnant silence fell over the group, to give everyone enough time to grasp the meaning behind the words. The Lords could bid farewell to any chance of large support from the aristocracy. Cold and calculating, that was the Duke of Blakeburne the world saw. Straight back, emotionless eyes and no mercy in sight. Even Ivy, who had seen the man behind this powerful fortress, was feeling intimidated by him at that moment. In front of them was a man that could decide the fate of a nation with few words and a glare. He seemed unreachable, impenetrable, and implacable. He was splendid.

Markham and Thomson didn't seem to share her view. With a disdainfully whispered, "We'll see," they left. The atmosphere felt immediately lighter, even if some residue of the tenseness lingered.

"You really must think me a spineless halfwit for not defending myself," Bellmore said with uncharacteristic moroseness.

"Oh, not at all! Some people are meant to instil fear, others to inspire love. Who is to say which one is more powerful?" Bellmore looked wide-eyed at Grace, who immediately blushed a deep shade of red. The Duke didn't seem to hear her, his eyes still following the slowly retreating backs of the obnoxious men. Bellmore, instead, having regained his footing, grinned widely down at Grace. His smile was back to its usual mischievous self, but, behind it, there was a more vulnerable connotation. Ivy smiled to herself.

Sometimes the right words came from the most unexpected sources.

Looking at her friends and family, Ivy felt her heart full of calm optimism.

Chapter Eighteen

The news of Napoleon's escape from Elba travelled across Britain like a cannon shot, overshadowing everything else, including Markham and Thomson's parliamentary bill. As the weeks passed, everyone who cared to look could see the situation was becoming more and more worrisome. The spectre of what had happened on the Peninsula was clouding the air. Each morning, the Duke of Rutherford-Blythe's silence at the breakfast table became longer. When he finally put down the morning paper and talked to his family, the situation he depicted didn't look promising. Napoleon's march across France was met with support from the local population, dissatisfied by the reinstalled sovereign. In Vienna, diplomats were still working on configuring a new Continent, but their handlings weren't enough to put everyone's mind at ease.

Meanwhile, days went on as usual for Ivy and the rest of the *ton*. Let it not be said that something as trivial as the return of the French

Emperor could come between them and entertainment. Ivy wanted to scream at their shallowness. If they wanted to forget her name, fine — up to a point—, but to act as if the prospect of war didn't concern them was indecent in her book. The House of Lords was resonating with speeches of those who had decisions to make. The same men who, however, would not send the heir to their title to fight the enemy. With some notable exceptions. Every time Ivy had seen Gabriel, she had dreaded hearing he had been called away. Not that she had seen him all that much. Parliamentary sessions took up most of the time of those who took their seat. Which were most of Ivy's titled family and acquaintances. The pleasant days spent between stimulating conversation and even more stimulating company were long gone.

She had been unfair. The *beau monde* talked about the war: how inconvenient it was that Napoleon could not stay put and how tiresome it would be if the shop in Bond Street had to reduce their stock because of another blockade. Ivy wanted not only to shout at them but to slap them silly to boot. How could they not understand the impact all that would have on people's lives? On Ivy's life? Yes, because, looking at the earnest face of the man who was now talking with a group of older gentlemen at Lady Nash's party, commanding their respect despite being years younger, Ivy came to a horrifying realisation.

She had fallen in love with him. Quite desperately.

She could have seen it way before that moment, but clearly, her mind didn't want to accept what her heart was browbeating it into. The realisation wasn't a welcome one. Even if too many kisses and caresses had been shared to make her doubt she stirred at least *something* in him, the timing couldn't have been worse. *Thank you, Boney, for making my life difficult,* Ivy thought, immediately feeling like a hypocrite for criticising the *ton* for its selfishness.

Ivy looked at Gabriel again. Had she realised she loved him just a few weeks before, she would have reacted with less panic. Now, it wasn't only the risk of heartbreak that frightened her but also the very real risk of having him taken away from her permanently.

Her gaze must have carried some weight because he raised his head nodded politely her way. What he saw on her face made him raise an eyebrow in question. Wasn't falling in love supposed to feel like floating on clouds or something equally sugary? It wasn't supposed to be accompanied by all this dread.

"Ivy?"

Oh, dear. Oh, dear. Oh, dear.

"Ivy! Are you listening to me?" She startled, looking away from a puzzled Gabriel, who was still placidly talking to those gentlemen as if it wasn't his fault that Ivy was now in that predicament.

"Yes, yes, of course, I'm listening, Victoria." She forced a smile for her friend, who wasn't fooled even for a second. *Blast!*

"What's amiss, Ivy?"

"Nothing, nothing! Everything is absolutely fine!" Now, if she could say it without squeaking, maybe someone would believe her.

"Who were you staring at?" Victoria looked over Ivy's shoulders, curious. "I don't see anything out of the ordinary. There is the Duke of Blakeburne talking and sending looks our way. That's hardly surprising—"

"Shh, Victoria. Don't let him hear you!"

"Why? He's on the other side of the room. Besides, I don't see the problem. You two are often seen conversing." Victoria smiled teasingly. "If you want my opinion—"

"I love him!" Ivy blurted out. Fortunately for her, Victoria was right in saying they were out of earshot of almost all of that afternoon's attendees. Her friend gaped at her for a second and then gently patted her hand.

"Of course you do, my dear. Anyone who looked under the surface could see it. It's high time you realised it."

"No, Victoria, you don't understand. It's a disaster!"

"I never knew you to be so dramatic. It's a good thing!"

"No, it isn't!" Ivy shook her head. "He is the Duke of Blakeburne!"

"A fact you sure have been aware of for quite some time, I assume," Victoria said slowly, proceeding cautiously in the face of Ivy's evident distress.

"A Major in His Majesty's Army!"

"Yes…and?"

"In the Army!"

"I heard you the first time! Why does it matter if…Oh!"

"Yes, Victoria. *Oh*, is right."

Realising what the real issue behind all that was, Victoria grabbed both Ivy's arms and made her look into her eyes.

"You don't even know if he is going away. Have you talked to him? You should," she added when Ivy shook her head. "I don't know if words of betrothal have been spoken, but—"

"Of course not! And now certainly is not the time. What if he's called away? What if he doesn't return? We're not talking about a grand tour here!"

"Breathe, Ivy. Don't get ahead of yourself."

"What's going on here? My Lady, are you well?" The stern voice interrupted Victoria's attempt to calm Ivy. With great effort, she regained her composure and turned to face the man who had the nerve to make her fall in love with him.

"Nothing out of the ordinary, Your Grace. Just chatting. You know how we women like gossiping." Ivy thanked the fates that she was born in the family she did. If she had to tread the stage for a living, she would have starved to death.

"With all due respect, my Lady, you are not the gossiping kind. And even if you were, you would not look as white as a sheet while doing it. I demand to know what the matter is about." Victoria elbowed her lightly. Despite the warm feeling pervading her knowing that he had noticed her distress from the other side of the room and had come to make sure she was well, she could not reveal the reason. Not just yet.

215

"I assure you I am well, Your Grace. Thank you for enquiring. It must be the fact that I haven't eaten since breakfast." Another lie. "As soon as I'll partake of some food, the colour will be back, I'm sure."

Blakeburne didn't look convinced. "See that you do. Lady Victoria, ascertain yourself of the fact if you please. Now, since I'm here, I also bid your farewell. I've other matters to attend to. Lady Everleigh, Lady Victoria, good day." He spun on his heels and walked away while summoning a servant to retrieve his greatcoat.

"Well, I never thought I'd say that, but the Duke of Blakeburne is sort of sweet. In his high-handed, standoffish way. But sweet nonetheless," Victoria commented as they watched the Duke leave the room.

Ivy, on her part, just sighed resignedly.

Esteemed Major Eastham,

I am sure this letter comes as no surprise. As you know, the situation in Europe doesn't allow us any other choice than to take immediate action. Wellington himself has sent out missives to his most trusted officers to gather enough men to fend off that pig who couldn't stay where we put him. Enclosed you will find the official summon. I write this note to ask you as a personal favour to answer in the way I am sure you already plan to. There is no room for mistakes anymore.

Colonel W. Stattford

Gabriel laid the letter on his desk, slowly, not really seeing what he was doing. The brusque disposition that characterised Colonel

Stattford oozed from the few lines he had just read. After weeks of waiting, the summon had finally arrived.

Restlessness was escalating quickly, and even ballrooms were becoming stifling, especially when he had to call to every ounce of patience he had left and listen to self-appointed military savants, whose closest things to a uniform they had ever touched was a red-embroidered waistcoat.

Dukes don't argue with those they deem inferior, but they nonetheless let them know what they think of them. Gabriel had come to hate his father's precepts, but he had to admit that sometimes they came in handy. Especially when he didn't want to skewer half of the *ton* with his bayonet. Or pulling his hair in frustration at the worst time in history for hostilities to resume. He was finally coming to terms with his resolution to ask Ivy to marry him. It had not been easy putting aside years of firmly believing that, at the right time, he would have taken a meek, undemanding wife. Which, despite what she thought —and it really was a joke that— Ivy Kington most certainly was not. At the same time, it had been surprisingly easy to accept. Her smiling face came flashing before his eyes. Her supple body under his hands. He suppressed a groan.

He had to admit that part of the restlessness he was feeling was due to the looming prospect of the marriage proposal. He didn't like not being able to predict the outcome of something he had planned. Or was trying to plan. Who knew so many things had to be considered before asking a lady for her hand in marriage?

And then, like a disease infecting a body, everything had been tainted. Britain was at war once again.

Gabriel put aside Stattford's letter. Sure enough, on the other piece of paper, he was asked to be in Dover in three weeks' time. Where he would go from there, it didn't say, a testament that things were far from clear.

A knock at the door announced his butler. "His Lordship Viscount Bellmore for you, Your Grace."

"Thank you, Jenkins. Send him in," Gabriel replied needlessly, as Bellmore was already walking past his servant, who bowed and retreated, not before sending the Viscount a butler-version of an exasperated look.

"Thank you, my good man." Bellmore made a quick beeline to the liquor cart before sitting in front of Gabriel's desk, crossing an ankle over his knee.

"Did you receive yours?" The question didn't need any preamble or context. Not only because Gabriel currently had the very letter in question in front of him, but also because few things swiped all the humour from Sebastian Sinclair's face. War and carnage being two of them.

"Yes, right this morning. Stattford included a few lines in which he kindly asked for my presence. I ought to be insulted. I am a Major. I don't need to be reminded of my duty."

"The cantankerous whoreson wouldn't be pleasant even to the King. If it makes you feel better, I too have been the fortunate recipient of a charming note." Gabriel wasn't at all surprised. It might be strange for a Colonel to approach a lower-ranking officer personally, but Bellmore wasn't a simple Captain. And it showed in times like those.

"What did he write?"

"Not much, really. Basically, he asked me to be ready to —I quote — 'put that pretty mug to good use'."

Gabriel himself didn't know the full extent of Bellmore's role. What he did know was that, as an officer, he recognised the enormous sway he held on the soldiers' spirits and how crucial he was. As a friend, he feared what would happen to him if something like what happened on the Peninsula repeated itself. He looked at him closely. His gaze was met with an unwavering one on the Viscount's part. Gabriel wouldn't make the mistake of suggesting he sold his commission again. He could respect that.

"Stattford must really want you there if he called you 'pretty'. I've heard him insult his own mother once."

Bellmore snorted. "If you heard only that, then you've been lucky. Anyhow, at least the summon doesn't state the date of departure yet. That gives us some time. I had put some plans in motion with the idea of being home for a while. What is it?" It seemed the Viscount knew him better than he thought. Or he wasn't as imperturbable as he once was. To answer the question, he handed Bellmore the summon. He quickly scanned it and whistled.

"Bollocks. Three weeks?" He looked up at Gabriel in confirmation. As if he could change the days on the calendar. He nodded.

"I believe they want to see if the whole things can be contained first. If that fails, they'll deploy real strength. And the man who can influence the mood like no other. You."

"The court jester, you mean." Gabriel pinned him down with a hard glare.

"You know better than anyone how far from the truth that is." Bellmore shrugged, brushing away Gabriel's words.

"Fine, fine. Put that scowl away, Blakeburne. No need for it. Now, have you told the Duchess all this? I doubt she'll be thrilled, you going away again. And, if I may be frank, ruining her big plans for you." Mischief restored; he sipped the rest of the spirit in his glass.

"Not yet. I haven't had the chance to. Not looking forward to it, honestly."

"Can't say I blame you. '*Hell hath no fury*' etcetera."

"I'm not sure this is what Congreve meant, but there certainly will be fury involved," Gabriel said it with so much seriousness, Bellmore couldn't help but chuckle.

"I'm glad you find it entertaining."

"Very much so, old chap. What about the lovely Lady Everleigh?"

Just like that, Gabriel's frown was back in place.

"That's another conversation I am not looking forward to. You remember what happened last time I told a woman I was leaving."

Bellmore shuddered dramatically, but then an earnest expression took over.

"The Countess is not Arabelle Ingram, Blakeburne. She will understand."

"And if she doesn't?" The question carried more meaning than the four simple words implied. Gabriel hated the vulnerability he was feeling.

"Then, my friend," —a dramatic pause followed—, "prepare to duck."

No amount of ducal breeding could have stopped Gabriel from rolling his eyes. At the same time, in his mind, he made a quick inventory of all the knick-knacks in the Rutherford-Blythe Townhouse, relieved that there seemed to be no shepherdesses with pointed canes that adorned the mantels.

Chapter Nineteen

As predicted, the conversation with his Duchess mother didn't go well. Oh, nothing as undignified as tears or hysterics. Just a few 'loving' reminders of how the late Duke had opposed his military career and how, once again, Gabriel was jeopardising the Blakeburne line, doing something reserved for the lower class. Gabriel refrained from pointing out how officers were mostly part of the aristocracy, either by birth or thanks to their success on the field.

On top of that, his mother had continued, if he hadn't been so stubborn, he would at least have a wife and possibly an heir underway. But no, even that was too much to ask. Needless to say, his mood was foul when he ascended the front steps of the R-B Townhouse. Someone could have questioned the wisdom of having that dreaded conversation with both his mother and Ivy, one immediately after the other. Usually, he would have scoffed and told them he didn't have time for such trivial things like protecting feelings. Even if they were his own. This time, however, while he waited for Ivy in the tastefully decorated drawing-room, he started to see the merits of those imaginary people's reasoning. After a last look around to make sure there weren't objects that could be made into ammunitions, he went to stand by the window. The back gardens were lovely and well-maintained, but Gabriel was not really seeing them. Rather, he was thinking about the last time he had been in that same room and how he had come to crush any interest Ivy had in him. His lips twisted in a sardonic curve in contemplating how the tables had turned in such a short time. What was even more ironic was that, despite his change of heart, he still couldn't marry her. Not now. Selfishly, he was glad he hadn't asked for her hand yet. It made what he had come to say easier. *It doesn't feel that way, though.* He could have spoken to her in a more public setting, informing her of the new development during one of those times. They had talked about the volatile situation more than once, always ignoring the stormy cloud over them that was his direct involvement.

She deserved better. Like she deserved better than a rushed wedding put together in two weeks, to leave him enough time to meet his appointment in Dover. And it was also better than waiting for an intended who didn't know when, and even whether, would come home to her. No, it was better for her to be free. The *ton* would wonder. One had to be blind and deaf not to have noticed that he and Ivy had started to attract gossipmongers' interested stares. It was bound to happen. Gabriel prided himself to have never read a gossip sheet in his life, but he would wager his fortune than the two of them were mentioned more than once in them. A bachelor Duke and a very eligible Countess could not be spotted repeatedly talking —at least they have been seen just talking, thank God— without setting tongues wagging.

What if, now that the ton has finally noticed her, you come back to find her on another man's arm?

He chased away the unpleasant thought and the jealousy that accompanied it. No, no, it was the right decision. He would not be swayed from his course.

He turned at the sound of the door opening behind him. "Good morning, Your Grace. What a pleasant surprise." Gabriel bowed to the Duchess of Rutherford-Blythe.

"Your Grace. Thank you for receiving me."

"Nonsense. We always find time for our friends."

"Then I am doubly honoured. For being welcomed and for being numbered among your friends."

"I was led to believe you wish to speak with my daughter. May I enquire on the nature of the request?" The Duchess had a maternal air around her that made it easy to underestimate her when compared with her more imposing husband. Gabriel already knew not to make that mistake.

"I would also like to speak to the Duke if he's available to callers. I have news to impart."

"Oh. Good news, I hope?" There was a glint in the Duchess's eyes that made Gabriel uncomfortable.

"Well, Your Grace, I—" Before Gabriel could finish, Ivy's voice could be heard just outside the door. She was clearly talking to herself. Gabriel suppressed a smile, some of the unease leaving his shoulders.

"I always forget to ask Stevens in which drawing-room he put guests. One would think I should know it by now, but he clearly has some kind of rotation system. Or hierarchic system. And why wouldn't he tell me who had come—oh!"

"Lady Everleigh."

"Gab—Your Grace!" His smile broke free at the sight of her blush. It had become one of his favourite things to see. He especially liked the red hue of her skin after he had thoroughly kissed her. But he was digressing. The reason for his visit quickly wiped the smile off his face.

"Ivy, His Grace was telling me he brings news. He wanted to talk to you and then to your Father." The Duchess stressed the word *father,* looking pointedly at Ivy, charging it with deeper meaning. Ivy looked at her mother, visibly baffled, and Gabriel shared the sentiment, especially when she patted her daughter's hand and said, "I'll give the two of you a few minutes alone. But I'll leave the door ajar." She beamed at them and made her way to the door.

"Your Grace, there is no need to depart. I wouldn't impose in your home—"

"Nonsense, nonsense. I'll go and inquire whether Rafael is back."

"Mama, wait!" But it was too late. Ivy's protests bounced against an almost-closed door.

She turned to him. He detected a mix of nervousness and expectation on her lovely face. He must have betrayed his befuddlement because her expression slowly morphed into one of horror.

"I apologise in advance, but I admit you find me at a loss. Why did Her Grace run away like the house is on fire?" In lieu of an answer, Ivy brought her hand to her mouth, stifling any sound emerging. *Oh God, what have I said to upset her so?* He still hadn't touched the subject of his imminent departure yet.

"Ivy? What's the matter?" She pressed her palm more firmly on her mouth, head bent downwards. He covered the distance between them with the intent of taking her into his arms. But she wasn't sobbing. Oh, she was shaking. With laughter.

"What in the world?" Finally looking up at him, Ivy let all restrain go and openly laughed aloud. Tears spilt down her face. He was starting to feel affronted by the undignified spectacle, most likely at his expense. Stiffening his spine, he gathered his ducal hauteur. That didn't help, as another round of laughter overtook her.

"Oh, dear Lord! I'm so sorry! But...look at your face!" she gasped in between heavy breaths. "By now, Mother will have alerted the entire household that right this moment you are proposing to me!" If his countenance was rigid before, now it was positively carved into stone. And she continued laughing.

"I fail to see what you would find so amusing in that scenario."

"Oh, nothing, if it were the case. But you are not proposing, are you?" At the shake of his head, another pearl of laughter escaped.

"Ivy, I have to kindly ask you to refrain from laughing so hard. Put yourself together and explain yourself!" Ivy took a few deep breaths, finally bringing her inexplicable merriment under control.

"You are right. I apologise for my unseemly behaviour. Don't feel insulted, Blakeburne. I was laughing at myself, at the days that will now await ahead of me, when I'll have to disambiguate everyone in this household —from my family to the scullery maids, and believe me, Father employs many people— that you are not here to ask for my hand."

"And you find the prospect amusing?"

"Positively hilarious." Gabriel looked alarmed when she threatened to start laughing again. Was she foxed? She didn't seem like the type to imbibe, especially in the afternoon, but he had no other explanation.

"Oh please, don't look at time like that! You'll make me lose my composure again." It was too late. "I can't stop thinking about Mother almost hopping away with glee." She was now pressing her hands on her stomach, which likely hurt from the effort.

"Ivy, please stop and listen to me…."

"You are probably here for some mundane reasons, and everybody is thinking you are now professing your devotion to me." The broken dam had brought an unstoppable wave of what by now could be nothing other than hysterics.

"If you just—"

"Bother, let's hope a message has not already been sent to Gregory."

"Ivy! For the love of…I'm leaving for the Continent!"

Her laughter died.

Ivy wanted to crawl under a rock and hide forever. And, while she was there, she could welcome the urge to cry that overtook her. She didn't know whether she felt more embarrassed by her behaviour or afraid for him. She decided to concentrate on the embarrassment. It was less devastating.

Suddenly fascinated by the intricate pattern entwined in the Aubusson carpet, she said softly, "I was afraid the time would come." She took a deep breath. "I apologise for my behaviour. It was really unbecoming." Ivy didn't know what had come over her. When she had entered the room, she had let her mother's barely veiled glee infuse her with a sense of expectation. Her heart, which had ambushed her by falling in love with Gabriel, had somersaulted seeing the Duke in all his unsmiling magnificence.

Moreover, that treacherous organ had sided with her mother. Looking into his beautiful, confused, green eyes, she had quickly realised her mistake. He had no intention of talking about marriage. The bubble of laughter had been impossible to stop. She was laughing at herself, at her once again foolish heart. He was probably thinking she was stark raving mad. But it didn't matter. It would have been better than what he had really come to say.

"I'm more interested in knowing what has originated it. Something was already off at Lady Nash's." Ivy had thought her explanation three nights before had been satisfactory, but she clearly hadn't convinced the observant Duke.

"Don't spend another thought on it, Blakeburne. It's a female peculiarity being capricious." Ivy cringed inside for the choice of excuse. She had always hated when a man dismissed a woman by labelling her of 'capricious nature'.

"You are the least capricious person I have ever met." He raked a hand through his hair, something he only did when he was extremely discomposed. At the sight, any thought about embarrassment flew out of the window. What did it matter if she had once again made a fool of herself in front of Gabriel? He had a very uncertain fate in front of him, and nobody and nothing could guarantee that he would come back. To her.

"When will you leave?"

"In three weeks," he replied, matching her sombre tone.

"So soon. Is the situation so dire, then?"

"I'm afraid so. Napoleon is amassing an army along his way, and we would be fools to underestimate him. We already made that mistake."

Ivy nodded. It corresponded to what her father was saying.

"And before you say anything, I will not sell my commission. I have a duty towards my country that I cannot ignore. Not even for you." Where did that thought come from?

And what's more, *not even for you*?

"Making such a demand would mean greatly overstepping the boundaries of our acquaintanceship." At his disbelieving look and raised brow, Ivy started to feel annoyed, the one emotion she hadn't yet felt that afternoon.

"I would *never* ask you such a thing. I'm aware that choosing to go must not be an easy decision. Especially since your income doesn't depend on it and you already have so many obligations to oversee here. It doesn't mean I wouldn't prefer to know you are safe and warm at home, within reach, but I respect your decision. I respect you. You are an honourable, heroic m—" Gabriel interrupted what was starting to become a lovelorn list of his qualities with his mouth, pulling her close. She hadn't noticed he was getting one step nearer for each word she said. The kiss went on for a while, a passionate mating of tongues and breaths, but it was nonetheless over too soon. And it was she who put a stop to it.

"What made you think I would have asked you to leave the Army?" she asked, a bit breathless, still in his arms.

"Others would have. Others did."

"The Duchess of Blakeburne? I am sure she's simply worried about your welfare. It's what mothers do." Gabriel shifted without releasing her, suddenly uncomfortable. Ivy narrowed her eyes at him.

"But you were not referring to her, were you?"

"My mother wasn't exactly overjoyed by the prospect of sending the Duke of Blakeburne once again off to war…." Ivy waited without saying a word. "But no, I had an unpleasant experience back before leaving England for the Peninsula."

"Your paramour didn't like the thought?" Ivy tried to sound nonchalant and worldly but couldn't hide the jealousy that laced her question. The image of a faceless woman pleading with him with doe eyes and a voluptuous body didn't sit well with her.

"It's not a topic suitable for a gently bred lady."

"Oh, please, Gabriel, don't start with that nonsense. Not when you came here expecting a tirade."

"You are right, Ivy. My humblest apologies. I shouldn't have let my past with Lady Ingram colour—" Gabriel must have immediately realised his mistake, but it was too late.

"Lady Ingram? You are comparing me to that horrid woman? Need I remind you who was who saved you from her clutches?" If her jealousy had been bad before giving a name to his past ladybird, now it was like acid in her stomach. Lady Ingram. The scheming, manipulative, rude Lady Ingram. The fact that he had even thought she would behave like her was the highest of insult. She was so incensed that she didn't even miss the warmth of his arms when she took a step back.

"If I weren't the gentle bred Lady you pointed out I am, I would slap you."

"At least it would be an improvement from the ceramic figurine she threw at me…."

Ivy barked out a laugh. "Is it that what she did? If you were so insufferable back then as you are now, I can't say I blame her. Wait...is that why you kept looking around at the furniture?"

He had the grace to look sheepish. Or as sheepish a man like him could look. It was pretty adorable. Ivy didn't want to let her anger go. If she did, the reality of the situation would swallow everything else. He was leaving. It was the right thing. For Britain. And even though she knew it, even as she said it, a selfish part of her wanted to lock him in a room —possibly hers— and keep him away from any danger. Suddenly overcome by desperation, Ivy brought her hand on his nape to pull him to her. They kissed frenziedly, their bodies touching everywhere. They were pouring everything they were too proud to say in their caresses.

I can't ask you to stay, but there isn't anything in the world I wouldn't give to keep you safe.

I can't stay, and there isn't anything in the world I wouldn't give to protect you and the life you know.

Please come back to me.

Please wait for me.

Gabriel was taking one step after the other, forcing her to walk backwards. She didn't stop touching him, his shoulders, his back, until they reached their destination, which was the drawing-room door. She pressed her against it, closing it with a soft click, effectively isolating them from the outside world by turning the key in the lock. And all without breaking the kiss. The man was nothing if not efficient. The hardwood was the only thing preventing her from dissolving into a puddle of lust on the floor, especially when his mouth started a descent along her neck and then her collarbone, leaving behind the gentle sting of small bites and kisses. His clever hands preceded his mouth in its journey downwards, cupping her breasts as if staking their claim on them and stimulating their already aching points. Her own hands, instead, had left him to press against the door, useless. Her breath and heartbeat were erratic, and all her strength went to suppress her moans that were getting louder and louder as his ministrations continued. When he finally raised his head to look into her eyes, the green of his orbs was almost completely taken over by a dark hunger that held her hostage. It didn't scare her in the least. He was surely able to see her permission to proceed. He raised the layers of her skirt, pulling it to her waist.

"Keep them up for me," he groaned, his voice the deepest she had ever heard. Ivy waited with anticipation for a repeat of the night of Lord Whiteridge's ball. When he dropped to his knees, she had just the time for a whispered "Oh dear," before his mouth latched on her core, licking, and sucking, lapping at the wetness he found there. His hands were now caressing her thighs while keeping them open against her instinct to close them. He was feasting on her, groaning like a man presented with all his favourite dishes. She looked down and was enthralled by the sight of his dark head moving rhythmically between her legs. She felt a surge of power accompanying the staggering pleasure he was giving her. The oh-so-proper, remote, powerful Duke of Blakeburne on his knees committing that scandalous act and thoroughly enjoying himself if the noises he was making were any indication. As for herself, she was reduced to sensations, chanting his name with every twirl of his tongue on her folds. When he suddenly added a finger, plunging it inside her and simultaneously sucking on that bundle of nerves that seemed to be the trigger of the shock shooting through her body, Ivy couldn't suppress a cry. She bit on her closed fist when it overtook her, making her knees give out. Joining Gabriel on the floor, she closed her eyes, her head pressed against the door. He gathered her to him, tucking the hair that had escaped her coiffure behind her ear, the gesture so tender it made her press a kiss on his glistening lips. She tasted herself on him, and the thought made her already pleasured body come alive once again. She deepened the kiss. This time it was he who stopped her. He brought them both back on their feet, but there wasn't an inch of space between them. Ivy could feel his hardness pressing against her belly. The desire to make him feel the same pleasure he had given her overtook everything else.

She pressed a hand against him, feeling him shudder. Staring into his eyes, ablaze with green fire, she said, "Let me do the same for you."

He sent a prayer heavenwards and staggered back a step, effectively preventing her to reach the fall of his breeches.

"I would give up my Dukedom for your lips on me." His expression was pained, his hair in disarray.

"No, you would not." It was a preposterous assumption. One that, knowing him, betrayed how much he was still under the fog of lust. His eyes —which were slightly unfocused, Ivy had noticed, and for which she was proud to take credit— regained some of their sharpness. A small smile curved his lips.

"You are right. I wouldn't. But I would be sorely tempted. As much as it pains me to stop you, the Duchess has been gone for a while and could barge into the room any moment now, and God knows whom she will bring with her. I won't put either of us in that situation. We have flirted with scandal many times. Now it would be more dangerous than ever." Ivy had to agree with his rational reasoning, but she wasn't any less disappointed. She pouted slightly, and he barked out a laugh, hugging her close once again. For the last time, at least for a while. She borrowed against him and mumbled something, muffled by his waistcoat.

"Care to repeat that, my Lady?" She looked up at him reproachfully, but behind it, her eyes were full of something way more tender.

"Don't compare me to Lady Ingram ever again." His grin was something only she was able to cajole from him. He cupped her face with both his hands.

"You, my beautiful madness, are unlike any other Lady. I am duly chastened for my mistake."

"I forgive you."

"I am in awe of such magnanimity."

Ivy breathed deeply before saying, "You are really going?" It wasn't a question that required his answer. "I have been dreading this moment, carrying around a sense of inevitability that has been clouding even the most glorious sunny day."

His eyes, those enthralling green eyes, so unlike any others, held her captive while she witnessed the change in them. From warm and open to hard and determined. Major's eyes.

"I will fight them even harder for having taken away the life I've lived since meeting you. But I will give my life if it would mean you will get to live yours as you deserve. And that means I won't make promises I can't keep. That was what I've come to say. I won't ask you to wait for me."

"With all due respect, Your Grace, that is not for you to decide." He seemed taken aback by her firm refusal. He thought she would simply accept his dictate and send him on his merry way? After what he had said? And…after those other wondrous things his mouths had just done to her?

"Ivy, I…"

"Now listen to me, Gabriel. I will not ask you to stay. I will not ask you to make a commitment to me." He opened his mouth to argue, but she stopped him. "It wouldn't be fair to either of us. But you can't ask me to go on like a part of me will not come with you." There, she had said it. They have tiptoed so much around one another that that veiled declaration had the force of a bullet. None of them said anything for a few moments. In the end, it didn't change anything. She finally broke the silence.

"I will write to you, and you will accept the letters with good grace. You'll even answer them as much as you are able, so you'll let me know how you are faring. I don't expect regular correspondence, but I need you to do this. Otherwise, I may be forced to come to see that you are safe myself. Is that clear, Major?" He chuckled at her threats and rested his cheek on her head.

"Crystal, my Lady. I will do my best, as long as you will not be disappointed by my epistolary effort."

"Oh, believe me, I'm familiar with your writing style. Let's just say, your talents lay elsewhere." She looked at him, sure that he could see the love shining in her eyes. Taking a step back was almost physically painful, but their time was over.

"You had better leave now, Gabriel. Let me spare you the trouble of having to explain to the Duke and Duchess that you are not to become their son-in-law."

"I will stay if you need me to." He appeared as reluctant as she was to put an end to their encounter. "I don't believe we will be able to meet again before my departure. I have to settle various matters in different estates."

"I totally understand. Now, go while you still can." She stood on tiptoe and kissed his cheek. "Godspeed, Your Grace."

He bowed deeply at his waist. "My Lady." His words, laced with regret and longing, were more than a simple honorific. They were a vow. In a few strides, his long legs reached the door, and in a few more, he was outside.

Ivy was still staring vacantly at the door when her parents filled the space through which half of her soul had disappeared.

"Here we are! I apologise for keeping you waiting, but Rafael— Where has the Duke gone? Ivy?" Ivy couldn't answer. Her legs gave out. She slumped into the chaise behind her and burst into tears.

Chapter Twenty

True to his words, Ivy —and the entire *ton*— didn't set eyes on the Duke of Blakeburne for the following three weeks. For once, the blasted man could have contradicted his own words. She didn't want to be angry. But she was. She floated around from one soirée to the other, from one inane promenade to the other, carrying rage like a cloak. She wasn't angry at the fact that Gabriel was making his vital contribution to the fight against Napoleon. Of course not. And neither was she enraged that in twenty days, he hadn't found the time to send a measly note. He had told as much.

She was furious at the time they had wasted, circling around one another, denying the truth before their eyes. She hadn't told him she loved him, and he hadn't delved too much into his own feelings yet. Had they both been less stubborn…So yes, she was angry. Only the fact that she was always surrounded by friends and family had spared Baron Whintrope a dive into the Serpentine for looking at her without a hint of recollection. She was fighting against an invisible, sly monster whose sharp claws were sinking painfully in her heart.

She felt helpless in front of the reality that she, for all her title and wealth, was still 'simply' a woman who could do nothing but wait and pray for the best. She couldn't fight alongside the man she loved, keep him safe. And she hated that.

Now it was the end of the month. And he was gone. Had she been a more dramatic person, she would have trashed her room, breaking things in a fit. Her mother lately looked at her worryingly, preparing herself for the moment she would finally break. But she hadn't. She was hanging on to her anger like a lifeline. Letting it go would mean making room for fear, for sadness. For the regret for a future of which she had had only glimpses. A future that might never come to pass.

❆ ❆ ❆

About a fortnight later, Ivy received the first letter. It was short, more a note than a letter.

> *Dear Lady Everleigh,*
>
> *I hope this letter finds you well. I am writing to let you know that, after an uneventful journey, I arrived safely on the French coasts. The air here predicts that that will most likely be the last uneventful thing we will be blessed with. I will write to you again upon reaching our final post so that you will know where to address your reply.*
>
> *With all my regards,*
> *Blakeburne*

Brief as it was, that letter helped dissolve the Gordian knot that had settled firmly in her stomach.

Ivy waited impatiently for his following letter, to which she would be finally able to reply. Meanwhile, life went on as usual for the British *ton*, whose superficiality didn't disappoint. That time, however, Ivy took comfort in its unswerving predictability. She rode in the Park; she attended the opera and different balls.

When the following letter finally came, she discovered that Gabriel and his Colonels would lead a smaller regiment not too far behind Wellington's troops. They could move faster, if needed, and could join Wellington in a few hours. At the same time, they would find themselves in the front-line in case of a surprise manoeuvre on Napoleon's part. For now, they were observing their surroundings, planning.

Ivy was thankful. Descriptions of day-to-day activities helped keep her over-imaginative mind under control. If all she had were the official reports in the papers that her father unsuccessfully tried to hide from her, she wouldn't have been able to go through her days. Gabriel's letters were always very informative, if not very passionate.

Except for one.

One morning, Ivy was sipping her tea when Stevens brought her the day's correspondence. Upon seeing the familiar scrawl on the slightly crumpled sealed paper, she immediately put her cup back on its saucer and started to read. From the very opening, it was clear that the tone was going to be very different.

> *My dearest Ivy,*
>
> *Yesterday we decamped and marched North for a few miles through the countryside. It was all very peaceful and picturesque, with fields of colourful flowers basking in the first May sun. Halfway through, I saw a woman standing on the side of the road. She had brown hair and dark eyes, just like yours. She was cradling an infant in her arms. Her eyes went wide when she saw the red*

coats. *She stood there, terrified. I made sure we passed without accident, and she resumed walking as fast as her legs could carry her. I know it because I watched her until she was just a dark blur. I put the peculiar feeling that that brief moment had left me with out of my mind as I went about overseeing my men set up camp. But then came nightfall. And the dream. I dreamt of the woman with brown hair and dark eyes looking up at me with terror-stricken eyes. I tried to give her my hand, to beckon her closer to me, to keep her safe, but she wouldn't let me touch her. I soon realised that it was me she was afraid of. Only, the woman wasn't an unknown peasant. It was you, Ivy.*

The next morning, I learned that the bridge we passed before we met the woman had been hastily blown up by the French to prevent us from going back to our last post, down the only trodden road. Nobody had been warned. Not even those who happened to walk by it. They blew it up two hours after we crossed it. How long do you think it takes to cover seven miles on foot while carrying a child? And when you are running away from the dangers of foreign soldiers?

With my deepest wish to never see that fear in your eyes,
Yours,
Blakeburne

Her hands shook so much, she had to put the letter down. Had it been the teacup, it would probably be shattered on the floor. Whoever held her heart had not been so sensible because it felt like it had splintered into million pieces. It ached for Gabriel, and it ached for the unknown woman and child, whose fate had been wagered in an unfair game they had slim chances to win. Ivy rang the bell, and the ever-solicitous butler appeared in the doorway.

"Stevens, can you please fetch me some ink and paper?"

"Right away, my Lady."

Ivy couldn't do much for Gabriel from London, but at least she could answer his letter immediately.

Dear Gabriel,

Can souls really become insensitive to the loss of innocent lives? I really should hope not. Otherwise, I despair for the future of humanity. It makes you the man you are, my love, that something others would fail to notice could still make an impact after having seen so much worse. I would like to think that the woman had stopped her walk to let her child play in one of those colourful fields and had looked up the sky, wondering where the sound of thunder had come from on such a sunny day. And maybe, she remembered the officer with the sombre green eyes who had let her through safely and who is fighting to avoid that a woman far away, who looks a little like her, had to stand on the side of another road, afraid. Your world is full of uncertainties, my love, but know one truth: I will never look at you in fear.

Yours,

Ivy

She set the letter down to let it dry. She had essentially told him she loved him but couldn't bring herself to regret it. The proud man needed comfort, which was the most natural thing in the world, even if he probably wouldn't see it that way. So, she had put *her* pride on the line. And it was the truth, after all.

If she had known it was going to be the last letter she would receive from him, maybe she would have written it clearly.

❖ ❖ ❖

Gabriel put down the quill, sanded the last missive and stood. He had finally exhausted all his correspondence. It seemed to him he had written to everybody in England and a good portion of his fellow

238

countrymen there on the Continent. Besides the obvious dispatches he exchanged with other officers, it appeared that suddenly every one of his men of affairs and stewards couldn't make a decision without consulting him first. At least he had something to do to pass the time. As he had written to his brother —there were also letters for his family among those neatly stacked on the corner of the desk— after encamping on a hill not too far away from Wellington's troops a week before, they had been doing nothing but wait. And observe the French. What usually was a peaceful, almost idyllic landscape was interspersed with tents and bivouacs. A gentle wind caressed green grass, its colour made more vibrant by rain droplets still clinging to the blades. At least it had stopped raining. What was even more tedious than being left hanging in an indefinite wait? Being left hanging under pouring rain. The few timid rays of sunshine that had greeted them had been a welcome respite. One that wasn't meant to last if the dark clouds in the distance had their way.

"Major? Permission to enter, sir?" said the silhouette outlined against the fabric of Gabriel's tent.

"Come in, Captain."

Despite being of average height and appearance, Captain John Harris was one of Gabriel's most trusted officers, whose skills would surely result in a stellar military carrier.

"Major, I have come to collect today's post if it's ready."

"Where's Rivers?" Usually, correspondence was a task assigned to Lieutenant Rivers, the most organised person Gabriel had ever met. Seeing the usual unreliability of delivering letters during a war, he had personally appointed the man to avoid adding further unpredictability.

"He has been detained, sir. I took on the responsibility of collecting the post for today." Another testament of the general inaction, if the Captain started going around gathering letters. "I can come back later if you are not finished."

"No, it's fine. I just finished replying to the last letter." Gabriel felt the annoying pang that he had come to expect when he thought about anything related to letters.

"Here, Harris, thank you." The Captain took the proffered stack of papers and left.

Gabriel's hand automatically went to the breast pocket of his uniform jacket, touching the single unanswered letter that burned a hole through the heavy fabric. He had read it so many times since he had got it that he didn't need to take it out to know what it said. It was the reply to a rather maudlin letter he had penned in a moment of weakness, but he wasn't too proud to admit that seeing that woman on the street had left him unbalanced. Upon spotting her, he had thought he had finally gone mad. It was Ivy, carrying a small child and dressed like a peasant, trying to go unnoticed by the British soldiers. He had blinked rapidly, and, getting near, the woman's features had come completely into focus. Apart from the colour of her hair and eyes, the resemblance wasn't that strong. The hardship of life had already started to take its toll on the young woman, who was desperately scanning her surroundings for a place to hide. Unsuccessful, she had let her paralysing fear overtake her. Gabriel had shot an uncompromising look at his men, promising retribution if even one of them approached the woman. No one had dared utter a word.

Well after that chance encounter, he was still thinking about it. Not much about the woman, who was just one of many, but about its effect on him. His heart had practically stopped beating the few moments he had irrationally thought the Countess of Everleigh was in a war-ridden Europe. That irrationality was worrying. Irrationality brought a loss of control, which, as maddening as it would have been normally, there it was downright dangerous.

He had woken up with a start, only to learn of the blown-up bridge. It was part of the war they were living in. He shouldn't have given it a second thought. Instead, he had penned Ivy that letter, full of nonsensical ramblings. He had immediately regretted sending it.

Who was he, Byron? With all that talk of dreams and fear-stricken eyes? Yes, he missed her like air in his lungs. But reality was that she distracted him too much, even from afar. That episode had been the final straw. He couldn't allow it, not when he had the lives of his men to think about. Not to mention a war to win. When he compared that with the prospect of breaking a promise he had made, there wasn't really a decision to make. He would focus on defeating Napoleon. He would not reply to Ivy's letter anymore, even if her words were what kept his dubious soul together. As his father would say, *nothing is more important than duty. Put everything else in its place, which is out of your mind.*

Chapter Twenty-One

Everything was fine back in London. Breakfast was eaten as usual every morning. Calls were exchanged at fashionable hours and for the appropriate lengths of time. Shopping expeditions filled the hours until dinner and the following evening engagements. Everything was absolutely fine. It wasn't as if the papers every day reported the uncertain progression of the hostility on the Continent and the inevitable rising number of casualties. And it wasn't as if the days went by, and Ivy hadn't received a single letter from Gabriel in weeks. Everything was fine. Right? There wasn't anything to worry about. Her parents, and her brother, *and* Victoria, *and* Grace, *and* Elizabeth, they were all convinced his letters were just being delayed or, at worst, they were lost somewhere between the front and England. Ivy agreed with them. After all, what other explanation could there be?

Then, at the beginning of the third week of silence, Ivy met two of the Duke's blood relatives during a morning ride in the Park. The

Marquess of Addington and Lord Eastham greeted her politely. Ivy scanned their faces searching for a sign they shared her worry and apprehension for Gabriel's health. Finding none, she was able to keep quiet until the initial pleasantries were over.

"Have you heard from your bother, my Lord?" From the slight nudge her mother —who had accompanied her as usual— gave her, she had to work on her subtlety. It wasn't proper to enquire about a man you weren't related to in such a direct way. Ivy would put an advertisement in the paper to let everybody know how much she cared about propriety at that moment. Which was not at all.

"Why yes, my Lady. I was just telling Charles here that I received a letter just yesterday. The poor man is going out of his mind with boredom." Lord Addington chuckled, and Ivy's shoulders relaxed as she breathed a bit more easily for the first time in days. Everyone was right: there must be some mishaps with the correspondence. What really mattered was that he was fine.

"How so, my Lord?" her mother asked. It was Lord Eastham who answered this time.

"It's a waiting game what they are playing now, Your Grace. At least from where they're standing. A waste of a great military mind, leading a detachment, if you ask me." Nobody asked you, Eastham.

"Surely you wouldn't prefer your cousin amid constant bloodshed, would you?" remarked Ivy.

"Of course not, Lady Everleigh. I only think that a man like Blakeburne would rather act than idly wait for orders."

"That is certainly true," confirmed the Duke's younger brother. "He said it so himself. I believed he wrote something on the line 'if I had wanted to spend my days writing letters to any- and everyone, I would have stayed at my desk at home, which is so much befitting that the one I have here. At least the exchange is still fast and regular.' The chap is at his wits' end. He hates writing." The two Lords laughed again, unaware that the joke was on Ivy. When their laughter died down, they finally noticed she hadn't joined in the merriment.

243

"Are you well, my Lady?"

"Oh dear, look at the time! We have to return if we want to make it in time for our engagement," the Duchess exclaimed, preventing Ivy to have to come up with an answer. There wasn't any engagement that Ivy was aware of, but she gladly went along with the excuse.

"You are right, Mother. I almost forgot." She turned to the men, noticing that Lord Eastham was studying her intently. "If you would excuse us, my Lords. It was a pleasure seeing you."

"The pleasure was ours, my Lady. Good day Your Grace," Lord Addington said, touching his hat in farewell, mimicked by his cousin. With nothing else to add, they parted ways, Ivy following her mother along the path. When she raised her eyes, she was surprised to see they were already entering their stables. Her mind was miles away. To be precise, it was with a man who, seated at a modest desk, miles away, with nothing to do but writing letters, had decided not to answer to the one in which she had poured her heart out.

She tiptoed into the library, careful not to wake neither her family nor the servants. She had no idea of the time, but given that they had come home well after midnight, it wasn't farfetched to assume that dawn wasn't too far away. The nightmare had been so vivid that she had woken with a strangled scream in her throat. Even now, she shuddered, the dark tentacles of unreality refusing to leave her. The dream had started by reliving the previous night's event. She and Victoria had attended another soirée at Covington House, with Gregory acting as reluctant chaperone. Lady Covington simply *loved* organising rendezvous. They had talked, danced —mostly Victoria— and everyone around her had made a point of mentioning Blakeburne and his letters. Or so it had seemed to Ivy. From then on, reality had become distorted. She had left the room to walk in the garden. Only, the garden wasn't really a garden. It was a field. A green field, basking in the sunlight. A lone tent stood in the distance. She had tried to make her way to it and suddenly found herself inside. It was night again, a candle casting light upon a man writing at a desk, his back to her. Her heart pounded, recognising him before her mind did. "Gabriel," she had tried to say, but her voice had remained stuck in her throat. She had then walked to him and peered over his shoulders. Gabriel hadn't heard her nearing, too intent on writing. The ink had shined bright red in the candlelight, like…blood? He was writing one single word, over and over again. *Forgettable.*

"Gabriel!" she had repeated, more forcefully. He kept writing and writing. *Forgettable.* To make him stop, she had put a hand on his shoulder and made him turn to her. Only to be confronted with a gruesome sight that would haunt her forever. Vacant eyes, not green, but white, the life gone from them. The same colour as his skin, marred by blood gushing from a head wound and flowing down his neck and right arm. Until it reached the fingers that held the quill. His head had lolled on the side, and she had screamed.

Realising it would have been impossible to fall back asleep after that, Ivy had thought to find some solace in the library. She was met with cold and darkness, a mirror of what was feeling inside. It felt like she would never be warm again. No fire had been left alight, and no moonlight was filtering through the drawn curtains.

The sky suddenly decided to take upon itself the task of lighting the room. Lightning flashed. Everything became white for a moment.

White, unseeing eyes looked up at her.

Ivy muffled her startled scream with her fist. The air that left her lungs seemed unable to find its way back in. Try as she may, Ivy's breaths were becoming shorter and less satisfactory by the moment. Her head was pounding mercilessly, and the sound of thunder exploded right inside her skull. The skies opened, and torrential rain started beating against the windowpanes before dripping down the glass. Another lighting.

White, unseeing eyes looked up at her, blood dripping down.

Ivy looked around frantically, her once safe place now sinister. *It's just a storm. No demons are hiding in the library. It's just a storm.* The crack of another thunder splintered her open. All the fissures she had been keeping together with her bare hands couldn't contain what was inside her anymore. Images flashed before her eyes, dreams and reality becoming one distressing thing.

Gabriel smiling at her, touching her, kissing her. Gabriel turning away. Gabriel, dead, alone, far away.

All her worries, insecurities, fears gathered in the strangled sob that escaped her. After the first, there was no way to stop. Shoulders heaving, her frame rocked with uncontrollable shudders. She crumbled to the floor. Feeling the hardwood of bookshelves on her back, she drew her knees to her chest and put her head on it, gasping for air. Her tears were soaking through her shift. She had never felt so alone. Alone in her fears, alone in her love. It was like being underwater, where nobody could reach her. The storm continued raging outside, and she was lost. Adrift.

She didn't hear the door opening. She didn't hear the light footsteps nearing.

"Oh, Ivy…" was all her mother said before gathering her into her arms.

"Everything will be all right. You'll see."

If only it were true.

The following morning, Ivy felt marginally better. She didn't know for how long she and her mother had remained in the library. When she had finally stopped crying, she had looked up in her mother's eyes and had seen profound concern for her. The Duchess had wordlessly taken her to her bedroom and helped her back to bed. Ivy didn't even remember touching the pillow, completely drained of strength. Now, the excruciating pain in her chest was slightly dulled, and at least she was feeling confident that she could face the new day. Both her parents were already sitting at the table, their expressions cautious and worried. It was to be expected when a mother had to witness a daughter break down in the middle of the night. That didn't mean Ivy looked forward to the conversation ahead.

"Good morning, Mother, Father. Anything new in the paper?"

"Ivy, please sit. You know perfectly well it's not what we want to talk about," the Duke said. It was worth a try. Ivy sighed.

"Yes, I know. Is there a possibility that we could forget about it? It was only a bad nightmare. Please don't worry about it." Her eyes were pleading. Neither of her parents was convinced, even if it *was* partially true. For some miracle, they let it go easily, with just "You know you can talk to us about anything, do you?" At her nod, the topic really turned to the articles in the morning paper.

"This is really indecorous, let alone dangerous. It should be prohibited to place such advertisements," said the Duke, annoyed, pointing at the advert section of *The Times*.

"Can you please expand on what you are talking about, Rafael?" his wife asked patiently.

"These gentlemen —and I use the term loosely— offer trips to the Continent to whoever is willing to pay. Now, in the middle of a bloody war!"

"But who would want to make such a journey?" asked Ivy.

"You'll be surprised how many men yearn for the thrill of finding themselves in perilous situations. Young bucks with more money than sense."

247

"If they wanted the thrill, they could always enlist...." Ivy replied, piqued.

"Ah, but you see, my dear, they want the *thrill*, not the actual risk being skewered by a bayonet." Ivy scoffed. What a ridiculous notion.

"I can't fathom so many ask for these men's services as to make it profitable."

"Mmm..." Ivy's mother didn't completely agree with her husband. "I think there's another reason that could bring people to make such decisions."

"And what would it be, love?" asked her father.

The Duchess's eyes were sombre when she said, "Desperation."

❈ ❈ ❈

The modicum of balance she had managed to achieve started to waver as days passed, and she was faced with something way worse than Gabriel not replying to her letters.

Ivy had just left Edward Eastham, Lord Addington, after he had shaken his head solemnly. They had met in Hyde Park almost every day for a fortnight. At first, their casual encounters had been pleasant. Seeing the same high cheekbone, broad shoulders and proud —even if a bit diluted— stance as Gabriel had made her stomach knot. The vague connection Gabriel's younger brother represented and the longing she always felt were infinitely preferable to the weight that had started settling on her heart when Lord Addington, on his horse in the mid of the crowded path near the Serpentine, had informed her that he, too, had stopped receiving replies to his letters to the front. That day was no different.

Ivy had started slipping again into that dark place where reality wasn't much different from her nightmares. Her sleep wasn't peaceful, and she could often be found pacing in the dead of night. It went without saying that her disposition wasn't benign to begin with. And it certainly didn't improve when her cousin Eleanor and aunt Evelyn decided to delight her afternoon with their charming presence. Ivy had almost reached the Park's gates, her mother by her side and two footmen trailing behind. The two sisters-in-law greeted one another congenially. Then it was the younger women's turn.

"Ivy! I didn't expect to find you here!" Eleanor exclaimed. "I thought you had left for Everleigh or Wildrose Manor." Right, because she hadn't been travelling almost the same path many times a week recently. *Lord, give me strength.*

"Indeed, here I am. What a strange world!" Eleanor narrowed her eyes, Ivy's sarcasm not lost to her. She felt *slightly* guilty until…

"You must have passed so unnoticed that even I, your own cousin, have overlooked you." Ivy reared back and stiffened on her side-saddle. They have never been each other's favourite person, but they had never been openly hostile towards one another. She looked at her lovely cousin, clad in a lilac riding habit enhancing her figure. Her expression was affable, and her voice low enough not to attract their mothers' attention.

"Now that the Duke isn't here to force others to see you basked in his reflected glory, you are back in your rightful place. It makes no difference whether you are in London, at Everleigh, or anywhere else. Nobody would miss you." Ivy was left speechless, only able to look at her mother and aunt, stunned that so much venom would not pervade the air and reach them. Then anger took over. She was feeling irritable, touchy, and very, very tired. So, she struck when she knew it would hurt the most.

"I thank you so very kindly, Eleanor," Ivy said sweetly, enjoying the confusion on her cousin's beautiful face. "You have just reminded me of the appointment that I have with *my* steward on matters concerning *my* estate." She heaved an exaggerated sigh. "One of the many obligations a *Countess* has, you know. But wait, you don't know."

Before Eleanor could retaliate, Ivy turned to her mother and reminded her too of the appointment. Which, to set the records straight, she really had planned. She didn't look forward to arguing with Mr Wallace for the sole reason her ideas came from someone not wearing breeches, but it was better than remaining there and letting Eleanor sharpen her tongue on her without letting her know how close to Ivy's sore spot she was. With one last icy look from her cousin, they parted ways.

Back home, Ivy did her utmost to go on with her day as usual. However, even after the meeting with Mr Wallace and the headache it caused, Eleanor's words swirled around her mind like a broken carillon, taking up more and more space. She was so out of sorts that she didn't see the maid turning the corner of the hall until she crashed into her, sending a pile of newspapers flying.

"Oh! I am so sorry, my Lady! I didn't mind where I was walkin'." The maid, Sandrine, apologised profusely, curtsying, despite it being entirely Ivy's fault. Sandrine crouched to pick up the old editions of the paper and gasped horrified when Ivy bent to help her.

"No, no, my Lady, there is no need for you to do that! It'll take just a moment."

"Nonsense Sandrine. If one goes around not looking where they're going, it's only fair they help straighten the mess." Sandrine was relatively new in the Duke's household and still unused to the peculiarity of the Kington family. Clearly nervous, she started rambling.

"I was bringin' these papers to the servants' quarters, as Mr Stevens said. He's teachin' us to read. In our days off, obviously." Ivy was aware of the man's undertaking, one she wholeheartedly supported. She stopped paying attention to what the maid was saying when her eyes fell on one particular page. It was the advertisement section. The one in which men promised safe and adventurous trips to the Continent.

The few lines placed by some greedy strangers somewhere had unlocked other words from another moment.

I will write to you, and you will accept the letters with good grace. You'll even answer them as much as you are able, so you'll let me know how you are faring. I don't expect regular correspondence, but I need you to do this. Otherwise, I may be forced to come to see that you are safe myself.

No, it was out of the question. That she was even considering it showed how jumbled her mind was. It would be irresponsible, dangerous, if not lethal. And for what? To ascertain that Gabriel was alive, sure, but a small —maybe not so small— part of her wanted not to feel so powerless anymore. So invisible. *Forgettable.*

No. It was complete madness, just like Gabriel had called her many times. Endangering her life just to feel better about herself. But while the rational, sane part of her brain was making an endless list of the sound reasons to forget all about the idiotic idea, another part, one that had remained dormant until that moment, was already formulating a plan.

"Have you completely lost your mind?" That wasn't the first time Victoria had said something along that line since barging through the door of Ivy's sitting room. Ivy was actually surprised by how many ways there were to say it.

"No. It's me. I must have caught a strange ailment that has made me daft. Because I could swear you're saying you want to travel to Belgium and find Blakeburne." Victoria rummaged in her reticule, producing a familiar folded note. "Ah, wait. I have this lunacy in writing!"

Ivy knew perfectly well what was inside it. That very morning, with a clarity that belied the impulsiveness of her actions, she had understood that, if she wanted even a small chance to succeed, she would need help. Before she could change her mind —or come back to her senses, depending on how one wanted to look at it— she was at her writing desk, penning three letters. One to Victoria, one to a strange man residing in Dover, and the third, the most difficult one, addressed all the way to the battlefield. Predictably, the most immediate consequences were in the form of a Victoria-shaped whirlwind.

"There is no need to shout, Victoria. If I could just—"

"Oh, I apologise, but it isn't every day that your friend asks you to cover for her while she goes gallivanting in the middle of a war!"

"Shhh! Please keep your voice down. I know it seems foolish—"

"Foolish! Foolish is hoping Prinny wears a sombre waistcoat! This is dangerous!"

"I know."

"You could die!"

"I know!"

"Not to talk about the fact that, if someone discovers it, you would be utterly ruined. Not that it would be worse than you dying, but still...."

"Don't you think I already know all that?" Ivy, who had begun pacing back and forth while her friend was submerging her with fair argumentations, finally managed to say. She stopped right in front of Victoria and looked straight at her. "Believe me, I would feel like you do if the roles were reversed. But you don't understand. I have to go. I have to know, Victoria."

She waited for the rant to resume, but instead, Victoria suddenly deflated.

"I *do* understand what it means to cling to hope for so long, only to see it slip through your fingers without understanding why." Victoria's voice was now low and forlorn as if she were talking from experience.

Ivy was at a loss for words. They had known each other their entire life and, still, she didn't know what had happened to make her say something like that.

"You just want to know the reason why. Putting aside for the moment the fact that you may not even be able to leave the country, once you find him, it could be the beginning of a love story to rival any Minerva Press novel. But Ivy, have you considered that you may not be prepared to face what you'll find?" Ivy nodded, looking at her feet, not quite able to stomach the doubt in her friend's eyes.

"Even if it were true, it wouldn't be your fault, Ivy. War changes people."

Ivy took a deep breath and did something that came very difficult to her. She laid her deepest fears bare for Victoria to see.

"I'm scared of what I'll find. Of course, I am. But as afraid as I am of everything —the journey, the enemy land, Gabriel himself— it's this silent void I'm most scared about. I've been hurting myself for years, well before meeting him, filling the silence with the worst doubts. This time, instead, I would fill it with certainties. Whatever they may be. And if certainties are even more terrifying than my fears, I will deal with them when the time comes. But I have to do something." Victoria listened, aching inside for her friend and knowing there was still one last thing to say.

"There is another possible outcome. What if he is...."

She hesitated, but there wasn't any need to finish the sentence.

"Then I'll bring him home."

At that moment, Victoria understood that she couldn't do anything to persuade her friend that that was a bad idea. Ivy already knew. Resigned, she prayed she wasn't making a huge mistake.

"What do you want me to do?

Chapter Twenty-Two

Secrecy and plans were not for her. Ivy had felt confident after a trip to the bank that had not raised any question, thanks to her unconventional family. And she had felt victorious re-emerging from the attic with two of Gregory's old travel bags without anyone noticing.

It all went up in smoke when Poppy, her lady's maid, barged into her room while she was trying to fold some clothes and said, "Whatever you've in mind to do, my Lady, you can't do it on your own. I'll come with you."

Ivy might have been a little off-kilter, but she wasn't stupid. As she had explained to Victoria while she was outlining her plan, it would be reckless even to think about travelling without protection.

"Just like I'm not going to put myself in the hands of strangers who could rob me blind, kidnap me, or God knows what else. I'm going to purchase their alleged

knowledge of the land." Hence the trip to the bank. *"I have already sent a letter ahead."*

"I still think you should talk to your family. Or ask Gregory to accompany you. It seems something someone like him would do." Ivy frowned at Victoria for more reasons than one.

"It's true I have more freedom than many other ladies, but my parents would draw the line at this. And even though Gregory has always been on my side, he won't condone me putting myself at risk. Just like I him."

Therefore, Ivy had enlisted Henry's help, one of the burly footmen that usually accompanied her out, as well as the Coachman's. She hadn't told them their final destination yet. She would do it in Dover before boarding the ship. Then they will have the right to choose what to do.

"Henry told me that you plan to leave tomorrow at first light." Apparently, that loyalty didn't extend to keeping quiet. Ivy continued folding her clothes, seeing no reason to hide anymore. Never underestimate the servants.

"I apologise if I'm oversteppin', my Lady, but you need me. First, you don't fare well in long carriage rides. Second, wherever it is you're goin', a Countess cannot show herself in public without her lady's maid's help." Ivy doubted anybody would care how she dressed where she was going. On the contrary, she was purposely packing her most serviceable and plain dresses. A thing that didn't escape her efficient maid.

"Jesus, Mary, and Joseph! What are you packin'?" The horrified and accusing looks she sent the abundance of brown and dark green clothes were hilarious.

"I could dismiss you for your defiance, you know," Ivy said without heat, and Poppy knew it was an idle threat because she continued, "Where on Earth are we goin'?"

Ivy found herself telling Poppy everything. She couldn't let her come without knowing what awaited them. She had not planned to take her maid with her, but the stubborn look on the other woman's face didn't leave much room for being vague. Any excuse she had tried to come up with went flying over Poppy's head.

"I don't like it one bit, my Lady, let me tell you. Not one bit. Still, I won't let you embark on this absurdity only with Henry and John Coachman." The matter was settled.

Before she knew it, Ivy was ensconced in the third-best Kington's coach, listening to Poppy sharing her thoughts on the endeavour for the first hours on the road.

"His Grace and Lord Burnam will catch up with us before we even leave London, mind me word. You'll be back before dinner, and we'll put all this behind us."

But, as they put miles between them and London, Poppy fell silent. Ivy's thought wandered to her parents and whether Victoria had done her part. Her friend had to have the letter Ivy had written for her family delivered by midmorning. Ivy hadn't wanted to lie, so she had explained her intentions the best she could, but she had bought herself some time by not letting them find the letter until she had had at least a five-hour head start.

Ivy hoped to reach Dover the following morning. That meant stopping only to change horses and for unavoidable needs before nightfall. It was Ivy's personal version of hell. She had always been prone to sickness while travelling, no matter how well-sprung the conveyance. And, thanks to that year's exceptionally rainy spring, the roads were the cherry on top of that mud cake. She spent most of her time with her eyes closed, keeping her breath under control. She wouldn't want to be delayed by having to cast up her accounts all over England. Her inability to read, embroider, or do anything else really, had left her with only one thing to do. Think.

Despite her resoluteness, she was scared out of her wits. The odds that everything could go to hell —she could literarily die and go to hell — were much higher than the ones of a perfect reunion worthy of her favourite books. But each time Gabriel's beautiful face entered her mind, she knew that she would travel every bumpy road on the planet to see it again. *Providing that he's alive and will want to see you.*

"You love him very much, don't you?" Ivy opened one eye. Now Poppy could read her mind.

"The Duke. You must really love him for doin' this. For riskin' everything for him. Not many would do what you're doin' for someone else." Ivy looked right into the maid's light blue eyes.

"Yes, I love him. And I know many wouldn't, and that makes me sad. And angry. Everybody deserved someone willing to walk to the end of the world for them, don't you agree?"

Poppy smiled, a hint of gloom in her eyes.

"I do, my Lady. I really do."

Wretched weather for a wretched plan. Ivy rubbed the shoulder she had just bashed against the wood panel of the coach.

"Sodding hell!" she exclaimed, uncaring of how blasphemous she was being. She was alone inside the carriage, Poppy riding on top. The day before, she had discovered that her maid and footman had been courting for at least a year. That explained how Poppy had learned of her plan so soon after she had put it in motion.

With her stomach still dancing at the rhythm of every pothole the wheels fell into, Ivy had shooed Poppy away to spend time with her sweetheart and leave her alone in her misery. Reluctantly, Poppy had agreed, making her promise to knock on the roof if she felt sicker. Ivy cursed her weak constitution again. She didn't want to think about the channel crossing that awaited her. *Gabriel, you are lucky you are worth it.*

After a night spent at an inn and a healthy meal that had calmed her blasted insides, they were finally reaching Dover. The air was changing, carrying the first sea scents. At least it wasn't raining, but the road conditions were atrocious, as attested by her smarting shoulder.

"There's a smoother streak ahead, my Lady!" John Coachman shouted, his voice barely audible above the noise of the horses and conveyance.

"Thank God," Ivy would have said back if words hadn't been drowned by a terrible sound that made all the previous ones seem like a lullaby.

Wood broke and splintered. Ivy, who was already bent to answer the Coachman, was violently propelled forward. The open window spared her head.

Then the carriage started to tilt to the opposite side, sending her flying, her body opposing as much resistance as a rag doll. She slammed against wood and glass.

Her luck was clearly over. The glass window shattered into sharp splinters, but Ivy didn't have the time to feel the nagging pain that shot through her leg when one particularly big piece of glass sliced through the layers of her clothes, reaching her flesh. A brass hook, so cleverly placed to hang coats and whatnots without bothering the travellers, hit her left temple so hard Ivy went momentarily blind. She could hear Poppy's and the men's desperate cries. They were trying to keep the coach upright and the horses under control. It was all pointless. Something else snapped with a sharp crack. Ivy was thrown once again. Almost bent in half, she escaped the wooden death trap by being tossed through the unhinged door. Mercifully, she had already lost consciousness when her body hit the muddy ground with a sickening thud.

Chapter Twenty-Three

Sebastian Sinclair was sitting at a table in the communal room of The Limping Duck, an inn just outside Dover, sipping a tank of strong ale. He wasn't in any hurry to leave, and the ship that would bring him to the Continent wouldn't set sail until the day after. He wasn't looking forward to going back to the hell on Earth that was the front, but his country and his fellow soldiers needed him. That didn't mean he would not get royally foxed before boarding the ship. He was just starting to work on it when a high-pitched voice disturbed the relative quiet of the half-empty inn.

"Is it possible to have a decent cup of tea around here? Really, it is not to be borne. Not only the travelling conditions are awful, but I have to suffer mediocre fares and hospitality as well!"

What was Lady Eleanor Kington doing there? The Season wasn't over yet, and Rutherford-Blythe's niece had always struck him as a social butterfly.

259

"Eleanor, it was your decision to leave London for the country," said another, more moderately clad, older woman, supposedly her companion, stepping inside after Lady Eleanor. Sebastian then remembered that the Earl of Northcott's country seat was somewhere in Kent.

"You know why I had to leave!" Eleanor said with dramatic flair. "It was, however, *not* my decision to take the longer route to Northcott."

"As we've already told you," the companion tried to say patiently, apparently not for the first time, "the choice was between remaining stuck on the road or a slight detour—"

"Yes, yes. Is there someone who works here, or do I have to die of thirst?" Lady Eleanor's eyes scanned the room, and Sebastian too late realised that that brought him directly in her line of sight. Her undeniably beautiful face cleared of any irritation. He groaned. And he was still sober.

"Lord Bellmore! What an extraordinary coincidence to find you here, so far from London!" *Extraordinary indeed*, thought Sebastian, rising to his feet to greet the young Lady.

"One would be hard-pressed to find a happier one, Lady Eleanor," Sebastian replied automatically, while inside he sighed when she took a seat at his table, while her companion —a woman he was sure he hadn't met before— sat quietly beside her. After finally getting the tea she was loudly clamouring for, she started enquiring about his destination, frowning when he explained he was meant to join his regiment.

"What a dreadful business. I'm sorry to hear you'll be leaving England."

Sebastian was gratefully spared from replying by a commotion just outside the inn. And to think that the kind innkeeper had extolled the peace that could be found at The Limping Dunk.

His relief soon morphed in alertness when a muddy and dishevelled young woman, dressed like a maid, burst inside.

"Help, please! Someone fetch a physician! Please hurry!"

Sebastian shot to his feet just as Mr Swan, the innkeeper, came rushing from the back. Keeping his distance but ready to be of service if needed, Sebastian couldn't understand much from the agitated speech and rushed words. He only gathered that there had been an accident on the road, which, seeing their conditions, wasn't that farfetched. Mr Swan vehemently motioned to come inside, simultaneously shouting for his son to fetch the local physician. Sebastian's blood went cold when two men carried inside a woman's lifeless body. They were clearly involved in the accident, as proven by the torn clothes and various cuts and scrapes adorning their faces. But they had certainly fared better than the woman. He jumped out of the way, not before noticing the bad shape she was in. Her face was turned away from him, and all he was able to see was blood encrusting her brown hair and neck and trickling from a nasty gash on her right leg, leaving a macabre trail on the floor before mixing with English mud.

The maid who had first rushed inside was shaking violently, looking at the woman who was being taken upstairs. As she made to follow the procession led by Mr Swan, she finally noticed Sebastian. But it wasn't him who made her gasp.

"Lady Eleanor?"

Sebastian looked at the Lady in question who, at some point, had come up to him. No flicker of recognition appeared on her face.

"Yes?"

Sebastian had never believed in premonitions, but he sensed he wouldn't like what the maid was going to say next.

"I'm Poppy, my Lady. Lady Everleigh's maid."

Fuck.

Besides not believing in premonitions, Sebastian didn't believe much in Divinity either. His life had not given him many reasons to be devout. But that day, sitting in a corner in a communal room, hands joined between his legs, head bent down, he prayed. He prayed for another possible explanation for what he had seen, for Lady Everleigh's maid's presence. She could have been travelling to visit her family, or the Duke had given her a few days off...He had misheard, and it was another unfortunate woman lying broken upstairs.

To confirm the futility of his efforts, when the country physician came down the stairs, he asked for a "female relative to follow him inside Miss Kington's room" while asking the maid to fetch some clean cloth. Sebastian didn't know why nobody corrected him on the right form of address, but he didn't really much care. His eyes followed a pale and silent Lady Eleanor until her back disappeared up the staircase, leaving him alone with her plainly clad companion.

Time passed, and for each minute that went by without knowing Lady Everleigh's conditions, his worry increased. He had seen enough bloodshed to understand with a swift glance when a situation was dire. Head wounds and blood loss were never auspicious, in and out a battlefield. Lives were lost for less. He really hoped the physician was doing his job right because the man didn't fully understand the implications. More than one life was at stake.

His friend's rare smiles flashes before his eyes. Sebastian had never seen the Duke of Blakeburne so riled up in all the years he had known him. Gabriel lived his life according to exact standards and with a serious approach to everything, thanks to his arsehole of a Father. But since meeting Ivy Kington, he had seen his friend unsettled, nervous, incensed, impassioned...happy. A complete arse sometimes and his own worst enemy, but Sebastian had been confident that, given time, he would have come up to scratch. Or Lady Everleigh would have forcibly dragged him towards happiness. But time was a luxury that many didn't have.

When noises came from the staircase, Sebastian realised he had been completely lost in his thoughts. Lady Eleanor appeared and, upon seeing him still there, made a sudden beeline for him, said something on the line of "My Lord, what a tragedy!" and collapsed in a dead weight in his arms.

Heart heavier than lead, he deposited Lady Eleanor on a wing chair and, with the aid of her companion, waited for her to recover from her fainting spell. He was becoming impatient and had decided to search for the physician himself when she finally opened her eyes. Only to deliver the coup de grâce to any hope he was still harbouring that everything was going to be fine.

"Oh, dear. Now I must go back to London. Poor Uncle…" She went on talking about making arrangements, but Sebastian had heard enough. He rose from where he was crouched in front of the wing chair and, with a brief farewell, left Lady Eleanor in her companion's capable hands. Every step he took felt like an enormous feat, every heartbeat like a bullet going through him. It was time for him to board a ship that would bring him in front of the man he considered a brother. To tell him what Sebastian was leaving behind him in an inn on the road to Dover.

She was the light that shined in Gabriel's eyes. And he would be the one to douse it forever.

❖ ❖ ❖

Oh, for fuck's sake! What were they waiting for? Leaving Stattford's tent after yet another useless conversation that resulted in "let's wait for Wellington's orders," Gabriel was letting out his frustration and boredom by personally rubbing down his stallion. He was losing his bloody mind waiting for a decision on how to proceed. Any decision. It was true that many great military strategies in history involved waiting. Hell, *his* strategies were often based on it, and, without false modesty, he was one of the best. But that was bordering on ridiculous. While Monarchs and Tsars bickered, his troops were simultaneously bored and anxious. It wasn't an easy feat creating that kind of atmosphere, he had to give the rulers that. What was worse, one of the few things that kept the men going, letters from home, had become sporadic and irregular. It drove organised Lieutenant Rivers crazy, seeing his pride and joy succumb to its own fragility. For his part, Gabriel didn't miss the remainder of his broken promise. He missed her, though. And that partially contributed to his frustration. *More than partially. Fair enough.*

At least they would soon be joined by the rest of the men. The air was slowly shifting.

As if he had evoked them, the sound of voices drew his attention to the rear side of the camp, where men were uproariously greeting each other with pats on the back. At the centre of the melee, obviously, was Bellmore. The man was able to galvanise the soldiers through his presence alone. He maybe didn't instil deference as Gabriel did, but he didn't command any less respect. When Bellmore finally spotted Gabriel, he immediately made his way towards him. As he came near, Gabriel saw his countenance change completely. His shoulders seemed to bend as if carrying the weight of the world. He had seen his friend that way only once before, and foreboding fell on him. When Bellmore couldn't meet his eyes at first, he knew something was wrong. And the moment he did, ghosts from the past came back to haunt the present. Something was *very* wrong.

"Dear Lord, what happened?"

Chapter Twenty-Four

*D*ead.

She was dead.

His very reason for breathing was dead.

It was funny how he had never really understood the depth of his love for Ivy until that very moment. Until it turned into devastation.

He looked at Bellmore, a man who had always been a good friend to him.

"I don't believe you. How can you know this? She is in London; she wrote to me."

"She must have written her last letter weeks ago. I'm so sorry. I was there when they brought her inside the inn, after...." His voice trailed off, leaving the sentence —and its implication—hanging heavily between them.

"How did it happen?" he whispered. Or maybe shouted, to rise above the single word resonating in his ears: dead.

Dead.

"I don't know why she left London. Something must have triggered her departure..."

Gabriel didn't want to believe it, but he already knew why. She had told him, hadn't she?

It was his fault.

"I don't believe you. It's impossible! She's in London, where I left her. Safe and unharmed. And *alive.*" He almost choked on the last word.

"I'm so sorry, Gabriel. I was there. I would give everything not to be the bearer of such news and—"

Gabriel didn't let him finish. At any other time, he would never have condoned that kind of behaviour in others, but he didn't care. If what Bellmore was saying was true, nothing mattered anymore. God, why had it become so hard to breathe?

"How did she...?"

"Does it really matter? Gabriel, take a moment. Don't torture yourself...."

"TELL ME!" he shouted. His world was falling apart. Crumbling, like the ruins of the old Abbey that stood on his land. Useless. Derelict. And Sebastian thought *that* was torture?

Dead. Ivy was dead.

"Here is what I know. I was on the road to Dover, and, despite the travelling conditions, I made a good time, leaving me with some time to kill. So, I stopped at this inn to spend the night. The next day, I was sipping my ale when somebody was carried inside by a footman and a man looking like a coachman. A maid was asking for a physician to be summoned, but all I saw was dark brown hair belonging to a woman, and blood. A lot of blood."

Gabriel paled. Not at the thought of blood, but at the thought of *Ivy's* blood. Of life draining from her drop after drop. A knife was slowly and painfully going through his heart. He welcomed the pain.

He would have taken the excruciating pain again and again if it meant it wouldn't touch Ivy.

"I stayed out of their way as they carried her upstairs. After a while, twenty minutes or so, the physician arrived and shut himself inside the room they had put her in, only reappearing to summon Lady Eleanor inside."

The faint flame of hope that stubbornly resisted within him, wishing that the whole story was only a sick joke or that Bellmore had mistaken another woman for his Ivy, began to waver. He didn't even think of questioning Ivy's cousin's presence.

"Lady Eleanor had been pestering me with conversation before they arrived, but became utterly useless when, after talking to the physician, seeing me, in a melodramatic fashion, she exclaimed, 'My Lord, what a tragedy!' and, launching herself through the room at me, fainted."

Gabriel listened to this part of the story with mounting impatience, a cluster of emotions swelling inside him and reaching the surface: anger, disbelief, desperation and, above all, pain. A lot of pain.

"I don't give a fuck about Lady Eleanor or her theatrics. She could still be laying on the floor for all I care."

Bellmore gave him a stricken look and continued, his voice low, "I know, I'm sorry, Gabe. Naturally, I wanted to make sense of Lady Eleanor's rumblings. So, after I left her, I walked up to the coachman, who was talking to a farm boy, and the fellow explained to me that there had been a terrible accident on the road. He didn't know how it had been possible for both the carriage hinder axle and the splinter bar to break at the same time. He'd blamed the roads. This fucking weather. But no one could dissuade Lady Everleigh from undertaking the journey, regardless of the dangers."

With each word, the knife was slowly embedding deeper and deeper in Gabriel's heart. He deserved it.

"John Coachman tried his damnedest but couldn't slow the horses down and, with a broken splinter, it was impossible to save the carriage. When it overturned, he, the groom, and the maid —who were travelling on top as well— were able to jump down, and they got away with only a few scratches, but Lady Everleigh..." Bellmore hesitated, swallowing hard, "She was thrown out of the carriage and was lying on the road when they went looking for her."

Gabriel was staring, unseeing, at the sky outside his tent, unable to speak, to move. Which was surprising, seeing the tangle of emotions raging inside him only moments before. Only some of Bellmore's words registered in his mind, but the Viscount continued to finish his shattering story.

"Before I left, Lady Eleanor told me she was going back to London to inform her family and 'make arrangements for her cousin'. I had to come here to tell you in person before the news travelled on its own."

Gabriel still hadn't said a word or moved a muscle. In his head, the chaos was reaching an alarming level. He wanted to shout at Bellmore that he was mistaken, that Gabriel would have felt something if her heart had stopped beating. And why hadn't the Viscount insisted on seeing her for himself and staying with her, so that she wouldn't have felt alone, even after she...Oh, God.

Dukes don't show joy or despair, dukes don't show affection or pain.

Ironically, Gabriel held on to his father's mantra like a flicker of light in the darkness threatening to swallow him whole, even if that light was cold and unwelcoming. It was all he had left.

Something must have shown in his eyes because Bellmore took a step towards him. Before Gabriel could say anything to stop him, Lieutenant Rivers entered the tent, oblivious to what was unfolding.

"Begging your pardon Major, the post finally came, and there's a letter for you."

Gabriel took the letter from the soldier's hand and froze. Immediately, he recognised the handwriting. He went to open it, but his hands were shaking. *Strange that.* His hands never shook. At the second try, he succeeded in tearing the seal open.

My dear Blakeburne,

It is my deepest wish that this letter finds you well. Of the last few weeks, I will always remember the state of worry that accompanied me until news of your well-being reached London. I was scared. Scared of what your silence could have meant. I have started this letter a thousand times in a thousand different ways, and my fireplace will be the only keeper of all my failed attempts to translate my thoughts into words. My first instinct has been not to bother you with my letters anymore, for surely by now, you would have realised that I am not an important enough part of your life to waste your ink, or even your thought, on.

The thing is that, unfortunately, or not, I won't accept it anymore. I will not stand in the corner of my life, waiting for others to realise that I am worth the effort of caring about, of staying, of coming back, or that simply I deserve the consideration of explaining why I am not enough.

I will be brave. I wouldn't dare compare this to the battles you are fighting, but I still think it takes courage to face one's deepest fears. So, I am coming to find you. I promised you long ago that I would, did I not? Lots can happen between now and the moment I'll finally be with you again, but I'm certain we'll meet again soon. Even if it is only to say goodbye. I won't even contemplate the alternative reason for your silence.

See you soon, my love. Forever Yours,

Best regards,

I.K.

Gabriel read the letter, each word like a drop of acid on his skin. Ironically enough, it wasn't what was written that finally broke the iron manacles on his control. Rather, it was what was stricken out. Those six little words crossed over with a bold black line, probably carelessly written but carefully concealed, just visible enough to be seen by someone who was searching for them.

See you soon, my love. Forever Yours,

Everything shattered, inside and out. Gabriel swept a furious hand over his desk, sending everything flying. Documents, quills, ink, all created a cacophony of noise crashing on the ground, all too similar to what was happening inside Gabriel's head. The shards of glass were not the pieces of his heart breaking, but rather his very soul splintering into tiny fragments, forever lost, impossible to put back together.

Lieutenant Rivers took a reflexive step back and shot a worried look at Bellmore, who, after a stunned moment, was trying to reach Gabriel. He put what was meant to be a comforting hand on his shoulder, but Gabriel shrugged it off as if it burned him.

"Leave me," he whispered.

"Gabriel..."

"I said, leave me! The both of you!" he roared.

"Gabe, I don't think—," Bellmore insisted, but he didn't get to finish his sentence. With a shove, Gabriel moved him away from him and exited his tent. He shouted for someone to saddle his horse, starting however to walk in the opposite direction, immediately forgetting the issued order. He walked across the campsite, not really seeing where he was going, oblivious to the soldiers respectfully greeting him, while the smartest ones jumped out of his way.

After much aimlessly roaming, something permeated the fog that was enveloping Gabriel. Lieutenant Colonel Huntington's and Colonel Stattford's voices.

"Two days from now, at dawn, we will lead a surprise attack," the Colonel was saying.

"Agreed. It will be brutal, but it's the best course. We can't spend more days here without doing anything but giving more time for them to organise themselves," replied Huntington.

"Let's call a meeting with the other officers and start dividing the men to..." Gabriel stopped listening and moved away from the tent. An hour ago, it would have been welcome news. The wait was over.

Yes, the odds of dying in battle were high, but it would also have meant the time to go home was drawing nearer. Home to Ivy.

Now...now it only meant the end.

I'm certain we'll meet again soon.

Chapter Twenty-Five

*D*id they stay above a blacksmith's shop overnight? That was the first thought crossing Ivy's mind when she tried to open her eyes. It was the only explanation for the brutal hammering resounding inside her skull. What time was it? The earlier they started the journey, the sooner they would reach Dover.

Wait, something wasn't right. Where was she? She didn't remember stopping. Slowly, the room came into focus, but nothing Ivy laid her eyes on looked familiar. The room, basked in what looked like the afternoon light, was sparsely furnished, with the bare necessities for a night stay: a simple table and two chairs near the fireplace, a mirror, and a basin at the far side of the room. Ivy slowly turned her head towards the open window on her left, from which the sounds of horses and coaches mixed with voices. A coaching inn then.

"How did I..." she whispered hoarsely to no one in particular.

"My Lady! You are awake!" Poppy's familiar voice came from near her head. Her maid sat on an uncomfortable-looking wooden chair at her bedside. She immediately put her embroidery down and stood.

"Poppy, where are we?" Ivy asked. She tried to sit but stopped as a stab of pain in her leg joined the pounding in her head.

"Oh, my Lady! We were all so scared! You were layin' there, in the middle of the road and you weren't movin'..."

Ivy remembered the ominous crack and John's shout before the carriage tilted dangerously. She touched her head and winced when her fingers brushed against her temple. She decided to pay attention to her body and catalogue her injuries, concluding that, besides her head and leg, everything else seemed to be intact. Some other aches here and there. Well, it could have been worse.

Poppy was still talking about the accident, and Ivy forced herself to pay attention and fill the void.

"A farm boy, Bernard's the name, was workin' nearby and heard the crash. He came runnin' and brought us to this inn. John, Henry and I luckily are uninjured —a bit black an' blue. John's blamin' 'imself for not noticin' that somethin' was off with the carriage. The physician 'as already been 'ere and Lady Eleanor 'as told anyone how worried she was for you!"

Ivy was grateful that nobody else had been hurt. Her fuzzy mind struggled to absorb everything Poppy was saying, some of which didn't make sense.

"My cousin is here?" What was Eleanor doing there while there were still entertainments in London? It was true that Uncle George's estate was in Kent, and the road to it, up to a certain point, was the same as the one to Dover, but still, what were the odds? Ivy didn't doubt that her cousin had used this unfortunate event to show her flair for the dramatic at its finest. She immediately scolded herself for her spiteful thought, but, in her defence, she was still a bit foggy from the head wound, and it was difficult to summon equanimity when the blacksmith inside her head was forging armours for every medieval knight that had ever existed.

"Yes, my Lady, she was here and mighty worried, she was," Poppy was saying. "She was the one talkin' to the physician after he examined you. She insisted on going back to inform your family of your accident."

Great, thought Ivy. If ever her family was not already descending on her in a cloud of aristocratic wrath, learning of her accident would surely push them over the edge. Nothing could have stopped Eleanor from pointing out how much more of a proper lady than Ivy she was.

"When did she leave?" she asked, battling with the need of sparing her family any needless worry. Maybe she could catch up with her.

"Almost two days ago." Ah well, Ivy couldn't very well go back all the way to London to stop her cousin from being petty.

"Have I been unconscious for so long?"

"You hit your head pretty hard. The physician said it's normal."

Poppy went on expressing her relief that she was alive by chatting animatedly. Ivy was listening with half an ear when her maid said, "Then somethin' a bit strange 'appened. I don't know what exactly, but when I stepped in the communal room for a moment to bring John somethin' to eat, I saw Lady Eleanor approachin' Lord Bellmore with a sad look on 'er face."

"What? Lord Bellmore was here as well?" Ivy exclaimed, wincing as pain pierced her head. Had her invitation to the blasted garden party hosted in this inn been lost in the post?

"Is he, at least, still here? I would like to talk to him."

"No, my Lady. That was what I was tryin' to tell you. When Lady Eleanor left the physician, she was lookin' very forlorn and rushed to Lord Bellmore and fainted. It must 'ave been too much for 'er delicate sensibilities." Ivy really doubted that. "I wondered why she did that when the physician was confident you'd recover. When she came around, she said some garbled things, but I don't know what went down because I came back to your room. The only thing I know is that

274

Lord Bellmore left immediately after. I saw His Lordship from the window."

That was strange, admitted Ivy. What could Eleanor have said to make Lord Bellmore leave in such a hurry? "Poppy, do you remember what my cousin said to Lord Bellmore? Try to repeat the exact same words, if you can, please," Ivy asked with a sense of dread.

"It was somethin' like 'makin' plans for you', my Lady. No, I'm sorry, it wasn't makin' plans, it was..."

"Making arrangement?" Ivy completed, silently sparing a few chosen words for her dear cousin.

"Yes, exactly, my Lady! Arrangements, that's what she said."

Ivy's heart was pounding in a staccato worse than the one in her head. What Eleanor had carelessly —she refused to believe she had done it on purpose— said was what people delicately said when they had to organise a funeral.

"Do you know where the Viscount was headed?" But Ivy already knew the answer. Unlike her cousin, Bellmore had a valid reason for being there. To cross the Channel and join his regiment.

"John said he was bound for the port," confirmed Poppy.

"We must find a carriage. Immediately. I imagine ours is unserviceable. We have to leave," Ivy said frantically.

"But, my Lady, the physician said you must rest for at least a sennight, and your leg is..."

"Poppy, I don't care. I have to go. I have to reach him." She had to reach Gabriel or at least catch up with Bellmore before he reached Gabriel. Because Ivy was sure that he was headed in his direction. To tell Gabriel she was dead.

Everybody tried to stop her from leaving, especially after Ivy had ordered Poppy to stay behind. Even the stern grey-haired physician, who had come to check on her, had firmly forbidden her from leaving the bed, let alone to order a carriage and board a ship. Poppy begged her to write a letter and have it hand-delivered instead, but it would have been difficult to find someone willing to brave the perils to reach the camp and, truth be told, she didn't have the heart to ask someone to do it. Moreover, she wanted to be sure Gabriel saw her in the flesh.

In the end, she compromised by spending another night at the inn, seeing that, because of all that arguing, the sun was already setting. Being a Countess, however, had taught her that, in the end, she had the upper hand. The innkeeper reluctantly agreed to find a carriage and have fresh horses readied for the following day.

Ivy still hadn't left the bed, but her imminent departure required some level of independent movement. So, in a rare moment alone, she tried to stand up on her own. The first few steps gave her a sense of confidence, promptly shattered when she went to open the door, turning slightly to the side. She cried out, losing her balance right through the door. Her fall was mercifully stopped by a warm body, smelling of…bread?

After a surprised grunt, firm hands steadied her.

"Miss! What are you doing out of bed?" Ivy was sure she hadn't met the middle-aged woman who stood in front of her. Her apron indicated that she was employed by the inn in some capacity, as did the fact she apparently was aware she was injured.

"I'm so sorry, I—"

"Poor dear! You shouldn't be up and about! Come sit near the fire and let me bring you a nice hot cup of tea. I'm Mrs Swan." Her firm grip on Ivy's arm didn't leave her many choices.

Once seated with a cup of tea warming her hands, Ivy discovered that Mrs Swan owned the inn where she was staying, The Limping Duck, together with her husband. She found it very amusing that the Swans had named their establishment The Limping Duck. Or maybe it was the brandy lacing her tea. "For a quicker recovery," the older woman had said.

When the grandfather clock struck seven, her cup was replaced by a plate of beef pie, the slice bigger than anything she could ever eat.

"Now, my dear, you have to eat it all. Then, you'll finally tell Mrs Swan what happened to a sweet thing like you to bring such sadness to your eyes. And do not try to pull the wool over this ol' woman's eyes. It has nothing to do with the accident." Ivy suppressed a smile at Mrs Swan's lack of deference. She had soon discovered that nobody had informed the innkeepers that she was a Countess, probably in a desperate attempt to salvage her reputation. Ivy didn't bother to correct them. Mrs Swan's sincere motherly concern made Ivy tell her a brief version of the events.

"So, you see, this is why I have to reach him as fast as I can." At the end of her tale, Mrs Swan was all teary-eyed. She patted Ivy's knee and rose.

"I've seen many people passing by in all my years here. I've heard many stories, so let me tell you something. He'd be a fool not to appreciate what a treasure you are."

Ivy fought back tears at the innkeeper's kind words. You would think that the most important people in your life would be the ones to leave a profound mark on you. Which was mostly true. Sometimes, however, we could see ourselves clearly only through the eyes of someone truly unexpected. The first impression from a stranger, a remark made by someone you hadn't seen in years. People who would never know the role they played in your life.

"Thank you again for everything, Mrs Swan. For staying up so late, for listening to me..."

"Oh, don't worry about it, Miss. Sleep well, and let me know if you need anything."

"Goodnight, Mrs Swan."

Careful not to put too much weight on her leg, Ivy went back to bed. Her mind wouldn't stop going back to Gabriel. Had Bellmore already reached him? She closed her eyes and pictured his face, trying to think about anything else that wasn't the pain in her leg, in her heart, or what she would do when —*if*— she would find Gabriel.

After what seemed like seconds, a knock at the door alerted Ivy that it was time to go. Time to finally find him.

❊ ❊ ❊

When someone tells you that when there is something really important you have to do, you feel neither hunger nor fatigue? Well, they lie, mused Ivy. *You feel everything, every mundane need of your body.* She was exhausted. Her head felt slightly better, the pounding less insistent, but the carriage rolling wasn't improving her dizziness and nausea. She tried to look on the bright side. Land was back under her feet. Crossing the Channel had been one of the worst experiences of her life. And Ivy wasn't one prone to exaggeration, unlike someone who was probably already in London raising a breeze.

At least she hadn't had problems obtaining the information she needed from the men who put the advertisement in *The Times*. The letter she had sent ahead might not have been enough, but the fat purse she had sent with Henry at the tavern where they were to meet was. With the delay her accident had caused, Ivy wasn't sure they would still be able to find her Mr Smith. A reluctant Henry had gone to the meeting place and, when he had come back, had even more reluctantly handed her two pieces of paper, one containing a roughly drawn route for the continental side of her trip and one with the name of a boat, dock number, and date. The latter being the morning after.

What she had found had been a medium-sized mercantile, whose Captain hadn't batted an eyelid when a woman boarded his ship. *Ah, the wonder of golden coins.* Henry had been harder to convince. Especially when she had declared he was to remain in Dover.

"You have to stay here waiting for the Duke and Marquess's possible arrival to stop them from crossing as well." Henry was shaking his head while she was talking. She hadn't told him that that had been her plan all along. The fewer people she put in danger, the better. She would have done the same with John Coachman, but when she had tried to talk to him, the man had given her a look that was so outraged Ivy had relented.

"I'm not leaving you alone, my Lady," Henry insisted. Ivy was forced to use the heavy weapons at her disposal.

"I'll not be alone, Henry. Poppy, on the other hand, will be left on her own so far away from home…." Ivy had been satisfied to see that the affection between her footman and maid had trampled any obligation he was feeling.

Once on board, the Captain had quickly informed her they would be having a smooth sailing, "if they don't decide to try to sink us." Ivy was aware of that real risk, but she would have hoped to keep her head under the sand for a while longer. At her anxious look, the Captain let out a guffaw.

"If you're worried now, you should have seen the Channel during the blockade. Now, then it was fun dodging the French." *Well, what could she possibly say to that?*

Unfortunately for the Captain's entertainment, the sea journey had mercifully gone without a hitch, apart from the small matter of her constant seasickness.

Ivy was now tapping her uninjured foot on a hired carriage's floor, fear and helplessness added to other, more physical, discomforts. Each mile seemed to stretch longer than the previous one. Her thoughts were divided between mentally urging the horses to run faster and the fear of what she would find. A stab of pain went to her heart at the thought of how Gabriel would react at the news of her death. Even if Ivy wasn't sure of Gabriel's feeling for her, of one thing she was sure:

Gabriel was honourable to a fault. He would blame himself for her death, knowing that the accident took place on the road to him.

Ivy would not allow it. She won't let him walk around carrying unnecessary guilt and maybe even jeopardising his safety because of it. She would show him that she was alive and well, and then she would punch him. If someone was going to hit him, it had better be her, for his callous treatment, not the French.

And then…if she had to, Ivy would say goodbye to him and go back to London, where she would start to learn how to live without him.

Breathe Ivy, come on, in and out, in and out.

Everything was going to be all right in the end. It had to be.

Inside the officers' tent, strategies were being discussed down to the finest details. The discussion among the highest ranks was very animated. Gabriel was sitting next to Lieutenant Colonel Huntington, trying to pay attention to aspects that could be crucial for the soldiers he led.

He had asked his second in command, Captain Harris, to attend. He wanted to make sure every word would be heard by someone levelheaded. He certainly was not, but even in the state he was in, he was sane enough not to put his men's lives at risk like that. He already had too much blood on his hands.

From the outside, he was displaying his usual stoic expression, arms crossed over his chest. Only upon a closer look one would notice that his eyes were vacant and empty.

"So, anything to add? Gentlemen, tomorrow is the day we finally defeat those bloody French." Nobody said anything, the finality of

Colonel Stattford's statement effectively putting an end to the discussion.

Officers dismissed, everybody exited the tent. The night before a battle was always a sort of spiritual moment mixed with the profane. Some soldiers would play a round or two of cards and dice; others would drink or be entertained by the women who always followed the regiment; others still would find a solitary spot to write a letter home. What they all had in common was that every soldier, down to the last one, was feeling that that night was a time for reflection. It was always the same on nights like those. Dreams fulfilled, hopes squashed, pain caused and suffered. Things left unsaid, and things yelled in anger. People never forgotten, and people neglected. All that was in the air that night. Gabriel could feel it in his lungs with every breath he tried to take.

"Major, would you like to join us for a cup?" hollered a young officer, spotting him.

He shook his head and moved on, sitting by a fire, mainly because nobody else was there. Gabriel stared at the flames dancing restlessly in front of him, feeling a warmth he didn't deserve. His thoughts obviously went to her, his Ivy. He couldn't understand how she could be gone from his world and he hadn't perceived it, how his heart had continued beating. He could still feel her with him, hear her voice, those surprisingly witty comments you didn't expect from somebody so quiet like her, but that made you laugh harder for it. How they argued, the tears he had caused when he had unintentionally hurt her with his coldness. His hands upon her and the pleasure of hers upon his skin. And the most painful thing of all: the regret for the choice he had made that had started the chain of events that had led to the tragedy.

He didn't know how much time had passed with him lost in his personal hell of longing and guilt before Bellmore sat beside him. Gabriel felt his friend's gaze on him and his struggle to find the words to say. In the end, Sebastian chose to remain silent, his familiar profile silhouetted in the black shadow. There wasn't anything to say, really, so they sat there, two men thinking about death.

Bellmore finally rose and, before leaving, turned to Gabriel. With a serious expression on his face, he said, "Try to get some rest, for tomorrow you owe to your men to be the leader they deserve. She wouldn't have wanted to weigh on their fate like that, least of all on yours. Say your goodbyes now, Gabe, and honour her by staying alive and bringing your men home." He then turned around and left.

Gabriel looked at the flames again. Bellmore was right. He had to ensure that his men had the best commanding officer they could.

His mind made up, he then started thinking about all the letters, whose dispatch depended on tomorrow's outcome, that were being written in that exact same moment, and wondered if they contained expressions of love, forgiveness, hate, or if the soldiers decided that in the end, all that mattered was saying goodbye and show someone that, even when tomorrow could bring only savagery, their thoughts were with them.

A letter, or the lack of one, was what had led Ivy to her journey to find him. A piece of paper and few drops of ink, and a lot less selfishness on his part, could have meant that Ivy would now be smiling at something someone was saying, safe in her family's bosom. Gabriel stood and walked towards his tent. He didn't sit at his desk. He instead stood, quill in hand, leaning on one arm over a piece of paper. It was too late to write the things she deserved.

He knew he was addressing his letter to someone who would never read it. In a fair world, it would have been her to receive the news of his death and not the other way around. She would have mourned him, he was sure, but war was war, and men died. She would have found peace and gone on and —Gabriel's heart constricted painfully at the thought— found someone worthy of her. He put the quill to the paper and wrote one single word:

Farewell.

❄ ❄ ❄

The morning should have seen the sun rising in a blue sky, prelude to a hot summer day. Instead, rain was pouring down on them like a punishment from the Gods. Despite the inclement weather, the camp was buzzing with activity, alive with anticipation. They had avoided preparing too much beforehand, maintaining misleading indolence. The plan was fairly simple if compared to great strategies in military history. Each officer would divide their soldiers into two units, one smaller than the other. They would then launch the attack with the first smaller groups, leaving the more numerous rear to add an element of surprise. It was risky, as all the surprise attacks usually were, but, on their side, they had the advantage of a bored enemy, hopefully, unaware that they had been gathering the bulk of the men in the past seemingly uneventful weeks.

Gabriel exited his tent, soul tired, with bloodshot eyes, looking around at the busy men with a sombre yet resolute expression on his face. His night had gone as one could have expected, with little to no sleep. Every time he had started to drift off, he had been plagued by nightmares of him running down a sloping hill while all around him a battle raged furiously. The clang of swords and the blast of firearms were deafening him, but the only thing he could do was run forward, an unknown force beckoning him. A woman stood alone, watching him. Ivy. When he had finally been near enough, however, Ivy had turned her back to him without a word. No matter how fast he had run, he couldn't reach her, to explain, to tell her he was sorry for the role he had played in her death. To simply tell her he loved her. He had woken each time with tears in his eyes and a pounding heart. He had then given up all thoughts of sleeping entirely, focusing instead on the details of his plan.

283

Now he was searching for a particular man amid the soldiers. Upon finding Captain Harris, he beckoned his second in command to him. Harris, having heard of Gabriel's outburst the previous day, approached warily. *Not a good start for a day of battle*, Gabriel thought darkly, *if you are scared of your own Major*.

"Captain, there's been a change of plans for our unit. Please, send someone to gather our men. I'll have a quick word with them. And while we wait, please come inside my tent, and I'll explain your new role as of today."

"Yes, Major," answered the ever-loyal but puzzled Captain Harris.

About ten minutes later, Gabriel was looking in his men's eyes, all gathered to listen to what they assumed were last-minute instructions. The downpour had reduced to a drizzle, making it possible to look at their trusting faces. He was more and more convinced of what he was about to do.

"Gentlemen," he began. "Today's an important day. You'll have to assume your position shortly, so I'll be brief. I will not lead you in battle today." Surprised murmurs rose from the ranks. "Due to reasons I will not divulge, I'm not in the frame of mind to be a good leader to you today. Suffice to say, I will not jeopardise the operation, and your lives, while I'm aware that my attention will not be one hundred per cent on my role. Therefore, as Major, it is in my power to leave the command to Captain Harris, a man I trust with my life and whose valour and military skills you all know and admire. I'm firmly convinced that the outcome of this battle, and maybe of the war, will not be compromised under his lead, but instead, the chances of victory will only increase. Something I can't, in good faith, guarantee, were you under my command."

A voice rose from amid the men. "Running scared, are we, Major? What will you do while we fight for our King and Country?"

"Who said that? How dare you speak this way to your Major!" shouted Captain Harris, leaping to Gabriel's defence.

"It's all right, Captain," appeased Gabriel. "It's a justifiable question. They have the right to feel this way. However, I haven't said I will not fight alongside you. Just that you'll answer to the Captain here and not to me. In fact, I will stand with the infantry. We want to surprise the enemy, and surprise them we will."

Shocked gasps met his last announcement, and even the soldier who had insubordinately raised his voice was rendered speechless. Looking closely at Major Eastham, Duke of Blakeburne, they all saw the same thing. A proud man who appeared haunted, putting his men before military glory. Nobody raised any objection.

"Everything has already been cleared with Lieutenant Colonel Huntington. Therefore, now that you are all aware of the change in command, we can all take our position and resume our preparations. Thank you, gentlemen and good luck!"

The soldiers scattered, mostly in small groups, discussing the strange and unforeseen development. It didn't change anything for them practically, but such a decision coming from a man widely known for his courage and honour, paired with his strange behaviour the day before, surely meant that something dire had happened to him. Leaving the relative safety of the officers' ranks in favour of the front line was dangerous and, possibly, fatal. Speculations began to fly wildly, but the distraction was cut short by the realisation that the hour was drawing near and that, maybe, there were better chances of victory, and survival, with a man not chased by demons as their leader.

Gabriel watched his men go and, turning towards Captain Harris, said, "Good, now that this's done, I have to talk to Captain Sinclair. See you out there, Captain." Harris acknowledged Gabriel's words and took his leave.

Gabriel turned and started walking in the opposite direction. He hadn't been completely honest either with Captain Harris or with his men. What he had said was true. He wasn't the right man to lead his soldiers and was sure of his decision to put the Captain in his stead. The young man had served under him for a long time and knew what to do. What wasn't true was the Colonel's approval of him stepping down or even his knowledge of Gabriel's real intentions.

He had used the last strength he possessed to talk to the troops like a Major. Now he was drained and hanging on by a thread. He couldn't even stand to talk to Bellmore and see the compassion in his eyes. Walking through the camp, he noticed that everything was ready. It was almost time.

He didn't have to hide his desolation anymore. With his shattered heart reflected in his eyes, he started walking towards the open field.

Chapter Twenty-Six

Ivy reached the outskirt of the camp just as the sun was starting to rise in the sky. Or, better said, when the light started to make the outline of the tents visible. *So, this is a battlefield*, she thought, alighting the carriage at a fair distance from the bustling men in uniform. John had stopped the carriage a good quarter of a mile away from the external tents that marked the perimeter of the British camp. Her less than graceful descent was accompanied by the squishing sound of her boots hitting mud. It hadn't stopped raining since her arrival on the Continent, belying the fact that it was supposed to be June.

"They won't allow us to go further, my Lady. Someone ought to notice us soon, and they'll ask us to leave, mark my words," said John with a mulish expression. "Can't blame them, really. We shouldn't be here; you shouldn't be here, my Lady. It's too dangerous. Maybe it's for the best that they'll send us on our way in a couple of minutes," the Coachman continued stubbornly. John had adamantly refused to remain behind, but that didn't mean he was happy with her and their destination. And he wasn't shy about voicing it. It wasn't just the rain that hadn't stopped since they had set foot on that side of the Channel.

"Truth be told, I'm surprised we even came this far, John. I expected more soldiers patrolling the area. Something must be happening in the camp," Ivy conjectured. "I might as well try to walk in there. Well, limp in there." She was frustrated by the slowness of her steps and by the heavy limp she was sporting because of her injury.

"Somebody will stop you, my Lady, right when you step foot in the camp."

"Good! The sooner I can attract someone's attention, the sooner they will bring me to Blakeburne. Now, John, you stay here and tend to the horses. You have to be ready to leave immediately if needed!" Ivy shouted, already walking away from him. She would not put John in danger because of her gamble.

John's words proved to be true. If she had ever felt invisible in her life, now the opposite was true. Each step she took attracted the attention of different soldiers, who stopped in their tracks to stare at her. Because of her limping gait or simply because she was a woman in a military camp, she didn't know. Their surprise, however, worked to her advantage: nobody approached her, too stunned by the sudden apparition of madwoman inelegantly rushing through their camp. *Fine, I don't look remotely my best, but this is hardly flattering. Come on fellows, you are at war, shouldn't you be a bit more responsive to incursions, for God's sake?* Ivy decided to approach the soldier in front of her.

"Excuse me?" she said loudly, to be heard above the noise of the men moving about. The man turned, startled by the sound of a female voice. He was pleasant-looking, blond, with brown eyes. He stood only a couple of inches taller than her, but he exuded an aura of calm and confidence that immediately made Ivy trust him. Not that she had a choice, really.

"Who are you? How did you come to be here, madam?" he asked without preamble, suspicious.

"I'm Lady Ivy Kington, Countess of Everleigh. I'm here for the Duke of Blakeburne or, more aptly in this case, Major Eastham, so if you would be so kind as to show me where I can find him, I would be most obliged and—"

"Listen, madam," the man interrupted brusquely, "I'm not a fool. What would an English Countess do here, during a war? I don't know how you know the Major or if you are his ladybird, but I cannot let you stay here now, and I won't certainly show you around."

Before Ivy could reply to his impertinence, another man spoke from behind her shoulders.

"Captain Harris, I thought you said all the women who entertained the good soldiers last night had been sent on their way. So, what is this dove still doing here? No offence, love."

Recognising the owner of the voice, Ivy turned, relieved. "I will tell you if none will be taken if you help me, my Lord Bellmore." Upon seeing her face, the Viscount turned white as a sheet. He looked like someone had punched him in his midsection. He even took a step back. Only seeing a ghost would have stunned him more. Well, in that case, it was as if he was seeing one.

"Lady Everleigh, but...I saw...You are dead!" Bellmore exclaimed. She would have laughed at his accusing tone, but she didn't have the time.

"As you can see, my Lord, that's not the case. A bit battered, for sure, but alive. I would very much like to hear how you came to think that I had departed this world, but that will have to wait. Now, if one of you gentlemen could please tell me where I can find Blakeburne, I've already wasted too much time," Ivy said curtly.

"So, *she* is the reason why the Major was in such a state yesterday and this morning," the Captain said knowingly, perusing her openly from head to toe. Quite rudely, in her opinion. Maybe it was Ivy's preconception, but he didn't seem impressed. At Bellmore's nod, Ivy's patience snapped.

"Listen to me, gentlemen, and listen very carefully. In the past days, I've travelled more miles than I care to count. A carriage accident has almost killed me and has left me even now standing on only one good leg and with a splitting headache you're worsening. And now I must stand here while two men are staring at me, cataloguing my physical attribute and wondering what all the fuss is about? You will either tell me where I can find Blakeburne, or I will find him myself. Even if I had to search each tent personally. Have I made myself clear?" Ivy was very proud of her little speech and even more so when she saw the men's abashed expressions.

"My humblest apologies Lady Everleigh," Bellmore said regretfully, followed by a deeply ashamed Captain Harris.

"You are right, my Lady. There's no excuse for my behaviour. Please forgive me. Now, if you would be so kind as to wait here, Captain Bellmore and I will fetch the Major for you. He should be among the men on the north side of the camp. However, what I, rather tactlessly, said is true. This is no place for a Lady."

"Thank you, Captain, I think," Ivy replied, watching Bellmore falling into step with him and saying something she couldn't catch.

Ivy watched the men go, hoping they would find Gabriel quickly. The hustle around her could only mean that something important was about to happen, and she was in the way, standing there, unmoving. After the third soldier carrying ammunition apologised for bumping into her before stopping, wide-eyed, to look at the strange creature out of place like a prizefighter at Almack's, she decided to step aside.

Lovely, it seems they are ready to attack. Her timing was perfect. After months of indolence, they had to launch an offensive *that* day. After a few painful steps, she stopped under a tree. From her standing point, she could understand why they had chosen that place for their camp. The plateau allowed an unobstructed view of the sloping hillside, where everything, and everyone, was easy to spot, even from a fair distance. On sunny days, when the air was clear and no fog hindered the eye, no instrument would be needed to see into the enemy's camp.

Ivy could still discern men on the other side going about their mundane activities. Nothing more menacing than what she supposed were everyday tasks during warfare: cleaning swords and rifles, moving cannons around, taking care of horses.

Ivy was perusing the French tents, noticing that someone must have been paying attention to the changes in the behaviour of the soldiers this side of the front, after all. The calm was being disrupted by running sentinels.

Then, a movement caught her eye. A splash of colour amid the green of the grass. A lone man, wearing a red uniform, was slowly walking down the hill, alone. He seemed to be in no hurry to reach his destination, whatever it may have been, as if out for a stroll. What was an English soldier doing, parading unprotected like that?

Wait, that… Ivy's blood turned into ice, and fear gripped her heart in a vice. *No. Oh, God. Please, let me be mistaken.* But she knew that man. She would recognise him everywhere, even from afar. The proud stance of his shoulders, the elegant walk, his short dark hair. Gabriel Sherborne Eastham, Duke of Blakeburne, Major Eastham, and a series of other minor titles, one of the most influential and respected men in the British Isles and the love of Ivy's life, was walking alone down the field, like a moving practice target for the enemies' rifles.

"Bloody hell!" she shouted. "No, no, no!"

Before realising what she was doing, Ivy started to run.

Unhurriedly, Gabriel descended the hill. In a short while, it would be the theatre of a battle that could decide the fate of the war, and all he could think about was how peaceful it all looked. Even the rain was gentle. As if it understood. He stopped in the middle of the field.

Gabriel was pretty indifferent to all things religious, but now it seemed a good time to have a little chat with Himself above.

"Tell me, what was the meaning of all this? What was the point of making me feel like this, disrupting my perfectly orderly life, to then take it all brutally away?" Gabriel's hoarse voice was rising, eyes dry but unfocused. "She would *have* to cross my path, upturn my life! Then, You, fate —whoever is responsible for us miserable souls— had to take her away. What was the fucking sense of it all? You took her and left me here! But I am going to rectify the mistake."

Breathing deeply, Gabriel swept his gaze over the horizon towards the enemy's camp. He hoped his plan worked. He had failed the only person he had vowed never to hurt. Maybe his suffering would serve someone. The enemy would spot a lone man and puzzle over why he was there, whether some intricate plan was afoot. They would focus on the British camp, looking for signals. That little distraction would give the British a little more time to bring the men forward, slightly off the side. The French would surely fire upon him to eliminate any possible surprise. Then the battle would start. Gabriel would not be there to see it, but it was as it had to be. The Army had little use of an officer with no will to fight.

His thoughts went back to Ivy again. He remembered the first time he had seen her. How those intelligent eyes had sparkled up at him, surprised and embarrassed. How her deeper vulnerability called to him, asking him without words to care. How strong she really was when the time came to fight for the people she loved. He then thought of those forbidden, passionate moments they had shared and allowed himself to imagine a future they would never have. A future neither of them would see. What would she say if she saw him like this? A weak man whose influence and wealth didn't mean a thing in the end. She would be ashamed of him, perhaps, but she would never point the finger at him, blaming him for her death. Gabriel just knew it because he knew her heart like he knew his own.

It was time. The French must have noticed him by now. Giving in to his pain, he stopped and closed his eyes. "Forgive me, my love. If I could, I would let you breathe the air I've left in my lungs. Breathe what life still resides in me," he whispered. And waited.

Suddenly something hit him in the back, making him stumble forward a step before catching himself and standing upright again. *How was it possible?* he thought. Surely the blast would have come from the opposite direction. And where was the noise? The pain? He thought being hit by a grenade would feel a lot different. Not like two arms embracing him. And then he felt, more than heard, a mouth moving against his shoulder blades.

"Gabriel! I'm here! Come, turn around and look at me!"

Ivy threw her body against Gabriel's back, unable to stop the momentum gained from her run down the hill. Immediately after spotting him, and just from the stiffness of his shoulders, she had understood with clarity what he was going to do. And she couldn't allow it. She couldn't believe her death had brought such extreme devastation, but it was the only possible explanation. After slamming against him, she had put her arms around him and was squeezing with all her might, scared to death for him, and herself, but also happy to be able to hug him again, to feel his powerful body in her arms.

"Gabriel, it's me, Ivy. It's all right, my love, look at me," she said soothingly, hesitant about what reaction he would have to a body thrown against him.

"I'm hearing voices now. It's almost as if I could feel you around me. I'd give everything to talk to you again, Ivy, but I know it's impossible. I'm so sorry. For everything," he said, his voice breaking, his eyes still closed.

"Gabriel, please, turn around." Finally, he turned within the circle of her arms. What Ivy saw broke her heart. Utter desolation reflected in his face. His beautiful green eyes, strangely glassy, were fixed on her, but it was clear he didn't believe he was looking at a real person but at something conjured by his mind.

"You are so beautiful," he said with heart-breaking tenderness and a soft smile on his lips.

"Gabriel! I'm here. I'm alive! Please, believe me." Ivy tried gently touching his cheek, but Gabriel shook his head, that odd smile still on his lips. He lifted a hand to touch her cheek in return, the gesture so loving that it brought tears to Ivy's eyes.

He didn't believe her. Wonderful. That wasn't working. Caresses and soft words were letting him believe she was some sort of apparition, a figment of his imagination. Well, then, time to change tactics.

"What the hell, Blakeburne? What in the bloody hell do you think you are doing? You come back to me this instant, you big oaf, or I am going to kick you in your shin until I pulverise it. I have pretty sturdy boots on," she shouted at him, shaking his shoulders for good measure. She had to admit that, even if she was doing this for him, it felt liberating for her as well, finally being able to express some frustration.

That seemed to sort some effect. Gabriel's eyes began to focus, blinking a few times.

"Ivy?" A kaleidoscope of emotions crossed his face. Disbelief, incredulity, hope, love even, only to set, pretty disappointingly, on horror. "*Fuck!* You are alive! How...what are you doing here? It's dangerous...."

BOOM!

An explosion resonated, too near for Ivy's taste.

"Bloody hell," Gabriel muttered.

Chapter Twenty-Seven

His plan had worked. All too well. Not only the French were aware of his presence on the field and had decided to eliminate a possible threat by firing at him, but Gabriel could see the British Army advancing from the right, rifles ready to fire. Looking down at the woman holding him, for a moment he lost himself in a sight he hadn't thought he could ever see again. Ivy was looking up at him with her beautiful brown eyes.

Yes, his plan had worked, but it had also spectacularly backfired because of one unforeseen factor: Ivy, alive and well, and now in real mortal danger, again, because of him. Damn Bellmore and his good intentions of rushing to his side in the moment of need. Damn Gabriel for being weak. And damn Ivy and her mad idea of saving him. The last wasn't true, Gabriel thought, still looking at her. She was the most beautiful thing he had ever seen, even with his rumpled clothes and bruised face.

"Ivy..." he tried again, his mind working furiously to evaluate all the possible ways to bring her far away before the two armies collided and the battle began in earnest. And crossing out each one of them. Looking around desperately, he evaluated that they only had a few more minutes. In the end, Gabriel decided to do the simplest of things. Run. Taking Ivy's hand in his own, he started running back towards the camp, scrutinising his surroundings for possible dangers.

❊ ❊ ❊

"They nearly hit us! We have to find cover!" she shouted, trying to keep up with him.

"We are on a bloody battlefield!" countered him. "Of course they have! They're firing from bloody cannons over there, aiming at us! You shouldn't be here..."

"Thank you very much for pointing it out, Gabriel. I didn't realise it on my own! What were *you* thinking? Of all the reckless, foolish things to do. I would have wanted you safe, regardless..." She decided to stop talking. It was too painful to think about what was going through his mind when he had decided to walk down the hill. Better save her breath for running. Her leg was hurting like hell, making her stumble every few steps, and she feared the stitches were giving out. But Gabriel, unaware of her injuries, was pulling her arm, willing her wordlessly to go faster. Maybe, if she had stopped to think, she would have realised that someone with two working legs would have been a better choice to be sent to stop Gabriel. He, however, would not have believed she was alive unless he had seen her with his own eyes. And even then, it had taken some convincing. Now, here they were, trying to save themselves from being killed. The irony wasn't lost to her.

In between these thoughts, Ivy was aware that Gabriel was still talking, mostly to himself. The noise was swallowing most of his words, but he was rambling about saving her. As if she would let him leave her side for the next twenty years, after that exploit.

"*We* will be safe. I'm not going without you. I came here to save you from committing the greatest mistake of your life," she panted, out of breath.

"You shouldn't have come here, for me..." he said, still looking ahead.

"You can't be serious! You did not expect me to do nothing, knowing that you..."

BOOM!

The enemy's aim was getting better now that all the attention was on the battlefield. They weren't the only target anymore, but now they were firing from different directions with multiple weapons. Ivy started to doubt they could make it, not with her slowing them down. Even her dark humour had deserted her.

Gabriel cursed foully when a bullet whistled near his head. *Too bloody close.*

Then it happened.

A violent blast hit the ground near their feet, a few inches behind their backs. The strength of the explosion sent them flying forward, and Gabriel couldn't reach her fast enough to break Ivy's fall. He could do nothing more than pull her in his arms before hitting the ground.

"I would much rather die this way than by being thrown out of a carriage," she whispered with a thread of voice before losing consciousness.

"Blakeburne! Eastham! Damn it, Gabriel! Lady Everleigh! Where are you?" Sebastian was restlessly searching among the bodies lying on the field for a sign of Gabriel and the Countess. He was shouting, alternating between calling for his friend, the lady, and cursing everything to hell. The battle was over, the British had won, but for Bellmore, the agony had just begun. He wasn't oblivious to the part he had played in that day's debacle.

"You had better not be dead, you two," he muttered under his breath. When he couldn't find Lady Everleigh where he had left her that morning, he had hoped she had decided to end that foolishness and go back to her carriage and off to the nearest town. Seeing the empty vehicle in the distance quickly disabused him of that notion.

Around him, the smell of death was unbearable, the sights gruesome. As always in those cases, the price to be paid for victory had been very high. The death count was still rising, and many more would die from the consequences of their wounds. He hoped he had not to visit two particular families in London upon his return.

After hours of search and almost blind by the rain pouring down in buckets, Bellmore was starting to lose hope. He coursed again when he almost stumbled in a hole in the ground, one of many created by the bast of firing cannons. Catching himself in time before falling headfirst into it, he straightened and, turning northwards, his eyes set on a sight that tore what was left of his heart apart. There, on the ground, laid Gabriel and Ivy. They were side by side, and his arms were around her. He will forever remember the look of peace that graced both their faces as if everything was finally all right.

"Oh hell." His voice wasn't more than a whisper. He reached them, hoping against hope to find any sign of life. Touching his friend's shoulder to turn him around, he was almost knocked out of his feet when Gabriel emitted a low moan and slowly opened his eyes, blinking slowly.

"You arse. I knew it. You are too stubborn to die this way, you son of a...."

Gabriel didn't know how long he had been out cold, but he certainly didn't welcome Bellmore throwing insults at him as first thing. After the initial shock of finding himself sprayed out in the open, he remembered where he was. *Ah yes, battlefield.*

He took stock of his conditions before moving. He was pleased to notice that, apart from the multiple bruises he would certainly sport soon, he seemed fine. Something was blocking his left arm, however. He looked down.

Ivy.

It all came rushing back, and he joisted up in a sitting position, pulling his arm from under her, careful however not to move her.

"Easy, my friend," said Bellmore. "We know nothing about your or Lady Everleigh's conditions."

Gabriel looked down and gently touched Ivy's cheek. "My love, please, wake up," he whispered desperately. He checked her body for injuries, despairing when even that didn't cause her to stir.

"No, God no..." Gathering his wits, Gabriel finally moved aside her hair, exposing her throat, to check for a pulse. The silence around him was broken only by his long exhale when he finally, *finally*, felt the weakest of heartbeats. A sound that caused the strongest surge of relief he had ever felt in his life.

"She is alive," he said in wonder.

Glad to have been spared from witnessing his friends falling apart for the second time in so many days, Bellmore sprang into action. "Gabriel, let's take her away from here. I'll bring the horses around. Are you able to stand?" Without turning and looking at Bellmore, Gabriel nodded. He didn't want to take his eyes away from Ivy and risk missing even the smallest sign that life was still in her. Her face was eerily pale, emphasising the contrast with a red cut and a dark purple bruise above her left temple. She wasn't bleeding, however, so it must have been the consequence of the carriage accident. "Come on, brave lass, don't give up now."

Bellmore returned, leading two horses, his chestnut stallion and a grey mare, which looked as tired as their human counterparts. Gabriel, now crunching down, picked up Ivy, a hand under her neck and an arm under her knees, wincing at the discomfort of his battered body. The movement seemed to be even more unpleasant for his precious cargo. Ivy emitted a low moan. Gabriel was relieved that Ivy was regaining a bit of consciousness but didn't relish causing her more pain than what she had already endured. Gingerly taking a few steps, Gabriel approached the grey horse, wondering how to mount it without putting Ivy down.

"Here, let me help. Give her to me." Gabriel traded her gently into the Viscount's arms. "Maybe it's better if I hold her."

"No!" The denial burst immediately from Gabriel's lips, louder than necessary. Straddling the horse with a groan, he insisted, "Give her back to me, now." Knowing it would be futile to argue, Bellmore silently put Ivy back in his arms and, mounting his own horse, together they started towards the camp, paying attention not to stumble on carcasses of other horses or weapons and keeping an eye for wounded soldiers. The atmosphere around them was one of death. Death of men, but also death of innocence, of heroic dreams. For those who were alive, looking around was like a punishment for their actions, a taste of what hell surely looked like.

The bouncing of the horse elicited another moan from Ivy. Looking down, Gabriel saw her eyes flutter open a sliver. Blinking, Ivy looked around and then up at him. "Are we dead for real this time? I hoped to be more comfortable, to be completely honest."

Gabriel let out a short laugh, surprised, making Bellmore turn his head around as well. "No, my dear, we still have things to do on this earth."

"Oh well, I better rest for a while longer then," she decided, her eyes already drifting shut. Gabriel kissed her forehead, "Rest, my love, I won't let anything else happen to you, I swear."

Ivy opened her eyes, blinking furiously to fight off the light. For the second time, she wasn't certain where she was.

It's becoming a habit. I'm not sure I like it. Pulling herself up on her elbows, she looked around, realising immediately she was alone, lying on a straw mattress covered by a sheet in a tent. She could hear low voices, sometimes swallowed by coughing and moaning, but she was separated from them by a makeshift screen made of other sheets. She was among wounded soldiers. As one of the few women probably present, the screen must be an attempt to save her modesty.

Probably hearing the rustling of bed sheets, a female head peeked at her side of the tent.

"My Lady, you are awake! How are you feeling?" the woman asked in a kind voice.

"Fine, I think. My head hurts. It's difficult to move my legs, but all that ailed me already before. My left side is very sore, though."

"That's hardly surprising. You fell on that side of your body, reopening the wound on your leg. You're very lucky. According to what Major Eastham told the physician, you are both lucky to be alive..."

"Gabriel! Is he well?" Ivy asked frantically, trying to sit up, only to be intercepted by the woman, who gently put a hand on her shoulder, preventing her from rising. Not that she could have accomplished it, feeling the sharp pain that shot through her.

"Now, none of that, my Lady. You have to stay abed; you are too weak to stand. Major Eastham is fine, only a little battered, and very worried about you. He's been here by your bedside from the moment he carried you here. Captain Bellmore had almost to manhandle him to convince him to leave you and be examined himself. He only relented when the Captain threatened to knock some sense into the

Major. He'll be upset he wasn't here when you woke up. He stepped outside half an hour ago to go change his clothes and eat something."

Ivy felt a profound relief knowing Gabriel was alive, well and mostly unhurt.

"Thank you, mmm...May I ask your name?"

"It's Christy Thomas, my Lady," answered the young woman. Ivy took a moment to look at her. She was really young —around eighteen, if she had to guess— and very pretty with red hair and big green eyes. She wondered what her story was, to be there, with the Army.

Suddenly, a commotion started from behind the screen, and Gabriel appeared. He looked, for lack of a better word, a fright. Oh, his clothes were pristine, his military uniform perfect. Those were, however, the only things that the man before her had in common with the Duke of Blakeburne she knew. His dark hair was in disarray from the many times he had run his hands through it, soft dark locks falling over his forehead. His face and neck were covered in dark bruises, contrasting dramatically with the green of his eyes. Ivy's perusal stopped there. Behind them, a multitude of emotions was raging war to seize control, and Ivy wasn't sure which one was going to win. The relief of seeing her reasonably well was shadowed by an overbearing mix of guilt and fear, looming over any tender feeling towards her. So intent she was on deciphering Gabriel's emotions, she saw the exact moment his self-control squashed everything, allowing him to approach her in a manner befitting a Duke. Or a Major.

"Lady Everleigh. I'm very glad to see you awake. How are you feeling? Is there anything you need?" Ivy was almost disappointed in having to deal with all that ducal politeness until he said, his eyes never leaving hers, "Miss Thomas, I believe Mr Phillips is asking for you. Something about dressings or bandages, I believe."

"Bless the man. A brilliant physician, but he can't find a thing without someone pointing at it. I'll come to check on you in a bit. Rest, my Lady, and don't try to get up." With a smile, she left them alone, not worried about the propriety, or the lack thereof, of the situation. The moment Miss Thomas turned around the screen, the mask fell off Gabriel's face, leaving everything exposed. She stopped breathing. In two steps, he covered the distance between them and crouched. A heartbeat after, he was kissing her. His lips were urgent on hers as if he couldn't help himself. Like a man needing air. Ivy didn't mind, though. On the contrary, she linked her hand around his neck and brought him closer, kissing him back with all the pent-up emotions she was feeling.

"Oh my God, Ivy," he said in between kisses, never lifting his lips more than a couple of inches from hers. "I thought you were dead. I was in hell, and I didn't want to crawl out." He then lifted his head to look at her face.

"How are you feeling?"

"I'm fine. I'll be up and about in no time." She tried to sit straighter up again, only to wince at the pain. Gabriel's eyes darkened.

"You are not fine! Don't you dare say you're fine!" Gabriel shouted. Ivy was taken aback by yet another sudden change in Gabriel. It seemed that now anger was commanding the troop. Anger towards what, she wasn't sure. Maybe her.

"Gabriel..." she started.

"No, Ivy. What were you thinking, parading through a battlefield like that? Bloody hell, what were you thinking travelling all the way here, alone? Do you know how stupid it was? Look at you, now." He waved a hand up and down her body.

Ivy was starting to lose her temper. She understood that probably Gabriel's rage was an outlet for his fear, but she had had enough. She was laying there, on a straw mattress, injured, and she wasn't in the mood to be berated only to let the man vent.

"What was *I* thinking? I was thinking about you, you idiotic oaf! I was trying to save your life. But had I known I would overcome all this only for my efforts to be called stupid, maybe I should have stayed in

London!" They were both shouting now. If only they had continued kissing forever, instead of talking.

"Exactly! London is your place, not here! Why did you even come? I don't want you here!" At these hurtful words, she recoiled as if he had slapped her. The fight went out her, emotional tiredness piling on physical aches. One moment it felt like the very breath he took depended on her. The next, they stood right at the beginning, arguing and insulting each other.

"Go away, Blakeburne. Surely there is something you would rather do, rather than be here. I need to rest. The sooner I recover, the sooner I can be on my way to London, where I belong, out of your hair." Ivy managed to utter these sentences coolly, piercing him with a glare.

"I'm not going anywhere, I—"

"I said. Leave. Me"

The anger on his face developed in absolute frostiness. "Fine, I will leave you to your rest, Madam." Gabriel bowed rigidly and left Ivy alone, aware that everyone in the tent had heard their heated argument. A few sheets weren't much for isolation. She sighed loudly. She wanted to punch him in the face for behaving like a self-centred idiot, but, barring that, she decided to concentrate on the next best thing. Getting better, to be back on her feet as soon as possible. After all, Gabriel was very tall, and she had to stand upright to reach his nose with her fist.

Angrily flapping the tent open, Gabriel marched outside, murmuring to himself, "Lord saves us from stubborn women." At his

304

approach, soldiers moved aside to let him pass for fear of being trampled by very polished boots belonging to a very angry man.

"Blakeburne! Oh, Blakeburne!"

Gabriel stopped, annoyed, at the sound of Bellmore's voice. By the tone of it, it wasn't the first time he had called him.

"What?"

"How is Lady Everleigh? I would have thought you couldn't be found far from her side, you two making doe eyes to each other." The man had the audacity to smirk. Not funny, old chap. Not funny at all.

"Ah! Let's just say, the latest events didn't put Lady Everleigh in a good mood. And to answer your question, she's laying in a straw bed, a leg bandaged, a head wound that is only now beginning to heal properly and countless other injuries. All because of me. No wonder she sent me away."

"I should say she isn't in a good mood. Who would? I find it odd, however, that she would show animosity towards you for no reason. Well, besides the fact she launched herself down the hill to stop your sorry arse from being killed." Gabriel felt bile rising at the thought. "You didn't, par chance, say something to upset her, did you?"

Gabriel regarded his friend with narrowed eyes, suspicious of why he would leap so readily to her defence. "How could you possibly know how she would react?"

"Well..." He appeared suddenly sheepish. "I may have spoken to her when she first arrived. She was so determined to find you that we, Captain Harris and I, relented and agreed to search for you. Let me tell you, Blakeburne, I envied you there. She was a force to be reckoned with. Didn't waste any time to put us in our place, all to find you," Bellmore finished, admiration clear in his voice, which Gabriel didn't like, not one bit.

"Be as it may, I simply asked her what she was possibly thinking in coming here. I also stated that I'd have preferred she stayed in London, where she'd have been safe, and not doing stupid, dangerous, things like this one," Gabriel repeated, in his opinion, reasonably.

"So, let me see If I understand correctly. To an injured woman, who literally walked through a battlefield for you, after being thrown by a moving carriage —her Coachman told me what really happened by the way— and forgoing the rightful time to recover, you say, let me paraphrase, that she is unwanted here and that her actions are stupid." Bellmore crossed his arms across his chest and regarded Gabriel with a raised eyebrow as if waiting for him to reach an epiphany.

"Of course, I didn't say she was unwanted! I...Oh, bloody hell." Gabriel closed his mouth, cursing himself. Could he be more of an arse? He had let all the weight of his worries overcome his good sense. He had shouted at a bedridden woman, for God's sake! After almost attacking her and kissing her without warning. He groaned, rubbing a hand on his face.

"Ah, I see you have seen the errors of your ways. I'm sure not everything is lost, my friend. Anyway, I came to find you for a reason other than inquiring about our lovely Lady. Colonel Stattford wants to see you."

It was to be expected, thought Gabriel. He hadn't foreseen that part of the plan because there shouldn't have been a time after the battle for him. He sighed again.

That was bound to be pleasant.

"I should make an example of you, Major! You could have cost us the victory! The war! Weeks and weeks of careful planning could have gone to hell because of your daft decisions!"

Gabriel had been standing for the last twenty minutes, listening to Colonel Stattford ranting about his actions and all the possible disastrous repercussions they could have had. He couldn't blame the man. Gabriel's plan *had* been sheer lunacy.

"Were it up to me, I would have you horsewhipped and squandered!" The Colonel's grey moustaches vibrated from the vehemence infused in his words. Spit was flying from his mouth, and a vein was throbbing worryingly in his red neck. He reminded Gabriel of a ferocious bulldog one of his tenants had when he was a lad. Gabriel stood silent, however, acknowledging the rightness of his accusations and ready to face whatever punishment his superior officers deemed fit for him.

"You should be executed!" Stattford took a deep breath, and the vein slowed its pulsing. "However, that ridiculous move of yours created a distraction we didn't know we needed," he added begrudgingly. "It seems to have helped surprise the French. Everywhere there is talk of heroism, maybe even of making you Colonel. In my opinion, this is all horseshite." He stabbed his index finger on the desk. "Something smells rotten here. Your actions spoke of something different than heroism. Those were self-destructive actions of a desperate man with nothing to lose." Nothing to say to that.

"Still, I can't deny the role you played in today's victory. You are one lucky fellow, Eastman. We are all lucky because, now that the war is almost over, you can go home and save His Majesty's Army from other *heroic* gestures." Ending his tirade, Colonel Stattford sat heavily on the chair behind his desk, weary from more than Gabriel's behaviour.

"Colonel, I agree with you. Were I in your shoes, I wouldn't tolerate an act of disobedience like this one. I'm ready to face the consequences of my actions. I can only explain myself by saying that in a moment when my life had lost its meaning, I had hoped to give one to my death, increasing our chances of victory." Gabriel held his head high, the proud stance the one inherited from generations of ducal ancestors, even if the other man was looking at him as if he was a raving madman. "Rest assured, Colonel, I will politely decline any promotion offered my way."

"At last, you show some sense. Now go, Major, you are dismissed."

With a nod of his head, Gabriel turned to exit the tent, only to be stopped on the threshold. "Oh, and, Major, what is this tale I hear about a woman, dressed in green, sprinting down the field? Is the entire world gone mad or what? Was she real? Somebody is even saying she's an avenging angel."

Gabriel turned towards the Colonel and smiled. "Oh, she is real. She's not an angel, but the next best thing."

Chapter Twenty-Eight

The following two days passed with Ivy seeing neither hide nor hair of Gabriel. It was really for the best, and she *had* asked him to leave. It gave her time to cool her anger, gather her strength and reflect on the next step to take. She told herself she wasn't hurt by his indifference, but she couldn't lie to herself. The seed of doubts, planted before coming to the Continent, was quickly blossoming in thorny vines infesting her mind.

Ivy had spent those two days in relative isolation, divided from the soldiers for modesty but able to hear their voices behind the screen. She came to recognise the kind timbre of Miss Thomas's voice, who stopped by her bed every spare moment she had to keep her company. Ivy was quickly becoming very fond of the girl, who tried to cheer her up, especially after her argument with Gabriel.

"Don't cry, my Lady," Christy had said, seeing the tears in Ivy's eyes, "All men are insensitive beasts. It's a wonder we women didn't decide to have nothing to do with them ages ago, putting an end to humanity." And on that line, it went for the following days. Miss Thomas had very clear opinions on the matter of menfolk.

Then there was Mr Phillips, the physician. A serious man, a little over thirty, who came to check on her on regular intervals and declared her quite lucky, all things considered. He had prescribed rest and to avoid physical exertion, paying particular attention to strong headaches.

"We are often at a loss when dealing with head wounds. We don't know for sure how serious the damage is when one receives a blow to the head. So, try to avoid stressful situations. It shouldn't be too difficult. Your leg will heal properly in a couple of weeks, keeping you from hazardous situations in the meantime."

Mr Phillips couldn't even assure her that her injury would not leave permanent damage, saying that only time would tell. That was what worried her most. She tried to show a brave face, but inside, Ivy feared what that meant, whether she would have to walk with a limp for the rest of her life. Another thing she had brought on herself when she had decided to enter that reckless journey. When questioned, the physician had denied the possibility of a loss of mobility, but he had warned against reopening the wound for the third time.

"It's not like I did it on purpose," she objected, pouting at Mr Phillips's back after he had repeated again how she had worsened the situation by falling on the leg after the explosion.

Even though she was well taken care of, Ivy found herself with too much time on her hands. Inevitably, her mind went to Gabriel and, especially, what all meant for her, for them. She didn't know anything anymore. She only knew one thing for sure. She needed answers. What she had written in her letter still held true. She had ascertained he was alive. If it came to that, now she would say goodbye to Gabriel, go back to London, and be strong enough to mend her broken heart and create new dreams for her future.

On the afternoon of the second day, Ivy was chatting with Christy about London and its sights during one of her rare breaks from her duties when Viscount Bellmore appeared at her 'bedside'. His approach was preceded by warm greetings by the other wounded soldiers, as it seemed the man was as well-liked among soldiers as he was in ballrooms. Upon seeing him, Ivy smiled in welcome. "My Lord, how nice to see you. What brings you here?"

"I couldn't forgive myself if I didn't personally wish you a full and speedy recovery." He really was too charming for his own good. "Moreover, I wanted to see how you were faring, knowing that the soldiers think of you as an angelic apparition." He grinned unrepentantly at her.

"They *what?*" Ivy asked with a startled laugh.

"You surely are aware of the story circulating among the men. Even Colonel Stattford asked Blakeburne directly what was about a woman appearing from thin air. Surely he told you?" He looked around, expecting to find him hidden somewhere. "Where is he, by the way?" An uncomfortable silence fell over them. Ivy pressed her lips in a thin line.

"He didn't, did he?" the Viscount said, shaking his head in exasperation. Ivy didn't know what he was talking about, but whatever it was, not having seen Gabriel for a while, she was pretty that *no, he didn't.*

From the corner of her eye, Ivy saw Miss Thomas shift nervously on her feet. The silence was as thick as the fog on a winter day in London.

Focusing on Bellmore, Ivy gathered her pride and raised her chin. "To answer your question, my Lord, no, I haven't seen nor heard from Blakeburne in the last two days. I hope, however, that he's faring well."

"I thought I've seen all the idiotic things the man could do in his life. Apparently, I was wrong. Pardon my language, my dear, but our Blakeburne is a fool and a stubborn one at that."

"You won't find objections here, my Lord. How is he?" Seeing her dejected face, Bellmore approached her bed and took her hand in his.

"He is well. As well as expected, given the situation. He was summoned by the Colonel to explain his behaviour, but he came away with only a slap on his wrist, so don't fret. I don't know the details of your relationship, but I've never seen him like that. When I mistakenly reported the news of your death, it was like seeing a man robbed of the light, facing a lifetime of darkness. I will forever be sorry for the part I played in this, but I'm asking you, as his friend and, hopefully, yours, not to give up on him, not now."

"I won't. At least not before confronting him." A combative light entered her dark eyes, bringing a smile back on Bellmore's face.

"You are one of the finest ladies I've ever met. You know that? Would you like for me to summon him for you?"

"Thank you, my Lord, but no. I've some planning to do."

❆ ❆ ❆

Bellmore found Gabriel ensconced in his tent, sitting behind his desk, poring over papers. News of Wellington's victory at Waterloo had travelled across the camp faster than a bullet. Many struggled to believe the war was really over, but a general undercurrent of hope lightened the mood. Well, not everyone's. Gabriel didn't glance up, even if Bellmore was sure he had heard him enter. Lady Everleigh had asked him not to bring him to the tent, but she had said nothing about giving him a piece of his mind.

"What can I do for you, Bellmore? As you can see, I'm very busy right now. The post came, and I must deal with the consequences of Napoleon's defeat. That *he* isn't tortured by a mountain of useless dispatches, but *I* am, is preposterous." Gabriel shuffled through his papers, still not looking up.

"Nice to see you are not fatally injured or bedridden. I started to wonder. What you can do for me is stop being an arse."

"Do you need something, or you just came here to show how overrated your sense of humour really is?"

"There is nothing wrong with my charming self, while the same cannot be said for you, I'm afraid. A certain lovely Lady could attest that. I had a nice chat with her..." At that, Gabriel's attention was finally torn away from the documents on his desk. His head snapped up, and he shot the other man a deadly glare.

"You went to see Lady Everleigh?" If possible, his voice would have caused frostbites. He stood up and watched his friend with narrowed eyes. Ah, now Bellmore had him.

"Of course, I did, since the man whose hide —it seems I have to constantly remind you— she saved, is holed up here and isn't deigning her of his venerable presence!" His voice rose at the end. It seemed Ivy had gained a new champion.

Ire sparked in Gabriel, mixing with an unsolicited dose of jealousy. "I'm trying to give her the space she needs. Need I remind you that she asked to be left alone? She needs time to come to terms with the fact that the man who cares about her above anything else in the world put her in mortal danger!" He pounded his fist on the desk and then ran his fingers through his hair, frustrated.

"To use your own words, this is stupid. Do you know what I saw when I talked to her? I saw a woman who put on a brave face but is afraid that everything she's done so far meant nothing to you!"

Gabriel came around the desk and took one threatening step towards him. "You know nothing!"

"Enough!" Both men turned, surprised, at the sound of a forceful feminine voice. Ivy took one tentative step forward with the aid of a cane, which Miss Thomas had begrudgingly produced when she had stubbornly refused to stay abed one minute longer. Her green gown was clean, if wrinkled beyond repair. Her hair was pulled back in a simple braid. However, what she lacked in immaculateness, she made up in regal determination.

"Ivy!" Gabriel exclaimed. "What are you doing here? You can't walk around like that!"

"Charming as always, Blakeburne. I think this is my clue to depart. My Lady." Bellmore bowed to Ivy, who acknowledged him with a distracted nod, her eyes never leaving Gabriel.

"Blakeburne, I've had enough of you telling me where I shouldn't be. It's becoming tiresome." She feigned boredom, while inside she was a nervous wreck. Time was up, time to face the truth. She regarded Gabriel, taking the time to really look at him. He was as perfectly put together as she remembered from London. Gone was the dishevelled man she had briefly seen. In front of her stood a Duke, in all his magnificence. His dark hair was combed back without a single lock out of place, exposing the sharp, closely shaven lines of his face. The contrast between his appearance and her rumpled self couldn't better represent the chasm that stood between them. But even in the presence of one of the most handsome men in the realm, what she really wanted to see was what resided behind his eyes. Since the beginning, she had sensed that they held all the man's secrets. Now she tried, unsuccessfully, to decipher what was hidden in them. The argument she had overheard between Gabriel and Bellmore gave her hope. Only to have it brutally squashed by his next words. Would she ever learn?

"Do you ever do what others tell you? I start to think I preferred you as a mousy little thing, too afraid to speak your mind." Ivy could only stare at him. *Really?*

Then, before she knew what she was doing, her hand came up and slapped him right across his left cheek. And she didn't stop there. All the pent-up anger and frustration surfaced like the eruption of a volcano, unstoppable and fed by boiling pain. Letting the cane fall to the ground, she started hitting his chest with all her strength. Once, twice, three times. He was so much stronger than her, so it didn't have a great effect, but it was immensely satisfying.

"You arrogant man!" *Punch.* "How can you do that to me!" *Punch.* "You almost killed yourself!"

"Ivy, stop." *Punch.*

"I don't care what you think of me anymore, but you don't get to do something like that!" She couldn't even bring herself to say it plainly.

"Stop! Ivy, for the love of...." Gabriel encircled her in his arms, bringing her flush against his body, steadying her with a hand on her nape. Ivy struggled against his hold, against the feeling of rightness. Her face pressed against his coat, and Ivy was finding it hard to breathe. Until she realised it was her throat that didn't work properly because of a giant lump. *Oh, no...* She broke down in sobs, the last thing she had sworn not to do in front of him.

It tore his heart apart, seeing her like that. He kissed the top of her head and held her until she calmed down. If he could, he would keep her there forever, safe from everything.

After her sobs quieted down, she lifted her head and looked at him, taking a step back. That time he released her, even if it caused almost physical pain.

"Maybe you are right. I shouldn't have come here. It has caused so much pain, so much suffering, to both of us." Her voice trailed off and, even if her words reflected his, he felt the loss of her conviction that had led her to this point.

Gabriel had so much to say but remained silent.

"Initially, when you stopped writing, I thought that maybe your letter went lost —HM post isn't known for his reliability after all— or that you faced more immediate problems, like, I don't know, win a war. Then I started worrying about everything that could have befallen you. My head was full of gruesome images." She shuddered and then raised accusing eyes to meet his.

"Imagine my surprise when I encountered your brother in Hyde Park, and he kindly reported how bored you were, sitting idly waiting for something to happen, for the enemy to set in the best position for you to attack. He even told me that in one of your letters you wrote that you had more time to pen letters than at home while managing your estates!

"I tried to rationalise it. I really did. After all, I would have preferred a thousand times your indifference than for your inability to answer to be due to a wound or, God forbid, worse. But then I became so angry at you, Blakeburne, it consumed me. How could you do that to me? It couldn't be possible that you had forgotten what it means to me to be an afterthought. Especially you, who knew how hurt I already have been by this kind of behaviour. But never mind that. You left me in the dark, sick with worry about your wellbeing!"

Gabriel had heard enough. She couldn't have misunderstood everything more. His actions may have been selfish, but, deep down, he had done it for her. To come back to her. To the future she had allowed him to envision. "Ivy, it was never my intention to hurt you, you must know that. I will forever blame myself for the injuries you sustained. After the last letter I wrote, I realised you were taking up too much space in my mind. I wanted —no, needed— to be completely focused. The more I was concentrated on what I was doing, the higher were the chances of coming back alive. To you. I didn't think this small matter would have caused such a strong reaction on your part."

For a great military man, he really was obtuse. "You could have simply told me!" Ivy exploded. "Can you imagine what it was like not knowing if you were all right? If I would ever see you again?"

"Of course, I know! The last few days have been agony!"

"Then I really don't understand you. There are times when you make me believe I mean everything, or at least something, to you, but the rest of the time, you wield your words like a sharp knife! Well, I congratulate you, your aim is true!"

316

Knowing she came all the way from London prepared to face his indifference gutted him. His brave Ivy. Looking into her eyes, he could see the damage he had brought. They weren't alight with fight, with the strength they were usually infused with. He had to bring it back, make them sparkle. I wasn't sure he really knew how. So he went, saying exactly the wrong thing. "Don't be so dramatic. I think you are overreacting."

She inhaled sharply. "Well then, that seals it. It seems my journey has been fruitful after all. I'll go back home with a limp I'm not sure will ever go away, a scar on my forehead and the awareness that the man I lo...did it for thinks of me like an unwanted, pitiful, dramatic, stupid woman. All of this could have been avoided if you had written to me, 'Dear Ivy, I am sorry, but I have to stop writing for a while. Don't worry, you'll hear from me soon. Or maybe not, but what's important is that I am not dead.' Hardly the narrative effort!"

If Gabriel wanted her anger, he had certainly succeeded. The fight was back in her eyes. He only hoped that she wouldn't give up fighting for him. She deserved a better explanation for his actions than a couple of ill-fated sentences. She couldn't carry on believing she meant close to nothing to him. It was laughable how far from the truth it was. He had almost let himself get killed when he thought she was dead. He opened his mouth to speak, but she wasn't finished.

"Listen, I promised myself we would let it all out before moving on." Moving on? From him? Over his cold, dead body. "With a more levelled head, maybe —and I say maybe— I will find my words unfair to you. Unfortunately, I can't help how I feel right now. I hear from the other soldiers that the war is almost over. Take me home, please. We will have plenty of time to talk, to unravel this tangle."

She spun around to leave, intent on putting distance between them.

The sudden movement caused a wave of dizziness that threatened to overcome her. Failing to find any kind of purchase to steady her, she prepared to meet the ground. Gabriel sprang into action, his arms circling her from behind. Before passing out, he heard her whisper, "Mr Phillips will be mighty put out with me."

❁ ❁ ❁

As it turned out, Mr Phillips didn't dare be 'mighty put out' with Ivy. Not with Gabriel's glare weighing down on him. The physician couldn't do anything but repeat, his frustration barely contained, how Ivy needed rest if she wanted to avoid permanent damage. She felt sorry for him. Upon all the other wounded he had to treat every day, he had to deal with a stubborn Countess who couldn't seem to care about her wellbeing and an intimidating Major-Duke who glowered at him with his frosty gaze.

Frosty was also a good description of the situation between Gabriel and Ivy. Continuing their discussion had been impossible. They were never left alone for more than a few minutes at a time and, even then, other soldiers were just a bed sheet away, with nothing better to do than be entertained by a lovers' quarrel between the officer who single-handedly started the decisive battle and the Lady —not an angelic apparition after all— who, also single-handedly, brought him back alive. That was the tale circulating.

Time was spent in frustrated silence. A few times, they opened their mouth to break that ridiculous impasse, but what came out was usually some short conversation about the situation, most to the soldiers' exasperations. More than one groan from the other side of the partition followed a particularly inane comment. The only bright side of the situation was the bond Ivy was forging with Christy Thomas. Like with Mrs Swan back at The Limping Duck, the peculiarity of the situation had shoved Ivy's usual shyness to the back of her mind. The young woman's easy-going and sunny personality made it easy for Ivy to feel at ease. It allowed her to focus on something else rather than her injures or Gabriel. In a word, on her pain. She eagerly waited for the nurse to come checking on her to hear the anecdotes of her busy day. Her favourite was the one about the one time a soldier had asked for gin to numb him before being stitched back together. Not convinced of the wisdom of the decision, she had nevertheless allowed him to drink the spirit. Only to be subjected to a series of awful —if endlessly amusing— limericks his foxed mind had conjured. "We were all laughing so hard, we couldn't in all conscience go near him with a needle. Even Mr Phillips had to stop treating him to wipe away tears. In the end, he recovered from the wound in his leg and went back to Devonshire to delight his wife with his poetry." Ivy loved those stories and loved hearing them from Christy. She still didn't know how she came to be there. Christy was an unstoppable chatterbox, only to fall silent when faced with questions about her origins. After days in her company, Ivy knew only that she hailed from a lost corner of Cornwall. The rest was clearly a sensitive topic, so Ivy decided not to pry further.

Until curiosity, mixed with utter boredom, made her change tactics. "So, Christy," formalities had been abandoned after the conversation about drunken soldiers, "what will you do now that the war is over?" Ivy asked one afternoon while the nurse was bandaging her leg with fresh linen.

"I really can't say, Ivy. I haven't thought so far ahead." She didn't lift her eyes, concentrating on Ivy's injured limb.

"You don't plan to go home?" She had witnessed her tending to her injury like it was second nature, whereas now she was cutting the bandage with the same focus medieval monks would use to draw a miniature on a Bible.

"No, I won't go back. That I know for sure." Seeing that even that last attempt had come to nought, Ivy now was sure that, behind her cheerful facade, everything wasn't right in her world. If Christy didn't want to confide in her, Ivy would have to respect her wishes. However, one thing she could do. She took her hand.

"If you ever find yourself in need of help, promise me you'll come to me in London, at Rutherford-Blythe House. I'll leave the address with you. It's the least I can do, after how good you've been to me in the past days."

"You are too kind, Ivy."

Ivy patted the hand she was holding. "Nonsense, my dear. Just promise me that, if you ever find yourself in trouble, you'll turn to me for assistance."

"Very well, I promise," Christy finally yielded. Ivy smiled at the young woman, her mind a little more at ease. She couldn't imagine what it felt like not having a family you wanted to go back to. She also knew that it left a woman with few choices. It was a small gesture for Ivy to make, but it could mean the world for someone like Christy.

"In the meantime, I've still got work to do here, to put those soldiers back on their feet. There are more than a few wives and sweethearts waiting for bad poetry!" The two women laughed, the heavy moment behind them.

❋ ❋ ❋

One morning, four days after the episode in Blakeburne's tent, Ivy woke up feeling definitely better. The blinding headache was now reduced to an annoying throbbing. Even Mr Phillips pronounced her firmly on the mend.

"Am I able to travel home?" Ivy asked hopefully. The last four days had been weighing on her for more than her bedridden status.

"Your leg is far from healed and is bound to bother you, but I can't forbid you from leaving anymore. If you don't overdo it, your convalescence will certainly benefit from a more stable environment, far from a battlefield. So yes, you can go, my Lady, provided that you'll pay attention to any sign of aggravation of any of your injures." *These words should be written in a poetry book*, Ivy thought, because she had never heard anything so beautiful in her life. She clapped her hand and emitted an unladylike but happy squeal. Impulsively, she threw her arms around the man, straining from her sitting position on the bed. "Thank you, Mr Phillips! Thank you!" Clearly uncomfortable with her sudden joyful manifestation, the physician patted her left arm fatherly. "You are welcome, my Lady."

"What the hell is happening here? Unhand her immediately." Blakeburne's voice resounded from behind the shorter man, cold like a winter night. Ivy, not intimidated by him, slowly released the man, smiling up at him. Quite different was the physician's reaction. He turned towards Blakeburne, nervously straightening his coat and shifting on his feet. "Major Eastham, I was just telling the Countess—"

"He was telling me that I can go home! Isn't it wonderful news?" Ivy smiled broadly. Blakeburne didn't return the smile, serious.

"Are you certain she's recovered enough to travel?" he asked, looking at Mr Phillips. "We will not jeopardise her full recovery by hasting our departure. Only four days ago, she fainted in front of me." Mr Phillips impressively stood his ground under Gabriel's unmerciful scrutiny. It seemed he drew the line at hearing his professional judgment put into question.

"I assure you, Major, that if I weren't sure that Lady Everleigh could travel safely, I wouldn't have given my consent. Like I was saying before your arrival, at this stage, Lady Everleigh has better chances of a speedy recovery in a household attended by family."

"Lady Everleigh is a responsible adult who will take all the necessary measures to assure her safety during and after her travels," interjected said Lady Everleigh, letting the men know how much she appreciated being left out from a conversation about her.

"Mr Phillips, thank you for your help. I'm sure that you have much to do. Lady Everleigh and I have a lot to talk about in preparation for our departure." The man nodded at the clear dismissal, relieved to have escaped the repercussion of that untimely hug. Moving the sheet to the side, he left Ivy and Gabriel to their relative solitude.

Gabriel looked at Ivy, eyebrow raised. "Have I interrupted something?"

"Oh yes, you have. I was planning to show Mr Phillips the depth of my gratitude. It's unfortunate that you arrived when you did. It was just getting to the good part." Ivy saw Gabriel clench his jaw hard, his eyes angry, but couldn't help taunting him.

"Don't play with fire, my Lady," he said slowly through his clenched teeth.

"Don't ask ludicrous questions, Your Grace," countered Ivy.

"I don't like entering here and finding you in the arms of another man." The dangerous glimmer in his eyes sent shivers down Ivy's spine, despite her irritation. That man was a sight to behold when angry. And when serious, and when happy. He was leaning above her, his closed fists creating indentations in the straw. Everybody else would have cowered when confronted with his stance.

But not Ivy. On the contrary, she felt empowered by it. They were looking into each other's eyes, their breaths mingling, trapped in a staring contest, both unwilling to lose. Both unwilling to admit the stakes they were playing for.

Without breaking eye contact, Ivy whispered, "I was carried away by the good news and hugged the physician. If either one of us took it for something even remotely like what you and I shared in the past, someone's memory must be faulty." There were getting closer and closer, only a hair's breadth dividing them.

"Because, as I remember it, it was nothing like that, and everything like this." Ivy wound a hand around Gabriel's neck and drew his mouth to hers. Her bold move took him by surprise, letting her lead the kiss. He recovered fast though and, with a groan, became an active

322

participant. As always, when they were concerned, they poured everything they couldn't say in that kiss. How could Gabriel ever think that that innocent hug with Mr Phillips even vaguely resembled *that?* She couldn't think straight when she was surrounded by him. Everything became meaningless, except for him.

The sound of a metal object crashing to the ground startled them out of their passion-induced bubble. A soldier accidentally knocking off a meal tray or someone dropping some medical equipment. It didn't matter what; it was enough to separate them. Gabriel raked a hand through his hair and took a step back, inhaling deeply. A kiss was a pleasant interlude, a way to reaffirm their physical connection. It always ended too soon. Each meeting of lips, each touch, unravelled them, leaving them exposed to each other, vulnerable. What followed was usually worthy of a play, often a tragedy.

"This isn't the time nor the place for that." His words were enough to douse Ivy in a dose of cold reality. Nothing had changed.

"Gabriel, I think it's time to..." Time to what would always remain everyone's guess because Blakeburne suddenly turned on his heels and spoke from above his shoulder.

"Given that you have medical consent, I'll go arrange for our departure. Your Coachman has been tending to your pair and carriage. I'll go speak with him directly. At least we have a comfortable conveyance at our disposal. If you could be ready to leave in the morning, I'd much appreciate it. Only a few officers still remain on site. Bellmore already left three days ago and must be more than halfway through the journey."

"I'm sorry to have inconvenienced you, your Grace. I'll be ready in the morning." Ivy's words were openly sarcastic but, by God, the man was able to infuriate her. Blakeburne didn't react to her jab. Instead, he acknowledged her insincere apology with a regal nod, leaving her to deal with her inner outrage.

※ ※ ※

After bidding farewell to Christy, making her renew her promise to come to find her if she ever needed help, Ivy left the tent, shooting a dirty look at one bedridden soldier. The man had the cheek to mumble under his breath, "Drat, now we won't know how it ends. We lost our entertainment today."

Ivy was walking, leaning heavily on Blakeburne's side, refusing to make use of the cane, but she heard the words clearly. Fortunately, she had been the only one. Or, if they had, nobody else showed any reaction.

They spent the first day in the carriage mostly in silence, looking outside the windows, each lost in their own world. Ivy didn't know the direction of Gabriel's musings. For her part, she never thought that the first time they found themselves completely alone, without fear of interruption, would be spent ignoring each other. She didn't dare dream of a scene out of her novels where the hero professed his undying love to the heroine, begging for forgiveness. But even an argument would have been better than this deafening silence. After everything that had happened in the past days, you would think a journey around the world would not be enough to fully explore the meaning behind their actions. She had promised him they would talk, but Ivy couldn't find the words. She had been right in her belief that he would have been plagued by tormenting guilt for her presumed death. Even seeing her in the flesh, alive and relatively well, hadn't erased it completely.

She set a surreptitious look in Gabriel's direction, examining his profile. The cuts and bruises that liberally adorned his face, residue of that ill-fated day, were healing and slowly fading. He looked as handsome as ever, with his aristocratic lineaments, daring the bruises to mar his appearance more than he allowed. What Ivy didn't

324

appreciate was the ducal persona he had firmly in place. She knew the more he barricaded himself behind it, the more his emotions were warring for supremacy. She wanted to reach out to him, but, even after everything, she didn't know if she could. Lost in her thoughts as she was, she jumped when he spoke.

"We should reach an inn shortly. I think it would be better if we stopped there for the night. We are in no hurry to reach London, and I'd prefer for you not to overdo on the first leg of the journey."

She nodded. She agreed. She was tired from more than the carriage ride along the uneven roads. She felt a different kind of exhaustion. She had assumed that her mad rush across the country and the even madder rush across a battlefield represented the crescendo of her story. Instead, she was still scrambling.

That set the tone for the following days. Nothing seemed to shake Gabriel out of his deep pensive mood. Their interactions were limited to primary needs. Ivy was ashamed to admit she had wasted many chances by spending her days sleeping. It had been the only way not to disgrace herself by emptying her stomach repeatedly on the roadside. Or overboard. And every evening, they each retired in their separate chambers.

Now, back on the English soil, she was feeling better. Physically. Mentally, she was feeling the weight of each hour that was bringing them near home. To face the consequences of their —mostly hers— actions.

The carriage stopped once again. She didn't know how much time had passed. Gabriel descended fist. He turned to help Ivy, taking first her hand in his, then putting both his hand on her waist and bringing her to the ground. Ivy raised her eyes to meet his when he didn't immediately release her. His eyes were troubled as he opened his mouth to speak. *Really Gabriel? Now?* Before he could utter a word, a woman's voice resounded loudly in the courtyard.

"Miss! You're back! I told my husband so. The ol' fool called me silly. Now, who's the silly one?" Ivy felt the first genuine smile in days tug at her lips. With all her preoccupations, she hadn't noticed they had stopped at The Limping Duck. She was so glad to see Mrs Swan again that she was in danger of tearing up. The older woman came racing towards her and enveloped Ivy in a big embrace she didn't even know she needed. Ivy felt Gabriel stiffen beside her, but she returned the hug wholeheartedly.

"I'm indeed back, Mrs Swan."

"Come inside, my dear! I see you've found your young man." She eyed Gabriel appreciatively. "And what a fine man he is. Now I understand why you travelled all that way to retrieve him."

Before Ivy could follow the dear woman inside, Gabriel stopped her with a hand on her forearm. "I would appreciate if you addressed the Countess with the respect due to her station. I'm the Duke of Blakeburne, and we are here to spend the night if you have rooms available. I'd like to reserve two chambers and a private parlour."

Ivy regarded Gabriel with disbelief. Never, during their acquaintance, he had wielded his title with such uncalled-for snobbery and rudeness. Ivy was mighty irritated by his behaviour. Her irritation became anger when she saw how horrified Mrs Swan was. Her cheeks lost all their rosy colour, and she looked at Ivy with wide eyes. "Countess? I—I thought…You never said…I'm so sorry, my Lady." The poor dear was stuttering. She dropped in a deep curtsy and was clearly at a loss for how to undo the offence she had unwittingly inflicted on a Duke.

Ivy took her arm gently, making her rise. "No, Mrs Swan, none of that. I deliberately omitted to tell you my title. Don't worry. You couldn't have known.

Now, I'm parched. If you'd be so kind as to prepare a cup of tea for me, I'll tell you everything that happened after I left your inn."

"Oh, of course, my Lady! But I couldn't possibly sit with you and His Grace…."

"Don't worry, Mrs Swan, the Duke is going to the stables to arrange for our horses to be groomed and fed," Ivy replied without looking at Gabriel. She was so incensed she couldn't look at him without unleashing her inner shrew or causing him further physical damage. Ignoring her protests that his son would take care of that, Ivy led Mrs Swan inside, leaving Blakeburne behind.

A pleasant smell of roast meat pervaded the air inside the building, emanating from the kitchen. Uncaring that it went against Blakeburne's wishes, Ivy led a distraught Mrs Swan to a wing chair near the fire, taking a seat in front of her. The poor woman was mercilessly wringing her apron with her hands. Ivy started to fear the Duke had caused her a profound shock when Mrs Swan couldn't stop apologising for her improper welcome. "I'm so sorry, my Lady, I really am! I didn't know you're a Countess. I meant no disrespect, I swear!"

"Stop worrying, Mrs Swan, please. No one has taken offence. You couldn't possibly have known...."

But there was no stopping the litany of Mrs Swan's distress. "Oh, but the Duke! We've never had such distinguished guests —oh, that nice Viscount once and a couple of Barons who live around here sure —, but a Duke! And a Countess! Mr Swan will be furious with me when he hears how I offended you!" Exasperated, Ivy realised that, no matter how many times she reassured her, Mrs Swan wasn't going to calm down any time soon. She tried to appeal to the innkeeper in her.

"Mrs Swan, you know what would make me feel better about this? A cup of tea. And maybe some of your wonderful pie. Would you be so kind as to bring some?"

That seemed to work. Thankfully, Mrs Swan stopped castigating herself and shot up, her back so ramrod straight that she could have made Blakeburne proud.

"Of course, my Lady! I'll go fetch it immediately. I've baked my famous pie today. You just wait, my Lady, you've never tasted any better. I'll be right back, my Lady." The old woman curtseyed not less than three times while covering the distance between Ivy and the door, finally turning the corner and hurrying to comply with her request. Left alone, she sighed and slumped against the back of the wing chair.

Damn you, Blakeburne! Ivy didn't need a subservient person. She needed someone to talk to, to help her make sense of her tangled thoughts. She would try again with Mrs Swan, but if she was going to 'my Lady' her during the entirety of their conversation, Ivy wasn't sure she could refrain from searching for Blakeburne and strangle him.

When Mrs Swan returned, balancing a tray loaded with teapot, cups, and more slices of pie she could possibly eat in a week, she seemed to have regained her bearings, for which Ivy was most grateful. Agitation replaced by kind interest, Mrs Swan observed her from above the rim of her teacup.

"So, how do you fare, my Lady? I'm sorry for not enquirin' before. I see you've acquired even more bruises than the last time I saw you if you don't mind me sayin' so. It wasn't the Duke that struck you, was it?" The woman's eyes flashed with anger. "Because if it was, I don't care if he were the King himself, I won't have it!"

Ivy was moved by her fierce protectiveness for a person she had seen her only once before. She immediately put her worries to rest before she started a tirade on the repercussions she had in mind for Blakeburne.

"No, no, Mrs Swan. Rest assured, the Duke had nothing to do with my injuries. We were…Ahem…caught in the middle of the action back there. I'm fine now." Ivy tried to downplay her mad rush to save Gabriel.

"With all due respect, ol' me doesn't think you're fine. And it's more than looking like you were set up by ruffians." *Why, thank you, Mrs Swan.* "You seem sad. When we met, you could barely stand, had been thrown by a carriage, and had only uncertainties to face. Despite all that, there was a sparkle in your eyes. I saw determination lookin' at you. Now, I'm sorry to say, it seems like that sparkle is fading."

She took a sip of her tea, looking at the other woman, who was waiting patiently for her to answer. Ivy decided it was time to unburden herself with someone. Putting the cup back on its saucer with a light ting, she placed it both on the table, using the few seconds to gather her thoughts.

"After I left the inn, I was able to reach the British camp...." Ivy related the past weeks' events, realising how close she and Gabriel had come to death. A shudder went through her when she came to the part when they had found themselves surrounded by the blasts of cannons and the cries of soldiers. Skipping hurriedly ahead, she tried to convey all the relief she had felt when she had ascertained Gabriel's wellbeing and the confusion, the hopelessness and self-doubt that had followed. Mrs Swan listened, making noises of dismay when she heard how they fought after the battle.

"So, you see, Mrs Swan. I know it was foolish. That, in reality, it was me who started the whole mess. But, deep down, I can't regret it. I foolishly thought, however, that one way or another, I would have had my answers. If my life were a novel, after I saved him and she saved me in return, we would have come home and lived happily ever after. Instead, I am no closer to unravelling my doubts than I was when I left London. We seem unable to let each other go, but I have come to doubt we are right to each other. Look at us!" She gestured to her face to get her point across.

Mrs Swan patted her knee, comforting her. "This isn't a book, my dear. If it were, Mr Swan would stop coming in the kitchen with muddy boots." Ivy had to laugh at Mrs Swan's practical view of life. She was right, though. Reality was very different from what you find within the pages of a book. You could not end a chapter or suddenly change the scenery when the heroine found herself in a difficult situation, or the author didn't know to go on. You must see it through, even if you didn't know exactly how.

"I wouldn't lose hope yet. It seems to me the Duke cares a great deal about you...."

"How can you say that? You've barely met him! And he was extremely rude to you!"

She waved a hand dismissively. "Oh, pish posh. If I had a penny for every ill-mannered customer, I would be a very rich woman. Besides, he was right in reprimanding me." Ivy opened her mouth to contradict her, but Mrs Swan stopped her.

"No, no, my dear, it's true." Ivy noted she had finally dropped the 'my Lady'. "But that's beside the point. What I wanted to say is that a man wouldn't go through the hell he faced if he wasn't destroyed by the thought of havin' lost someone important, no matter how honourable he is. And don't try to sell me the story of him feelin' guilty! You love him, right?"

Ivy nodded. It was her only certainty. The strength that had propelled her forward.

"Don't give up, my Lady. Talk to him, fight with him again. Fight not for him but for yourself. It will be worth it."

First Bellmore, now Mrs Swan. Everybody was asking her not to give up on Blakeburne. Ivy didn't share their optimism and started to feel like a female Don Quixote tilting at a very stubborn windmill.

"You are very wise, Mrs Swan. Mr Swan is a very lucky man."

"Oh dear, believe me, he knows. I tell him every day." Ivy laughed again. And it felt good.

Ivy didn't see Gabriel again until after dinner. She had pled exhaustion when a maid had come to fetch her to lead her to the parlour, where the Duke had arranged for them to dine. She had instead asked for a tray to be brought to her chamber, hoping to regain a bit of perspective, before facing him again. They had enough on their plate without this new unpleasant side of him she couldn't dismiss, despite what Mrs Swan said. She wanted to believe the long journey had weighed on him too. She would be pacing back and forth across the room if she wasn't still unstable on her injured leg. As it was, she slowly reached the door when she heard knocking and, thinking it was the maid to retrieve her dinner tray, she opened it without hesitation.

"Why didn't you come down for dinner? Are your injuries bothering you?" Gabriel said by way of greeting, entering her bedchamber as if fully entitled to do so. Her choices were to move from the threshold or be trampled.

"My injuries aren't what is bothering me, thank you very much."

"What is it then? The innkeeper's wife told me you were exhausted, but you aren't in bed."

"Mrs Swan really is a brave woman. After the way you treated her, I don't know if I'd have dared approach you."

"After the way *I* treated her? She was the one overstepping every boundary. To address a Countess with such familiarity…."

"She didn't know I was a Countess! We purposely didn't tell her. I was alone, injured and in need of a friendly face. A simple Miss could have that without drawing too much attention. Do you think these people see peers and peeresses every day?"

"Now they do. If it makes you feel better, tomorrow I'll leave a substantial compensation for the woman."

"You know, Blakeburne, I really don't like this condescending side of yours." His face hardened. He straightened his back, Duke firmly in place.

"That's too bad, my Lady, because you are saddled with me."

"What do you mean? A few more days, and we'll be in London."

At his raised brow, Ivy's heart began to beat faster. He could not mean what she thought he meant.

"Come on, Ivy, you know better than me that we will have to marry immediately after we reach London. You are an unmarried Lady who decided to travel halfway across Europe alone and had been away for weeks. Your family will be frantic. Not to talk about the fact that your cousin took upon herself to inform them of your whereabouts. The only way to salvage your reputation will be to marry. Seeing that you did all that because of me, it's only fair that it would be me to help you out this predicament."

Ivy blinked repetitively. She knew he was right. It was the sensible thing to do. After everything that happened, the thought of what awaited them in Town hadn't figured much in her mind. Just like the fact that Poppy and Henry weren't there, where she had left them. Her father must have come after her, and they must have been able to convince him to turn around. Even so, she doubted a pleasant reunion was in her immediate future.

She really felt a haft-wit for not realising sooner that that was what had been weighing on him. Looking at Gabriel, she saw the dream that she secretly harboured in her heart become within reach. What she didn't foresee, however, was that the only proposal she would happily accept would be uttered in such a way. The blow to her head hadn't managed to knock the ridiculousness out of her. And their spectacularly poor choices weren't nearly enough to base a marriage on. Nor was her love for him. Her pride didn't let her prostrate at his feet in gratitude. Especially after their recent behaviour towards each other.

"I'm sure there's a way out of this mess that doesn't revolve around us getting married. The *ton* hardly took notice of me before, I don't see why they should start doing it now. I will go to the country for a few months perhaps. All will be forgotten in no time. And I don't think anyone outside those near me would link my absence to you."

Gabriel straightened his waistcoat and crossed his arms over his chest. He looked offended by her words. How dare she refuse the mighty Duke of Blakeburne, the catch of all catches? Ivy would have laughed at his ruffled feathers if her future wasn't on the line.

"Setting aside the fact that you stubbornly continue to believe the *ton*'s disinterest towards your actions, how do you think your family will react upon you —our— return?"

She knew her parents and brother would never turn her back to her. Each one of them had —or had had— their fair share of scandals and eccentricities. This, however, was not the small matter of hiding behind a potted plant with someone during a ball or racing at dawn in Hyde Park. She wasn't sure she would be able to look at them for the rest of her life and see disappointment reflected in their eyes, the what-ifs.

"They will stand by my side, whichever decision I will make," she said with more conviction than she was actually feeling.

"It may be as you say, but why subject oneself to Society's scorn when there is a simple solution at hand? Moreover, my honour could not allow it. We will be married by special license immediately after reaching London." Gabriel's voice broke no argument. Ivy briefly closed her eyes, the will to fight leaving her. They had made their choices. Now they would pay the price. Looking at his boots, Ivy nodded. She heard Gabriel exhale deeply.

"Good. I'll leave you to your rest. We leave at first light. Goodnight."

He didn't wait for her whispered "Goodnight" and was already out of the door. Task completed, on to the next. Ivy sat on the bed and looked out of the window. It was a clear summer night, the moon shining brightly.

Happy ever after, indeed.

Chapter Twenty-Nine

After a night spent tossing and turning, Ivy found herself back on the road to London. She had left a tearful —and very well compensated— Mrs Swan with the promise to write soon, despite the 'inappropriateness' of a Countess writing to an innkeeper.

Blakeburne had decided to ride beside the carriage for the final stretch of the journey. They were still keeping a sedate pace, mindful not to tire her too much. She was feeling fine but didn't bother correcting Gabriel. Cowardly, she wasn't in any hurry to reach London. What awaited her were tirades and more well-meaning tirades. Oh, and let's not forget the prospect of marriage to the man she loved. The man who in the past had openly told her he would not marry her and was forced to do it to save her probably tattered reputation.

But he was ready to die when he thought you were dead.

It had only been a few weeks, but to Ivy, it already seemed like those days belonged to someone else. Just like all those moments, a few lifetimes ago, when they had stood in each other arms in dark corners and gardens. Looking outside the windows, Ivy let herself remember the feeling of his hands on her flesh, of her hands on him. Of his mouth on hers, on her…

As if reading her mind, he turned to her. She felt her cheek redden. Did he ever think about it? Does he ever burn for her touch? For her kiss?

Ivy was sure she was in love with every facet of his character. The serious man, the mighty Duke, the respected Major, and the passionate Gabriel. She missed the man and wondered if she would ever meet him again.

If he had his way, she would have a lifetime to find it out.

❁ ❁ ❁

"Ivy Emmaline Kington! Do you have any idea what you have put us through?"

"I am sorry, Mama—"

"I thought I'd seen everything with Gregory's escapades!" She pointed at that said son. "You've always been my sweet, quiet girl I could trust not to do something rash. More fool me! What do you do? You up and go right into war! Leaving behind only a meagre note saying not worry! Not to worry??"

Ivy opened her mouth again—

"What is there to worry when you then find out —after chasing her halfway across the country— that your daughter has been hurt in a terrible carriage accident? And that, despite that, she still went on and carried out the most reckless plan I have ever heard? And then—"

335

"Georgie, love, she knows all that. She was there." *Thank you, Father.*

"I know Rafael, but maybe if she hears it from someone else, she will understand how foolhardy it really was."

Put that way, her mother was right. But so was her father. Her injuries and aches constantly reminded her.

"And everything for *Blakeburne*? I knew you fancied him, but isn't it a bit...*extreme*?" Obviously, even her brother had something to say. Then his face darkened. "Where is he, by the way?"

That was a good question. Ivy had envisioned an argument awaiting her when she told him she would have preferred facing her family alone. Instead, he had simply nodded and had gone back looking outside the carriage window. They had just reached the outskirt of London, and the overcrowded streets had become so bad that Gabriel had decided to leave the horse and climb inside the carriage.

In deep contrast to that stimulating conversation, Ivy had hardly had the time to gingerly climb down the carriage steps when the door of her townhouse had been thrown open, and she had been ushered inside by the Duchess herself, who had forced Stevens aside. Ivy had only heard the carriage pull away, taking the Duke of Blakeburne with it. Her mother had started leading her by her arm, gasping when she had seen her limp. At a much slower pace, they had entered the family drawing-room, where the male half of the Kingtons awaited expectantly, both standing and with arms crossed on their chest while asking Stevens to fetch the family physician. Ivy had hugged them both and felt their posture relax slightly.

"I'm so sorry for making you worry," she had said, borrowing into her father's chest. Sensing a storm brewing at her apology, Ivy had scrambled for a distraction.

"Before you say anything, may I have something to eat? I'm famished."

That had bought her some time, but nothing could have stopped them from exploding. Hours later, after a fortifying meal and a bath, they were once again all gathered in the same room, and Ivy was giving them the rightful chance to vent.

Gregory's had been the first question requiring a real answer from her. An answer she didn't know.

"I have no clue where His Grace is right now."

"He'd better make an apparition soon, or I will pay him a visit...."

"Gregory, don't go overreacting—"

"Overreacting? Me? How is it that, in all this absurd story, *I* am the one overreacting when the cad has—"

"His Grace, the Duke of Blakeburne," Stevens' booming voice announced. And indeed, there he was, perfectly turned out, his face adorned with a smile. *That would have been nice.*

In reality, his expression didn't betray an ounce of emotion as he bowed to the people in front of him. He wasn't fazed by the hostile looks he was receiving from the Kingtons. And neither he was when Gregory charged towards him.

"Gregory, stop right this instant!" Ivy interjected sharply. Their drawing-room would not become the theatre of a brawl. Or the aristocratic version of it.

"Why? Give me one reason not to rearrange his face." Gregory's eyes were flashing with animosity towards the Duke, but he nonetheless stopped a few feet away from the love of Ivy's life, who had yet to say a word.

"One, because it's not the Duke's fault but entirely mine if he —we — are now in this situation." From the corner of her eyes, she saw Gabriel's jaw clench in sharp angles. Why should he be displeased by her defence she didn't know. Or rather, she knew. *Pride.*

"From where I'm standing, he played more than a small part in this debacle. And who knows the real extent of his *involvement* with you." His not-so-subtle allusions were clear for all present.

"Gregory!" cried the Duchess. His son didn't pay much attention to her, locked in a staring contest with the man who had invented glaring.

"You can think what you want of me, Burnam, but if I ever hear you try to cast aspersions on your sister's character again, you will have a bigger problem at hand than a wedding to attend." Those were the first words out of Gabriel's mouth since Stevens had announced his arrival. A threat. *Wonderful.*

As Gregory took a menacing step forward, the Double Duke finally decided to intervene.

"You are aware, Your Grace, those rumours are spreading like wildfire right as we speak."

"Thank you so much, Eleanor," Ivy whispered, not quietly enough. Her father sent her a warning look.

"Despite some members of our own family's unfortunate contribution...." Another pointed look in her direction, and Ivy refrained from adding anything else. "There are some things I cannot overlook. I may disagree with Society's way of determining people's worth, but I won't allow it to take away my daughter's choices. She has to be free to attend balls, or not, as she wishes. She has to be free to walk down the streets and shop without whispers following her. But, in order for her to have choices, I'm afraid I have to take away yours."

The Duke of Rutherford-Blythe's words hit Ivy like a punch in her stomach. It was nothing but the truth. She could hide behind the memories of their shared kisses and half-said declarations, but stronger than those were the memories of the many times he had told her he had no wish to marry her. And then back at The Limping Duck, where he had scorned her belief that the outcome could still be different. Looking now at the man she loved, she found it difficult to draw breath.

"Father, I—"

Gabriel didn't seem perturbed by the prospect. Instead, his elegant hand went to his breast pocket, drawing out two folded papers and handing them to her brother, who was still the nearest person to him. Gregory opened one, revealing an official document.

"As you can see, all this…." He let his voice trail off to imply their heated —from the Kingtons' part— discussion. "Was hardly necessary. I had already sent a letter ahead to the Archbishop of Canterbury while on the road. After I brought the Countess home, I went to collect the special licence I requested. I also sent an announcement to *The Times,* of which you can find a copy in the other sheet in your hand, Burnam. The Duke of Blakeburne and the Countess of Everleigh's betrothal will be in the paper tomorrow morning. I hope you find my dealings satisfactory." Only then Gabriel looked briefly at his new fiancée before focusing again on the Double Duke.

"Now, there are few legal matters to discuss. If His Grace could spare me few minutes of his time, I'd like to iron them out immediately." At the older Duke's nod, Ivy spoke up.

"The Countess of Everleigh would very much like to be present at the discussion."

"Ivy, dear, don't you think you should let the Duke and your father deal with such things?" said her mother, who, until that moment, had observed everything attentively.

"You all forget that only I have the final say in what pertains to Everleigh, so I have to be present. Furthermore, my decisions have brought us here today. I will have a say in those that will shape our future too."

Chapter Thirty

There wasn't a single drawing-room or parlour in London that didn't resonate with animated voices speculating about what was going to be the wedding of the Season. Of the century, according to some. Matrons and young ladies alike couldn't stop talking about the events that had brought the austere Duke of Blakeburne to wed the Countess of Everleigh. Somehow, and much to the surprise of both the Easthams and the Kingtons, the scandalous tale of an unmarried woman who went traipsing around Europe during the war against Napoleon to find an Army Major became the most swoon-worthy love story of all time, where nothing, from physical injuries to bloody battlefields, could stop two people in love from finding each other. Still scandalous, but wasn't it romantic?

"Yes, Your Grace, isn't it oh-so-romantic?" Bellmore sighed dreamily, a hand on his heart, repeating Miss Ashton's words, who had just left them to continue her promenade down Rotten Row. The gel had made Gabriel slightly uncomfortable by looking up at him with twinkling eyes and fluttering eyelashes while his friend was shamelessly enjoying the show. The Viscount laughed at the scathing look Gabriel shot him.

"You tell me, Bellmore. You were there. Was it romantic swiping the field among corpses, or what was left of them, searching for us? And finding us —her—more dead than alive, her faint heartbeat barely detectable?" Gabriel instantly regretted his words when he saw Sebastian flinch and the colour drain from his face. He regretted it also because it brought those moments back, which were already playing in many of his nightmares.

The Viscount quickly brushed it all away in typical Bellmore fashion, buried who knew how deep. "I personally think your story should become an epic poem rivalling any other ever written. You, the broody hero, who saves the fair maiden. Or is it the other way around? One never knows with you two." Gabriel sent him yet another dark look that was met with yet another laugh.

For him, it wasn't even remotely funny. The *ton* had already been a nuisance when it thought he was unapproachable, like a sort of demigod among mortals. Now everyone viewed him as a modern knight in shining armour, rescuing ladies from atop his white horse. And not metaphorically either. The tale was getting more exaggerated each time he heard it. The situation was becoming unbearable. *And my horse is black, thank you very much.*

He didn't have a romantic bone in his body. Just ask Ivy. The 'fair maiden', whose marriage proposal —if one could call it that— had consisted in first being told she couldn't be so naïve as to think she had a choice in the matter, followed by having a special licence almost slapped in her brother's irate face. And let's not forget the arid discussion that had taken place shortly after in R-B's studio. *Really, the stuff as dreams are made on.*

Could he really blame her for trying to find a way out of it? Gabriel refused to let it affect him. They will marry, end of story. It was unacceptable that she continued saying that it was all her fault, that her actions alone had brought them to their impending marriage. Gabriel could concede, if hard-pressed, that nobody had forced Ivy to take upon herself to find him, a thought that even now made his skin crawl. But all those moments alone, in gardens, in drawing-rooms and libraries, when her hands had explored the contours of his body, of his cock, when he had put his fingers and mouth on her most private place...all had built towards their marriage. He had already meant to offer for her after all.

So yes, it was irritating that she had tried to wriggle her way out of it. She had relented in the end. She had even looked at him with eyes brimming with emotions when he had told her and the Duke that he had no use of her dowry and she could use it for Everleigh, which she will continue to personally oversee. Of course, she would. He didn't need another estate to add to his duties. And Ivy was perfectly capable of handling it herself like she had been doing for years. All Kington's properties enjoyed a level of prosperity, and Everleigh wasn't any different. So, he had told them as much. If that was all it took to put that look of happiness on her face, Gabriel would give her hundreds of other estates to oversee. Even R-B had looked at him approvingly for the first time since he had entered his townhouse.

It had taken some time for him to let go of his well-laid plan of an unchallenging wife who wouldn't disrupt his orderly life. But in exchange, he would get Ivy. His Ivy. His beautiful madness.

His chest constricted. What kind of husband would he be? He, the boy who had looked at a father hugging his son like it was the most extraordinary thing. The man who had been taught that kindness was a weakness if it didn't serve a purpose.

"So, Gabe, are you nervous? Ready to be a blushing groom tomorrow?" How was he still friends with Bellmore was a mystery.

"Of course, I'm not nervous. What is there to be nervous about? It's a wedding. The sooner it's done, the sooner all this absurdity will be over."

"Let not Lady Everleigh hear you refer to your wedding as an 'absurdity'. You already walk on thin ice when one looks at your past interactions with your fiancée." *Oh, for the love of...*

"I wasn't referring to my wedding! I was talking ab—" Gabriel was interrupted by a group of giggling ladies who came upon them on the Row, forcing the two men to acknowledge them with a tip of the hat. Gabriel didn't spare them a second glance.

"—about all this brooding romantic hero horseshite."

"I hear Byron is green with envy."

"Sebastian, in the name of all the years of our friendship, I ask you to cease."

"Aaaw, you sweet chap, you love me. I love you too." Bellmore dried a non-existing tear from his eye.

"I swear to God, I'm this close to braining you with my walking stick."

"All right, all right. No need for violence in Hyde Park. Just one last question."

Gabriel sighed and waited, dreading what the Viscount would say next.

"Are you ready?"

"For what?"

"To finally claim your Duchess."

He had been nervous. Now that the wedding ceremony and breakfast were over, Gabriel could admit it to himself, if not to an exasperating Sebastian.

Ivy Kington, Countess of Everleigh, was his wife.

The affair had been fairly simple. Or as simple as it could have been when two families that 'together took up more than half of Debrett's pages' merged together. Bellmore's words, not Gabriel's, even if it was only a *slight* exaggeration. He had to thank his new wife for keeping the two Duchesses of Rutherford-Blythe and Blakeburne — now Dowager— on a short leash. Otherwise, who knew what kind of grandiose fête they would have put together. Gabriel shivered at the thought.

They had been married at St. George's —that had been non-negotiable, and Gabriel agreed— and the Archbishop of Canterbury had officiated the ceremony as befitting the members of such distinguished families. But, apart from that, everything else had been tastefully limited to family and friends.

He *had* been nervous, but when he had seen her walking towards him, clad in an ivory gown that had shined not because of its gold embroidery but because of *her*, calm had settled over him. Looking into the deep brown eyes that had carried him through the worst days of his life, he had made another promise. The first one had been many years ago, that his brother never felt the late Duke's heartless disregard. That day in St. George's, Gabriel vowed that she would never let doubt lead her actions ever again. He would spend the rest of his life showing her how valuable she was. How essential to him she was.

Now, seated in front of his legally wedded wife on their way home from R-B's townhouse, where the Duchess had insisted on hosting breakfast, Gabriel was looking forward to shedding the heavy mantle of their past and finally being with her. And that involved shedding their real clothes as well. His blood boiled just thinking about it. He had already tasted her, and now he could repeat the experience. And more. Hell, it was his duty to do so. Both the law and society demanded that he spend the following hours disrobing his wife, learning the shapes of her body, pleasuring her —and she him— until they dropped, exhausted. *Wasn't it warm in the carriage?*

"Gabriel? Are you well?" asked Ivy, looking at him strangely. Now that he thought about it, she hadn't said much since finding herself alone with him.

"Yes, my dear. Why do you ask?"

"You suddenly seemed, I don't know, fidgety."

"It's been a long day."

"It has. When we arrive at your townhouse—"

"*Our* townhouse"

"Sorry. At *our* townhouse, I will ask the servants to draw us both a bath if it's not too much bother...." *Ivy, naked, sliding a wet cloth up and down her body...oh fuck it!*

"...and then we...Gabriel oooff!" He smothered her next words with his mouth while simultaneously pulling her on his lap. Their kisses became immediately wild, hungry. The same hunger seemed to be consuming her as well because, a heartbeat later, she was straddling him, her gown gathered at her waist.

"I am not the least tired," he managed to say when they came up for air. He then groaned when she ran her hand through his hair and gently tugged.

"Thank God," was her only reply before taking his lips with hers again. Their tongues waltzed together in a dance without rules nor polite distance. He started sliding his open mouth down her jaw and her neck, aroused to the breaking point by her soft moans. The carriage stopped, and it was a good thing he already had his hands on her, or she would have fallen unceremoniously on her bottom. He gently put her back on her seat just as the door opened. Not really giving her time to adjust herself, Gabriel alighted the carriage and proffered his hand to her.

"Your Grace."

"Your Grace," Ivy gifted him with a small smile, her beautiful face alight with pleasure. Her bruises and injuries had healed, and nothing remained of those fateful days. Apart from her name indelibly engraved on his soul. The hand he was now holding had unwaveringly brought him back from the bottomless pit of hell. Images started flashing before his eyes, but he brutally chased them away. She was there with him. *His*.

Urgency overcame him once again. If it weren't very undignified, he would have run up the front stairs. As it was, his pace wasn't *that* slow, and he was grateful for more reasons than one that Ivy was able to keep up with him. Her limp was mostly imperceptible those days, and his —and Rutherford-Blythe's— physician had confirmed that it would completely disappear once Ivy regained confidence in the sturdiness of her leg.

"Gabriel! The servants!" Ivy warned from behind him, laughter in her voice, her hand firmly clasped in his.

"They're celebrating our nuptials. It's just you and me. The only one here is Jenkins, but he's retiring to his quarters now." He didn't turn around to see if his butler, who had opened the door and welcomed them, was actually doing that. He knew he would.

"How very...considerate of them. Lead the way then, Your Grace."

❅ ❅ ❅

Ivy didn't have the time to appreciate the magnificence of Blakeburne townhouse, not when she was being led to the upper floor by a very determined Gabriel. She didn't mind it at all. She had behaved like a wanton back in the carriage, but who could blame her? Just look at the man she could now call *husband*. Impossibly handsome in dark green coat and ivory embroidered waistcoat that fortuitously matched her wedding dress. But it had been the look in his emerald eyes when he had first spotted her in St. George's that had made it

346

almost impossible not to run to him, propriety be damned. It was a look that said *I would run through a battlefield to get to you.*

I already did, she was sure hers said in response. She had refused to wear a veil covering her face. The exquisite lace confection her mother had given her —her own wedding veil— was pinned back with a comb. She had wanted to make sure nothing obstructed her face. And her view of him. They had gone through too much not to look straight into each other's eyes while speaking their vows. And could the *ton* have a good look at the face of the woman who was marrying the most eligible Duke of the Season, the same face they always seemed to forget? Yes. So what? She had never claimed to be above smugness. Or a saint. How much of a saint she wasn't was even clearer when, just a few steps inside the ducal chamber, Ivy was already pushing Gabriel's coat off his broad shoulders, letting it fall unceremoniously on the floor.

"I fear you'll find my service as a valet somewhat lacking, Your Grace."

"Not as much as mine as a lady's maid." The words were just out of his mouth when Ivy heard fabric tearing. She gasped, but it was soon forgotten when Gabriel started opening the laces on her light corset. She, in turn, was first undoing the buttons on his waistcoat, then removing his white shirt. Finally, his chest was under her fingers. Warm skin, lightly dusted with dark hair, was pulled on defined muscles. Ivy couldn't stop herself from caressing those hard planes and ridges, marvelled by the goose pimples that appeared on his skin with each stroke. Soon, the mounting pile of clothing on the floor was joined by her corset. And thank God for that because Ivy sorely needed more freedom to draw breath. It was short-lived, however. Leaning down to kiss her, he swept her off her feet, eliminating that tiny distance that separated them. She instinctively wrapped her legs around him, hindered only by the transparent shift she had still on. That position gave him easy access to her breasts. Gabriel started playing with the hard points with his tongue, and Ivy was swept away by pleasure. She didn't notice he had sidestepped the clothes on the floor and carried her across the room until she felt herself being lowered to the high bed. Pushing up on her elbow, she took her time admiring Gabriel shedding the rest of his clothes.

The Duke of Blakeburne was all-powerful. Major Eastham commanded respect. The man in front of her was...*hers*. And splendid. A masculine, sensual creature obliterating all the layers and masks he presented to the world every day. His hair was ruffled and not in frustration. His heavy-lidded green eyes bore into her, leisurely perusing the length of her body.

And that was the moment when her insecurities stormed back. *Oh no.* She had to stop thinking about all her flaws that were worsening by the second. And what if she couldn't please him? She didn't really know what was going to happen. Instinct had guided her in the past, but as much as she wasn't the typical sheltered young miss, she didn't know if she would measure up. *No. Stop it, Ivy. Concentrate on the expanse of that male skin, that rippling muscles, on Gabriel's hands that are opening the fall of his breeches...why is he stopping?*

"Ivy, are you well?"

"Come here, Gabriel." Ivy rose on her knees and grasped his nape once he was within reach. She kissed him intensely, her tongue seeking entry. She was forcing all thoughts of inadequacy away, trying to capture that warm sensation that engulfed her each time she kissed Gabriel. She trailed open-mouthed kisses along his jaw and strong neck. She must have been more desperate than she thought because Gabriel cupped the side of her face and looked directly into her eyes.

"What's happening right now?"

"What do you mean? I'm kissing you."

"And there are few things better than your mouth on me. But there's something else." *Devil confound it.* Ivy tried to avert her gaze, but he held her firm. She swallowed hard.

"What if I am...not enough?"

Ivy immediately felt the loss of his touch when he took his hands away. He rose from his bent position and started pacing. Ivy hadn't foreseen her words would cause such a vehement reaction.

"Tell me you are not serious right now."

"I'm sorry, forget I said anything. Come back here." She didn't sound desperate, did she?

"Ivy...You are killing me right now. Not enough? It's the most ludicrous thing I've ever heard. Have you forgotten how we've come to be here? I almost killed myself when I thought you had been taken away from me forever!" A pregnant pause followed, both lost in their personal nightmare. She had not wanted to resurrect those memories on their wedding night, but they were part of their story. She looked at his rippling back while he paced. Back and forth. Far from her.

There was not going to be a magic cure for a life spent believing she was so inconsequential it was normal for people to overlook her. But at that moment, she had to choose. She could let it taint everything that ever happened to her. Or she could be the same woman who fought the odds for what she wanted. Even if it was frightening. And that meant...

"I love you." Her voice was surprisingly strong. Maybe it was to be heard above her heartbeat pounding in her ears.

That effectively made Gabriel change the course of his pacing. He now charged towards her with single-minded purpose. His expression was almost feral. In two strides, he was on her. Ivy wasn't afraid of him, never that, but the light in his eyes made her start babbling.

"I do. I really love you. That was why I had to find you. That was why I—" Her voice trailed off when his big hands slowly pushed her shift higher and higher. They started from her ankles, up to her knees, to her thighs. Up, up, until it came off completely. His hands then caressed down the opposite path, stopping to pay homage to her breasts. A touch on her belly, light as a feather. And lower. He cupped her mound possessively before parting her and finding her wetness, ready for him.

"Touch me," he ordered, his voice deep with desire. Ivy gladly complied, tracing the contours of his chest and abdomen before following the same path with her tongue. The room was resonating with their laboured breaths and strangled sounds, creating the most beautiful melody Ivy had ever heard. Her fingers met the fabric of his half-open breeches, and she tore at the reaming buttons. Something ripped, but it was just fair. He had ruined her wedding gown. She burrowed inside, meeting the warm hardness she had touched only once before. After a few strokes, he stopped her. He grinned at her embarrassing pout but stepped back to remove his boots —luckily, he was able to do it without the help of a valet— and his breeches. Now they were both naked. He made her lie down on the bed before climbing on top of her. After a brief peck on her lips, he kissed a burning trail across her whole body, not leaving any spot untouched. Ivy raised her head to see if he was leaving burns in his wake, so hot was his mouth. He was murmuring something against her skin that sounded like *fucking finally* and *mine.*

She, in turn, was stroking his shoulders, but she gripped his hair with a startled "Gabriel!" when his tongue swirled around the sensitive bud of nerves between her nether lips. He worked mercilessly until she shattered with a cry. He had been watching her the entire time, and, at the smug look on his face, she tugged at his soft locks and pulled him up. They kissed, her sated body immediately wanting more.

"Take me, my love," she whispered against his lips. Intense emerald pools of desire met her. His hips ground against hers, his hard cock — yes, she knew the word— creating delicious friction along her sensitised flesh. She jumped when his hand brushed her nub while guiding himself at her opening.

"I will be gentle, but it will hurt. I'm sorry." Ivy kissed him.

"I know. It can't be helped." She smiled at him. "What's a little pain when I get you in return?"

"You humble me, Ivy. You reduce me to nothing." He started pushing inside, and Ivy gritted her teeth at the sharp stab of pain. He stopped and looked at her with concern.

"I can stop…" he groaned, his chest heaving.

"No." He let out a sharp chuckle at her one-word reply but simultaneously buried himself to the hilt. He touched her forehead with his and waited. After a short while, her pain was replaced by an insistent throbbing and…want. Their eyes locked, their souls and hearts pouring from them. She nodded. He groaned from deep in his throat and started moving. First slowly, then faster when she started matching his rhythm stroke for stroke. Sweat dripped from him and pooled on her breasts, mixing with hers. And when it all became unbearable, when her body was becoming too tight to contain everything she was feeling, she exploded. That time she didn't run from the blast, though. She welcomed it. And he was right there with her. Closing his eyes, Gabriel burrowed his face into her neck, smothering the shout that burst from him when he found his release.

He collapsed on her, replete. She ran a soothing hand down his spine, and he shivered. She didn't mind his weight on her, even if she was feeling a touch smothered. Too soon, he lifted himself with a tired grunt, falling on his back and pulling her to him.

"Are you well, love?" he asked, placing a kiss on her hair.

"I'm perfectly content. Thank you. And you?" Her voice was drowsy, her eyelid already closing.

"I've never been better. You've deprived me of all my strength, Your Grace. But I can fall asleep peacefully, with you near, knowing I performed my duty."

Her eyes snapped open. *Duty*.

351

Chapter Thirty-One

The first week into the marriage between the Duke and Duchess of Blakeburne brought a welcome confirmation. Ivy had been right all along. His standoffish, aloof Grace wore a mask for the whole world to see. A mask Ivy wanted to seize, tore into million tiny pieces, and fed to the fire. Then she would take its ashes and give them to seven sea captains to spread in the farthest seas. And then she would find the mould from which it had been forged and fuse it into a badge of honour she was going to wear everywhere. Why? Because underneath that mask, there was the real man the world deserved to meet. The man who walked around in his shirtsleeves, who was passionate about ancient literature, horseflesh, and his tenants. Oh, Gabriel had still much in common with the Duke of Blakeburne. He was undeniably intense and powerful. And when he turned that intensity towards his new wife, Ivy knew she was doomed. If she had fallen in love with the Duke, she could fall hopelessly in love with the man.

Ivy was given an entire week to enjoy that side of Gabriel. The morning after their passionate wedding night, and after he had reminded her in great details what exactly had come to pass, he had informed her that he had not dismissed his servants only for the day but for the entire week. Together they had decided not to go on a honeymoon since not much time had passed since their return from the Continent. Both the Kingtons and the Easthams heaved a sigh of relief at that news.

To make up for it, Gabriel had planned for them to entrench in the townhouse instead. Apart from Cook and a very stubborn butler — who had at least conceded to remain within his domains— they were left to fend for themselves.

So, no footmen in the dining room to witness the Duke dragging his Duchess from her chair to his lap, where she promptly started opening the Duke's shirt before being spread on the table among the clatter of plates, cutlery, and glass. No butler announcing visitors while the Duke seated proudly behind his chair in his study, the Duchess between his legs opening his fall. And no lady's maid remarking on how few garments the Duchess required during the day and how the Duchess's bedchamber still remained untouched since her arrival.

The morning marking the end of their 'honeymoon' started with the typical noises of an aristocratic household. Servants' light steps going about their tasks, oiled doors opening and closing. Murmured voices coming from the dressing room. Ivy opened her eyes just as the connecting door opened, and an impeccably dressed Gabriel entered, a gentle smile tugging at his lips when he saw her watching him.

"Good morning, my dear. May I ask you what do you find so offensive about my attire? You are glaring at it." Ivy *was* looking at it rather bitterly.

"You are wearing a waistcoat. And a coat."

"Yes, and of supreme quality, I may add."

"I wouldn't care if they were made of spun gold. They represent our return to the outside world, with which I necessarily have to share you. And so do the return of the servants. But I can't go around glaring at them for working dutifully, can I? Therefore, I will turn my wrath on your waistcoats."

Gabriel chuckled at her impeccable reasoning.

"If it makes you happy, you can do what you want with my wardrobe. Just not let my valet hear you. Everybody knows never to displease a gentleman's valet."

Ivy flopped back down on the bed with a huff. Gabriel bent to kiss her pouting lips.

"What are your plans for the day?"

"I am to meet Victoria, Elizabeth, and Grace in…show me your timepiece. At least the waistcoat has its uses." She blinked rapidly. "In an hour! I'd better hurry. Gabriel, please let Poppy in!"

"Immediately, Your Grace." He made a leg to her before doing her bidding and opening the door. Efficient as ever, on the other side stood Poppy, waiting for permission to enter, while a ball of fur made his way inside, not before hissing at the man who stood too near his mistress.

"Colonel!"

"I brought him with me this morning, Your Grace," Poppy said, still on the threshold.

"Explain to me again why this feline —that clearly cannot stand my presence— had to follow you here."

"He hasn't left my side since I returned. Mother said he has started clawing at the upholstery the day of our wedding." Gabriel regarded the striped cat, and the animal looked back directly at him, unimpressed. After that staring contest, Colonel clearly decided Gabriel didn't deserve a second thought and jumped on a chair near the fireplace. Gabriel, with a similar expression, made to exit the room. Finding everything hilarious, Ivy couldn't refrain from saying, "Do try to get along. Don't make me choose between you two. If one wants to look deeper at the situation, Colonel outranks you, Major."

Ivy was pretty sure the Duke's mumbles on the other side of the now-closed door weren't meant for gentle ears.

※ ※ ※

Despite what she had told her husband, Ivy was in an exceedingly good mood when she met her friends near the Serpentine. Summer was slowly giving way to autumn, the burnished reds and yellows winning the battle against the brilliant greens, perfectly matching one of her favourite walking dresses. She smiled brilliantly at the three women, who curtsied deeply at her approach.

"Your Grace. You honour us with your presence," Victoria said, her eyes alight with merriment. "After a week without a word, we started to think we were now too far beneath you for your notice." Ivy was ready to meet the good-natured mocking in kind but was interrupted by a curious Elizabeth.

"What have you and the Duke been doing alone holed inside the house for an entire week? Weren't you bored?" Ivy wouldn't be able to contain her blush if her life depended on it. What have they been doing…

"I have one word for you, dear Elizabeth," interceded Victoria, "Newlyweds."

"Yes…And?" When it became apparent Elizabeth was really clueless about what had gone on behind their closed doors, the others burst into laughter.

"What? Why are you laughing? Mine was a reasonable question!"

"Oh, dear." Ivy dabbed the corners of her eyes. "You and I will have a chat soon."

It was all well and good that they shared a laugh between friends, but too many women entered marriage without any idea of what was expected from them in the conjugal bed. Ivy could help fill that unfair void. She had been lucky to have been raised by parents who didn't share the general idea of female sensibilities. And now to have a husband that had shown her in practice with his body. And mouth. And fingers…

"Isn't it warm in here?" Ivy asked, her body tingling at the memories her shameless brain had conjured.

"We are outside, Ivy. So no, it isn't," Grace pointed out logically. "Anyway. How is married life going? I daresay very well. You look beaming with joy."

"You would be too if you had the Duke of Blakeburne eating from the palm of your hand. Only Ivy could make a man like him fall in love with her."

"I don't think the Duke would ever eat from anybody's palm, Victoria." Ivy deliberately didn't address the second part of her friend's statement. It was true, she was happy. So what if Gabriel hadn't said anything even close to her love declaration in return. Or if their bodies hadn't yet cooled down before he had referred to their lovemaking as 'duty'. For once in her life, she would focus on the positive things, shoving any hesitations so far away that nobody would be able to find them. Gabriel didn't exactly have a silver tongue, as many of their past arguments showed. *Therefore, fears, deep down you go.*

"I second Victoria's view of things. He is—" What he was would forever remain unknown because another shrill voice drowned Grace's.

"Cousin! Just the Duchess I was dying to see!" Ivy turned and was faced with the most baffling group of people. Her cousin Eleanor was on the arm of…the Earl of Covington? Behind them, two people that didn't rank very high in her estimation. The woman who had tried to trap her husband, Lady Ingram, and her new cousin by marriage, Lord Charles Eastham, who Ivy still had not completely forgiven for his words at the now Dowager Duchess of Blakeburne's ball. Apart from Covington, she could have lived without meeting that party.

"Eleanor. To what do I owe such enthusiasm?" *Which you never had before.*

"I was just curious about how my newly married cousin was faring. We didn't have the chance to talk at your wedding."

"Lovely ceremony. I hope you received my note in which I thanked you and the Duke for including me in what was clearly a gathering of close friends and family." *Sweet Covington.*

"We are happy to include you among them, my Lord." That earned Ivy daggers from Lady Ingram, who *hadn't* been invited. *One wonders why.*

"We were all surprised that you could plan a wedding in such a short time. A two-month-long engagement is not the norm and certainly often not enough to arrange a ceremony." Eleanor's false praise was getting on Ivy's nerves. How dare she imply it was a rushed wedding. *Wasn't it, though?* It didn't matter.

"As per the Duke's and my choice. We were lucky enough to have two of the *ton's* most celebrated hostesses by our side."

Eleanor clearly decided to change tactics. "Well, I, for one, am pleased to see you so content. After all those rumours."

That was it. "Rumours *you* started spreading."

Eleanor gasped. "It wasn't me who embarrassed our family by travelling alone halfway across Europe!"

"You could have at least not misled Lord Bellmore into thinking I was dead!" Ivy was past caring if everybody heard.

"Ladies, I think it's time to continue with our promenade," interjected Lord Eastham, getting one step closer to forgiveness by preventing a brawl in Hyde Park. Much to the disappointment of Lady Ingram and the malicious glint in her eyes. "Please, bring my regards to my cousin."

"I will, my Lord, thank you. Lord Covington, Lady Ingram. Eleanor." Ivy forced the farewell out, followed by other, awkward ones from the others. As she watched them walk away, she wondered again at that odd group.

Then Eleanor, from her place on Covington's arm, fired one last parting shot. "I really hope you'll be content in your marriage, Ivy.

The *beau monde* may think your story is worthy of a poem, but then why, when I passed by the Duke and Viscount Bellmore here the day before your wedding, was he referring to it as an 'absurdity'?"

※ ※ ※

Her squabble with Eleanor was just the beginning of the collective effort to drain every drop of Ivy's contentedness. She had been able to banish her cousin's malice from her mind. History showed Eleanor was hardy reliable when she had to report facts. But having barely set eyes on her husband since arguing with his waistcoat didn't help her mood. She was realistic enough to know Gabriel was an extremely busy man. She had plenty to do with one estate, she could well imagine having to make decisions on several, spread all over the Empire, on an everyday basis. Add that to parliamentary duties and a role of royal advisor for the Prince Regent, and it wasn't strange that she would see him only at dinner. She understood, but that didn't mean she had to like it.

She didn't want to add herself to his endless list of worries or, God forbid, *duties*. Therefore, she cherished the time she got to spend with him. Gabriel accompanied her to perfunctory events —even if he spent an inexplicable amount of time glaring at the Earl of Covington — but they both didn't love Society enough to submit themselves to it more than necessary.

Now that she was the Duchess of Blakeburne, she wasn't invisible anymore. She resented the fact a little. Was it too much to ask that people remember her for herself and not only because now she was married to the Duke? When Baron Whintrope, embodying the best the *ton* had to offer, asked her where she had been hiding all that time, she had realised that yes, it was too much to ask. She had had to restrain her husband from attacking the Baron, allowing him a ducal glare. Ivy had made sure to express her appreciation for that in the carriage on the way home. Thoroughly.

Those were her favourite moments, and not only for the pleasure she drew from them, but mostly because among the clothes left in a heap on the floor lain his mask. So, the Duchess's chamber still hadn't seen anyone sleeping in it. And Ivy didn't care that he rose every morning without waking her, never to be seen again for the whole day. Or that she hadn't told him she loved him again after that first night, too proud to expose herself that way again.

Her days were divided between visiting her family and friends and forging a relationship with her mother-in-law. She had been particularly useful in shedding light on what made Gabriel the Duke of Blakeburne. Hearing about his sire made her understand the rigid rules by which he abided. But, where the Dowager saw the perfect thirteenth Duke of Blakeburne, Ivy saw dark tendrils of coldness that still enveloped his successor.

Then the study accident happened. Ivy had just met with the Dowager and, after another story from his childhood in which Gabriel had spent Christmas morning in the nursery conjugating Latin verbs instead of being outside playing in the snow with his little brother, she had decided to go see him. Jenkins had confirmed the Duke was at home. Maybe she could convince him to take a 'nap' in the middle of the afternoon like they had done that first pleasure-filled week. Although, she did have a practical reason for seeing him in the form of the letter from her steward in her hand.

Knocking gently, she entered the study. There he was, his dark head bent on his desk, quill in hand.

"Jenkins, if it's Mr Watt, tell him he's early and make him wait in the parlour. I expect for those in my employ to be able to read the time."

"My, my, husband, what a strict master you are." He finally raised his head at the sound of her voice.

359

"Ivy. What can I do for you?"

Ivy regarded him, cataloguing every part of him. Not a hair out of place, his ducal perfection made her want to make him come undone. She placed the letter on the mahogany surface before forcing him to lay back on his chair by climbing on his lap.

"Um, let's see, what can you do for me?" Her voice was sultry while she ran her hand over the expanse of his chest. She kissed him. After a few strokes of his tongue, he broke away.

"Ivy…"

Misinterpreting it as an encouragement, she bent her head to expose her neck while peppering his jaw with light kisses.

"Ivy! Stop!" He pushed her away, not violently, but forcefully enough to bring her back on her feet. "What's got into you? Don't you hear Jenkins is knocking?"

She hadn't heard, too caught up in the moment. Her embarrassment was complete when he looked at her slightly dishevelled appearance, disgusted. "Your gown is wrinkled," he pointed out.

Raising her chin despite feeling humiliated by her own husband, she looked at him in the eyes. "I came to tell you that I might have to travel to Everleigh in ten days or so." She turned with a swish of her skirt and went to open the door to their butler, who was patiently waiting on the other side.

"Jenkins, please come in," she said to the servant. "Let's not disrupt His Grace's day."

"Ivy…" The man had the gut to say her name in the same breath as an exasperated sigh.

"I'll see you at dinner, husband."

Later, Jenkins informed her Gabriel wouldn't join her for dinner. So, since the Dowager had acquired her own residence and didn't live with them, for the first time, Ivy dined alone. She asked the housekeeper, Mrs Jenkins, to serve it in one of the smaller rooms. There wasn't any need for formality between her and herself.

When it was clear the Duke would not appear at all that evening, she decided to retire. Passing the study, light was visible from under the closed door. Her husband really burned the candles at both ends. She was tempted to go in and to force him to leave his desk, but her pride didn't allow her to risk another embarrassment. Ivy had always known Gabriel didn't have much time to spare. Hell, he organised his day to the minute, and Ivy would never fault him for his commitment. She couldn't deny, however, that his easy dismissal hurt a bit. But she would get over it. She had years of practice with dismissals.

Moving away from the door, she went to her dressing room, where Poppy readied her for bed. She looked at the Duchess's chamber's closed door, but she couldn't make herself go inside.

She was later woken by the scorching heat of lips and hands on her neck and down her side. Eyes still closed, she turned. Her hands were met by soft skin. She welcomed the deep kiss he bestowed on her. She helped him open the row of tiny buttons on her nightshirt and laid on her back, savouring his attention on every inch of her body. His restless focus eased only when she came apart with a muffled cry. Only then she did open her eyes. And there he was, Gabriel, the man who looked at her like she was the most precious thing in his life. He entered her with tortured slowness until there wasn't even a breath of space between them. His thrusts were controlled at first, then the rhythm became lost in a frenzied need so intense she had no choice but to follow him over the edge again. Lying there, chests heaving, they still hadn't said a word to each other.

They turned to face one another, and Gabriel's eyes shone while his hand caressed her cheek. He had left the Duke back in his study, among stacks of papers. The sight wasn't as welcome as it usually was. When she had hesitated before and left him alone, something had started changing. Because, while he was able to shed his mask, she was afraid that one was being forged for her to wear. Permanently.

Ivy Kington, Countess of Everleigh, was becoming the Duchess of Blakeburne.

Chapter Thirty-Two

Ivy considered herself an intelligent person. Not quite a bluestocking, even if the number of books she had acquired since learning how to read could cast doubt on that claim. And what did intelligent people do when faced with a most maddening situation? They either lived with a constant headache, or they learned to adapt. Ivy —not liking the idea of adding to her already frequent migraines — decided on the latter. In the span of a few days, she became the epitome of what a Duchess should be. It wasn't even that difficult. She was already the daughter of one. During the day, she was poised, elegant, and independent. At night, she used her husband for her pleasure. If said husband had noticed that the woman who had faced the threat of the French for him was slowly disappearing, he didn't comment on it. And that was what she wanted. *Wasn't it?* It sometimes earned her an odd look from her friends and family, but it was all right.

Circumstances changed, and so did people. She did try to save her *duchessy* behaviour for Gabriel.

That day, she was waiting for Jenkins to enquire if the Duke had the time to see her —because that was how it was done. In two days, she would leave for Everleigh to settle some disputes only she could address. She had informed Gabriel of her plans at dinner a few days prior, but he still had to let her know if he intended to accompany her.

"His Grace will see you now, Your Grace."

"Thank you, Jenkins. You can go. There is no need to show me the way. It's my home." The butler bowed, hiding the slightest twitch of his lips. She liked Mr Jenkins and his wife, the housekeeper. They had met when they had been respectively footman and scullery maid and had been in the household since Gabriel had been a child.

She entered the study. She hadn't done that since that day, more than a week ago.

"Good morning, husband."

"Good morning, wife," he said, rising on his feet from behind his desk. "It's a good thing you decided to come to see me. We have to talk about our plans for leaving London."

"Yes, exactly." He could have informed her sooner, but at least he was preparing to travel with her.

"I have to go to Blakeburne Manor. I will leave in three days. You should accompany me. I think it's time you see your ancestral estate." Ivy blinked. And then blinked again. She opened her mouth and then closed it again. Finally, she managed to say, "I beg your pardon?"

"I know it's a bit sudden, but I confide you can pack in time." Ivy couldn't decide if it was more insulting that he thought she couldn't pack in three whole days —he had seen that she had no problem travelling light— or that he had failed to notice that her trunks were almost ready. For another trip. Which he had forgotten. Or discarded as meaningless.

"Gabriel," she tried again, this time successfully. "I will leave for Everleigh the day after tomorrow. I told you as much the other night if

363

you recall." She was talking slowly, even carefully, her mind swimming in astonishment.

"Of course, I do. I just didn't think it was a sure thing. Be as it may, can you not postpone your trip?"

"Can you not postpone *yours?*" she retorted. They stared at each other, clearly at an impasse.

"Blakeburne Manor gives the Duchy its name," Gabriel pointed out as if it were enough to end the discussion.

"And Everleigh gives *me* my name."

"Not anymore."

A red haze started to fall over her eyes at his condescendence.

"I may be the Duchess of Blakeburne now, but I will always be the Countess of Everleigh first."

"And I respect that. But, as my wife, your first duty will always be to the Dukedom. To me." There it was that word again. *Duty.*

"And *your* duty? Will your first duty always be to the Dukedom, above all else?"

"Of course. You knew it when you married me."

Right that moment, an explosion occurred inside her. Eleanor's words, her doubts, and all the things she had shoved deep inside went flying like shrapnel. Before she could think better of it, she asked the question that really mattered.

"Did you *want* to marry me? It's no secret this wasn't what you wished. *I* wasn't what you wanted." Gabriel's spine shot ramrod straight, his eyes hard as real emeralds.

"I won't dignify that question with an answer. That you even have to ask it's preposterous."

A knock at the door interrupted what was quickly becoming a bloodbath. Jenkins, temporary saviour of marriages.

"Your Grace, I'm sorry to interrupt. Miss Winter has arrived and is waiting for you in her carriage."

"Jenkins, tell Miss Winter the Duchess will be along shortly."

364

"Nonsense. Jenkins, I will be right there. There isn't anything else to say."

"The conversation isn't over, Ivy!" It was Gabriel's first sign of emotion since she had entered the study. Since well before, really.

"We will continue it tonight. Good day, Your Grace."

❖ ❖ ❖

Ivy was still fuming in the carriage. She had stormed out and had slumped in her seat with the grace of an irate elephant. She had barely greeted Grace before she had started murmuring to herself like a self-respecting bedlamite.

"'I won't dignify that question with an answer,'" she parroted, deepening her voice.

"'The conversation isn't over'. Of course, Your Grace, let's examine how you are an arse!"

"I gather something happened with the Duke?" asked Grace, who had that far remained silent, subjecting herself to Ivy's gibberish. It wasn't Grace's fault Gabriel was an obstinate numbskull. She didn't deserve to have her day ruined by her foul mood.

"I'm sorry, Grace. I'm going to stop now. Let's not waste any more breath on hopeless circumstances."

Grace wisely agreed with a nod. "As you wish. But let me just say that I'm glad to see you like this."

"Foul-mouthed and irritating?"

"Animated. Don't take it the wrong way, but of late, you've been somewhat...dull."

"I don't think there is a right way to take it. And I'm not *dull*. I'm poised and distinguished."

"You were all that already. But you were also *more*. Now I see only that if that makes any sense." Ivy regarded the quietest of her friends closely.

"You are too perceptive for your own good. You know that?"

"It's a cross I have to bear," she said with a dramatic sigh, making Ivy laugh.

"Apropos of cross, let's go pestering Mr Davies for refusing to order us those novels."

"Wasn't that already the plan?" Ivy laughed again, thankfully more than words to have her in her life.

❃ ❃ ❃

"Have a nice day Mr Davies! And thank you!" They left a beleaguered but considerably richer Mr Davies with two piles of books to deliver to the addresses he was already very familiar with. Ivy's frame of mind had considerably improved. She was ready to go home and talk calmly with Gabriel again. He had to thank his lucky star that equanimous Grace and The Turning Page's atmosphere she loved so much were able to cool her down.

Grace was chatting away, animated by the day's findings, when she abruptly stopped on the pavement. "Drat! I've forgotten my reticule. I must have left it on the counter," Grace said with an apologetic grimace.

"Let's go fetch it before Mr Davies decides to ban us till the end of time."

Grace stopped her. "Oh, there's no need to bother. I see the carriage there, just around the corner. I won't be more than a moment." Ivy could indeed see the rear of the carriage parked a few feet away. They had left their footmen with it, not deeming them necessary for the short walk to the shop. Ivy nodded at her friend with a smile and started towards their conveyance.

She wasn't really paying attention to where she was going, her mind already on how to deal with the complications at home. She was already around the corner when she thought she heard Grace saying something from the distance. She turned, but a brawny arm snatched her from her waist, making her stumble directly against a mountain of a man. The hand that came up to cover her mouth was so massive it almost spanned her entire face, effectively blinding her. Trying to wriggle herself free was proving useless, as was trying to scream. What emerged were nothing more than muffled sounds smothered by the sweaty flesh of her unknown assailant.

She was pushed inside what was clearly not Grace's carriage.

It had all lasted mere seconds. People continued strolling up and down the road as if she were not being taken against her will in the middle of the day in a fashionable part of London. In one last desperate attempt to escape, Ivy regained her footing and launched herself at her captor standing on the carriage step, filling the space between her and freedom. It was like trying to move a mountain by blowing on it. Hands that had seized her now pushed her ruthlessly back. The momentum sent her violently against the wooden interior. For the second time in her life, Ivy felt her head collide with the merciless material and lost her battle with darkness.

People still continued with their day when an unmarked, but well made, carriage was lost in the busy street.

Gabriel adjusted his gloves, his walking stick under his arm. The door of his solicitor's office closed behind him. Mr Rutledge had not been happy to see him. He had told him in no uncertain terms that, Duke or not Duke, he wasn't at the whim of 'pompous nobs', to use his words. It was one of the reasons Gabriel had chosen him to manage his affairs in Town. The fact that he wasn't on half of the *ton*'s payroll was another one. Hardly anyone knew that the Duke of Blakeburne shared the solicitor with professionals and tradesmen. *The horror!* The state of his coffers disagreed.

They had an appointment two days hence, but Gabriel was feeling restless. It had nothing to do with his investments and everything to do with his wife. He couldn't believe his ears when she had asked him whether he wanted their marriage. That his wife, his madness, his life, doubted it even for a second meant that he wasn't handling his new role as well as he thought.

That first week of their marriage had left him deeply satisfied. And not only physically. Those days had started to fill a void he wasn't even aware he had. She had taken the rules his sire had instilled in him and had obliterated every single one without even knowing it. When she had told him she loved him, he had suddenly seen how deeply those rules had shaped the man he was. Because, despite how they had hit him with the force of thousand cannon blasts, he hadn't said anything back but had made love to her like it was the only thing keeping him anchored. And it was.

But honeymoons didn't last. Each time he had walked by his study during that week, he had felt a physical itch looking at the growing mountain of papers on his desk.

Once back to his normal life, he had been pleased to note that he could keep his days just as they were before their marriage and fill his nights with Ivy. The pleasure they found together had surpassed his wildest dreams. Just like that day in his study, when, with a herculean effort, he had forced himself not to take her right there, with the butler and one of his men of business waiting outside the door.

But something had changed right under his eyes. Each time he looked at his wife, little by little, he saw her changing, not retreating in the shy shell he had seen in the past, nor embracing that inner fire that he knew simmered inside her, but morphing into the very Duchess he had thought he had always wanted. The one who went about her days dignified and collected, not bothering the Duke in his important tasks. And the void inside him had come back.

He had been so intent in studying her that he had not listened that night when she talked about Everleigh. And that brought them to that very morning. After she had left, he hadn't been able to concentrate on anything except how it was possible she didn't know how deeply in love with her he was. After everything they had faced together. It had taken some time for him to realise it himself, he had fought it even, but it had all been useless. And now it was undeniable.

Without informing anyone, he had escaped his house and started walking. After a while, he had become annoyed by how much time he was wasting just wandering around, without his thoughts being any clearer. Finding himself near Brook Street, he had decided to anticipate his appointment with Mr Rutledge.

He was starting his walk back home when he heard his name being called urgently.

"Blakeburne! Fucking finally!" He turned towards the man freely cursing down the street. His brother-in-law was almost running towards him, Bellmore close on his heels.

"Where the fuck have you been?" the Marquess of Burnam continued with his profanities.

"You are deuced hard to find, old chap. Bloody inconvenient," added a slightly calmer Bellmore, unhelpfully. Gabriel wanted to say that what he did was none of their business, but Burnam had no time for that.

"Make haste! Our carriage is parked right there."

"Someone cares to explain what the hell is going on? Why were you looking for me?"

The Marquess was already walking towards the carriage like the devil was chasing him. It was Bellmore who answered him. He looked straight into Gabriel's eyes without breaking his stride. Gabriel found himself back at the Army camp when the Viscount had come bearing the news that had made his world go temporary black. Cold sweat started running down his spine.

"The Duchess has been kidnapped."

Chapter Thirty-Three

Ivy was rudely shoved inside a room, probably a cellar. Even if she hadn't been forced down the steep stairs, she would have known it by the stale odour and the dampness that permeated the sack her kidnappers had put on her head, making it hard to breathe. She hoped being in a closed place meant she would soon regain her eyesight. She was near panicking as it was; being able to see meant regaining an ounce of control. Her head throbbed with the by now familiar pain of a head wound.

Her only hope was that by now —whenever it was— Grace had raised the alarm. She imagined Gabriel pacing up and down his study, organising a search party. To everyone else, he would seem callously fully in control of the situation. Only those who knew what to look for would see the storm brewing inside him. Thoughts of her husband were comforting, and she managed to bring her breath under control. Questions started to swirl and overlap in her mind. Why had she been taken? Who could have a reason to do such a thing? Ivy couldn't think of anyone who would go to such lengths. Up until a few months ago, she was hardly deemed worthy of a second glance. Now someone had concocted a plan to kidnap her. It was a bold, hazardous move. For, however unappreciated she had been, Ivy was a Countess and the wife a Duke, a powerful one at that. The consequences of discovery would be very dire. Their motivations had to outweigh the risks. But what were those motivations? Ransom?

There was no forthcoming answer. The only thing that had changed lately had been her marital status. Could her marriage be at the core of all that? A former lover who hadn't come to terms with the Duke of Blakeburne not being available anymore? Ivy couldn't envision it, but it remained a possibility. There would be time to try to make sense of the situation, but at the moment, she had more pressing matters. Namely what her kidnappers had in store for her. She could sense someone in front of her. Despite that, she was startled and tried to take a step back when a hand touched her shoulders. She started to struggle again to avoid her kidnapper's touch and against the rope binding her hands together.

"What do you want from me? Let me go!"

"Shh, don't be afraid. Nothing bad will happen to you if you behave."

Ivy froze in her struggle, unable to move a muscle, her cries stuck in her throat. Surely, she was wrong. It had to be a trick of her mind. It couldn't be…

"Now, my dear, I'm going to remove this ugly sack. Be still." Actions followed his words. Ivy blinked furiously, trying to see something. Panic threatened to swallow her when she couldn't see anything at all. What had they done to her? She was blind! Did they drug her? What kind of substance rendered you blind?

Just before panic overcame her, pulling her under in a sea of irrationality, her eyes caught a sliver of light on the floor. She wasn't blind after all, but the room was cast in total darkness. That dim light had to come from under a door, marking it the only source of illumination, oxygen and…freedom. Her relief was short-lived when the person —clearly a man— spoke again, throwing her in a nightmare from which she had no hope of waking.

"There, isn't it better? I know these accommodations are a far cry from what you are used to, but they have to do for now." A long finger traced the contour of her cheek, and Ivy had to suppress a shiver. "Now, if you promise to be the quiet, little mouse I know you can be, I'll leave you to get settled. After all, this is going to be a lengthy stay for you. One could even say that this is the ideal place for a mouse." Ivy felt him move away from her, his retreating steps in the direction of the door. Her eyes were fixed on his back, trying to find out even the slightest hint that disputed what her dazed mind was trying to tell her. She hoped the candlelight stemming from outside would be enough.

The retreating figure was tall, well-built, and wearing dark clothes. Anything else was still enveloped in darkness. He stopped on the threshold and, without turning, left her with parting words that froze the blood in her veins.

"Now rest, my dear. There is so much I have in store for you."

The clang of the metal door closing resounded deep inside Ivy. Like a thread being cut by scissors, that sound severed the connection with everything she thought she knew. Falling on her knees, she forced her mind to clear, to function enough to make sense of the unexplainable. His height, his shoulders, even his scent, all led to one explanation. If that wasn't damning enough, his words continued to repeat themselves in her mind. Not their meaning, but how they were uttered. The truth she was facing —and she was trying to deny with all her might— was horrifying. That voice. The voice that had become as dear to her as her own belonged to Gabriel.

❊ ❊ ❊

Left alone in the pitch-dark room, Ivy tried to get an inkling of her surroundings. She took tentative steps to her right, careful not to bump into any piece of furniture, or anything else, stored in what she was now sure was a cellar. It took more strength not to stumble on her own feet than she would have liked, bringing it home how vulnerable she really was. Her hands, still tied together, finally pressed against the cold and damp surface of a wall. It was a relief to have something solid to lean on when everything else around her seemed to shake right to its foundations. She sagged against it, depleted. Her mind was still clouded by the blow, and the shock of what had just transpired had left her completely off balance. Was it real or just a cruel hallucination? She shook her head, trying to clear it, but nothing came to her aid. She slid down the damp surface, bringing her knees to her chest. In the back of her mind, a feeble voice was warning her to be rational, to examine the room in search of anything that could help her escape or at least understand what was going on. But she couldn't move. She was a prisoner of her own head, where she couldn't escape images of her husband. Images of their life together, of what had led to their marriage. Sweet memories to which her mind was trying desperately to cling on. The effort was rapidly becoming too great. Each and every one of them was slowly being tainted by others. By the times she had felt alone, not enough to be loved, cherished, and protected. The shadow darkening her memories swallowed everything else until it became too difficult to discern what was real and what was a product of her mind. Until only darkness remained.

She was running on the grass, trying to reach Gabriel before something terrible happened. She didn't remember what, but she was sure it was a matter of life or death. That part was real. She was sure of it. It had really happened. But something was off. The grass under her feet was lifeless brown, dead, crunching under each one of her hurried steps. The sky was a different shade of reddish-brown but without the warmth of a sunset. It cast a sick light around, making everything indiscernible. She must have been running for a while, her breath was laboured. All that didn't matter because, there, in the distance, stood Gabriel. His back was to her, and he was wearing a black cloak, a hood covering his head. When Ivy finally reached the figure, she urged him to turn around, a hand pulling his arm. She looked at his beloved face. What she saw was not it, though. In its place, nothing. A black shadow, a phantom face hidden underneath the hood. She took a retreating step, scared by the single feature visible among the nothingness. Green eyes, shining with cruelty. "Did you really think I cared for you? That I loved you?" The voice was deep, hollowed, but controlled and cultured. Unmistakably Gabriel's. "You've always been too naïve to understand what was going on around you. Not everything is as it seems." He was walking towards her, slowly but inexorably. She tried to raise her arms to stop him, but it was like lead manacles were blocking her movements. "You should have done us all a favour and died in that carriage accident. Now I wouldn't be saddled with you for life."

"Gabriel, no. This isn't you." Silence met her protests. One step forward, then another. For each one of his, Ivy took a matching one backwards. Suddenly the scenery changed around her. She was now standing in her own drawing-room at Blakeburne House, opulence and elegance in stark contrast with the lifeless field. Still, the shadow was advancing menacingly. And still, she retreated, an opposite force to his stronger, darker one. Her knees and back met the balustrade of the balcony. Rather than the protective barrier of hard stone, her body went through it as if it were made of soft butter. Nothing stood between her and the ground below. Ivy didn't know what awaited her, but the last thing she saw was Gabriel, his face now clearly visible, standing motionless on the balcony, watching her fall with an unconcerned expression. She tried to scream for help, for him to do something, but her voice was swallowed by his. "Maybe it will not be for long, after all."

Ivy woke with a start. She took a couple of deep breaths, not knowing what else to do. It was all pointless when a new wave of panic washed over her, making bile rise in her throat. The abduction. The cellar. Gabriel. Oh God, was it Gabriel who was keeping her confined?

She couldn't fathom how she could have fallen asleep, letting her guard down. Shaking her head, she was comforted that the pain had lessened. Her head was clear for the first time after who knew how long. She realised that what had woken her from her nightmare-filled slumber had been the metallic click of the lock and the creak of the

375

opening door. She thanked heaven for being vigilant, ready to face any threat. The candlelight from the doorway outlined the shape of two figures, one very different from the other. One was plump, petite and obviously female. The other, more worryingly, was a giant. The man who had taken her from the street. Easily more than six feet four, the mountain of muscles carried a lamp held high in his right hand, illuminating the face of a bruiser. Thick blond brows dominated deeply set dark eyes that regarded her intently. His large nose had undoubtedly been broken more than once. His mouth was set in a thin line, a thin scar on the left side of it giving a perpetual downcast tilt, not exactly cruel, but not kind either. After her nightmare, the ensemble did nothing to help keep her panic under control.

Ivy was so intent on warily watching the man that she didn't notice the smaller figure approaching until the voice directly in front of her made her jump.

"The Master has ordered to bring you dinner."

"And who might your Master be?" Ivy asked, in a desperate attempt to have everything she had seen and heard disproved.

"Please, sit at the table and eat your dinner," the woman said, setting the tray on a small rectangular table on the opposite side of the room. Now that the light-bearer man stood in the middle of it, Ivy could see that the wall against which she had leant was the only void of furniture, sparse as it were. Facing the door, there was a straw mattress on the floor, covered with white and —from what she could see— clean sheets. On its right stood the plain rectangular table with a chair, and in the corner, a bucket. That was the extent of the amenities in her prison cell.

"I'm not hungry, thank you. Please, can you tell me what's going on? Where am I? Why am I here?"

"Eat lass. Dae yerself a favour an' eat whit's in th' plate. Ye willnae like it if I mak ye." Those were the first words that came out of the giant's mouth, spoken in a melodic Scottish brogue. His massive presence was made even more threatening by the game of light and

376

shadows playing on his face. She fancied she could hear a strange note behind his tone. Something like reluctance and... resignation. Like he wasn't totally on board with this. Her mind hadn't proved itself to be totally trustworthy of late, however. She decided to temporarily set her stubbornness aside and try to put something in her stomach. She needed all the strength she could muster. Especially if it meant they would free her hands. She sat in the old chair, her posture the same as if she were sharing her repast with royalty and not in a cellar, surrounded by dubious characters. She was the Duchess of Blakeburne, Countess of Everleigh, and nobody had better forget it, least of all herself. It was her only certainty.

The cold meal consisted of undetermined roasted meat and a slice of bread. A small jug of water made her realise how thirsty she was. She guzzled it down in two healthy swallows, but her empty stomach threatened to rebel. *That was a bad idea*, Ivy thought, following it with a piece of bread, hoping not to disgrace herself with a mad rush to the bucket. Once certain the crisis had been averted, she picked the meat apart with the fork, constantly aware of the two behind her, watching her like hawks. Or vultures, more aptly.

"Do you have to stand there, sinisterly watching? I am eating, am I not?" Silence met her outburst. With a glare and a huff to uphold her aristocratic exterior and hide her fear, she resumed her meal. She wasn't sure whether it was lunch or dinner. Hell, maybe breakfast. The absence of windows didn't help discern what time, or day, it was. The only possible source of information were the two mostly unhelpful people in the room.

"Can you at least tell me what time it is?" Ivy didn't want to let them know she wasn't even sure if a day, or two, had passed since she had been taken from the busy street.

"It's past noon. Noo feenish eatin'." That from the giant, who didn't bother checking a timepiece to be a little more precise. 'Past noon' could mean anything. 'Past noon' most certainly also meant that she had been held there for at least a day, seeing that it had been mid-afternoon when she had exited The Turning Page. Could have been more, but she doubted it. That was the first meal she was presented with. If they aimed to starve someone, one didn't give them substantial sustenance. The food was simple, but not poor. The meat was heavily spiced, almost too much. And Ivy knew from the household ledgers, spices weren't inexpensive.

When she couldn't swallow one more bite, she rose from the table. She had to grip the back of the chair to remain upright. What was wrong with the floor?

The room swam before her eyes. After one tentative step, she stumbled, only to have a huge hand seize her arm with bruising strength. *Do humans have hands so big?* The man almost lifted her off her feet and moved her forward. *That's nice. Walking is very overrated. Where is he taking me? Oh, a bed. Good idea. What an outstanding gentleman. Let's rest for a bit, and all will be well.*

"Miss Winter, are you sure you can't tell us anything else? Even the most insignificant detail could help us." Grace Winter swallowed hard, clearly intimidated. Gabriel couldn't blame her. He had to cut a frightening figure, looming over her from across his desk, knuckles white from gripping the wood so hard it was in danger of splitting. Nonetheless, the young woman straightened her spine, looking right at him. He could see why she was friends with his wife. His heart constricted.

"You don't really think I would take the matter lightly, do you, Your Grace? I have told you everything I can. I forgot my reticule inside the bookshop. While I went to retrieve it, Ivy walked to my carriage waiting nearby. If I hadn't stepped outside to call for her to come back to have a look at a book Mr Davies had uncovered from a high shelf, I wouldn't have seen the big man with the brown cloak carry her away. Then again, if I hadn't forgotten my reticule, she wouldn't have been walking alone. It was my fault."

Gabriel agreed, but he refrained from pointing it out. One thing was sure. Once Ivy was safely by his side again, he would replace each one of the footmen who were supposed to guard her with so many mean-looking armed guards that Rutherford-Blythe's ones would seem like tin soldiers in comparison. *If he could find her.* No, he couldn't allow his mind to wander.

"In that case, you could have been taken as well, and we would still be oblivious to the fact," Bellmore was saying. Easy for him to be level-headed. It wasn't part of his soul that was missing.

They were all gathered in Gabriel's study. He, Bellmore, Burnam, and Grace Winter, who had come directly at Blakeburne House after witnessing Ivy's kidnapping, only to find it empty. She had then sent a messenger running to R-B. Burnam had wisely asked for Bellmore's help to find Gabriel, while the Duke started organising his men for the search. How much time had they lost to find him?

Burnam was pacing a hole in his carpet. "What reason could they have to take Ivy?"

"Ransom," Bellmore provided simply. "It's the most probable reason."

"Ivy has always had loads of money. Why now?" Burnam countered, who was getting on Gabriel's already frayed nerves with his constant pacing.

"Now she has even more. The Kingtons and the Easthams together could buy a small kingdom without putting a dent in their coffers. If I had to risk my neck, I would choose the fattest pigeon of all." Gabriel shot him a deadly glare, to which the Viscount shrugged. He wasn't completely wrong. Gabriel was already two steps ahead with his reasoning, though. He couldn't totally discard the money motive, but it seemed too hazardous. Kidnapping a Duchess in broad daylight? If

379

something went wrong, the culprit would be swinging before realising it.

"Or they have a personal grievance."

Burnam's head snapped in Gabriel's direction. "That's absurd. Ivy is the most generous-hearted person I know." The Marquess narrowed his eyes and finally stopped pacing, only to stride right up the Duke's face. "As opposed to *your* affable personality. I swear to God, Blakeburne, if this happened again because of you, I—"

"Let's not forget it's not in *my* family that it had already happened before." The two men were almost touching after Gabriel had gone around his desk to face his brother-in-law.

"That was different, and you know it." They were referring to the scandal that had surrounded the kidnapping of the now Duchess of Rutherford-Blythe, many years before.

"Cease!" The command came unexpectedly from Miss Winter. Grace was on her feet, her cheeks scarlet red, and her fists clenched. "This is hardly helpful. You'll have time to recriminate until you are both blue in the face after we find Ivy." She pinned Gabriel with a look that would have made any General proud.

"Let's bring your wife home, Your Grace."

"Hear, hear, Miss Winter," praised Bellmore, a slight grin on his lips, a heavy heart in his chest.

Chapter Thirty-Four

"Time to wake up, sweetheart." *Sweetheart?* Gabriel had never called her sweetheart. And yet, when she opened her eyes, it was that tall shadow that accompanied the deep voice. He was standing in the doorway. Whichever light he had brought with him had been left in the hall, not helping her glazed eyesight. What time was it? What *day* was it? She remembered eating that spicy meal and then…nothing more than swimming faces and darkness. The latter was still one trusted companion. She shifted on the pallet but tried not to make a sound, wary of what could happen once he knew she was conscious.

"I know you are awake. There's no need to rise on my account. I only came for a chat. How long do you think it would take for someone to notice you are gone? Hours? Days? Weeks? You've never been the brightest star in the sky, have you, Ivy?" Ivy couldn't bear her inferiority position any longer. She rose to her feet, swaying lightly.

"Let me go. Half of London will be searching for me by now, and the other half is being searched as we speak." Or at least that was what she wanted to believe. But if the shadow was the man she won't resign herself to believe he was, why would anyone search for her?

"Yet I don't see anyone here. Nobody even came to ask questions. And to think that it's so obvious." The last was said in that condescending way Ivy found deeply irritating in Gabriel. With each word, each gesture, she was losing hope that everything she was seeing was a horrifying nightmare and that she would soon wake up.

"Why are you doing this?" *Please, let me understand.* The shadow had turned to leave but stopped at her question.

"Why, my dear, you are nothing more than an inconvenience. You know how I hate when something disrupts my life. You really thought I wanted you?" He then addressed someone who had been standing just outside the cellar the whole time. "Do it."

The door closed behind the shadow. Only, the giant man stood on her side of the door. In the darkness, she couldn't see his face as he took the first step towards her.

Five days. Five bloody days since someone had taken Ivy away from him. Gabriel was at his wits' end. He had slept a few hours here and there, but the nightmares had been almost worse than reality. At least, when he was awake, he could do something. But it wasn't enough. He and R-B had hired every Bow Street Runner and private investigator available. Bellmore had used his unsavoury connections to search every slum and dirty corner. But nothing. They had asked questions as discretely as possible to avoid adding dealing with a scandal on top of everything else. That had been R-B's idea. Gabriel had wanted to punch his father-in-law out when he had said it. Who cared about gossip when he was close to razing the whole town to the ground?

Gabriel felt nauseous each time he stopped to think about what Ivy could be facing at the hand of the unknown degenerate, whose motives were still obscure.

A ransom letter would have meant Ivy was worth more alive than dead. But there had been no contact whatsoever. He felt ill at the thought of what that meant. This was worse than the time on the Continent. The danger there had been tangible, recognisable, fightable. This time, they were chasing a ghost, a threat that could assume any form.

Gabriel had threatened, bribed, promised favours, all to come up empty-handed. He was returning from another fruitless meeting with Bow Street. They usually came to him, but that day the walls of his enormous townhouse were closing on him.

Five days. He would not rest until he found her, but each tick of the clock was like a cut on his skin.

"Your Grace?" Jenkins brought him back to the present. The man had been even more sombre than normal, his worry etched on his face since the news had reached the household.

"Yes, Jenkins?"

"There's Lady Eleanor waiting for you."

What did his wife's cousin want with him? She was oblivious to what was happening. For obvious reason. She and her gossiping ways were one of the reasons he and Ivy got married in the first place. That he had got his heart's desire out of it was inconsequential. He would not trust her with the truth. That and the fact that she had been less than nice to his wife in the past didn't put her under a favourable light. She had been adroitly questioned by the Duchess of R-B and Ivy's friends, who had proven to be irreplaceable in making enquires among the female half of the *ton*. Luckily for her, nothing suspicious had arisen.

"Tell Lady Eleanor I will see her another time."

"I think you'd better listen to what I have to say, Your Grace," Lady Eleanor said, emerging from the drawing-room. Petite and beautiful, Eleanor Kington exuded confidence.

"What is so paramount that it cannot wait? I can't fathom what business you could have to discuss with me."

Eleanor tutted. "That's no way to treat family, Your Grace. Especially when I may know where to find your wife."

Ivy was being drugged. She had finally realised it after the fourth heavy spiced meal she had been served since the beginning of her 'stay'. She would have noticed it sooner if not for the aforementioned substances keeping her mind in a constant state of confusion. So, she had decided to stop eating. The wisdom of such a decision was debatable because any moment of clear-headedness she had gained was soon replaced by the haze of hunger. At least, she was able to keep the monsters at bay. Especially the giant, who had come to visit her every day. He hadn't touched her, thank God. He simply stood, or sat, inside her cell, looking at her, one lone, small candle casting more shadows than light around. Ivy never knew when, or if, he would move or hurt her.

Other times, he would rise and walk slowly around the room before sitting back down again. It was terrifying. After a while, he left without a word. The first days, he had left behind a fear-stricken, almost hysterical, Ivy. It became harder and harder not to break into sobs when the shadow came to retrieve the monster.

Once, she had had a glimpse of a blue coat, one she was sure she had seen Gabriel wear. Every time, his broad shoulders and slim waist mocked her, filling the doorway like an avenging angel, only to lock her in the dark again.

One thought alone occupied her mind, both when it was lucid and addled. She had to escape. Rescue didn't seem forthcoming, so she had to take matters into her own hands. She had tried pleading with the giant man turned monster and the old woman who brought food that Ivy left untouched. It had all fallen on deaf ears. She refused to beg the shadow. There was a part of her that hung to the hope that another explanation, even a far-fetched and implausible one, could be the truth behind her captivity. That it wasn't Gabriel, her husband, the love of her life. As the days went by, it was increasingly difficult to hold on to it. *Focus Ivy.*

She needed a plan.

She started walking up and down her cell, disheartened and not a little worried when her breath became laboured after only a few turns. The by-then familiar sound of the lock unlatching broke the silence once again.

"I'm glad to see you using your time to exercise. *Mens sana in corpore sano.* Isn't in how the saying goes? A healthy mind in a healthy body."

Plan be damned. Ivy threw herself in his direction. Her feebleness slowed her down, making her attack ineffective. With two steps backwards, he slammed the door shut, and Ivy's raised fists met hardwood. But not before the faint candlelight caught a flash of colour. The green of his eyes.

"Let me out!" she shouted, pounding until her hands were scraped by the repeated abrasion. He was still there, on the other side, listening to her. The monster was there as well, waiting to play his game. They talked briefly. They were arguing. Although her ear was pressed against the door, she couldn't understand what they were saying. Only disjointed words.

She should have come away from the door.

"…is madness. It cannot be condoned."

You are my beautiful madness.

She had thought she had already lost hope. But it hadn't been true until that moment. Until the darkness surrounding her seeped into her heart. It was a good thing that it didn't require her will to beat because she hadn't any strength left to infuse to it. It was her husband, the man who had made her discover she could be more than what the *ton* had planned for her. Whose smiles had been worth their rarity for their beauty. Who had worshipped her body to untold pleasure. The man she had brought back from the war.

The man who had told her time and time again he didn't want to marry her. Who had readily banished her to an item of his agenda. Who hadn't told her he loved her in return.

He had imprisoned her and hidden her away. He was mentally torturing her. He resumed her pounding, the pain in her heart making the one in her hands seem like a tingle. Tears were freely staining her face, but her voice was loud and clear.

"Do your worst! I'm here, at your mercy." She took a step back and spread her arms wide in surrender, even if he could not see her. "I've nothing left to believe in! You have threatened me, hurt me, made me doubt what I see with my own eyes. What is it that you want? Just be a man and finish this yourself, not using your servants. Let's get it over with, Gabriel." It was the first time she had said his name aloud. It tore away from her, a cherished word that she had guarded until the end.

Her stubborn heart continued working, its pulsation so loud it appeared to resound from outside her body.

But they weren't heartbeats she was hearing. It was Gabriel walking away.

"Lady Eleanor, why would I want to know something about my wife from you when I could simply ask her myself?" The clock was ticking. Five days and two hours had passed. And he was there, wasting time with her wife's cousin.

"Let's drop the pretence, shall we? Ivy has never been a diamond of the first water who attracted much attention, but it's unusual even for her to disappear for so long, especially since she has somehow managed to become the new Duchess of Blakeburne."

"I urge you to tread carefully when talking about my wife." More than a few judges would not convict him if she throttled her now, he was sure.

"A wife who isn't here. Whose mother and friends are even now running around asking questions. We might not be very close, but I don't want anything to happen to Ivy."

"What do you think you know?" Gabriel asked, slightly mollified. He might as well exploit her presence.

"Let's just say, I've made the mistake of befriending a woman you know well, Your Grace. Lady Ingram." *Arabelle?* "I found her worldly and sophisticated, but, deep down, she's just a spoiled child who wants what she can't have. Believe me, I recognise the type." She pointed meaningfully at herself. "The woman is positively obsessed with you and with becoming your Duchess." Gabriel perfectly recalled when Arabelle had tried to trap him by compromising them both. She would have succeeded if not for Ivy. But an abduction?

"I may agree with you, but it doesn't prove she has something to do with Ivy's disappearance."

"Maybe not. But if I told you she thinks that 'carriage accidents are unfortunate but sometimes unavoidable'? That's what she said when I told her about Ivy's misadventure on the road to Dover. Or that other time when she said that Ivy's absence would not even be noticed, were she to disappear? It's true I've said something similar to Ivy once, and I regret it, but it's different with Lady Ingram. She is more malicious. I think you should...Your Grace!"

Gabriel was already out of the room, shouting for Jenkins, before learning what she thought he should do. Burnam was right. It was all because of him. He had examined everyone who could hold a grudge against him but had not considered a former mistress to which he hadn't exchanged more than greetings in the past ten years.

Except, Lady Ingram wasn't home. And had not been for the last fortnight.

His feet were dragging, the effort of climbing the steps to his front door almost too great. Once inside, he was informed that Burnam, R-B, and his cousin Charles were waiting for him. He had sent a note to apprise the Kingtons of the new development, while he had not seen his cousin since he had asked the first round of questions.

He didn't even greet them before making a beeline to the liquor cart. After emptying his glass in two healthy gulps, he faced the men.

"Nothing. She wasn't home and had not been for a while."

"That doesn't exonerate her completely." Gabriel agreed with R-B.

"True. She either has nothing to do with this, and she's simply a spiteful woman, or her plan is far more complex and articulate. Either way, we still haven't a clue where the fuck Ivy is!" Gabriel raked a hand through his hair in frustration. He appealed to every ounce of sang-froid. R-B and Burnam appeared as tired as he felt, violet shadow circling their eyes. His cousin stood silent, a solemn expression on his face.

"Cousin, it's good to see you. I see you've taken my advice and availed yourself of my tailor's services." Gabriel eyed Charles's blue morning coat, similar to one he owned. *Oh, Lord, what the hell was he even saying? Who bloody cared?*

"Thank you, Gabriel. But that's inconsequential now. Tell me, what can I do to help?" The noose was tightening around Gabriel's neck. Charles was the second person who had been left in the dark to have come to him in one day. It would not be much longer before the news of the Duchess's disappearance started to spread. What would that mean for the kidnappers?

"Another set of eyes will not go amiss," Burnam answered for him. Gabriel nodded.

"You keep vigilant and report anything that even smells out of the ordinary. I'll go after Lady Ingram. I want to be sure she hadn't even breathed in Ivy's direction before discarding her." The Kingtons would continue their part of the search.

"I just wanted to say I'm sorry this is happening to you, Gabriel," Charles said. "Sometimes, it doesn't matter how hard we try. It seems it's never enough."

Chapter Thirty-Five

"Lass." It was the first time the mountain had spoken to her since that first day. Just like then, he was pressing her to eat. Strange priorities for a monster.

"This I teuk directly frae th' kitchen, frae mah own meal," he said, handing her a small loaf of bread. She rose from her foetal position, opening her puffy eyes, and looked at it with suspicion. The man sighed and took a bite, making a show of chewing it.

"It's guid, lass." The tone was gentle. At first, she had been too frightened to pay much attention to his Scottish lilt. Then again, he hadn't bothered talking in her presence, limiting himself to just looming menacingly over her or moving around, in and out of the darkness. He hadn't needed to lay a finger on her to frighten her out of her mind. Uncertainty was that powerful. Now, with the candle not playing tricks and fully lighting his face, Ivy saw that he wasn't as frightening as they had led her to believe. The scars that marred his face weren't pretty, but his eyes were. They weren't dark, but light blue and kind, under greying blond brows. They didn't hide any malice. But Ivy didn't trust her judgement anymore. Look at where it had led her.

"It isnae fair that he treats ye so. It wisnae th' plan. I wis tae tak' ye frae th' street tae send a message tae anither Sassenach that owed His Lordship money. That whit he said. Na body takkit about lockin' ye awaye. It isnae th' thing."

Ivy didn't disagree. Glimpsing a pale ray of hope in his disapproval, she decided to try her luck with the man.

"What's your name?"

"Duncan Munro. That wis mah da's name. He wauld tirn in his grave if he kent a Munro teuk part in harmin' an innocent lass lik ye. Na money's wirt whit Eastham's daein'."

Ivy's ears perked up, and not to better understand his thickening brogue. It was the second time that Munro had got Gabriel's honorific wrong. She had thought the first time —calling him His Lordship and not His Grace— had been an honest mistake made by someone not overly familiar with the peerage. But nobody had ever called Gabriel 'Eastham' outside the Army. He had always carried a title. It didn't make any sense.

Even if it were a deliberate choice on Gabriel's part, to mislead those around him, why not use a completely different name? It seemed too approximate for an intelligent man like him. That also meant they were not in one of Blakeburne's properties, where everybody knew him.

Unless…Hope hit her so hard it almost robbed her of breath. With it came a different sense of betrayal.

There was another man, always present but mostly at the fringe of her story. A man who admired her husband to extremes. A man who was *almost* like her husband, but not quite.

His Lordship, Lord Charles Eastham.

That would explain why she was being kept completely in the dark and why he had taken care never to come too near her. *But that was Gabriel's voice.* It wasn't any less absurd than any other theory, but it was like a gloved hand had started carefully gathering the shards of her splintered heart. She looked into the giant's eyes, and, after taking back her fate, she put it in his big hands.

"Well, Mr Munro, it's a pleasure to meet you. What about I help you make your father proud? What do you say?"

Munro didn't waste time in redeeming himself in his father's eyes. He did it in Ivy's for sure. She had learned that she had been kept captive for five days —she had thought something similar, but the lack of windows in the cellar had made it impossible to be sure. Fortunately, they were still in London, under Eastham's townhouse, nothing less. He was either being very smug or very confident that nobody would search for her there. Ivy loathed admitting he had been right. It was nonetheless providential for her escape. Being in the middle of nowhere would have added a whole lot of complications. She also learned that Eastham had let his butler know he would be gone until dinner. There was no reason to dawdle. With Mrs Keepers's help — the old woman who brought her food and who had been against Eastham's schemes from the beginning but who had complied when he had threatened her employment— Ivy was provided with a set of servant clothes. It was then a matter of creating a small diversion to distract the handful of servants who were either part of the machinations or would wonder about the appearance of a strange maid and ask questions. That was masterfully accomplished by Mrs

Keepers, who drew everyone to the kitchen by screaming 'Fire!' at the top of her lungs.

It was their signal. Ivy and Munro made their way to the servant's back door, acting as if they were going about their duties. Once outside, all it was left to do was cover the distance between the house and the street, where a hackney was waiting. It would have been an easy task if she weren't weak and blinded by the sudden sunlight after days of darkness. She was grateful for Munro's presence beside her, as a kitten could have ambushed her. She finally reached the hackney and mounted with the help of her monster turned ally. She was surprised when he followed her inside.

"I willnae leave ye alone 'til ye're sauf hame, lass."

Ivy shuddered to think what Eastham had in store for her that had convinced Munro to go against his employer so decisively. She didn't stop shivering for the whole duration of the ride. It had more to do with the emotional turmoil than with the drizzle softly drumming on the carriage roof. Rationally she knew it was very improbable that Eastham would come after her before she reached Blakeburne Townhouse. Forcing a hackney to stop and manhandle its occupant would make an even worst spectacle than her kidnapping.

Even in her frayed state, she could appreciate the irony of having her original kidnapper now look at her with concern.

"'I' is almost dune," he said, always keeping an eye on the passing streets. She simply nodded, her chest constricting with each yard that brought her nearer to Gabriel. The carriage finally came to a halt. There was something she needed to say before alighting.

"Thank you, Mr Munro." He didn't reply but unlatched the door and helped her down. The steps to the front door drained the last of her strengths. It was Munro who knocked, his enormous hands making the door shake.

When it opened, it was to reveal a mildly irritated Jenkins. "Please refrain from such display of—"

"May I come in, Jenkins?" Ivy said with a tired smile, wobbling dangerously.

"Your Grace!" the butler exclaimed before she collapsed into his arms. As they supported her, Ivy thought they weren't the arms she wanted to fall into.

❧ ❧ ❧

The world is full of imbeciles, Gabriel thought as his stallion sidestepped another upturned cart. He should already have reached the outskirts of London, towards Arabelle's country residence. Instead, he had to be hindered by the slowest and more inept people who had ever dealt with horses. At least he had the forethought to travel on horseback. If he were to be stuck inside a carriage, he would have gone on a rampage. No, much better to curse at strangers than to spend the time thinking about how he had not been able to keep his promise to himself and to Ivy just a few months into their marriage. He missed her. If something had happened to her, there would be no him anymore either. He had to live twice through the thought of having lost her forever now. Forget the armed guards, once she was back home, he would not let her out of his sight.

"Your Grace!"

First, he would hunt down those bounders who had dared touch her. Then he would spend the rest of his life making her forget, replacing those memories with happy ones.

"Your Grace! Blakeburne!" He stopped his stallion and looked around for the voice raising above the cacophony around him. Robert, one of his grooms, slowed Gabriel's fastest bay, coming up to his side. Panting, Robert handed him a folded paper.

"An urgent message for you, Your Grace." He took the note, dreading and hoping at the same time. As it turned out, he had good reason for the ambivalent feelings. The words were penned in Sebastian's titled scrawl.

The Duchess is home. She is fine, but hurry back.
A word of warning, my friend:
you won't like what you'll find.
-B

❀ ❀ ❀

He burst through his front door after throwing his reins at Robert.

"The family drawing-room," was all Jenkins said. The sun was setting down over the horizon, the room lit by the light from the fire and a great number of candles. Many people were standing just inside the room. His servants, Bellmore, a giant man he didn't know. Their soft murmurs quieted down when they spotted him. The atmosphere was one found at a wake.

He finally saw her, sitting on the settee by the fire. She sat there, unmoving, looking at the flames, lost. That was the word that came to him watching her. Lost. What little he could see of her eyes from her profile was an empty pool, no sign of his Ivy hidden in their depth. His wife, his love, who bravely faced the horrors of war to bring him back, had finally reached her breaking point. And he hadn't been there to protect her.

"Ivy," he whispered tentatively. "What have they done to you?" He spoke quietly from his position a few feet away from her, but not so low it couldn't reach her ears. She didn't turn her head towards him, but she stiffened at the sound of his voice.

Fury. Pure, unadulterated fury he didn't think he was capable of feeling came over him like an ocean wave, immense and unstoppable. Instead of going to her, he turned away and quietly walked up to Bellmore, passing the servants, some looking worried, others with stunned expressions, all loyal to his wife.

"Who?" His single word was like an ice stylet. Bellmore quickly debated the wisdom of revealing that information. In the end, he didn't think he had a choice.

"Your cousin Charles." Bellmore's words didn't register at first. Then, he calmly exited the room, asking for the carriage.

He didn't slam the front door open with a bang into the wall like he had done coming in. He gave the coachman the address before he could even stop in front of him. A flick of the rein and the horses moved forward while sounds came from the house he was leaving behind. In the red boiling rage clouding his mind, it seemed almost as if Ivy was shouting his name. He knew it wasn't possible. Before his eyes, there still was the image of her vacant eyes and broken spirit, like a porcelain doll a little girl had forgotten in a corner.

He opened the hidden compartment, taking out the pistol he kept there for fending off unknown enemies. He checked and loaded it, ready to use it against one enemy that was part of his own family.

"Gabriel! Gabriel!" Ivy cried, running outside. "Please, come back."

"I need you," she then whispered, accepting the futility of her actions.

"Come, Your Grace, come inside. It's cold," said Mrs Jenkins. "I've sent for your family and Lady Victoria. They'll arrive shortly. We've all been so worried for you."

Ivy let Mrs Jenkins take her inside. "I just wanted him here for me. I need to feel the difference," she said, almost to herself. She probably wasn't making any sense to the kind housekeeper, but for Ivy, it was of the utmost importance to be able to see, to touch, Gabriel.

"Come, sit by the fire. Now, you must not talk like that. You know His Grace loves you more than anything else in the world."

She wished she could be so sure. She just felt that each time she was struggling, she had to pick up the pieces and put them back together alone. And that time, again, she had to patch up the cracks in her armour and fight. Because she had to stop Gabriel. From her place near the fire, she had felt the moment Gabriel had lost the tight leash on his control. The heat in the room had risen dramatically, and it wasn't because of all the candles she had insisted were lit, not bearing the thought of a dark room. But as quickly as it had exploded, it had been taken away.

"You're right, Mrs Jenkins. No time to dwell on that. We must stop Blakeburne from doing something terrible. You saw the state he was in."

Mrs Jenkins was surprised by how attuned Her Grace was with her husband. She hadn't even been sure she had noticed his rushed entrance and even more rushed exit immediately after.

They were still standing in the hall when the front door opened again, and Jenkins let Gregory and Victoria in.

"Ivy!" Victoria cried, hugging her tightly. She returned her hug, tears filling her eyes. "We were all so worried! What happened? Oh, look at your face." Ivy gingerly touched the side of her head, where the bruise was still visible.

"I will tell you everything later. Now we have one more pressing matter."

Gregory came up to her and put an arm around her waist. "What could possibly be so important now? Where's Blakeburne?" He looked around for her husband, frowning when he didn't see him. Ivy would have desired nothing more than to have him by her side for her to lean on. Alas, that wasn't in her cards.

"He's with his cousin Charles."

"Why would he be, when your kidnappers are still out there?" Ivy waited and, after a blink, Gregory's expression cleared, only to be replaced by horror.

"Eastham? No. He—he was here earlier this morning!" So, there was where he went, to witness the chaos he had caused.

"But why?" asked Victoria. That was the question that echoed in Ivy's mind as well. What reason could Charles possibly have to do such a thing?

"I really don't know. What I do know is that I have to go after Gabriel. He isn't thinking lucidly."

"I don't think it's a good idea," Victoria said tentatively, while Gregory bellowed, "No way in hell you're going after him!"

"Jenkins?" The butler was still near, seeing that they hadn't moved from the entrance hall.

"Your Grace."

"Please retrieve the Duke's duelling pistols and fetch the other carriage." Her horse would have been faster, but she wasn't feeling well enough to ride.

The butler didn't appear very surprised by her request. "Immediately, Your Grace."

Meanwhile, Gregory was still ranting, "Ivy! Are you out of your mind?"

"Possibly. I'm furious. With Charles for putting me through hell for no apparent reason. And with Gabriel, for not being here. I want him to choose me. Above his honour, above revenge. Not because of an obligation. I deserve to come first. After days of Charles torturing me by making me believe the man I love was capable of hurting me, I just needed him to reassure me. And He. Is. Not. Here. So I'll go and save him from himself once again, then I can go back to fending for myself."

Gregory opened her mouth, but Victoria put a hand on his forearm. Ivy was surprised when it was enough to quiet him.

"You'll explain what Charles did later. But, you know you're not alone, Ivy, right?" Ivy nodded slowly, not really wanting to delve into that. Not when she had to go. But Victoria wasn't finished. "We were all terrified that something had happened to you. And Blakeburne was out of his mind. He would have gone to the world's ends to find you." Ivy said nothing. She simply turned and took the two pistols out of their case from Jenkins' proffered arms.

"If there's no way to talk you out of this, I'll come with you. You can barely stand."

"I'm fine." Her appearances surely didn't help corroborate her reassurance. She was still wearing the deep green walking gown she had donned five days before meeting with Grace. Looking down at herself, she saw it was wrinkled beyond repair and stained. Hospitality at Eastham's townhouse had left much to be desired. When she looked up, her eyes fell on the tall figure standing silently in a corner. Duncan Munro had refused to leave, even after making sure she was well taken care of. Her unexpected guardian monster. He nodded.

"Don't you worry, Gregory. I have someone on the inside."

Chapter Thirty-Six

She had to be the only abduction victim in history to willingly go back to where she had been kept prisoner less than six hours after escaping. She hadn't been able to convince Gregory not to come, but he had begrudgingly agreed to remain in the carriage and let her go inside alone with Munro. His mistrust towards the Scot was apparent by how his brother kept glaring at him. Ivy alighted as soon as the carriage came to a halt outside Eastham's residence, just behind Gabriel's.

"Your Grace, what—?" Ivy didn't spare a glance for Blakeburne's coachman up in the driver box. She knocked on the door, the street lamps casting Munro's big shadow over her. When someone finally opened it, Munro didn't give anyone the time to argue. He slammed his big hand on the wood panel, throwing it open. The townhouse wasn't as large as hers, but she hadn't the faintest idea where the men could be. Her safest bet was the study or a parlour. Her steps echoed on the marble floors.

No servants came to stop her. She made to turn and ask Munro where to go when voices reached her ears. Her hand went to the pistol in the deep pocket of her dress, silently thanking Grace for teaching them all how to use it the summer before. She had never shot anything other than inanimate objects, but she had never had any reason to. Ivy followed the voices and, as she drew near, she was able to discern the one belonging to her husband.

"Why? Why did you have to hurt her?" His words lacked any kind of sentiment, but Ivy knew that was when he was the most dangerous. When his mind refused to let emotions in, focusing with a single-minded purpose on the threat. Ivy tiptoed to the ajar door. It wouldn't be very wise barging inside like a madwoman, brandishing a pistol. And she was more than a little interested in Charles's answer.

"Oh, Gabriel, you don't get it, do you?" Charles' voice was equally calm, but it hid a hint of scorn. "It was never about her. It was about you. It always has been. She was a means to an end. An expendable pawn in the game, if you like."

He said it like it was the most obvious thing in the world. Ivy dared to peek inside the room —the study, she had been right— and was met with an alarming scene. The two cousins were facing each other. Charles stood behind his desk, Gabriel on the other side, near the shelves, both holding a pistol. The weapons were momentarily lowered, but a wrong move, a wrong word, and they both would have a clear shot. To be killed. To become murderers. The thought of that fate for Gabriel was what made Ivy step inside.

"Well, that's disappointing. One would think that an abduction would have least have *something* to do with the one who gets abducted." Both men turned towards her, but Ivy spared only a glance for her husband, who had whirled in her direction. No, her focus was on the other Eastham man, at which he aimed her own pistol.

"How kind of you to join us, Your Grace."

"I can't say it's a pleasure being here, Eastham. I came for my husband." She didn't know where her bravery came from, but she didn't even flinch when Charles raised his pistol and pointed it back at her. Immediately, the sound of the third pistol cocking came from Gabriel's direction.

"Lower your arm, Charles."

"It's our dear Duchess here who is waving a weapon. Where are your manners, Your Grace?" He seemed totally unconcerned with now having to look down two barrels.

How could she possibly have thought their eyes were the same? Yes, they shared the same unusual colour and shape, but the similarities ended there. Gabriel's could be sombre and difficult to read, sometimes downright cold, like in that moment. But they could also be alight with laughter and affection. Charles's, on the other hand...his were completely empty, vacant. She couldn't recall a time when she had seen even the tiniest sparkle of something warm in them.

His lips curled into a mocking sneer, but his eyes didn't change. "I must say, it's endearing seeing you like that. It makes me wonder what you did to inspire such devotion when you treated Lady Everleigh so abominably." Ivy felt chills run down her spine. She was looking at Eastham, but the voice was unmistakably Gabriel's deep one. A memory resurfaced: her husband telling her Charles had managed to pose as Gabriel to stir trouble between him and the late Duke. She had discarded it as a prank. There wasn't anything remotely funny in the current situation.

"Still up to the old tricks, I see." Charles didn't address his cousin's comment.

"I followed you, Blakeburne. Like I used to do when we were lads when I learned to do this." He turned to Ivy, thankfully going back to using his own voice. "Then I followed her too when that uselessly complicated courtship started. I observed you two closely.

It was apparent how he had the power to shatter you, my dear. You are so fragile, so insecure. It's been ridiculously easy to make you

402

believe everything I said was coming out of Blakeburne's mouth. Pathetic really, if you think about it."

"Why altering the food then? If it was so easy to fool me, why did you have to keep me in a constant state of confusion?"

He shrugged. "Although it had been remarkably simple to convince you you were being held prisoner by your own husband, I couldn't risk you seeing past the ruse. So, I kept lacing your food."

"But why go through all this trouble to make me hate Gabriel?" She felt her husband tense beside her. "After you killed me, all your games would have been over."

"Oh, but here is where you're wrong, Your Grace. It was never my intention to kill you. I only made you believe that your dear husband here cared so little for you he wouldn't move a finger to save you from that goon. On the contrary, that you've become a nuisance to him. Someone to get rid of. I'm pretty sure I did succeed in that, didn't I?" Ivy refused to answer. She didn't want to relive those terrifying hours when she had finally admitted that Gabriel was getting perverse joy in toying with her.

"What could you have possibly gained from it?" A mad light entered Charles' eyes at the question. For the first time, his true nature was showing.

"The fall of the mighty, perfect Duke of Blakeburne. Obviously. Nobody could ever measure up to him. We, mere mortals, can't do anything else but stand in his shadow, always coming up short in front of his magnificence. You should know this better than anyone else, Duchess." He was clearly lost in the world his deranged mind had conjured, where he could finally win this long-standing —and self-inflicted— rivalry with Gabriel.

"All my life, I had to endlessly listen to others sing his praises. My own father always repeated how he wished I was more like him. I went and doubled my family's fortune, and you know what my sire said? 'At your age, Blakeburne had tripled it.' When I did my duty as heir and didn't join the Army to make sure my family's wealth remained intact while others succumbed under the weight of taxes and the lack of men, did I get his thanks? Of course not, because Major Eastham had 'gone and become a hero, despite being a future Duke and not a mere heir to a courtesy title'. Which, come to think of it, it's ironic because the old Duke never approved of your choices." He was sneering at that point.

"To top it all, my dear, he went and took a wife —after a romantic tale that will be remembered for generations. And not just any wife, oh no. The Duke of Blakeburne had to choose none other than the titled —though overlooked— daughter of the double Duke of Rutherford-Blythe! Merging the two most powerful families of the Empire. My mother didn't stop talking about it for weeks!" Ivy could understand the frustration of never being enough, despite being everything it was asked of you. But Charles had shaped his whole life on trying to best Gabriel. He would have been a formidable opponent, were he aware of the competition. But her husband was looking at Charles like he had never really seen him before. It was clear he was completely unaware of the depth of the younger man's resentment. Charles had no chance to win if there was no rival aware of the game.

"Looking at you, everybody saw the perfect, blissful couple. I, however, looked deeper. And right there, I saw my chance. Because what matters the most to the fourteenth Duke of Blakeburne, even more than his lovely wife? His honour. What would society —and Parliament— say when they learned their hero mistreated the woman he seemed to be so enamoured of? Because there was no way in hell that the newly-appointed Duchess of Blakeburne —not to talk about her family of hot-headed aristocrats— would have let something like being locked in a cellar slide and kept silent. You would have gone down, Blakeburne, spectacularly. And the best part of it is, it would have been at the hand of the woman you claim to love." He laughed, proud of his own cleverness. He looked between the two of them, all three still holding each other at gunpoint.

Ivy could see the two men shared a similar mannerism. It was eerie. Her mind, still prey to the effect of the lack of nourishment and fatigue, was making it difficult to think clearly. Her vision was starting to blur, and she knew that soon she would have to lower her pistol. She had come to save Gabriel, not to put him even more in danger.

"Love is so fragile, isn't it? And so is trust. So difficult to acquire and so easy to lose. It needs nourishment and constant care. Otherwise, it withers and dies." Charles was continuing his rigmarole. "You, dear cousin, are unable to take care of it. You are incapable of keeping it alive. I only hastened what you are already accomplishing on your own. Its death."

Gabriel had evidently had enough of Charles's rambling because he started walking towards him while simultaneously stepping in front of Ivy.

"You spent so much time peeking behind curtains, and yet you failed to see the one important thing. *She* is the most important thing in my life. And you dared take her from me, putting her in danger. Did you tamper with her carriage axle too?" She had never second-guessed that the dreadful roads had caused her accident. But apparently, Gabriel had. He raised his pistol to Charles's forehead.

Everything stilled. She didn't dare to breathe.

"Of course not," Charles scoffed, unfazed. "I told you. My plan was much more sophisticated than harming your Duchess like an ignorant brute." Ivy believed him. A broken axle didn't fit with the rest. Gabriel had come to the same conclusion because he nodded.

"Were it for me, I would gladly put a bullet between your eyes. As you said, I am the Duke of Blakeburne. Nobody would gainsay me for a mere heir to a courtesy title." Gabriel cruelly used Charles's own words against him. Her husband was frightening right then. Ivy didn't like it, didn't like *him* that way. She would like to say she was sure he would stop before killing his cousin.

Charles hit the edge of his desk with his thighs. He swallowed hard. The earlier smugness was gone.

"But," Gabriel continued, "since it is my wife you unwisely decided to toy with, I'll let her decide your fate. I'd pray she'll be more magnanimous than me if I were you."

Ivy released her breath. Then she focused on her kidnapper, the man who had made the very foundation of her life shake and almost crumble.

"Banish him," she said coldly. "It's not worth the blood on your hand" —*and the stain on your soul*— "or the scandal that *we* would have to weather while he rots in gaol or swings for having kidnapped a Duchess."

"Let the gossipmongers talk. He *took* you from me. What he did is unworthy of the Eastham name." Gabriel still hadn't lowered his weapon, engaging in a battle with himself. Ivy put a hand on his arm, feeling the rigidity of his muscles.

"Gabriel." Her whisper was enough to turn the scales. He lowered his pistol.

"Your Duchess has a kind heart. But I don't see how you could force me to do anything. Even *you* don't have that kind of power." He laid his own pistol on the desk behind him. Charles wasn't a murderer. He was just a man lost in his own distorted world of resentment and envy.

"I won't test that theory if I were you. I will bow to my wife's wishes, but if I ever see you near her or if you even think about doing something remotely like this again, I will ruin you. You will be left with less than a farthing to your name and no one to turn to. Have I made myself clear?" Charles nodded.

Finally, every pistol was put away. Ivy felt lightheaded, mainly because it was really over.

"You will leave London immediately." Like in a well-rehearsed play, two big men entered the study and surrounded Charles. Henry and Jimmy, her father's men.

Gregory really is incapable of keeping his mouth shut.

"My Lord," Henry spat the honorific. "We'll escort you to your country estate." Weren't they gracious? Ivy waited for Charles to put on a fight, but he wisely decided to follow the two armed fellows meekly. *Thank the Lord*, thought Ivy. She had been ready for the whole ordeal to be over for a while now. He was almost out of the door — and their lives— when Gabriel spoke.

"How could you have possibly thought it would have worked?" It was obviously a rhetorical question, and he didn't wait for an answer. "Make my own wife fear and distrust me. You failed miserably."

Charles turned his head in her direction. His green eyes bore into her. What he saw made his lips stretch in a pleased smile.

"Did I?"

Chapter Thirty-Seven

Gabriel refused to let her go. He carried her outside Charles'
townhouse and set her on his lap in the carriage. He even somehow
managed to descend the steps without making them both fall on their
faces. Ivy had put her head in the crook of his neck and got
comfortable, trusting him. He fed and bathed her before putting her to
bed. Again, without any protest from her. Without many words at all,
really. Only once he climbed behind her and pulled her against the
warm cocoon of his bigger body Ivy felt him relax. She was asleep a
few heartbeats later, only to be roused in the middle of the night by his
mouth on her. Gabriel was kissing and stroking her, the earlier
peacefulness gone. His urgency, his need for reassurance, fed her own.
Soon their touches were like marks on each other's skin. When he
finally entered her, there was no room in their minds for fear and
worry, his frenzied thrusts chasing blissful oblivion. Once sated, they

fell back asleep, Ivy's head resting on his chest. But blissful oblivion didn't last.

That was the last time Ivy was able to sleep through the night. The nightmares that had gradually eased in the weeks after those hellish days on the battlefield returned. More gruesome and articulated. Dead soldiers' blooded corpses covered the floor of a dark, claustrophobic cellar. Enormous monsters ran after her in unfamiliar woods, silent and sinister. And more combinations of Ivy's worst memories. Every dream had one element in common. Every flight, every scream, was witnessed by a crowd made of members of the *ton*. And every time, among that immobile, rabid throng of people enjoying her terror, stood Gabriel, looking bored and uninterested. Never making a motion to save her.

Needless to say, her waking hours passed in a cloud of tiredness, even the most insignificant thing out of the ordinary causing hundreds of anxiety-filled questions.

The days in Charles' clutches had left, fortunately, few physical scars. The emotional wounds would take longer to heal if they ever would.

Every time she assured him she was fine, Gabriel became more and more worried. She caught him looking at her many times during the day, which he insisted on attending to his affair nearby. Physically, at least. There was a chasm between them, widened by the demons they each carried on their shoulders. Ivy knew her husband hadn't come away from her abduction unscathed, but she didn't know how to reach him. How did one lead someone else out of a labyrinth when they were lost too?

❋ ❋ ❋

409

He was losing her. Ivy was slowly slipping through his fingers, fading away. Even in the darkest hours, when he had been terrified for her, he had focused on what was in his power to do to bring her back. He had made many mistakes, true, but never before hadn't he had the faintest idea where to start, even to make other mistakes. She wasn't sleeping, and sometimes she retreated in an isolated, unreachable place that had been keeping her from him. He absolutely loathed it. It scared him. She seemed fine during the day, going about her everyday life. She met with her friends and family, managed Everleigh from afar. But the nights were another story. He was woken by her screams almost every night. He would pull her in his arms and wait for her frantic heartbeat to calm down while she apologised for troubling him. She *fucking apologised* for having nightmares about being abducted by his deranged cousin. She had even suggested they slept separately, something he had categorically refused. He had spent many hours thinking about Charles, about his rivalry with *him*. His heart broke at every scream, every shudder as if a stonecutter were chipping away at it, piece after piece.

Speaking of managing Everleigh, Gabriel had intercepted Jenkins with another letter from her estate manager.

"I'll take it to her, Jenkins."

"Very well, Your Grace."

It gave a plausible reason —not that he needed one— to seek out his wife. He found her in the library, one of her favourite places in the house, half-reclined on a settee, an open book on her lap. It wasn't an unusual sigh. What was unusual was that the world inside its pages couldn't capture her interest. He saw her profile was turned towards the window.

He went to gently caress the exposed skin on her nape. The times he had done the same in the past, they had ended up in a satisfied tangle of bodies and limbs on the Aubusson rug.

"Ivy, I have a—"

"Don't touch me!" She startled so much she jumped out of the settee, shouting. She turned towards him with wide, terror-stricken eyes, her pose defensive. He was paralysed with shock, his hand still comically raised to touch her.

"Gabriel!" Ivy said, panting as if she had just run two miles. *It's fear. She lost her breath because of fear. She's afraid of you.* All his years of wearing a mask had failed him, and Ivy saw the horror on his face.

"I'm so sorry, Gabriel. I didn't mean to scream." And there she was, apologising again. Only this time, it spiked a flicker of anger inside him. Ivy hadn't wanted a more severe punishment for Charles, but her bent head and downcast eyes made him wish he had put a bullet through him, cousin or not.

Your world is full of uncertainty, my love, but know one truth: I will never look at you in fear.

That was what she had written months before when he had felt the weight of a conflict far away from home. Her words had been the beacon that had kept him sane. He had kept that letter with him everywhere he went, burning a hole in his skin when he had thought she was dead. It represented hope, a reason to fight. And now their one truth had been belied.

"Why did you? Scream." He managed to keep his temper under control. She didn't deserve it.

"I...You...I didn't hear you come in. Your voice..." She didn't complete the thought, but the meaning was clear. And it was like wind on an open flame.

"You didn't really believe it was me that kept you locked in that cellar, did you?" When Ivy didn't immediately confirm it, something inside Gabriel broke.

"You did. You thought that I, your own husband who loves you more than his next breath, was capable of doing something so inhuman."

He turned away from her, the movement almost physically painful. But necessary.

411

"I can't even look at you right now." Gabriel prepared himself for her anger. He almost wished to have her insult him after the complete apathy of the past days. He knew he was being unfair and cruel, after all she went through. But, deep down, he had to admit his words rang true. Gabriel was deeply hurt by the fact that she had so readily believed he could do something like that. To anyone, but especially to her. But her scalding words didn't come. Instead, he heard the doors to the garden close and the latch click, louder than an explosion, the effect almost as shattering.

He wasn't sure that time they would survive it.

Her breaths became shorter and shallower. Her chest felt tighter. All the pain and anger threatened to burst free. She was suffocating. She needed air. *Breathe, damn it!*

The sky above was overcast, with heavy grey clouds. The sound of thunder perfectly matched what was happening inside her head. Humidity pervaded the air, hindering her attempt to draw breath. Before her eyes, Gabriel's upset face refused to leave. She hadn't wanted to hurt him by recoiling at his touch. She had been so lost in thoughts that hadn't noticed his presence until she had felt his light touch, accompanied by his voice. *That* voice. Her reaction had been visceral.

And when he had turned away, not bearing the very sight of her, she had felt a hand choking her.

He couldn't fault his accusing question, his anger. He could blame Charles for tarnishing even the first time Gabriel had told her he loved her. It had been said in anger, in frustration. She would never forgive him that.

Ivy had had to escape. Needed to.

She took a couple of steps in the unwelcoming weather, her slippers not making a sound on the wet grass. Every sound was swallowed by the pounding of her heart. The staccato was resounding in her ears together with her laborious breaths. And behind the strangled cacophony, voices. Familiar voices. They were memories overlapping in a painful sequence. They came unbridled, unstoppable, like an avalanche. And they started from the beginning.

Baron Whintrope sporting a confused look. *And who might you be, young lady?*

Her cousin shooting her spiteful words. *Nobody would miss you.*

And Gabriel, his beloved face a detached, disdainful mask.

I don't want you here!

A pity she is so...insignificant.

You are nothing more than an inconvenience. You really thought I wanted you?

Wait, something was not right. It wasn't Gabriel who denigrated her and ridiculed their marriage. Or was it? Images swam before her eyes, laughing at her, and she wasn't able to separate truth from fabrication. Mocking faces. Echoing voices, repeating again and again, *you are insignificant.*

Stupid.

Stupid.

She sagged against the outside wall and slid to the ground, hugging her knees, her head between them. She inhaled deeply, but the air was still not enough. Her heart constricted painfully, making her worry she was having some kind of seizure.

That was how Victoria found her, still huddled in a small ball.

"Ivy? Jenkins told me you— Ivy!" Ivy heard Victoria rush to her and crouch at her side.

"What's the matter, dearest? Are you hurt?" Ivy shook her still-bent head. Her breathing had started to calm down. A new, painful choice had been made.

Now, she only had to find the strength to stand up and carry it out. Finally, looking at her friend, she saw Victoria sigh deeply.

"I can't stand seeing you like that. There must be something that can be done. And where the bloody hell is the Duke?" Gabriel must have gone out immediately after they had talked. *After he told you he couldn't look at you.*

Ivy hadn't been able to explain to anyone the pain she had felt once she had given in and believed Gabriel was her kidnapper. A pain that hadn't gone away after her escape. Because *she* had been the one to fall for Charles' machinations. *She* had been the one who, in the end, had thought Gabriel capable of such things. Was an addled and deprived mind enough of an excuse?

"What's happening inside that head of yours? Let me —us— help you," Victoria said softly, taking a hand in hers.

That brought Ivy to the choice she had just made.

"I have to go."

If Gabriel had been anyone else, he would have got completely sotted. Instead, he had decided to use his time to pay another unsolicited visit to his London solicitor, who had threatened to disembowel him if he didn't start abiding by his appointments. He couldn't have known it would have been less painful than what was waiting at home.

"The Duchess is waiting for you in your study, Your Grace," Jenkins said as soon as Gabriel doffed his top hat. He was suddenly alert, not liking the subtle urgency in his butler's voice. Deciding not to waste time enquiring, he nodded and went to find his wife.

She was pacing up and down the length of the room.

"You wanted to see me, love?" She visibly stiffened as his endearment, but she soon gathered her posture. She turned to him.

"I'm leaving for Everleigh."

The constriction in his chest loosened slightly. He felt himself relax. Ivy had expressed that wish before the hell of the past weeks. It had been one of many times he had disappointed her during their short marriage. Gabriel started making plans in his head. It wasn't ideal but feasible.

"Let me confer briefly with my man of affairs. I can be ready to leave in two days. Why are you shaking your head?"

"I'm going alone."

"That's preposterous. Why would you do that? What's the meaning of this?"

"I need time. I can't allow what happened before with you to happen again. I think finding myself in a comforting, untouched place will help. I need to go to Everleigh."

"Far from me, you mean. I apologise, but I won't let you leave me."

"I am not leaving you. I can't. I love every inch, every different facet of you. I even love your fierce scowl." His heart skipped a beat in finally hearing those words again. She gave him a tender, but sad, smile before continuing. "He was right on one thing. You will always have the power to hurt me too easily." *Fucking Charles.* "And before you say it, it's not your fault. I've learned something from this. I can't base my worth on what others think of me. It would always be like walking on the edge of a cliff, where a gush of wind could make me fall. I am one of the most powerful women of the Empire —and I was it even before marrying you— yet I've always felt like I was walking alone, never enough. And I'm not talking about estate responsibilities or similar. No, I mean that I had to almost get killed on a battlefield, all to ascertain myself you cared for me. Hell, I was offended that, deep down, my kidnapping wasn't about me! It's time it stops. I must fight once again. For myself. And for us."

415

"Why don't you stay instead. We can find a way together. What happened to you was horrible."

"Don't you dare look at me in pity."

"I wasn't—"

"You know perfectly well that my insecurities are antecedent to my abduction. You commented on my behaviour in the past yourself. When I recoiled from your touch, I felt like they were taking over. I can't allow that. Let me go, please." There were many right things to say to make her stay, but Gabriel looked at her beloved face and saw it was pointless. He could only stand straighter, his last resource his ducal persona.

"Very well, Your Grace. If this is what you wish, I won't stop you. Have a safe journey." He turned his back to her and exited the room.

Chapter Thirty-Eight

"This is quickly becoming a regular occurrence, Blakeburne. Shall we give it a name? Something along the lines of 'The Pacing of inner Turmoil' or 'The Wife Epiphany'. No, I got it! 'Let's wait for wise Sebastian to enlighten me on my foolish Ways'."

"A bit of a mouthful, isn't it?"

Gabriel *had* paced the equivalent of the distance between London and Everleigh. Even Colonel, his wife's cat, had hissed at him and left his cosy settee with disdain. Now, with Sebastian following him with his eyes, Gabriel realised the futility of it and slumped unceremoniously in his wing chair.

"What can a chap do if his superior thinking is the only thing that stands between wedded bliss and a bottomless pit of despair? Yours, obviously." Gabriel speared him with a hard glare.

"I cannot wait for you to find yourself in a similar predicament. Then I will impart *my* advice. Never you fear." Sebastian laughed, the carefree sound grating on Gabriel's ears.

"Ah, that day will be long in coming. And I certainly won't need your advice. Now, back to the matter at hand. What are you going to do?"

"Do? Why, nothing."

Bellmore stared at him like he had told him he was going to sell all his properties and join a travelling company.

"*Nothing?*" When Sebastian realised Gabriel was serious, he emitted a frustrated groan. "I can't believe I must have this conversation with you. Again. Let me spell it out for you. And pay attention this time. You. Have. To. Follow. Her." His words were met with a mulish expression Gabriel would have called *resolute*. Mulish.

"She had stated very clearly that she doesn't want to be followed. I'm only doing what she asked."

"She doesn't really mean that."

"Of could she does. Ivy is a very rational woman."

"Is she really, though?"

Gabriel jumped to Ivy's defences. "I don't know what you are implying, but if you think I will stand here and let you insult my wife..."

"Smooth your feathers. I was referring to her action when *you* are concerned." When not even a flicker of understanding crossed the Duke's eyes, Sebastian continued imparting his wisdom. "Let me summarise your Duchess's behaviour since she's met you." He raised his little finger to start a list. "She went after you during a battle and saved you from certain death." Another finger. "She went after you to stop you from killing your scapegrace of a cousin."

"I know very well what she did." Sebastian didn't know how close he was to losing his fingers.

"But even that isn't the point...."

"And what, pray tell, is the point?"

"What did you do for her? Were you there for her when she was certainly scared out of her mind on the Continent? Were you there for her after Charles made her doubt everything she trusted?" Gabriel remained silent. He didn't have to explain his actions and his marriage to Sebastian.

Faced by the stoic wall that was the Duke of Blakeburne, Bellmore stood up and headed for the door.

He was almost there when Gabriel quietly said, "She wanted to be left alone. I am only doing what she wanted. I have to respect that."

"It seems to me you find yourself at a crossroad, old chap. You're honour bound to leave her alone as she asked. On the other hand, how do you imagine your life will be without her? Because some damages cannot be undone, even by the Duke of Blakeburne" Without waiting for an answer, Bellmore took his leave, not before seeing the look that came over his friend's face.

"I thought so," he whispered to himself, smiling, closing the door behind him. Blakeburne's butler appeared at his side, ever the picture of efficiency.

"Ah, Jenkins, my good man! What will our boy do without us?" The servant didn't react to the Duke of Blakeburne being called 'a boy', used to the Viscount's outrageousness.

"I really couldn't say, my Lord." His mouth curved slightly at the corners, the only concession at Bellmore's barb. "Shall I have your mount fetched, my Lord?"

"Yes, please, Jenkins. Ah, and I would keep the coach ready if I were you."

Bellmore had been wrong. Gabriel didn't ask for the coach to be summoned. After his friend had left, he entrenched himself in his study, morosely dissecting every chance encounter, every stolen moment he and Ivy had had since that first night. He tortured himself with the darkest point of their story and even more with the brightest ones. That opened a bleeding wound.

For all his promises, for all his efforts, he had become worse than his father. The thirteenth Duke of Blakeburne had been distant and cold and had tried to shape his heir in his image.

Love was a weakness. Gabriel had long known —since he had made that promise to himself about his brother— that his sire had been partly successful.

His detachment had made him the powerful Duke he was today. With Ivy, he had found that there was more inside him than, well, nothing. But while his father had been a distant, almost unworldly creature, Gabriel had been present in Ivy's life. Except for every time she had really needed him.

Sebastian had depicted it perfectly with just a few words.

Ivy had told him.

He had blurted out that he loved her while he was furious, feeling powerless and hurt. Then he had let her go without a fight, while she had done nothing but fight for him, even when he had given no indication her efforts were welcomed.

Gabriel looked down at his hand and noticed with surprise that he was holding an empty glass. How long had it been there? How long had *he* been there?

The sound of glass exploding as he threw it in the fireplace was deeply satisfying.

He had failed as a husband, as he had known all along. But the Duke of Blakeburne didn't condone failure. To borrow Sebastian's words, what was he going to do about it?

With a new purpose firmly in place, he tore the door open and bellowed, "Jenkins!"

420

The butler appeared immediately, and Gabriel suspected the man was lying in wait.

"Carriage."

"Waiting, Your Grace."

"Bags."

"Packed."

"We will talk about that smug look of yours when I came back, Jenkins," Gabriel said while he took the proffered gloves and hat.

"As you wish, Your Grace." Gabriel was almost through the door when Jenkins stopped him.

"Bring her back, Your Grace." Gabriel stared into Jenkins' serious eyes and nodded solemnly.

He was bringing his Duchess home. Once and for all.

❖ ❖ ❖

"I'm not evicting them. And that's my final word on the matter. If you don't like my way of dealing with things, I'm sure the Duke of Rutherford-Blythe *and* the Duke of Blakeburne will happily assist me in finding a new steward." Ivy hated invoking their names, but she had lost her last shred of patience. The Countess of Everleigh and Duchess of Blakeburne before him didn't impress the obnoxious man, but just the mention of the Dukes was enough to have the colour drain from his face. That was the really annoying truth of the world they lived in. Ivy didn't make a habit of threatening her employees, but she couldn't allow having her decisions questioned at every turn. Not when she already did it on her own. Like deciding to leave London. And Gabriel.

"Very well, Your Grace. We'll do it your way," the steward begrudgingly conceded.

"That was never in question, sir. Please, feel free to go back to the house. I'll take Empress for a ride." Meaning, *get out of my sight, you near-sighted dimwit.*

They were riding back from inspecting some of the smaller cottages at the far edge of the estate. One, in particular, needed repair, mostly because the family who lived in it had been too worried about the man of the house's injury and a fever that had been ailing their youngest child to take care of a leaking roof. They feared losing their home, but Ivy had quickly reassured them that she would send someone to take care of it and that they wouldn't go anywhere. Much to the steward's chagrin.

Once alone, she looked around the vast green expanse of her land. It was cold outside, but the sun cast a cheerful light that made everything even more peaceful. She had done the right thing in coming to Everleigh. No dark memories lurked in the shadows. She could finally breathe freely. But an invisible string was keeping her tied with the strength of a hawser, its pull inescapable. And she had realised she didn't want to escape it. She has told Gabriel she was going away to fight for herself and to save their marriage, but, as the days passed, that fight more and more resembled a flight. And that would have been fine too if she hadn't left a part of her behind. Her husband, her heart.

People liked to think everything was oh-so complicated. Sometimes it really wasn't. She had another choice to make. A simple one. She could stay where she was for an indefinite amount of time, hoping one day to wake up and find that everything had fallen into place, that her daemons had disappeared, and she had finally accepted the place the *ton* had put her in. A little box labelled 'unassuming, quiet Countess-now-Duchess'. The kind of wife the Duke of Blakeburne had wished for at the beginning. Unfortunately for him, there was another option. Reclaim the place that was rightfully hers. At his side, as the Duchess of Blakeburne, Countess of Everleigh. One of the most —if not the most— powerful peeresses of the Empire. It would not be easy.

Changes like that didn't happen overnight. She would falter and stumble. Things will still try to come and haunt her. But she had something few others in her position could say to have. She loved her husband, deeply and irrevocably. She would turn that love into strength.

See, the choice wasn't complicated.

While deep in thought, Empress had led her back to the stables without Ivy's contribution. Providentially, it was exactly where she wanted to go.

"Have the carriage readied for me tomorrow at first light, please." She told the head groom before handing him Empress' reins with a loving pat on her neck.

"Certainly, Your Grace. Where will you be headed, if you don't mind me askin'? 'Need to know to arrange for the horses to be changed, if you'd be goin' far, Your Grace."

She smiled at the groom, certainty reflecting in her eyes. "London. I'm going back home."

The man nodded at her reverentially, not really appreciating the depth of her statement, and went about taking care of Empress. She made her way to the house, where she would have to inform her staff of her departure, less than a week after their arrival. Her poor servants were travelling back and forth like mail coaches. She would make sure they were all well compensated for their trouble. At least she travelled light. She would have a mutiny on her hands if she started filling trunks…

"Yer Grace!" Ivy turned and saw Munro hurrying towards her. The big Scot had followed her there without leaving her a choice in the matter. He had been irremovably firm in appointing himself as her protector.

"*Leuk at thois scrawny laddies!*" he had said. "*Na, I dinnae traist thaim tae protect ye.*" He was lucky she had grown fond of him. Obsequious was he not.

He pointed at the front of the house.

"A visitor fur ye."

"Oh, I am not expecting anyone." She nonetheless started to make her way to see who had come to Everleigh. And to send them on their way. She had things to do.

She had just turned the corner when the door of the imposing black carriage opened. She would have seen the ducal crest, had she not been too focused on drinking in the tall man emerging.

"Gabriel," she whispered.

He heard her —or felt her presence— because his intense green eyes shot to her. They hid everything she was feeling. She obviously hadn't forgotten how handsome he was, but it struck anew how he affected her. The sun brightened his dark hair to deep mahogany and emphasised his powerful physique encased in a grey travelling coat.

Although she had been ready to rush back to him, now that he was standing there, she wasn't running to him and into his arms but waited for him to cover the short distance that separated them.

He came so near that he had to be able to hear the thundering pulse of her heart. He cupped her cheek with a tender caress, and she leaned into his hand. Ivy hadn't realised how much she had missed his touch until that moment. How her body had missed the nearness of his.

He had yet to say a word. So much still lingered between them.

After many long moments, without averting his gaze from her face, he said only three perfect words.

"Show me Everleigh."

Her smile was so wide it hurt. "With pleasure, Your Grace."

She was resplendent. The way she talked about her estate and the people who lived on it lightened her eyes in a way few other things could do. He had been one of them, once upon a time, he realised. He felt even more as an arse for dismissing her when she had talked about coming here before her abduction.

Looking around the large estate —far larger than the ones many other peers could claim to own— he recognised the sign of good and caring management. Everything was in decent shape, and the people he had passed on the road had been well-fed and in high spirit. His admiration for his wife grew even more, if possible.

"You've been doing a magnificent job, Ivy." He told her sincerely, loving the blush that came over her beautiful face. They had been riding for a while, with her pointing out interesting something or another. She was the most interesting thing around, with the pride she obviously took in Everleigh.

"Thank you. But the merit isn't sorely mine. On the contrary, I haven't been able to do much while in London. I can count on excellent staff and estate manager." The last was said with a quirk of her mouth. He would have lost it had he not been staring at her. He had been unable to look away.

"Why the grimace?"

She waved away his question. "Oh, it's nothing really. I just had an unpleasant discussion with the aforementioned manager."

He tightened the grip on his reins, affronted. If the man had disrespected his wife…

"Is he still on the premises? I would like a word with him—"

"Why are you here, Gabriel?" interrupted Ivy.

There it was. The crux of the matter. They had tiptoed around it for the few hours of the estate tour, but the lingering distance between them had slowly become an unwelcome chaperone. "It's not for interceding on my behalf with disagreeable managers which, as much as I appreciate it, it's unnecessary."

"Correct. Even though I'd really like to clarify some things with him."

"If it's to assess Everleigh's conditions and value, I hope you're satisfied with what you see."

"Of course, it's not the reason why I'm here. If you'd let me—"

"...then I *would* advise you to talk with Mr Wallace. Even it's not your responsibility—"

"Ivy! For God's sake, woman! I'm here for you! Only you."

She fell quiet and looked at him expectantly. And nervously. She had no idea of what he was going to say next, and that sent a pang of regret in his heart.

Now that he was granted the chance to speak, Gabriel found himself sharing her nervousness. He wasn't good at those things. He dismounted and went to help Ivy down her horse, finally able to touch her. He took it as a good sign when she didn't step back or ask him to remove his hands, still resting on her waist. He didn't know if he could have borne her recoiling from him again.

"To let you know how serious I am, I would say that I wouldn't care if the entire estate burned to the ground. But, somehow, I think that would result with your whip somewhere on my person."

"And you would be right, Your Grace." Her lips curved in a small smile that he yearned to capture with his own. Then they both looked at each other, and Gabriel knew that was the moment that would determine the course of their marriage.

"I'm the farthest thing from a poet you could get." That earned him a fervent nod. "But you deserve my best effort." He cleared his dry throat. "Do you know what I think when I look at the stars in a night sky? That they'll always be there. Sometimes you can't see them, but you know that they are there even in the darkest of nights. Behind the clouds, behind the filthy, smelly fog, they aren't going anywhere.

"That's what I want to be for you. The stars in the night sky. Not to look down on you. Not even to guide you. And certainly not to make you shine brighter. As if you needed me for it. But to be one of the few certainties in your life. Because the fact is, you don't need someone to save you. You never did. You save yourself. Since the first day we met, you've been saving *me* every chance you got. It's an unflatteringly long list. You saved me from being trapped by Lady Ingram. You saved me on that bloody battlefield. You saved me by stopping me from killing my cousin. And you saved me from a miserable, empty life and from becoming a sad, grumpy old man.

"But sometimes I can do it for you. Not because you cannot, but because I can. It's my privilege. To be there for you to lean on, as I failed to do so far. To lend you the strength you think you need or help you find it inside you. Because I love you, and I will love you for as long as the stars will adorn the night sky. Which, let me tell you, will be a fairly long time."

Silence met his heartfelt declaration. As it stretched, Gabriel started to feel warmth creeping from his neck to his face. He rubbed his nape, rapidly thinking about something else to say.

One second, he was feeling dejected, losing hope of being able to win Ivy back. The next, he caught himself before falling on his behind, a flurry of fabric and precious woman attacking him. Ivy crushed her mouth to his, first with light, fast pecks, then, with his enthusiastic involvement, in deep and passionate kisses. On their own volition, his hands fondled her supple curves. How had he even thought to let her go?

After a while, they came up for air. Despite his panting, Gabriel felt he could finally breathe properly for the first time since Charles had taken her.

"Next time, refrain from wishing for my estate to burn and from speaking about filthy fog," was what she said with swollen lips and sparkling eyes.

"That's all you gathered from me baring my soul to you?" Gabriel asked a little hurt.

"My love." That was a more auspicious beginning. "You may not be a poet, but I love you more for trying. Even if your astronomical description is a little simplistic. You are my brave soldier. My broody duke. My serious but passionate husband. My home. *My madness.*" He held her tighter at that.

"It took me some time to realise that maybe my fears of being invisible and inconsequential may never completely disappear. But now I know I can look your way and find what I'm looking for. It's your unique, unmistakable voice that leads me out of the dark." Those brief sentences were more important than she realised. She was starting to heal from the wound left by her abduction. "Thank you for coming after me when I didn't know I wanted you to."

A lone tear slid down her cheek. He caught it with his thumb. He would have hated the thought of her tears if her eyes didn't burst with hope and love. No traces of the fear he saw last time. A veil of vulnerability still lingered, but he had a lifetime to make it disappear. Another promise, another vow.

"Well, I had a little nudge," he admitted, letting his mouth tilt upwards slightly. Then he sobered. "I'm so sorry for not being there when you really needed me to. I'm sorry for every ounce of hurt I've caused you since the night we met. But I will spend the rest of my days making sure you'll never doubt that I love you more than my next heartbeat."

"I know you will. And you know how I know it? Because I discovered that to each one of those heartbeats you would give up correspond one of mine. And one is hard-pressed to find a stronger and more honourable heart than yours, my love." Another emotion appeared in her eyes. Determination.

"I won't let any insignificant war, kidnapping, or even ourselves and our mistakes come between us and the bright future we have ahead."

He had nothing to say to that. They had laid their soul bare to one another. Raw, vulnerable, but never stronger, they came together naturally, the invisible string that drew them together now tying around them with a tight knot.

Gabriel lowered her to the ground on the soft green grass and began working on ties and buttons that hid his wife from his touch. Ivy sighed languidly, the sounds then turning into gasps when he reached her bare skin, reacquainting himself with her smooth flesh. Soon Ivy was tugging impatiently at his clothes. He had to laugh at her frenzy, which earned him a glare. He wisely made quick work of divesting himself before covering her naked upper body with his own. Breasts to chest, they kissed for a while, the delicious friction quickly becoming insufficient. He slid his warm tongue over her neck and breasts, eliciting needy moans from his wife. She scratched his shoulders, grabbing his behind while simultaneously raising her pelvis to meet his hardness.

"Gabriel, hurry." Her urgency made his control snap. There would be many times in the future to love his wife slowly and tenderly. Right that moment, he needed the rest of her clothes off. He tore the fabric with a groan, unbothered by anything but his unquenchable need to be inside her.

So there, in an open clearing on Ivy's estate, he took his wife with powerful thrusts, showing with his body his love, his need, and everything else he still hadn't been able to tell her. And she took him in return. There was no going back from that. If they had to be honest, there had been no going back since the night a quiet Countess had made a serious, cynic Duke laugh at the sight of three mice. They reached their pinnacle together with a cry, finding that kind of peace only sacred things can infuse.

Gabriel was resting heavily on her, lazily kissing her neck. Mindful that he was crushing her, he searched for the strength to rise, only to be pulled back down. Ivy buried her face in the crook of his neck, inhaling his scent.

"Ivy, love, let me up." She mumbled something that sounded like *Idontwantto*, or so he presumed by the feeling of her lips mouthing the words on his skin.

"Someone may come."

Dontcare. He let out a laugh while rising on his elbows.

"Well, Your Grace, you may not mind others seeing me bare-arsed, but I will certainly be displeased if a farmhand or anyone else managed to see my wife without a stitch of clothes."

She grumbled but finally let him go. They dressed in silence. Ivy looked daggers at him when he restored an almost pristine appearance, except for a few stains, while her clothes were clearly unsalvageable. When he went to put his tie pin into place, she motioned to hand it to her. She managed to pin part of her skirts together, leaving a fetching slit that opened when she walked. He couldn't contain his grin that, despite her annoyance, melted Ivy's hard scowl.

"It's all your fault. You're lucky I adore when you smile." How could he have thought to live even a day without her? He patted her hair, trying in vain to restore a sort of coiffure. She swatted him away.

"How many estates do we own in total?"

Gabriel had to blink at the abrupt question.

"When we married, we reached the number of six and twenty. May I ask you why this enquiry?"

It was her turn to smile mischievously at him.

"And how many have secluded clearings?" He started to grasp where the conversation was going. And he liked it very much.

"A fair amount of them, I reckon. And if they don't, trees can be planted." He immediately started making plans for each estate.

"I really hope that our housekeepers know how to remove grass stains, then."

"You should know I pride myself on my superior staff. I don't foresee any problem in that regard. I applaud your practical thinking, though, my love."

"Well, I *am* the Duchess of Blakeburne." Another surge of love engulfed him at the proud way she made his name hers.

"That you are. And none other could be the perfect Duchess of Blakeburne, if not the Countess of Everleigh."

Epilogue

"**U**nbelievable," Ivy mumbled under her breath. "I've never seen so many people in the same room."

"It was to be expected. It's the Duchess of Blakeburne's Christmas ball," Victoria said, sipping a glass of champagne.

"*Dowager* Duchess of Blakeburne. I was more than happy to give my mother-in-law free rein. And now to give her credit for her success. When I learned that she and my mother had joined forces again for this ball, I gladly stepped aside and let them do their magic."

"It *is* magical," agreed Grace, looking around. After the previous year's success, Ophelia had decided to make the Christmas ball a yearly tradition.

Gabriel's protests had been left unheard. Therefore, Ivy was standing with her friends in an enchanted forest, but without the cold and dangers. Or the quietness.

"It would have been even more magical with a few dozen people less."

"Nobody, and I reiterate, nobody would miss a ball organised by the Blakeburne-Rutherford-Blythe." Alas, Grace's assessment was accurate.

"And miss welcoming you and the Duke back in Town." Victoria's eyes sparkled while she said that. Ivy felt herself blushing. She and Gabriel had been out of Town, touring their estates. That they had really done what they had hinted at that day back in Everleigh, grass stains and all, was nobody's business.

"Where's the Duke by the way?"

"He left to fetch me a glass of champagne and never returned. The crowd must have swallowed him whole. I am now a merry widow." She covered her face with her hand, faking desperation. Her friends laughed but soon limited themselves to smiles. She felt his presence before an arm surreptitiously circled her waist. Victoria and Grace still weren't completely comfortable in the Duke's presence. Ivy sometimes forgot that, while she saw the extraordinary man beneath, his formidable ducal mask was still in place for the rest of the world to see.

"You could at least be an 'inconsolable' widow, Your Grace." She took the glass he proffered with a nod of thanks.

"Still eavesdropping on other people's conversations, I gather."

"Still saying the most curious things, I see." He was looking at her with crystalline green eyes, and she smugly took all the credit for putting that serene light in them.

"Good evening, Lady Victoria, Miss Winter," he greeted when he finally tore his gaze from her.

"Your Grace." They curtsied before expressing their awe at the beauty of the room. Gabriel, always the gracious host, thanked them, but she had to laugh under her breath at his painful grimace when they started talking about draperies and decorations. Fortunately for him, the topic was exhausted reasonably quickly, and the party fell in companionable silence, observing the couples dancing. Ivy spotted

Elizabeth Winter dancing with the handsome and ever-grinning Viscount Bellmore. The two had a flamboyant dancing style, seemingly oblivious to the stares they attracted, simply enjoying the dance. Looking away, Ivy opened her mouth to comment on it, only to close it again when she saw the expression on Grace's face, her eyes still glued on the twirling couple. *Oh, dear.*

Her attention was soon drawn to another familiar, if still unusual, couple. The Earl of Covington was dancing with her cousin Eleanor. Ivy had talked to her cousin only once since the kidnapping when Eleanor had apologised for unwillingly misleading the Duke in his search for her. She had been sincerely upset, and Ivy couldn't in all conscience do anything else if not forgive her. Their relationship would never grow closer than it was, but at least she had not plotted to harm her. Small victories.

The Earl, usually a decent dancer, was moving curiously stiffly. *Maybe it's Eleanor's nearness.*

"Could you please refrain from staring at *dear* Covington?" Gabriel whispered in her ear.

"How many times do we have to rehash that night at the theatre?" Her husband had got over his irrational jealousy over the young Earl, although sometimes it reared its ugly head. "And I am not staring at him. I was just...."

Except she *was* staring at him. She stared at him when he suddenly halted in the middle of the dance floor, causing another couple to bump into him, creating a chain effect that effectively stopped the dancing.

Gabriel grumbled, "What the hell is he doing?" and stepped forward to intervene. He stopped after just one step when Covington got down to one knee and grabbed Eleanor's hand.

"My darling Eleanor," he started in a raised voice, attracting the attention of those who hadn't yet noticed the sudden end of the set, "you are the most beautiful jewel among a sea of paste." Well done, Covington. In a sentence, he had managed to offhandedly offend every other lady present. "Any man would be lucky to have you as his wife, but please say you'll make me the luckiest and happiest man in the world and have me. I love you. Will you be my wife?"

Ivy couldn't watch. She closed her eyes and refrained with difficulty from burying her face in Gabriel's chest. Poor shy, dear Covington. Her cousin would reject him publicly, and there was nothing Ivy could do to stop it.

"Yes! Of course, I'll marry you, you silly man! I've been waiting for a long time for you to ask me. Since that day in Hyde Park. Because I love you too!" *What?* Ivy opened her eyes wide, incredulous.

The happy couple accepted the round of applause and well wishes that were thrown their way. Arm in arm, they basked in the attention. Well, Eleanor basked, Covington suffered through it. A more unexpected, mismatched pairing she had yet to see, but the happiness on their faces made Ivy wish that nothing would ever tarnish it. She wished him luck with Aunt Evelyn as well, him being 'just' an Earl and all.

Then a thought struck her, and she looked up at her husband with a devilish smile. He regarded her warily.

"What is it, my love? If you wish for a similar display, I'm afraid I'm bound to disappoint you."

She kissed his cheek. "Don't worry. I would die of embarrassment if you ever did something like that. You are safe. No, I just realised that, with Eleanor married to him, Covington will become your cousin as well."

He stifled a groan. "Blasted Covington."

Ivy laughed and, with everyone else distracted, planted a kiss on his lips.

She might not have had a marriage proposal out of the pages of a book, but woe to anyone who tried to take away her chance to write the end of their story.

The End

434

Author's Note

Thank you so much for taking a chance on me and my book. If you enjoyed it, please consider taking a moment to leave a review on your favourite book site.

As you may know, this is my debut novel. And the first of many more, hopefully. I hope you had as much fun reading it as I had writing it. It is often said that if you look close enough, you can find the author hidden behind her characters. Writing this book has made me realise how true that is. But enough about me!

Ivy, Gabriel, and all my beloved characters live and love during the Regency era. You could find many typical elements, but with a personal touch. Some events are historically accurate, like, for example, the timeframe of the Napoleonic wars or the exceptionally rainy summer that Europe had in 1815. I, however, decided to take full advantage of the freedom granted by fiction, leaving history alone as much as possible. The battle in which Gabriel and Ivy take part is born from my pen, just like the viewing of Thomas Lawrence's work.

Very real is Ivy's constant struggle against insecurities and low self-esteem, something that transcends space and time. What Ivy experiences when "her head is a dark place" can be ascribed to mild depression and anxiety symptoms. Today we have ways to understand it and take a journey to overcome it, but I can't fathom it would have been the same back in the 19th century.

If you ever feel the same, what I can tell you is that you are not alone. And you are so worth it! Ivy had her happy ever after. Why shouldn't you?

Whatever it might be.

Love,

Val

About the Author

Val Guildthorne was born and still lives in Italy (alas, far away from the sea and the Alps!). Her passion for reading started when she was very young, feeding her lively imagination. She voraciously read everything from thrillers to the classics of Italian literature until she discovered romance, in particular historical romance.

After a master's degree in specialised translation and interpreting at the University of Bologna (aka Alma Mater Studiorum, the 'Nourishing Mother of the Studies', the oldest University in the world), she started working as a translator and interpreter. Her job, and her love for travelling, give her the opportunity to spend some time all over Europe, especially in the UK and in Germany.

When translating other people's words wasn't enough anymore, on the advice of her wise cat, she decided to follow her dream of bringing to life those stories that have always been there, in the back of her mind.

Get in touch:

valguildthorne.author@gmail.com

Twitter: valguild_author

Instagram: thatvalwhowrites

437

Contents

Printed in Great Britain
by Amazon

16846717R00255